THE LONG TRAIL

BRAD DENNISO

Author of

RETURN OF THE GUNHAWK **and**
THUNDER

Published by Pine Bookshelf
Buford, Georgia

Series
The McCabes #1

THE McCABES

The Long Trail
One Man's Shadow
Return of the Gunhawk
Boom Town
Trail Drive
Johnny McCabe
Shoshone Valley
Thunder

JUBILEE

Preacher With A Gun
Gunhawk Blood (Coming Soon)

THE TEXAS RANGER

Tremain
Wardtown
Jericho (Coming Soon)

PART ONE

DUSTY

ONE

His name was Dusty. Simply that. The only name he had ever known. He was twenty years old—still a boy, by the standards of some—but he had been doing the work of a man since he was twelve. Swinging an ax, working a shovel, shoeing horses. He was not overly tall, but he filled out his shirt with muscle.

He rode along, keeping his horse to a light canter, his horse's hooves kicking up a cloud of dust that trailed away behind him. The countryside was flat, stretching away to a line of low ridges to his left. To his right, the land simply faded into a distance hazy with heat. Short, brown grass grew, sometimes so sparsely that six inches of gravel was visible between each strand. Such was Nevada in the late spring.

A tattered Stetson was pulled down over his head to keep the Nevada sun from frying his brains, and shoulder-length hair caught the wind and trailed out behind him. He wore a buckskin shirt he had made himself, and the legs of his tattered Levi's were tucked into worn and scratched up riding boots.

A Colt .44 was holstered low at his right side, and tied down for a quick draw. A second one was tucked into the front of his gunbelt. They were each of the older cap-and-ball percussion design, not even in production anymore. Soon spare parts would be difficult to find. They had long been replaced on the market by the newer Colt Peacemaker, which was out of his price range. But his pistols were functional, well balanced, and with them he was able to shoot fast and straight. They had been given to him by the man who had raised him, along with the knowledge of how to use them.

Dusty's horse was the color of straw, and had been a gift from a man he had worked for in Arizona, a man named Cantrell.

"I think you're going on a fool's quest," the man had said. "But you're a good man, and I can't let you leave without a good horse to get you there safely and hopefully bring you back. And don't forget, your job will be waiting for you."

Mister Cantrell had let him have the pick of the remuda, and Dusty chose the gelding he was now riding. Dusty had ridden this animal many times, and thought it had sand. A cutting horse, actually. Not what you would normally want for a cross-country ride, but the horse could run fast and long.

Even now, the gelding moved along with spirit, its hooves tapping out a rhythm along the hard packed Nevada dirt, its mane waving in the hot wind.

A bedroll was tied to the back of Dusty's saddle, and packed in it was some ammunition, a skillet, a spoon, and a dented coffee pot. Draped over the pommel were two canteens. He owned nothing more in the world.

Dusty had left a small mining town the day before, and the bartender there had told him somewhere ahead would be a way station. Dusty would remain there just long enough to fill the two canteens and maybe grab a plate of beans, and rest his horse a little. Then he would continue on, covering as much ground as possible before sunset.

If the bartender was correct with his directions, sometime the following day Dusty would reach the town he now sought. And maybe-just-maybe, his long ride would come to an end, and he could return to his life in Arizona.

Dusty hoped the old barkeep was right about the way station, and gave a quick sigh of frustration at his own negligence to ask for more reliable information. One of his two canteens was already empty, the other only half-full. He had put fifteen miles of desert behind him since leaving that mining town, and if he did not find a stream or a well soon, he would be in serious trouble; he did not have enough water to make it back.

As he rode, he caught sight of a shape up ahead and off to one side, dancing in the haze. He was not about to get

his hopes up. Could be anything, he knew. A large rock. Even just a trick the sunlight was playing on his eyes.

Suddenly, his horse began increasing its pace, like a thirsty horse will do when it smells water. Whatever it was ahead, apparently water was near, or at least the horse thought so. Dusty gave the horse its head and held on for the ride.

As they drew closer, the thing up ahead began to divide into two shapes, a house and a barn, he realized, shimmering in a line of heat waves. The walls of each structure were made of wood that had been bleached by the sun; any paint or white-wash was long since baked away.

The way station. That old barkeep had been right.

An iron pump stood outside the house, and in a corral behind the barn were eight horses, larger than what you normally strapped a saddle onto. Used for pulling a wagon, which Dusty assumed was probably a stagecoach.

This place was not much to look at. But at the moment, he did not care. His eyes fixed on the water pump and the water trough it was mounted onto.

Dusty reined up at the trough, giving the reins an extra hard tug to hold his horse in check. His horse danced a bit in protest at being so close to water but denied its much-needed drink, but Dusty held his ground. He was not about to help himself to water without permission from whoever was in the house. Common courtesy aside, such a thing could get you shot.

"Hello, the house!" he called out.

He stepped from the saddle while he waited for an answer.

The horse shifted one hoof impatiently, eyeing the water trough. Dusty's own throat was raw with thirst. There was no answer from the house.

He decided not to make his horse wait any longer. He let go of the reins, and the buckskin pushed its muzzle into the water.

Dusty decided he could wait no longer, either. A metal dipper rested on the edge of the trough. He grasped it, then jacked the iron handle of the pump until water came gushing out and filled the dipper. He raised the dipper to his mouth and drained it.

The water was not cold, and tasted a little brackish, as the well was probably not very deep. But it was wet. That was all that really mattered, after fifteen miles of Nevada desert. He refilled the dipper.

"Howdy," came a voice from the shack.

Dusty turned his gaze in that direction to see a man standing in the doorway. He was taller than Dusty, and almost skeletal thin. His shirt and trousers were tattered and baggy. His jaw was covered with short, stubbly hair. At his right side a revolver rode low. Dusty knew there was only one reason to wear a gun like that—to be within easy reach. A little unusual for a man operating a way station. Most of those Dusty had seen were either wrangler or farmer types. Not that a man who was good with a gun couldn't operate a way station, but he struck Dusty as looking a little out of place. But Dusty was too thirsty for questions to fully form in his head.

"Sorry to be helping myself," Dusty said, "but I've been on the trail a long time, and I'm mighty dry."

"Go ahead. The water's free for the takin'."

Dusty tipped the dipper and drained it again. He then took the reins of his horse and pulled its muzzle from the water. It was not good to let a thirsty, tired horse have too much water all at once.

"If you got some oats, my horse could sure use some," Dusty said. "I don't have any money, but I could do some work in exchange."

The man shook his head. "Help yourself to the oats. Then come on inside. The woman's got supper on the stove, and you're more than welcome to some."

"Much obliged."

Dusty led his horse into the barn, and a stall. He loosened the cinch, then slipped off the bridle, and pulled a feed bag over its head.

He left his hat hanging from the saddle horn by the chin strap. He was not one to live with a hat forever on his head like it had grown there, like some cowhands he had known. He liked the feeling of wind in his hair, and the sun on his face.

He stopped at the iron pump for one more dipper of water. Now that he was not as thirsty, he had to admit the

water was not very good at all. A strong metallic aftertaste. Not at all like the cold, sweet water from the Cantrell well. He found himself looking forward to returning, more so than ever, once he was finished here in Nevada. He set the dipper down and continued on to the house.

The door was opened by the thin man, who smiled, revealing a row of blackened teeth. "Come on in, stranger."

Dusty stepped in, now registering the details he had overlooked earlier. This man had gunfighter stamped on him as surely as if it had been done with a hot iron. Dusty doubted he had ever worked as a hostler. Something about the man's manner, his stooped shoulders, a slight shuffle to his gait, a smile that was too forced with nothing behind it, told him this man probably did little work, except for maybe back-shooting and cattle rustling.

Seated at the table was another man, shorter than the first and chunkier. His shirt was also tattered, and stained from sweat and an overall lack of washing. Before him on the table was a plate of beans, and he was eagerly diving into them, making slurping sounds that reminded Dusty of a hog devouring slop.

A woman stirred a pile of beans in a skillet, her face flushed from the heat of the stove, considering the day was already hot enough to make heat waves rise from the earth. She was pretty, Dusty thought. About his age. Strands of chestnut hair had come free from a bun at the back of her head, and fell across gentle cheekbones. Pretty, but she seemed tired. Harried, maybe.

She tossed a nervous glance toward him, then directed her attention back toward the beans. Beside the skillet was a coffeepot, its contents boiling and hissing.

"Something to eat, mister?" the thin man said.

Dusty had to admit, now that his thirst was satisfied, his belly was rumbling with emptiness. "Yessir. I'm downright hungry."

The thin man, standing behind him now, landed a hand on his shoulder. This set Dusty immediately on edge. Never let a man touch your shoulder, the man who had raised him once said. And this man had known the tricks of survival like none other. Your shoulder is too near your neck

and throat, and when a man gets his hands around your throat, you are in trouble.

But the man's voice was calm, not threatening, his words a little distorted by the grin his mouth was pulled apart in. "Grab a chair then, stranger."

Dusty slid a chair from under the table and dropped into it. Something was definitely wrong here, he thought. The thin man and the slop-devourer seemed out of place, and the woman almost frightened. And more than that, things felt wrong.

Always trust your gut feelings—another lesson from the man who had raised him. A man's head is of little use to him, much of the time. You can think yourself out of a right decision and headfirst into a wrong one, but your gut will never lie to you.

"Woman!" the thin man barked. "Bring this here man a plate of beans. And some coffee."

Without a word, she grabbed a spoon and scooped some beans onto a flat dish, then fetched a napkin from the drawer.

The man at the table was eyeing Dusty. "So, where you from?"

Dusty shrugged. He had never considered himself as being from anywhere in particular. "Here...there...a little bit of everywhere, I reckon."

The napkin slid from the woman's hands to the floor in front of the stove, and she knelt to retrieve it.

The thin man said, "Come on, woman. Hurry up."

The woman set the plate in front of Dusty, and the folded napkin at his side.

Dusty took a fork full of beans. They tasted like the best he had ever eaten, but when you are hungry, your taste buds become less particular.

He could hear the woman pouring a cup of coffee. He also was aware that the thin man was still standing behind him. "Excuse me. I really don't like anyone standing behind me."

It was as he spoke that he became aware of black markings on the napkin. Soot from the stove, forming letters. HELP.

Dusty lunged from the table to one side, as the thin man swung the grip of his pistol toward where Dusty's head had been.

The girl, standing between the stove and table, a mug in her hand, tossed the scalding coffee into the thin man's face.

The man let out a screech like a wild cat, clawing at his face, taking a step backward.

Dusty rolled away from him and came to a stop sitting with his back against the doorjamb, the Colt from his belt in his right hand.

The fat man was now rising from the table, pulling a pistol from a holster mounted on his hip.

Dusty gripped the trigger tightly, and with the palm of his left hand fanned the gun's hammer and sent two rapid shots into the man's chest. The man stumbled backward, his foot catching on the leg of a chair. He went over backward, and his head slammed into the floorboards.

The thin man, still squinting from the hot coffee he had received in the face, snapped off a shot in the direction Dusty had fired from, the bullet tearing into the door jamb not a foot from Dusty's head.

Dusty fanned two more shots. From his angle on the floor, the bullets cut up and into the man's chest, lifting him and slamming him backward into a wall. The man's own gun went off again, firing into a floorboard, and he slid to the floor to lie motionless, his head propped awkwardly against the wall.

Dusty rose to his feet. Only one shot remained in his pistol, so he pushed it back into his belt, and slid his second pistol from its holster. He then checked the men to see if any life remained. There was none.

Dusty looked to the woman, who was standing by the stove. Both hands, slightly trembling, were clasped over her mouth.

"I take it they weren't friends of yours," Dusty said.

She shook her head.

"Are you all right?"

She nodded. Then with one hand she brushed back the loose strands of hair, smoothed her apron, and drew a

deep breath, composing herself. The trembling was gone. "I'm fine. I want to thank you for what you did."

"It was more luck than anything, but you're more than welcome."

"They rode in not half an hour ago. They didn't hurt me, at least not yet. They were so hungry they had to put food first. But I would have made them kill me before what they had in mind."

Odd thing, Dusty thought, as he dragged the two dead men outside. On the frontier, you almost never heard of a woman being abused. Such a thing could get a man lynched before he even went to trial. In a land where men outnumbered women by as much as ten to one in some places, even the most rough-mannered cutthroats treated a woman as though she were almost sacred. Usually. But apparently not this time.

When he returned, she invited him to stay and finish his meal, and she brought over the coffee he had missed the first time.

She said, "My father and I run this place. He's gone to town for supplies. He stays overnight when he goes, because Baker's Crossing is so far away."

"How far?"

"Maybe twenty miles. Why? Do you know anyone there?"

He shrugged. "It's where I'm heading. Whether I know anyone there, we'll see." Dusty was never comfortable talking about himself, and he especially did not want to go into why he was going to Baker's Crossing.

"Do you have any other family?" he asked.

She nodded. "Back east."

As she spoke, she cranked an iron pump handle, filling a kettle so she could begin cleaning the dishes. "I have a grandmother, and a couple uncles and their families. My mother died last year, and Pa thought it best to come west and start fresh. Pa wants to homestead. Maybe go to Oregon, where there's fresh farmland."

"You're a far piece from Oregon."

"Pa thought maybe to find a job in California for a year or two, first. Maybe save up some money. We got this far, and the job of running the way station was available, so he took

it. It can get dull here—there's a lot of time on your hands between stages, but I never thought of it as dangerous until today."

"Them two are unusual. Some of the worst back-stabbers I've ever met will treat a woman like the grandest lady, and woe be to anyone who dares otherwise. Women are rare out here, and women of marrying age, even more so."

She gave her name as Mahalia Anderson. From the Bible, she said. But her Pa and pretty much every one else called her Haley.

"Folks just call me Dusty," he said.

"Oh? Is that short for something?"

He shrugged. "I don't rightly know. I never knew my Ma or Pa."

When he was finished eating, he took a shovel from a tool shed and dug two graves behind the house, then rolled a body into each one. Before he dumped the stocky one into the ground, however, he examined the dead man' pistol, which he had pried from his fingers before dragging him from the house.

The gun was a Colt Peacemaker. It could be loaded with metallic cartridges, inserted through a loading gate at the rear of the cylinder. Unlike the cap and ball pistols Dusty carried, which were loaded through the front of the cylinder manually with powder and a lead ball or bullet, and primed with a percussion cap placed over a nipple behind each chamber. Reloading a cap and ball revolver was a lengthy process. Some men carried one or more extra cylinders and would simply remove the cylinder in their pistol and replace it as a method of speedier reloading. Others, like Dusty, simply carried two pistols.

Dusty had seen a few Peacemakers—Mister Cantrell owned one—but figured it would be a lot of years before he could afford one.

What the hell, he thought. The dead man wouldn't be needing it anymore. He had probably stolen it, anyhow, and it would be impossible to find the gun's rightful owner. Dusty could leave it for Haley's father, who would probably sell it to a stage passenger, or Dusty could simply take it himself.

He unbuckled the dead man's gunbelt, and slid it out from under him. It was made of finely tooled leather, with

twenty cartridge loops sewn into the back, each filled. The pistol was not a .45, as were most Peacemakers, but a .44-40, sized to take the same ammunition as the .44-40 Winchester. As such, if you owned both weapons, you could fill your cartridge belt with ammunition that could be used in either gun.

He unbuckled his own scratched up, worn gunbelt and dropped it along with his second pistol to the ground, and buckled on the dead man's belt. He adjusted it so the pistol would ride low on his right leg, then drew the gun and slapped it back into the holster, then pulled it free again. He would need to practice until his draw with the new gun flowed smoothly. He noted the pistol's balance, superior to those of his own.

Dusty finished scooping earth over the two dead men, filling the graves, then returned to the shack.

"I'd best be going," he said. "I have a lot of miles to cover."

She gave a sort of half shrug. "You could always sleep in the barn. It's getting late in the day. You won't make many more miles before dark."

"Thanks. But I don't think that would look proper."

"No. I don't suppose it would."

There was something in her eye, in the tone of her voice. Was Dusty imagining it? Was there just a hint of disappointment? Or was it just that he wanted to see disappointment?

That was a hard thing—trying to read a woman. It was too easy to see what you wanted in a woman's eyes. Haley was pretty, and she had that sort of frontier strength Dusty found so attractive in a girl. And yet, she was softly feminine, not hard and mannish like some women who had been made so by too many years of hard living. And she had a soft, whispery voice, and green eyes that seemed to reach into his soul without even trying. He didn't know if he had ever noticed the color of a woman's eyes before.

"Thanks for the beans and coffee. I'd best be riding on."

He went to the barn, tightened the cinch and removed the feed bag that had long been emptied, and led his horse out into the yard. He let it drink a bit from the trough, then

tethered it to a hitching rail, and went back to the front door. Not that he really needed to. He had said his good-bye. It was just that he wanted to see her one more time. To look into those eyes. To hear that voice one more time. She answered after a quick knock.

"I just wanted to say good-bye, and thanks again," he said.

"It's I who should be thanking you," she said.

"Think nothing of it. Really."

She shook her head. "I'll never think nothing of it. And neither will my Pa. There will always be a free supper waiting for you, once he hears about what you did. He'll never take any money from you."

"Much obliged."

She reached suddenly with one hand to the side of his face, letting her finger gently trace the contour of his cheekbone. "Do you really have to leave?"

He hesitated. He needed to get to Baker's Crossing. He wanted an end to his quest. And yet...and yet...

She pulled her hand away suddenly, her eyes darting downward. "I'm sorry. I don't know what came over me. You must think me brazen."

In these times, romance was a thing of subtleties and nuances, never bold or blatant except among those of poor reputation. And yet, here they were, just the two of them. There was no one else here to cast disparaging glances, or whisper behind their backs. He was lonely, and she probably was, too.

"I don't think you're brazen," he said, and touched a hand to her face. "I think you're pretty."

And he drew closer to her, and their lips met.

"Stay," she said.

"I've been riding for weeks," he said. "I must look like a saddle bum, and smell even worse."

"We have a bath tub. Enough room for two. The next stage isn't due until morning. Pa won't be back until sometime after that."

He liked the sound of that. Very much. He was young, with the needs and wants that come with his age. But there was Baker's Crossing. Business awaited him there, business he had been waiting to complete for as far back as he could

remember. As attractive as he found Haley, and as appealing as he found her suggestion, he could wait no longer to be on his way. It was true he had but a few more miles he could cross before dark, but at least those would be miles he would not have to cross come morning.

"I've got to be going," he said.

She nodded. "I understand."

Their gazes remained connected for a few moments more, as though by a rope that did not want to break, but then he forced himself to turn, and stepped down from the porch. He pulled his horse's rein free from the rail, and swung into the saddle.

She had followed him onto the porch. She raised one hand in a wave, and he nodded in response, and then touched his heels to the horse's ribs, and started away at a shambling trot

Two hundred yards from the way station; he stopped and turned in the saddle to look back. The porch was now deserted. A gust of wind scattered dust against the weathered building.

He shook his head, wondering if he was a complete fool. If Haley was correct, twenty miles of dust and dry brown grass not fit for a mule lay between him and Baker's Crossing. Suddenly, those miles seemed dreadfully long.

With a pull of the reins, he turned his horse around and kicked it into a gallop that brought him quickly back to the hitching rail in front of the shack. He swung out of the saddle, covered the distance between the rail and the porch in a few quick strides, and rapped on the door.

She opened it with surprise. "Dusty. Is something wrong?"

"Nope. It's just that, all of a sudden, the thought of that hot bath sounds awfully good, and the company even better."

TWO

Dusty stretched out on the soft mattress, the covers pulled to his chest. One arm was crooked behind his head, serving as a supplement to his pillow, and the other was around Haley's shoulders, hugging her gently as she slept, her head resting on his chest. He liked the feeling of her long hair as it spread wildly over his ribs, and his fingers gently caressed the soft skin of her bare shoulder.

He breathed easily. He was freshly bathed, for the first time since he had left Arizona, and with a beautiful woman in his arms, also for the first time since he had left Arizona. He felt all was right with the world. He was at peace with himself, or at least, as close as he ever came to it.

Haley had been concerned he might think inviting men into her bath and then her bed was commonplace for her, but he assured her he could tell by the look in her eye, by the warmth and sincerity of her touch, that such was not the case. Some women give themselves out of a need to somehow compensate for insecurity, forever seeking the touch of a man to convince themselves they are worthy of being loved. Yet the convincing never seems to last long, and they find themselves seeking it again and again. Other women seem to have a stronger emotional foundation, and it is these who give themselves only because they truly care about a man. Haley was of the second group.

Yet, despite this contentment which seemed to originate at the center of his being and radiate outward, he found he could not sleep. Despite the beauty and passion of the woman whose bed he was sharing, he found his thoughts returning to his reason for being in Nevada in the first place. His business in Baker's Crossing. His business that, once completed, would find him returning to Arizona, and hopefully his old job at the Cantrell Ranch. Though he had to admit, at the moment, he was not so eager to leave Nevada.

Baker's Crossing. What had the barkeep in that dirty, little mining town said about it? Not much. Haley, as they had talked before she drifted off to sleep, had said it was a small cattle town that served surrounding ranches, all of which managed to avoid bankruptcy because longhorns could survive on the dry, brown grass growing here in the

southwest. Though, Dusty had to admit the grass growing about him was some of the worst he had ever seen, and found it difficult to imagine even a longhorn could graze here. Most of the ranches in Nevada were further west, closer to the mountains, north of that mining town. The Tahoe area. Dusty figured the grass must be a little better there, probably because of the spring run-off. But he did not know from personal experience. He had never been to Nevada before, and from what he had seen so far, aside from Haley, there was wasn't a whole lot to make a man want to stay here.

He had left the Cantrell Ranch about three weeks ago, to find a piece of his past. To learn where he had come from. He had left for Nevada in search of a woman he had never met before. His mother.

Dusty had been raised by a man named Sam Patterson. An outlaw. The leader of a band of former Confederate guerrilla raiders who used military tactics to strike banks or trains. Sometimes they raided a farm or ranch for horses or supplies.

Dusty had never talked about any of this with anyone, even Mister Cantrell. Though he thought the old man knew there was more to Dusty's past than he let on, because of the way Dusty wore his guns.

Dusty had never been an outlaw. Patterson had never allowed him to have a part in his gang's criminal activities. He wanted Dusty to have a clear name, a clear conscience. But Dusty knew there was such a thing as guilt by association. He believed if the truth about his past became known, he would not be able to find an honest job, and might be forced to resort to Patterson's lifestyle simply to survive. And there would be no way a girl like Haley would want to be with him.

He eventually fell off to sleep, but found himself awake as the gray light of early dawn brought a ghostly glow to Haley's bedroom. They had both rolled over in their sleep, so that she was curled in a ball, and he was curled behind her, conforming to her position, his arm draped over her shoulder, almost protectively.

He slid out of bed, as easily as he could manage so as not to awaken her. He pulled on his jeans, slung his new gunbelt over his shoulder – Dusty never wanted to be far

from his gun, something he had gained from growing up on the run with the Patterson gang, and he padded out into the kitchen in his bare feet to make coffee.

Once the coffee was ready, he poured himself a cup and stepped out onto the porch to greet the morning. His gunbelt was now buckled about his hips, and his new pistol was riding low.

The barnyard was deserted. To the east, the sky was alive with crimson and orange. The breeze was still cool. He relished its touch, because by the time he rode out, it would be oven-like. He would be soaking with sweat and covered with dust, and that wonderful feeling of being freshly bathed would seem like a distant memory.

Dusty heard the hinges of the door squeak gently as it was opened behind him, and Haley stepped out in her bare feet. A blanket was wrapped about her shoulders, and pulled together in front to form a makeshift robe, which she held together with one hand.

"Good morning," he said.

She gently placed a kiss on one shoulder blade. "You know, we have a good three hours before the morning stage arrives."

Dusty rode out twenty minutes before the stage was due, but once his business in Baker's Crossing was finished, he would be back. This he promised.

"I'll be waiting," she said.

He followed the trail over a flat stretch for what he figured was three miles, then up along a gentle, sandy slope. The ridge dropped down, gradually melting into the countryside.

It had occurred to him he would probably pass her father on the way to Baker's Crossing. He thought maybe the idea of avoiding the man seemed preferable. At least for now. If Dusty were to tell him of the two outlaws who had been ready to victimize his daughter, once they were finished filling their stomachs, then the man would probably push his horses to their limit getting back to the way station as quickly as possible. But this was no longer necessary. The danger had passed. And Dusty did not want to do anything that would make Haley look bad. After all, her father would be able to do some figuring, based on the time of day and

how far Dusty was along the trail, and determine Dusty had most likely spent the night at the way station.

Was Dusty falling in love? He did not rightly know. He was not sure he knew what love was. But he knew he cared about Haley and what people thought about her, especially those close to her like her father.

Dusty decided he would let Haley tell her father as much as she wanted to, in her own time and way, and then he would meet the man later. Once his visit to Baker's Crossing was done. He turned his horse off the trail and rode for about a mile into the countryside, then turned his horse to ride in a parallel line to the trail.

The day was turning off hot, like he had thought it might. Sweat rolled down his back and soaked his hair under his hat. His horse's hooves kicked up little clouds of dust. As good as that bath had felt, it was like it had never happened.

In the distance, maybe a half-mile further along between himself and the way station, he saw a cloud of dust. More than would be kicked up by a rider, but maybe enough to match four wagon wheels and a team of horses. Most likely Haley's father. Dusty let the wagon move along for a couple of miles, then turned his horse back toward the trail, and picked it up maybe a half hour after her father had passed along.

Dusty rode on. The trail soon covered a long flat expanse, then went up another sandy slope. After a short time, the earth ahead suddenly seemed to fall away. At the base of the decline was a scattering of buildings. Single-level structures mostly, with walls of gray, sun beaten planks nailed upright.

This must be Baker's Crossing, he thought. Not too danged impressive looking.

One building stood two floors high, with a rickety looking balcony stretching the length of the second floor. Anyone stepping on that, Dusty thought, would probably soon find themselves at ground level. Even from this distance, he could make out the big, black letters painted on a sign mounted on the balcony railing. SALOON. This building would be his destination.

He amended that. His second destination, as his gaze drifted to the center of the town's lone street, and the well

house standing there. An iron pump was mounted on its side. His throat was dry, and he knew his horse could use the water, and his canteens were again empty.

Dusty touched his horse's ribs with his boot heels, and they started down the gravelly decline. Once at the base of the decline, the horse quickened its pace, as it had the day before when it smelled water at the way station.

Dusty reined up at the well, dismounted, and he let the horse push its muzzle into the trough.

A tin cup rested on the edge of the trough. Dusty filled it from the iron pump, and poured the water down his throat so quickly most of it spilled down over his chin and onto the front of his shirt. The water was cold. Wet. Refreshing, all the way down. It struck his stomach a little heavily, but he scarcely noticed.

He had not anticipated the water being this fresh. In dry country, what little water there was often ran close to the surface, tasting like it had back at the way station. He refilled the cup.

After his thirst had become but a memory, and his horse had as much water as Dusty dared allow it, he led the horse across to the saloon. He gave one rein a couple turns about a hitching rail, then stepped up to the boardwalk and pushed through a pair of batwing doors. One hinge squeaked from a lack of grease.

The room was deserted, except for a man behind a bar who was idly wiping dust from shot glasses and mugs. A dozen tables were scattered about, chairs turned upside down and mounted on them. At the far wall, a ramshackle flight of wooden stairs climbed to the second floor.

Dusty was tired. His back ached because of all the miles he had covered in the saddle between the way station and here, and his backside felt almost blistered. Yet, anticipation was rising within him. This could be where he would meet his mother. Finally. To, maybe, get to know her, find out what she was like. Of course, there also the chance she was not here at all. Maybe the old red-faced barkeep further back on the trail was wrong. Maybe no one here had ever even heard of a Rose Callahan. Then, what would he do? Where would he go?

Either way, he realized his journey was over. First, he would return to that little way station miles behind him on the trail, and to Haley. And then, it would be back to Arizona, where he would hit up Mister Cantrell for another job. He would then maybe start saving his money. Maybe start up a small cattle outfit of his own in a few years. Make a life for himself. And he would try to put the questions of his past to rest.

He had a quick flickering of an image in his mind—a little cattle spread he would operate himself, and of Haley waiting for him at the house when he returned each night. But he pushed that image away. It was way too soon for him to be having such thoughts.

The barkeep was a man of maybe fifty, with thinning hair, but his face was decorated with bushy sideburns showing flecks of silver. He wore a white shirt and a checkered vest, and an apron was tied about his middle. He looked at Dusty from under bushy brows.

"What can I do for you, son?" he said.

"You open for business?"

He shrugged. "It's early, but what the hell. What can I get you?"

Though Dusty had settled his thirst outside, he now thought a beer might taste good. And it gave him a moment more to procrastinate before asking the question that might end his long ride in disappointment.

"I'll have a beer."

"I don't serve boys under twenty-one. How old are you, son?"

Dusty looked at him coolly, annoyance rising inside him. He was tired to the bone, and if he felt like a beer, then he was danged well going to have one. "I'm old enough to have a beer without no sass from you."

The bartender grabbed a mug, and filled it from one of the tapped kegs that were mounted horizontally behind the bar. He was grinning, apparently finding something amusing about the situation. Or about Dusty. Dusty was filled with the gumption and spine that comes with being twenty, but he was too tired at the moment to take offense at being the source of anyone's amusement.

The barkeep said, "You got money to pay for this?"

Dusty reached into the pocket of his Levi's. He had seen a coin in there a few days earlier. He found it, a nickel, and dropped it to the bar. "There you go. All the money I have to my name."

"Your life savings, huh?" the barkeep snorted a chuckle. "That should cover it."

The barkeep set the mug on the bar before Dusty. "I hope you enjoy it, son, because with no more money, you won't be having a second one."

Dusty tipped the mug, pouring down a few gulps. Then he dragged the back of one buckskin sleeve across his mouth.

He found the barkeep was staring at him.

Dusty said, "You got a problem?"

The barkeep shook his head. "You look a little familiar, that's all."

"Ain't never been through these parts before."

"Never said you had. You just remind me of someone, that's all."

The barkeep went back to wiping glasses and straightening behind the bar, but as he worked he would steal an occasional glance at Dusty.

When the beer was finished, Dusty said, "Since I can't afford a second one, how about some information instead."

The barkeep raised his brows in sort of a half-shrug. "I'll do what I can."

"I'm looking for a particular woman. Might be about your age. I don't rightly know. Name of Rose Callahan."

The barkeep's good humor drained from his face. He eyed Dusty levelly. "I might. Who is she to you."

"Now, that's none of your dang business. I take it you know her?"

The barkeep said nothing.

"Do you know where I can find her?"

The barkeep was silent for a long moment, as though he were weighing the situation in his mind. He reminded Dusty of a card shark, deliberating over a hand.

Finally, the man said, "Up those stairs. First door on the right."

"Much obliged." Dusty turned and strode across the barroom floor.

He took the stairs one at a time, not in twos like he normally might. He found himself suddenly...he was not sure...scared? Maybe.

This was Rose Callahan he was about to see. The woman who had brought him into the world. She had given him up for reasons he did not know—reasons he hoped to learn. What he really wanted, he had to admit to himself, was to connect with her, to form a parent-child bond. He wanted his mother in his life.

A thought struck him—what if this Rose Callahan was not the one he was seeking? But he immediately dismissed this as irrational. The name was not that common. And in the west, there were so few women in general. It was so unlikely there would be two with the same name, working saloons in the same area.

Even though he had never met his mother, and had never known anything about her, he had learned a year earlier what her name was and what she did for a living. The last anyone had known, she was living in or near Carson City, Nevada.

His mother was a saloon woman, and that did not rest easily with him. How could it? But as the year ticked away, he had let the news gradually settle. Mister Cantrell had helped.

"It doesn't matter who your parents were, or what they did," he had said. "What matters is who you are. What kind of man you make yourself into."

This had helped. A little. In time, Dusty found a sort of acceptance of what his mother was, and it was then he decided to find her, with the first stop in his journey being Carson City, where he began asking questions. Questions that eventually led him to this saloon.

And now, he was climbing the stairs that would take him to her. First door on the right.

He did not know what he expected to gain from this, really. He knew what he wanted, but was he being realistic? After all, he and his mother were strangers. You cannot expect to gain an entire lifetime of bonding in one visit. And

maybe they would have nothing at all in common. Maybe they would not even like each other.

As the boy climbed the stairs and moved beyond the barkeep's line of sight, a woman stepped from a doorway behind the bar. Her hair was sandy colored, and piled atop her head in an assortment of curls. Her face was painted to hide the lines of hard living.

"It's him," the barkeep said, his eyes on the now vacant staircase.

She followed his gaze. "Who? I don't see anyone."

"Him. A boy who was just in here. Had a beer. Just went up the stairs. He looked familiar, I thought. I didn't think much of it, at first. After you've tended bar for so many years, you see more cowboys and miners than there are stars in the heavens, and it's not unusual for a customer to strike me as looking a little familiar. But the more I looked at him, the more I figured it out. He's about the right age. Then, when he asked for Rosie, I knew it had to be him.

"And the way he walks, the way he carries himself. The way he wears his gun like it's a part of him. The spitting image of his father."

"After all these years," she said with a sort of hushed wonder.

The barkeep sighed. "We knew he'd come looking for her someday."

The woman shook her head, her gaze fixed on the empty staircase. "I hope he's ready for what he's going to find."

THREE

Dusty stood before the door. He raised a fist to rap on it, to announce his presence, then he pulled his hand away. Here he stood, his face streaked with trail dust and sweat, his jaw covered with a half-inch of whiskers—he had bathed the night before, but not shaved since he had left Arizona. He was wearing his buckskin shirt, which was stained with grease and campfire smoke. He suddenly felt he should have been in a white shirt and tie. Maybe a jacket. After all, he was about to meet his mother. If the woman in the next room, answering to the correct name, was indeed his mother.

But he had spent his final nickel downstairs. His only options were to meet her looking like this, or not meet her at all. And he had ridden too far for the second choice.

He raised his fist again, hesitating for only a moment while he pulled his hat from his head, then knocked on the door.

There was no answer. No one was in there. Maybe she had gone out. No, that could not be. The barkeep downstairs had said she was here.

He knocked again. Still no answer.

He stood uncertainly for a few moments. Should he go downstairs and wait? Should he knock a third time? Should he simply stand out here like a fool?

He raised his knuckles for a third knock, but then thought better of it, and reached for the doorknob. This was wrong, Dusty thought. You don't just go into someone's bedroom uninvited. But he couldn't bear to wait, either. He found himself almost tingling with anticipation, and maybe even just a touch of fear. His knees felt weak. Here I go, he thought, and he turned the knob and let the door swing open.

He leaned forward to peek past the edge of the door into the room. A single bed was against one wall, and there was a small bureau with a basin and pitcher atop it. A window overlooked the street below. The smell of whiskey was in the air.

Someone was lying in the bed. A woman.

"Hello?" Dusty said.

There was no response. Dusty did not want to be caught stepping in here like this. These were prudent times, and such a thing would be unseemly. Less than gentlemanly behavior toward a woman could land you in a rash of trouble. Dusty himself wouldn't tolerate such an action by another man. Yet, she had not reacted when Dusty spoke. It wasn't odd for one to take a light nap during the day, but this woman seemed to be out cold. He thought what-the-hell, and stepped in.

The woman was maybe sixty-ish, her face lined, the flesh sagging at her neck and puffy beneath each eye. It was not simply the skin of age, he realized, but of illness. Her cheekbones and jaw line were starkly pronounced, her eyes deeply set, almost sinking in, giving her face a skeletal look. Her skin bore a tinge of yellow. He became concerned; was she breathing at all? She was lying so still.

He moved to the side of the bed.

"Ma'am? I don't mean to intrude, but the door was open," a little lie, "and I wanted to make sure you were all right."

No response at all, not even the flutter of eyelids, but at least from where he now stood he could see that she was indeed breathing. Lightly, almost silently.

He shifted a foot, and his toe touched something which rolled away. He reached down and under the bed, his fingers finding and curling around a glass bottle. He pulled it out, finding it bore a whiskey label.

There was no glass. She must have been drinking directly from the bottle. Drank herself into a drunken stupor, he realized. She might have finished the bottle, or it might have spilled when it fell. The floorboards were stained and discolored, and the smell of whiskey was strong.

He wondered if this could be the Rose Callahan who had been his mother. No, he decided. The name might be the same, the line of work might be also, but this woman was far too old. Her hair, flying wildly about the pillow, was salt-and-pepper in some places, snowy white in others. Her face was too deeply engraved with the lines of age. She must be sixty if she's a day, he thought. That would have put her at forty-three when he was born. You didn't see too many prostitutes that old. The younger competition usually forced them out of

a job long before they reached their forties. And you almost never heard of a woman giving birth at that age.

Dusty stood the bottle upright on a small stand by the bed, then turned and stepped out of the room. He closed the door behind him.

So, his journey was over. This woman, this Rose Callahan he had been pursuing, was not the one who was his mother.

He replaced his hat and stood outside the door, not quite sure how he felt. He had tried to find his mother, but had been unable to. Hell, it had been a long-shot from the start. And now he would return to the Cantrell spread and hopefully get his old job back. Now he could devote all of his attention to saving money and starting his own outfit, without his thoughts drifting any longer to his past. His unanswered questions would simply have to remain unanswered.

He supposed there should be some sort of feeling of completion. His journey was over. He should be glad. But he found he was not.

Was it so terribly wrong to want to know who your mother was? To know something of her background? Was it so wrong not to want to feel alone in the world? Sam Patterson had given him all that he could, been like a father to him, and because of Sam, Dusty thought he might know what it would be like to have a family. A home. But it had not been enough.

He turned and started down the stairs. He suddenly felt weary. Not the bone-weariness he had been feeling because of all the riding, but a deep-down-to-the-soul exhaustion. He took one step after another, his feet feeling heavy. This ride, this long trail he had been following, had all been for nothing.

He stepped down onto the barroom floor. Ahead of him was the door, and out beyond, his horse waited. But then, he caught sight of the bar with his peripheral vision, and a second drink suddenly seemed appealing. Something a little stronger than beer.

A saloon woman was standing at the bar, alongside the barkeep. Her hair was lightly colored, her age difficult to

guess because of all of the paint on her face. Dusty stepped up to the bar.

"I'll have another drink," he said to the barkeep. "Make it a whiskey this time."

"I thought you were out of money," he said.

Oh, yeah. Dusty had momentarily forgotten, in the wave of weariness and despair that had struck him outside the woman's doorway upstairs. He had spent his last nickel on a beer before he had gone upstairs. "I don't know...I'll work it off, or something."

"No, you don't have to. This one's on the house." The barkeep set a glass on the bar and poured a shot of whiskey. "You look like you could use one."

Dusty downed the whiskey in one gulp, but barely noticed its burn as it traveled down.

"Was she awake?" the barkeep asked.

"No," Dusty said quietly. "She was asleep the whole time I was there. It turns out she wasn't the one I was looking for. I made this whole ride for nothing."

"No. No, you didn't. She's the one."

Dusty had been staring at his empty glass, but now he looked up to the barkeep, curiosity suddenly rising like a tide, washing away the weariness.

As if in reply to an unanswered question, the barkeep continued. "She might not be what you expected, but when a man goes searching for his past, he'd best be prepared for what he might find."

"How did you know?"

"You wouldn't remember me. You were too young when she gave you away. My name's Lewis."

The saloon woman stepped over. "And I'm Annie McGraw. We used to work with you mother, years ago. About twenty years, actually. We sort of take care of her, now."

"But," Dusty said, "how can she be my mother? She's so old. She looks old enough to be my grandmother."

"She's not well, Dusty," Lewis said. "I assume you still call yourself Dusty?"

Dusty nodded. "It's the only name I know."

"Like I said, she's not well. Too much whiskey over the years. Her liver's about gone. So's her heart. She's dying."

"She's forty-six," Annie put in. "But sickness can age you. And she's done a lot of hard livin'."

Dusty said, "But I saw an empty whiskey bottle up there. Why are you letting her drink if she's as sick as you say?"

"The doctor doesn't think it will make much difference at this point," Lewis said.

Annie continued. "She's been out of her head, more or less, for weeks. The doctor says her liver is so badly gone it's poisoning her blood. About a week ago, she took a turn downhill. Sleeps most of the time, now. When she's awake, there are times she doesn't even know her own name. The doctor doesn't think she has much longer left."

"Forty-six," Dusty said. "I guess I've never seen anyone quite that sick. And I thought I'd seen a lot. I've seen a man die of a bullet wound. I've seen a cowhand dragged to death when he was thrown from the saddle and his foot stuck in the stirrup, and the horse started running. But I've never seen this."

"It's been hard. She, Lewis and me—none of us had a family, so we all sort of became each other's family. Took care of each other, when there was no one else to. Now, she's all but gone."

Lewis said, "We always thought you might come back. Annie and I always told her so. Even as a child you were so determined. That doesn't seem to have changed any."

"Lewis, Rosie and I bought this place years ago. Lewis tends bar, and Rosie and I would wait tables. No more whorin'. This gives us a chance to have a little more of a decent life."

"Why?" Dusty asked. "Why did she choose that life?"

"No one chooses it, Dusty. A woman has to do what she has to do when she finds herself suddenly alone in a land like this, where there are no jobs for unmarried women. I had met a man, a gold miner, through the mail. We corresponded for a year, then I spent what little money I had inherited from my parents to come west and meet him. Thought I'd surprise him, but he surprised me. When I got here, I found he had a wife and five children. I had no money to get me back east.

29

Not even enough to eat on. So I did what I had to, to keep from starving.

"Your mother, she found herself in a similar situation. She had been raised by her parents in a cabin in the mountains. When they died, she found herself alone, with nothing. Her father had been a mountain man, running a line of traps which was their only source of income. He provided food for the table mostly by hunting. Deer, rabbit, occasionally a bighorn sheep. Then they both died suddenly, and Rosie had to find a way to feed herself. Her father had never taught her how to hunt or shoot, and once the supplies they had in the cabin were gone, she had no choice but to go down to the mining camps and make a living."

"Don't condemn her," Lewis said. "She and Annie are two of the finest people I have ever met. You shouldn't judge a person by the things they are forced to do to survive."

Dusty nodded, and his gaze dropped back to his now empty glass. He had found his mother, after all. He had found Rose Callahan. And yet, he had still not found the past he had been searching for.

"There's still so much I don't know," he said. "So many questions I'd like to ask her. I started out to find myself. To connect with my past. But I don't really know much more than I ever did."

"What kind of questions?" Lewis asked.

"Like, who my father is. What my name really is. I don't even know my full name. I mean, what kind of name is *Dusty?*"

Annie smiled. "Your name is Dustin. Dustin McCabe. I never heard Rosie mention a middle name. Your father is Johnny McCabe."

Dusty blinked with surprise. "The gunfighter?"

She nodded.

Lewis said, "I see you've heard of him."

"Who hasn't?" Dusty asked. "They speak his name on a level with Hickok, Clay Allison, John Wesley Hardin." He was going to add, Sam Patterson, but thought better of it.

Annie said, "Most of his reputation was established long before he ever rode into Carson City, which is where she, Lewis and I were at the time. But occasionally we hear something about him. He had gotten married a year or so

after he rode through, and started a small ranch near 'Frisco. His wife died, three or four years after they were married, I think. They say she caught a bullet meant for him, but you know how stories like that are. They grow as time passes. They say he now has a spread in Montana Territory. He has a couple sons, probably about your age."

Dusty thought about that for a moment. "But how could anyone know for certain, considering..." he glanced to Annie, "no offense, but considering the line of work she was in. All the men she must have been with."

Lewis shrugged. "Rosie always said she somehow knew. She had a feeling. Women can tell that sort of thing sometimes. And we all saw the resemblance. Even now, looking at you, you're the spitting image of him. He wasn't much older than you when he swaggered into the barroom that night. The way your face is shaped, the way you walk. It's almost like looking into the past."

Dusty nodded slowly. "Johnny McCabe. I guess I don't know quite what to think about that. I hadn't been really expecting to ever find my mother, not really. I mean, it was a real long-shot. And even if I did, I figured finding my father would be out of the question. And I certainly wasn't expecting him to be someone like Johnny McCabe."

Lewis refilled Dusty's glass, and Dusty took a slug, then asked, "Where did she get the name Dustin?"

Annie said, "Her father—your grandfather. You were named after him. Dustin Callahan. He was a trapper, sometimes an Army scout. He took up with a Ute woman, and they settled in a mountain cabin in the Tahoe area."

"Did she ever mention having any brothers or sisters?"

"No. She was never one to talk much about herself, but I gathered by what she did say that she was an only child."

"So, I've got Indian blood in me," Dusty said. "And my father is Johnny McCabe."

He then asked, "Did he know about me?"

"No," Annie said. "He was in town just one night. He rode on the next morning. That was back when we were working out of a mining camp a couple days' ride out of 'Frisco."

Lewis nodded at the memory, agreeing with her account of the events. "Eighteen fifty-eight, I believe. Long before we bought this place. That was a year before the gold rush. The Comstock Lode. This was all just empty desert country, back then."

Annie gave a weary shake of her head. "Lord, those were wild times."

Dusty listened to the talk, but his mind was on what he was learning about his background. About his father, and how he came into the world. He was aware of the ways of the world; once he had learned his mother was a saloon woman, he knew the probability of how he had been born. But that was before he knew his father's name. He had never met Johnny McCabe, and most of what he had heard about him was probably tall tales, but at least his father no longer seemed entirely faceless. And as the facelessness vanished, Dusty felt a touch of anger rising. Even though he knew this anger was not rational, it was still very real.

"So," Dusty said. "He rode into town, got a little drunk, whelped a child, and rode on without even a backward glance?"

Annie said, "He didn't just get a little drunk. He sat down at a table and began pouring the whiskey down. How he ever made it up the stairs, I'll never know. The following morning, his brother and another man, Zack Johnson, rode in to get him. They had to practically carry him out."

"Zack Johnson. I've heard of him, too. A Texas Ranger, or at least he was at one time. That name comes up around camp fires every so often."

"Apparently he's a friend of your father's."

Lewis said, "Don't fault him none for that night, getting drunk like that. He had a powerful hurt riding with him. You could see the pain in his eyes the moment he stepped into the barroom. I was tending bar, and the look in his eyes, the pain, caught my attention even more than the way he wore his guns. He ordered a bottle of whiskey, dropped a fistful of silver dollars on the bar, enough to pay for a week's stay in the best hotel in town, and said to keep bringing the whiskey to him until he fell over.

"He didn't say what was behind the pain he was feeling, that he was trying to numb with all that whiskey.

And if he ever told Rosie, she never told us. But like I said, you could see it in his eyes."

"If it's any consolation," Annie said, "I don't think paying for a saloon woman was the usual way he conducted himself. You work the saloons enough years, you develop a sort of feeling about people."

"He didn't buy Rosie, either, if that's any consolation. Rosie told us she never took any money from him. And when those two men came in to fetch him, I called one of them over to the bar and gave him back the cash your father had dropped on the bar. I never could bring myself to even take out enough for the three bottles of whiskey he poured down."

"Dang," Dusty said, his sudden anger now fading. "Three bottles?"

Lewis nodded. "I've known men who drank themselves to death on less than that."

"What do you suppose? What do you suppose could have driven a man to that kind of hurt?"

"I don't know. But the look in his eyes kind of haunted me. For a little while afterward, I'd have nightmares about it."

Dusty finished his whiskey. Since taking something for free went against his grain, he insisted on sweeping up. Lewis and Annie told him he was welcome to remain as long as he was of a mind to. They considered any child of Rosie's to be family.

Dusty took a room upstairs, and Lewis paid to have his clothes washed at a laundry a few buildings down the street, and Dusty scrubbed away the trail dust and the sweat in an iron tub out back. He also took a straight razor to the whiskers that had been growing on his chin and upper lip since he had left Arizona.

He insisted on working about the saloon every day to pay for his keep, sweeping the floor and scooping up empty glasses and bottles, and after a time, pouring beer.

He would check in on Rosie, hoping to find her awake, but she never was. The town doctor, a thin old man in a jacket that sort of bagged on his bony frame, and with a bowler perched atop his head, would visit twice daily, use a stethoscope to listen to her breathing and her rapid, shallow heartbeat, and stare at his watch as he checked the pace of her pulse. Then, he would simply shake his head sadly.

Four days after Dusty had ridden into town, his mother died, without having regained consciousness. Dusty never had the opportunity he had ridden so far to find. To talk to his mother, to get to know her.

During her final moments, her face now deeply yellowed and her abdomen swollen with liver disease, she would utter words he couldn't make out, and her eyelids would occasionally flutter. The old doctor sat at one side of the bed, and Dusty at the other, holding her small, bony hand in his.

"I'm here, Ma," he said. "It's been a lot of years, but I'm here."

Annie, standing behind him, placed a hand on his shoulder. "We're all here, Rosie."

Lewis stood by the foot of the bed saying nothing, his eyes glistening with wetness.

Finally, Rosie took one shuddering breath, then another, and then she breathed no more.

"She's gone," the doctor said.

Lewis and Dusty buried Rosie behind the saloon. There was a small cemetery outside of town. Nothing more than a few graves dug into the dirt, with wooden crosses or head markers. Lewis and Annie wanted her buried behind the only home Rosie had known since the cabin she had been raised in. Dusty had insisted on doing all of the shovel work himself, and then using an iron poker heated in the saloon's wood stove, he burned his mother's name into a wooden plank. Her exact birth date was unknown, so below her name he simply burned, D.1878.

"You're welcome to remain with us as long as you like," Lewis said that night, as they shared a supper of beans and steak. "You'll always have a home here with us."

"Thanks," Dusty said. "That means a lot to me. But in the morning, I think I'll be riding on."

"Will you be back?"

"Probably. Eventually."

"Where are you headed? Back to Arizona?"

But Annie knew. She said, "Montana."

Dusty nodded.

Lewis said, "Good luck, son. I hope you find him."

The following morning, as the eastern sky lightened to a steel gray and the stars overhead faded away, Dusty led his horse from the livery stable. He swung into the saddle, thinking to turn his horse toward the edge of town, but on an impulse, he rode instead toward the saloon, and to the small grave behind it.

He sat in the saddle, his hat in one hand as he looked down at the plank, which struck him as seeming so small against a backdrop of a barren ridge that rose to a sharp-looking edge, maybe five miles in the distance. ROSE CALLAHAN. D.1878.

He wanted to say something. If nothing else, then at least goodbye. But a spoken word would somehow seem out of place. There was a sort of solemnity, almost a reverence, to the silence this morning. A silence that did not need to be broken.

He felt, somehow, she had known he was at her bedside, and she had known who he was. And she knew he was here now. Words did not need to be spoken.

He returned his hat to his head, turned his horse away, and left the town of Baker's Crossing behind him.

FOUR

There was one stop Dusty wanted to make before he lit out for Montana. A little way station a few hours outside of Baker's Crossing.

Dusty did not think he knew what love was. He thought maybe the word was used too much—by women who were lost in the romance of romance, waiting for their knight-in-shining-armor to come and save them from a life of loneliness, and by men who were simply trying to satisfy their needs in bed. Somehow, amazingly when you thought about it, despite the vast difference in the needs of men and women, many would find some sort of middle ground and make a life with each other.

Dusty had never used the word love simply to gain what he wanted. And he never intended to. Dusty knew what it felt like to be an unwanted child, a bastard with no name and no sense of identity. He would be danged if he would take a chance on bringing a child like that into the world. Sure, he had known more than one girl, and gotten intimate with some of them, but only when he cared about them. Never casually, and never with a saloon woman. Never to simply release animal passions.

He was finding he cared deeply about Haley Anderson. More so than had ever felt about any other girl before. He had last seen Haley five days earlier, and wanted to see her again before he lit out for Montana. He wanted to tell her of his background. Not only the information he had learned at Baker's Crossing, but also of Sam Patterson. If she would still have him, then once he had returned from Montana, they could begin making some sort of plans. He could return to Arizona, work for Mr. Cantrell for a while and save his money, and then he could start his own spread, and he and Haley could build a life together.

He had ridden away from that little way station with no knowledge of his background at all, other than his mother's name. Now, even though he had not quite met his mother, as she had never gained consciousness, he had been there when she died and he felt she somehow knew he was there. And from Lewis and Annie he had learned much about her. He now also knew his father's name, and for that matter,

his own. Dustin McCabe. He was thinking about maybe adding Callahan as his middle name. Dustin C. McCabe. A name he could sign, like when he was homesteading the land that would be the headquarters for his cattle outfit. The place where he and Haley would raise their children, if they would have him. And he now had a name he could give his children.

The sky was covered with a thin, steely gray overcast as he drew within sight of the way station. The day was hot, but not quite as severe as it had been when he had first ridden to this place. He dismounted in the front yard, and gave the rein a couple of turns about the hitching rail.

The front door opened, and a man stepped out. A little taller than Dusty, with shaggy white hair and a beard. He wore cover-alls, and a faded plaid shirt. "Can I help you?"

Haley's father, apparently.

"Yes, sir. Mister Anderson? I'm Dusty." He figured she must have told her father about him.

"No, my name's Timmons. The Andersons pulled out three days ago."

"Pulled out?"

"Yeah. Anderson—he quit his job. He and his daughter hopped the stage east, and were gone. Me, I'm a shotgun rider for the stage line. I'm runnin' the station until they find someone."

Gone? Old man Anderson must have been really shaken by what had happened to his daughter while he was away. But was he taking her to Oregon to farm, as was his original plan, or was he taking her back east? Either way, he would have taken the eastbound stage.

"Hey," the old man said. "Did you say your name was 'Dusty?'"

Dusty nodded.

"I got something in here for you. Come on in."

Dusty followed the man into the building. Timmons took an envelope from the table and handed it to him. Written on the front of the envelope was the word Dusty, in a flowing hand.

"It's from Miss Anderson," the old man said.

Dusty nodded. "Thanks."

"Well? You gonna open it?"

Dusty wanted to read it in private. He tucked it into a pocket in the front of his buckskin shirt. "Later. Right now, I need some water and oats for my horse."

"Water's out front. Oats are in the barn. Help yourself."

When his horse was comfortable in a stall with a feedbag over its head, Dusty sat on the hay strewn floor, his back against the stable wall, his hat resting on the floor beside him, and pulled the envelope from his shirt.

Sam Patterson had insisted he learn how to read. "A man can't get nowhere in life without knowing how to read and write."

It turned out Sam had been a bank teller before becoming a guerrilla raider during the War. He was an educated man, and though he had left that life behind him, his education still remained. It no longer showed in the way he spoke, but it was still there, lying in the back reaches of his mind. He insisted on sharing it with Dusty. There were no textbooks to use, but using charcoal on the flat side of a board, and sometimes simply a stick in the dirt, Sam Patterson taught the orphan kid named Dusty how to read and write.

Dusty tore open the envelope. Haley had flowing, beautiful penmanship. She was as skilled and artful with a quill pen as he was with a pistol. He was not surprised.

My Dearest Dusty, it began. *I know not if you will ever return to the way station, and as such receive this letter. I knew you for only one night, but it was the grandest night of my life, and I feel like I have known you forever. This said, I hope you will return, and find this letter.*

I told my father about how you saved me. I told him you slept in the barn. Forgive me the lie for the sake of discretion. But my father is no fool, he knows the ways of the world, and he knows I have come to care for you deeply in the short time I have known you.

She did not use the word *love*. Dusty found himself smiling.

My father said that he will be forever grateful to you, and hopes to one day meet you, but he cannot bear to remain at this way station a moment longer. Every moment here is one moment longer of subjecting me to danger, he said. Even

had he been home when those men rode in, he would have been helpless to stop them.

She used words well, he noticed. He liked that.

We are bound for Oregon in the morning. We have not had the time to save the money he had wanted, but he does not care. We will settle in, probably homestead, get a cabin up before winter, and put in a crop of alfalfa.

I do hope you come searching for me, Dusty. I cannot bear another day without you. You did not say how you feel about me, but I believe I saw it in your eyes, and felt it in your touch. I do so hope you will come to Oregon.

She signed it, *Yours forever, Haley.*

He liked that. Yours forever. He really liked that.

He figured if he lit out now, riding hard, he would be able to overtake them. But what about Montana?

He had thought his quest would end once he found Rose Callahan, but in fact it had only begun. Could he abandon it now? He had never dared even hope that he would be able to learn his father's name, and now he had a chance to actually meet the man. To look him square in the eye, to shake his hand. Could he simply turn away from this and ride to Oregon?

He supposed he could go to Oregon, spend some time with Haley and see if something permanent developed—he could never push a plow, but Oregon was also good cattle country, or so he had heard. Montana wasn't going anywhere. It would always be there, for a time when he was ready to go there and find Johnny McCabe.

Yet, he had the feeling if he went to Oregon now, the opportunity to go to Montana would simply never arise. Running a ranch, especially a little one-man operation, was a seven-day-a-week job, with no time off for vacations. And if Haley would have him, they would be raising children. The years would pass. Johnny McCabe would grow old, and eventually die, and Dusty would be in Oregon, never having met the man.

No, if he was to ride to Montana, he had to do it now. Then, once he had met Johnny McCabe, there would be Oregon. He supposed he could catch up to Haley and explain the situation, so she would know how he felt and not be left wondering, but he knew if he looked into those eyes one more

time, he would never be able to ride away from her, and he would always be left wondering about his father.

He decided he would ride to Montana first. He would cut overland, avoiding trails. This would give him a more direct route, and get him to Montana sooner so he could meet his father, and then be on to Oregon.

He considered writing her a letter. Leave it here at the way station for the next stage bound eastward. It would eventually get to her, probably, though it might take months. Mail delivery in the west was extremely slow, and he did not even have her address. Miss Haley Anderson, Oregon, was all he had. He could add, in care of her father. Dusty had not gotten the man's first name, but he was sure he could get it from Timmons.

But then he dismissed the idea of doing this. Even though Patterson had taught Dusty how to read well enough that he could decipher the flowing script of Haley's letter, his own handwriting was awkward, like a child's compared to her own. He would be embarrassed for her to see how limited his education was.

No, he decided. He would not write a letter. He would ride to Montana as quickly as he could. He would leave this afternoon. As soon as his horse was rested. And then, once he had met his father, and maybe spent a few days and got to know him a little bit, he would be off to Oregon.

Was he a fool? Probably. After all, what might be developing between him and Haley came along rarely. Once in a lifetime, and that was if you were lucky. Would his decision leave him with regrets? Maybe. Only time would tell. But he knew what he had to do.

He accepted a free meal of beans, bread and hot coffee from Timmons, then rode out, bound for Montana.

PART TWO

JOSH

FIVE

Pa had ridden out two weeks earlier. A cattle auction was being held in eastern Montana on a large spread near Virginia City, and he intended to look over the stock. If he found any that might be a good addition to the McCabe herd, he would offer a bid. If his bid was good, he would hire some hands and bring the new stock back to the McCabe range.

Pa never traveled by stage coach. He would instead saddle up and light out on horseback, seldom even taking established trails. He would often shoot his supper and roast it over a small fire. He would sleep under the open sky, almost never in a hotel room. Aunt Ginny, with her tiny spectacles riding low on her nose, and her brows dropped in a perpetual frown, a reprimand always cocked and ready to go, told him he would get himself killed doing fool stunts like this. Civilized people rode stage coaches when doing extensive traveling, and trains if they were available. But Pa told her riding through the wilderness, free of the trails and roads and all of the trappings of civilization, made him feel truly alive. It was the way man was intended to live, he would say. This would usually get a reaction of, "Oh, poppy-cock," and Pa would laugh.

This discussion had been replayed more times than Josh could ever count. It had been going on when he was a small kid, and now he was twenty and it was still going on.

Pa was a calm man, seldom speaking sternly, but instead had a sort of quiet power about him. Presence, Aunt Ginny called it. Leading came naturally to him, and people seemed to spontaneously flock about him, almost looking to him for guidance. The more demanding a situation, the more they turned to him. But when he was riding in the

wilderness, a sort of serenity fell over him. He still had the presence Aunt Ginny spoke of, but his eyes got a faraway look. Almost like he was in some sort of quiet communion with the mountains, the forests, the rolling grasslands. Josh did not quite understand this, but he wanted to. Yet, he also somehow knew it could not be learned. It was something he had to let come to him.

This was a big time for Josh, this time of Pa's absence. For the previous five years, Josh had been taking an active role in the operation of the family's ranch, working alongside Pa and the men. But this time, for the first time, Pa had left Josh in command.

Usually Josh accompanied Pa on business trips, meeting with prospective buyers such as mining company owners or sometimes the U.S. Army, or occasionally attending a livestock auction. Pa's right-hand-man, Zack Johnson, who had ridden alongside Pa in the Texas Rangers many years earlier, would take care of the ranch while Pa and Josh were away. But a year earlier, Zack had decided he would like to start his own spread, and so he had staked out a claim at the other side of the valley and began his own cattle operation.

Pa had not taken any of his journeys during the past year, but Josh knew he eventually would, and wondered who he would entrust the ranch to while he was gone. It had been at the supper table a few nights ago that Pa had announced his plan.

"You won't be goin' with me this time, Josh. With Zack gone, I need someone here to look after things. You're doing the work of a man. That makes you, in my eyes, a man. The ranch will be yours until I get back."

The fork had almost fallen out of Josh's hands. "I'll do my best, sir."

Josh reflected on all of this as he rode along. He had informed Aunt Ginny the evening before that he would be riding out to visit the cabin where the ranch's line riders were based. Pa sometimes referred to them as the floating outfit. Josh told her he would probably be spending the night at the cabin.

The floaters were ramrodded by a cowhand who had ridden for Pa maybe nine or ten years, and who went by the

name of Reno. On the frontier, you did not question a man's name. He told you what he was called. You accepted it, and never inquired further. Reno was a good man, but even so, Pa would ride out once a week to check on things. He felt it served to reinforce the fact that this ranch was a hands-on operation. The owner was also the main ramrod.

Reno was a good man, but he was known to drink a little too much. And when he was drinking, he was not such a good man. Get some whiskey into him, and he tended to throw responsibility out the window. This was maybe in the back of Pa's mind when he rode out to check on Reno and the boys, but he never voiced the concern. When Josh mentioned it to him once, all Pa said was he and Reno had an understanding.

Josh tended to ride out to the line cabin, make the customary appearance. Reinforce the fact that this was a hands-on operation. Maybe share in the work for a day or two, then return to the house. Nothing less than Pa would have done.

The night before Pa had ridden out, he stood with Josh on the front porch, overlooking five miles of meadow stretching out before them, forming the valley floor.

"This ranch will be yours one day," Pa had said, a smoldering pipe in one hand. "I want you to treat it like it's yours while I'm gone."

"What's the secret to being a good leader, Pa?"

Pa shrugged. "I don't know. Most of it is something you're born with, I guess. I've always seemed to fall into that role without even trying. I think you have those qualities, too. But the captain I rode under when I was with the Texas Rangers gave me some advice. Treat your men with respect, be honest with them, never talk down to them, and never ask them to do something you wouldn't do yourself. I was the ramrod of two other cow outfits before I started my own, and I've always applied those rules to my men. And I've done well."

Josh was about Pa's height, though more slightly built. He could move more quickly, but his wrists and forearms were more slender, and his shoulders didn't have as much spread. He had never been able to muster the bull-strength of Pa, and doubted he ever would.

Josh's hair was the color of corn silk, which he had gotten from his mother, and he wore it long, falling to his shoulders, like Pa did. Pa, Zack Johnson, and Josh's Uncle Josiah had once wintered in the valley with a band of Shoshones, a year or so before Pa had married Ma and long before Pa had moved the family here. It was from them Pa acquired his preference for longer hair, wearing it pulled back away from his face, and letting it fall to his shoulders, and sometimes tying it in a tail Indian-style.

Aunt Ginny was usually ready to go off on a scolding frenzy, and Pa's hair had been the subject a number of times throughout the years.

"Good grief, John, you look like some sort of half-civilized mountain man."

"That's what I am, Ginny," he would reply, which always drew a chuckle from Josh and his sister Bree.

Aunt Ginny's consternation had settled on Josh more than once after he had started growing his hair long—at first it was to be like Pa, and now he had simply gotten used to it. Aunt Ginny was forced to admit, though, there were worse things than for a boy to try to be like his father.

Like Pa, Josh was clean-shaven. The Shoshone had a name for a man with a beard. Dog-face. Pa and the others had ridden into their camp with a couple months' worth of whiskers decorating their jaws, but once he had found himself on the receiving end of that name, he sharpened his Bowie knife to a razor's edge and shaved away his beard. Though, Josh found that with his own light hair and complexion, not much grew along his jaw to shave, except for some light fuzz.

Josh wore a flat crowned hat with a brim that was becoming floppy with wear, and at his right side was holstered a Navy Colt.

Colt was the more popular brand of pistol, but among the old cap-and-ball revolvers, anyone who knew anything about shooting preferred a Remington for its superior balance and aim. Pa carried two of them, one holstered at either side. Josh had been intending to save his money for a Remington, but a couple years earlier Colt had introduced a new pistol, the Peacemaker, which was equal to the Remington in balance and accuracy, but quicker and easier to load. To buy

one of those was now his goal. Yet, no matter what he used for a pistol, he doubted his draw or marksmanship would ever be the match of Pa's.

When Pa drew, his gun seemed to almost leap into his hand, and his bullet would find his target almost like it had eyes and was seeking it out. Pa's skills with a gun seemed like he was putting no effort into it at all, as though the gun was simply his to command. He had said it felt more like simply letting his draw or his shooting happen, rather than making it happen.

Josh found being the son of Johnny McCabe wasn't easy. Not because of anything Pa ever said or done. But without even seeming to know it, the man cast a rather large shadow.

As Josh rode along, he let his gaze travel slowly over the terrain ahead and to each side, and turned periodically to survey the ground he had just covered. He was not expecting trouble, but Pa had taught him to always be alert. This was wild land. Remote. The nearest law was days away by horseback. And even then, the lawman had local authority only, his jurisdiction ending at the edge of town.

Josh had left behind the little valley they called home. He was now riding through long grassy hills that each covered a quarter mile of area, in a gradual rise to a rounded summit. Ahead, the land fell away to an even lower, longer series of hills. Behind him, visible when at the top of a grassy rise, were the foothills, now hazy with distance, and appearing dark due to the junipers and pines covering. Further back, the foothills would rise into forested ridges. It was in a valley amongst those ridges that the McCabe house stood.

Josh rode a chestnut colored mustang with a blonde mane and two blonde stockings. The horse was small, not more than fourteen hands, but was mountain bred and could run all day. It was Josh's first choice when going mustanging. The animal took naturally to pulling against a rope, which was beneficial when you were trying to hold a wild one at the other end of that rope after dropping a loop over its neck.

Josh had been letting the horse have its head, and for this horse, having its head meant running. The horse loved to

pound its hooves into the earth and let the miles roll by. Josh had not named the horse, but his sister, Bree, called it Rabbit because of its speed. Josh thought this was a stupid name, and his sister tended to be annoyingly cutesy too much of the time. Regardless, the name seemed to stick, and even Josh found himself, much to his own dismay, thinking of the horse by that danged name.

Rabbit had been moving at almost a full gallop for the previous three miles, and wanted to do more, but Josh reined up at the top of a grassy rise. Rabbit pounded his hooves a bit in protest, and let out a snort, but Josh held the reins firmly and Rabbit acquiesced. Despite the dumb name, this horse had brass.

Pa had said a good horse was often the difference between life and death out here on the remote frontier. Josh was more than willing to put his confidence in Rabbit.

Rabbit was lathered from running, so Josh let him blow. As he sat in the saddle, Josh let his gaze drift across the countryside below. It was just beyond the base of the long hill that a patch of earth looked somehow disturbed. Torn up. Like the earth can sometimes be after a herd is driven through, or a large group of riders has passed by.

Josh let Rabbit catch his wind for a few minutes more, then touched his heels to the horse's ribs to start forward, but kept the horse to a walk. As he approached the base of the hill, he could see clearly the sod had indeed been torn up by hooves. Riders, many of them, had passed through recently.

Before Josh had even learned how to read, he had been taught by Pa how to read sign. Pa claimed Josh had become one of the best trackers he had ever seen, though Josh knew Pa and Zack Johnson were still a few steps ahead of him.

Josh gave a tug on the reins to stop Rabbit by the torn-up sod, and allowed himself time to study these tracks. Many riders, indeed. Exactly how many, he could not tell, as the tracks of one would cross over those of another, and obliterate part of the trail.

Whenever he and Pa followed the trail of an animal— they had trailed many an elk through the mountains simply

for the practice—Pa would ask, "What can you tell me about the animal, just by looking at the tracks?"

Josh asked himself this now. What could he learn about these riders, simply by looking at their trail?

Well, they were not in a hurry. The horses were kept to a walk as they passed through—the hoof prints were too close together to have been made by running horses. At the very best, some of them might have been moving at a light trot. And they were all shod.

Josh found himself curious. A large body of riders traveling through the grasslands a few miles east of the ranch house. There were no trails to follow out here; the nearest would be the stage route, which was eight or ten miles south. Sioux renegades maybe, but not too danged likely. The Sioux, who had been living freely when Pa first brought his family to Montana, were now confined to reservations and gradually coming to take on the ways of the white man, but few rode shod horses.

Josh nudged Rabbit forward, keeping the horse to a slow walk as he examined the tracks a little further along. He had ridden but one hundred yards when he found a chunk of sod that had been torn completely free, and in the loose exposed earth was a track much more clear than those in the springy sod. An unshod hoof, and not that of a horse. The print of a cow. He also found, as he rode along further, not only horse droppings but some from cows, too.

These men were running cattle, and this was McCabe range. Eighteen hundred head of cattle grazed this range, along with about two hundred head of Zack Johnson's herd. Since Pa and Zack were considered themselves more brothers than friends, they charged no cost for sharing each other's range. More than three hundred head of McCabe cattle were on Johnson range at this moment, and had been since spring round-up. They had not been separated, because what was the point?

Josh could think of no good reason for this many riders out here in the remote hills. He wished he had brought a rifle along, but you normally don't when you're planning on working. A rifle sticking in the front of a saddle could easily snag a lariat. Josh decided he would follow the trail, but not come too close to those he followed. If it looked like trouble,

he would fetch Reno and the boys before engaging the riders. There were a couple of rifles at the line camp.

He estimated the tracks to be a day old. Partly by the condition of the tracks, and partly by the look of the droppings. He figured if he rode at a leisurely pace, he would run no risk of accidentally catching up with them.

The trail moved north for a couple of miles, then swung northwest, and then directly west and into the low wooded ridges. Further west within these hills was the valley Josh called home.

He had not been long in the ridges when another trail from off to the northeast merged with the main one. Two riders, and two or three more cows.

Shortly, he found the remains of a camp. In a depression between two low ridges were the blackened remnants of a large campfire. Off to one side, below a small pine, were the remains of a steer. Most of the choice cuts were gone, and what was left had been picked over by a mountain lion. And on the hide he found the brand of a letter M inside a roughly defined circle.

This was definitely a McCabe steer.

He turned his horse away, and he let him go at a shambling trot back along the trail. He would go to the line camp, get Reno and the boys, grab the rifles, and get those steers back. Reno was a large man, good with his fists, and though not fast with a pistol, he was a reasonably good shot. And more importantly, he had the kind of nerve that allowed him to keep his gun hand steady during a fight. A veteran of the late War Between the States, he had seen action. The other two, Tarley and Whitey, Josh knew less about, but they were good workers, and out here, you gave your loyalty to your employer, even if it meant taking up arms to defend the land or the herd. You rode for the brand.

Now that Zack Johnson had his own spread, Reno was the McCabes' best hand. When he was sober. Pa did not allow drinking on the job, and a couple years earlier he had found Reno with an open bottle in the bunkhouse during working hours. Whiskey tended to make Reno's temper flare, but he discovered while he was physically stronger than Pa, and was an excellent scrapper, Pa could punch faster and was a smarter fighter. Pa left Reno on the bunkhouse floor

with his face battered and bloody, one eye swollen shut, his nose broken. Reno had not allowed whiskey to interfere with his job since.

As Josh let Rabbit negotiate his own way down a slope to the base of a ridge, a question occurred to him: How was a group of riders able to rustle this many animals and not even be noticed by the floaters? It was the job of Reno and the boys to prevent just this sort of thing. Had something happened to them? Had this group of riders, possibly outlaws or raiders, killed Reno, Whitey and Tarley? When you were a line rider, you tended to ride alone for the most part, each man riding in a different direction to patrol and round up strays and watch for rustlers or squatters, only to reunite with the others at the line camp at night. Picking the floaters off one-by-one would not prove difficult.

Once the ridges were behind him, Josh held onto his hat and let Rabbit stretch his legs into a mile-eating gallop, quickly narrowing the distance between himself and the line camp. Josh stood in the saddle and leaned forward, to reduce the wind resistance and make Rabbit's job easier.

As he rode, he found himself filled alternately with feelings of urgency and dread. Dread that he might find Reno and the boys dead.

After a few miles, he reined up and let Rabbit blow. The horse was now greatly lathered at the shoulders and neck. Josh knew Rabbit still wanted to run, and he thought the horse had enough sense to ease off on his own before he ran himself to death, but it was imperative Rabbit have enough wind left to get Josh to the line camp.

After a few moments, Rabbit was pounding his hooves, dancing a bit to one side and snapping his head back and forth. He wanted to run.

"Dang, but you're a glutton for punishment," Josh muttered, then he let Rabbit have his head again, and they were off.

Two miles later, Josh topped a low rise, and beyond the base of the hill was a stream, and a couple hundred yards further on, the line camp.

Pa and Zack had built the cabin by cleaning away part of a low hill with shovels, and building a sort of dug-out that had three walls made of pine logs. The exposed earth of the

hillside served as the back wall. The roof was made of sod, and grass grew on it. A stovepipe protruded through a hole in one wall.

A stable, also made of pine logs, stood nearby, and horses milled about within the corral.

Josh dismounted far enough away to be beyond rifle range, ground-hitched Rabbit, then started down the hill afoot, his pistol drawn.

Chances were that none of the men stealing cattle would be at the cabin, but Josh did not want to take chances. He ran in a zig-zagging pattern, so anyone trying to draw a bead on him with a rifle from a cabin window would not have a steady target.

He stopped behind a short pine, waited a moment, then sprinted toward an outcropping of bedrock, diving behind its cover, his hat flying away behind him. There was no gunfire from the cabin.

He spotted a juniper atop a small hump of earth only ten yards from the corral. He burst from the cover of the rock, again weaving as he ran, bracing himself for gunfire at any moment. He dove, and came to a rolling stop behind the hump of earth. Still no gunfire.

He ran to the corral fence, and he glanced at the horses. All bearing the brand of the Circle M. It seemed to him if raiders had killed Reno and the boys, they would have taken the horses.

Josh now sprinted toward the cabin, covering the remaining distance in a few seconds, and came to a sliding stop before the door. He cocked his revolver, raised one foot and drove the door open. He burst in, ready to shoot at any gun barrels that might be aimed at him.

He found the cabin deserted. Three of the six bunks showed signs of having been slept in. Dishes crusty with dried food were stacked on an open shelf, and a coffee pot stood on the stove. On a table was an empty whiskey bottle.

Josh touched the side of the stove and found it warm. Men had been here not long ago. There was no sign that a fight had taken place. A couple Winchesters rested against a bunk, which meant the men were not expecting trouble.

Josh's eyes went again to the bottle on the table. He then noticed two others rolling under one of the bunks, and

began to realize the cattle were being taken from this range with no opposition.

Apparently Reno was back to his old ways.

Josh eased the hammer of his revolver back into its neutral position, and slid the gun back into his holster. Then, he strode from the cabin, anger rising within him, enough that he could not manage even a chuckle at how foolish he must have looked, diving from one source of cover to the next. He snatched his hat from where it had tumbled to the grass.

He led Rabbit to the corral. The horse was winded, and needed rest. Within minutes, a fresh mount was saddled. Josh had no way of knowing which direction Reno and the boys might have ridden away in, so he rode in a wide circle about the cabin, cutting for sign. He found what he had expected, a clear trail made as the men rode to and from the cabin. Some hoof prints were fresher than others, one set of tracks looking like it might have been made no earlier than this morning. Three horses, traveling east at a shambling trot.

Josh followed these tracks through a grove of tall pines, then across a flat grassy expanse, and up an incline.

He heard the sound of a pistol shot, small in the distance, brought to him on the wind. He nudged the horse's ribs with his heels, and the animal broke into a gallop. Again, he thought a rifle would have been handy; two were at the cabin, but he had stormed away in such an angry huff he had left them both leaning against the bunks.

He heard more gunshots. They were evenly spaced, not in a random sort of staccato rhythm that might indicate a gun battle. There was one gun only, being fired slowly but repeatedly. Then there would be a pause, before the firing would begin again. It reminded Josh of the sound of target practice, the hesitations being the time needed to reload.

When he had put a half mile behind him, he topped out on a low rise, and below was a small ravine which saw plenty of water during the spring run-off. Junipers and short pines grew, and sitting with his back against one pine was Reno, tipping a bottle, his adam's apple bobbing as he chugged its contents. Tarley was standing, aiming his pistol toward a pine at the far side of the ravine, squeezing off

shots. Occasionally his aim would be true and a branch would break free and fall, or a strip of bark would fly away. The third man, Whitey, was standing idly by while Tarley emptied his pistol at the tree.

Six shots. Two tree branches and a piece of bark. Tarley then flipped open the loading gate and dropped the empties from his revolver. That Tarley considered himself a fair hand with a gun was obvious; he wore his holster low on his leg, like Josh and Pa. The difference was that Josh, like Pa, wanted his pistol within easy reach, while men like Tarley wore their gun as such simply for show. A man who knew anything about shooting a pistol would not be wasting his shots on a target as far away as that tree was.

Josh gave his horse a nudge, and started down the slope. Reno was the first to see Josh approaching.

Reno was a man of thirty, but was considered old by cowhand reckoning. The range of ages on most ranches was usually eighteen to twenty-two. Reno's jaw was covered with short, stubbly whiskers, and his face was lined from having lived most of his life exposed to the raw elements. And Josh thought, Reno liked his whiskey and such a thing can age a man. He wore his gun high on his belt, where he could get to it if need be, but he had no pretense about speed.

"Hey, boys," Reno called to the other two. "We have company."

Tarley had just reloaded his pistol, and was sighting in on a branch. He and Whitey now turned as Josh reined up a few yards from Reno.

"What's going on here?" Josh asked.

Reno smiled, squinting into the sun. "What do you think is going on here, boy? My two compadres, here, are havin' a little target practice. And I'm washin' down the trail dust."

"It's pretty obvious what you're doing. It's also pretty obvious you're not doing your job. Some riders have been cutting through here, helping themselves to our herd. Now I see how they've been getting away with it so easy."

Reno shrugged, looking up at Josh, squinting a little into the sun. "What're you gonna do about it?"

"It's not what I'm gonna do about it. It's what we're gonna do about it. We're going to grab the rifles, and go after those cows."

Reno looked at the other two, who had ambled over. Reno said, "This here feller wants us to chase after some rustlers."

"Sounds dangerous," Whitey said nonchalantly, almost conversationally.

Reno returned his gaze to Josh. "No thanks, Mister Boss-man. We're cowhands, not gunhawks. If you're your daddy's son, why don't you take that big ol' hawg-leg you're wearin' at your side, and go run down them rustlers yourself?"

Josh said through his teeth, "When my Pa rode out, he left me in charge, and I'm giving you an order."

"If the boss wants an order given, he can come and give it himself. He don't have to send no runt to do it."

"Look, Reno..."

"No, you look, boy!" Reno shouted, raising his fist and aiming a pointed index finger at Josh. "When Johnson done quit this outfit and started his own place, that made me top hand. Whenever the boss is gone, he always leaves his top hand in charge. And now, that's me."

"You think I'm too young to be giving orders to a cowhand who's been around as long as you?" Josh's voice was climbing to a roar as he felt anger swelling inside. "Age should have nothing to do with it. Pa left me in charge, and if you work for Pa, you ride for the brand. It's a simple as that."

"No it ain't, boy. How do we know you got the sand for the job? Out here, you don't get nothin' just because of whose kin you are."

Whitey put in, "You ain't proved yourself, boy. You got the job only because you're the boss's son."

"That's right," Reno said, leaning back against the tree. "Respect ain't somethin' that's given to you. You gotta earn it."

"Reno," Josh said. "You're fired."

Reno raised the bottle to Josh as a sort of salute, and took another drink.

"Reno, I want you off this range. You've got just long enough to go back to the line shack and pack up your gear."

"You're gonna have to climb down from that horse and toss me off'n this range yourself."

Tarley said, "You're gonna have to toss us all off, boy."

Tarley was in his early twenties, and wore a black handle-bar mustache under a long nose, and his front teeth had long since been knocked out in a saloon brawl. Whitey had hair the color of Josh's, and it fell shaggily to his brow and over his ears. At his chin was a fuzzy promise of a beard.

Josh wanted sorely to step down from the saddle, yank that bottle from Reno's grip, and drive his knuckles into the big man's face. Josh's temper was a mean one, and he was athletic and gifted with his fists. Pa, who was as good a scrapper as Josh had ever seen, knew a bit about boxing, and he had filled a grain bag with gravel and hung it from a rafter in the barn, and coached Josh in the art of fisticuffs. Pa had taught him how to punch intelligently, from a solid stance, turning his shoulders and hips into it, rather than simply throwing wild hay-makers and hoping they connect. Pa had also learned something about wrestling tricks from the Shoshone, and Josh was wiry enough to be quite effective with them, also.

Pa had beaten Reno, perhaps the only man to have ever done so, and Josh found himself desiring the opportunity to become the second, but he knew to accept Reno's challenge would not be the right thing to do. Pa had said many times to think things through. Don't let you're temper do your thinking for you, and send you charging blindly into a situation.

Josh held a tight rein on his anger as he sat in the saddle, his gaze meeting levelly with Reno's. "No, Reno, that's just what you'd like me to do, but it wouldn't prove a thing. No matter which one of us whupped the other, you're still fired. You got half an hour to get your things packed and start ridin'."

Josh's glance then darted to the other two. "And you two can either mount up and ride after them cows with me, or join your partner. Which is it gonna be?"

Tarley let his hand fall until it hovered just above his holstered pistol. "You gonna make us, boy?"

"Leave that gun where it is, Tarley," Josh said.

Whitey looked nervously to Tarley. "Yeah. They say he learned how to shoot from his old man."

"Don't matter," Tarley said. "You either go for your gun, or turn your horse around and go home."

Josh stared silently at Tarley, his own hand falling to within reach of the Colt Navy resting at his side. Whitey glanced warily to Tarley, then moved back, away from the reach of any bullets that might stray.

The challenge had been made, and Josh accepted. He had shot many a can from a rail fence, and had exchanged rifle shots with raiders and renegade Indians, but this was the first time he had ever faced a man, ready to draw.

A strange calmness overtook him, and he was breathing slow and easy.

Tarley was smiling. He believed himself to be the faster gun, and that this fight was over before it could begin.

Josh watched Tarley carefully, keeping his gaze on Tarley's eyes, not his gun hand. Always watch a man's eyes, Pa had said. His gun hand will move too fast for you to react to, but his eyes will betray his movement a moment before he makes it.

The passage of time seemed to slow as the two faced each other. Josh's horse lifted one hoof and set it down out of boredom. A gust of wind wobbled the brim of Josh's hat, and the sun felt warm on his shoulders.

Then, it happened. A flicker of intent in Tarley's eyes. This is it, Josh knew! And each man reached for his gun, Josh a second of a fraction behind Tarley.

Both pistols cleared leather, but Josh overtook Tarley and gained the lead as each brought his pistol up to fire. Josh fired first, his bullet digging into Tarley's shoulder. Tarley's gun went off and Josh felt the bullet's wind as it whizzed past his cheekbone.

Tarley spun with the impact of Josh's bullet and fell to the earth, his revolver still in his grip.

The whole thing had taken maybe two seconds.

Josh's horse, suddenly startled, began to rear up on its hind legs, but Josh pulled tightly on the reins, and it returned to all fours.

Josh cocked his pistol, and said, "Let go of the gun, Tarley."

Tarley was gripping his shoulder with his left hand and he let the pistol fall to the earth.

Whitey's mouth was hanging open. "Just like his Pa."

"Now," Josh said, "you men get him into the saddle and into town before he bleeds to death."

SIX

Josh knew pride was a useless thing. Dangerous, even. Aunt Ginny had told him many a time pride is nothing more than artificially inflating your sense of self-worth based on accomplishments, which is not the same as feeling self-respect because of who you were. What kind of ethics you had, or beliefs. Or philosophies. Regardless, pride was what he felt as he rode toward the valley. A man never knows how he will react to a situation until he faces it, and Josh had handled his first gunfight like a man. Like a McCabe. He had not become afraid, with a trembling voice and shaking hands, and turned to run, as he had seen some men do. He had calmly faced his opponent, and let skill prevail. And nerve.

Pa had taught him that it takes more than simply skill to win a gunfight. Growing up on the frontier, Josh had seen Pa forced into a gunfight on four separate occasions, and believed there was none faster. But Pa claimed to have faced more than one who was faster than he was. It was not speed, Pa had said, but nerve that enabled him to win. It takes skill to be able to pull a gun from a holster in less time than it takes to talk about it, without shooting your foot in the process, but it requires a steely nerve to hold the gun steady when another man is aiming a pistol at you, and to make your shot count.

Josh found he had that nerve. He had proven it to himself this day, and to Reno and to Whitey. And most of all, to Tarley, who would probably regain most of the use of his right arm. But he would remember.

Josh had been shooting to kill. He would be a liar to claim he had not tried—intentionally trying to wing a man only, or shooting a gun from a man's hand, was the stuff of legends and bad dime novels. Don't get fancy, Pa had told him. I hope you never have to use your gun against a man, but if it comes to that, don't try any trick shooting. Shoot to kill. Because that's what your opponent will be doing to you.

However, he was not above admitting his shot had strayed a little, landing not in Tarley's chest as intended, but his shoulder. But Josh was glad. Even relieved. He had killed before, and had not liked the feeling. A small band of Sioux warriors had struck the ranch two years earlier, swooping

down from the wooded hills to the valley floor where the house stood. Josh, the lightest in weight, was sent to the peak of the roof with a rifle, while Pa, Zack, the wrangler and a couple cowhands manned windows at each side of the house. With a Winchester in his hands, Josh had dropped two riders.

Once the fight was over, Josh went to see close-up the men he had killed. One was a boy only a year or two older than he was, lying with lifeless eyes staring skyward.

Josh felt a strong hand on his shoulder, and he looked up to see the ocean blue eyes of his father, the strong jaw, the face lined like a war map from years of riding into the sun and wind.

Pa said, "It's not a pleasant thing, even though you had to do it."

Josh shook his head. "No, sir. It ain't pleasant at all."

"You became a man today. And you made me proud."

Josh didn't understand Tarley, who risked death simply to prove a point. Some might have felt Josh reckless for accepting the challenge, but he knew if he had backed down, he would have been as good as dead. On the frontier, courage meant everything. Survival was often a group effort, like when the Sioux warriors had attacked. A man without courage might become a detriment to those around him. A cowardly act could stay with a man his entire life. Any hopes he might have of making something of himself and holding his head high when in the presence of other men would be lost.

Things will not always be this way out here, Josh thought. Already, the streets of cities like San Francisco and St. Louis were paved with cobblestones, and telegraph wires stretched to many parts of the west. Just nine years earlier a railroad track had been laid clear to the Pacific. Civilization was creeping its way westward, and would one day come to these mountains. But that time was not yet here.

In a way, Josh hoped it would not be here for a long time. The raw frontier could be a place of violence, but here a man could be truly free. With his horse beneath him, his gun at his side, and his wits, courage and ingenuity, he had all he needed to meet any trouble that might arise. Josh did not

need, or want, civilization with all of its restrictions. Its limitations.

Josh reined up atop a steep ridge. Below him, a thick pine forest trailed away, to meet a flat expanse covered with lush, green grass. Two miles away, straight ahead and due west, the grassy plateau met with pines again, which blanketed another ridge. This was the small valley the McCabes called home. It was fifteen miles along, and at the southern end stood the McCabe Ranch headquarters. At the northern end of the valley was Zack Johnson's ranch.

Josh started down the ridge, once again riding Rabbit, letting the mountain bred horse find its footing as it went.

Pa had always said never to come back the same way you leave, so anyone who might be watching cannot discern a pattern to your habits. It seemed to Josh that Pa lived in sort of a state of war much of the time, almost as though he expected an enemy force to come attacking at any moment. Zack Johnson had explained that comes from having been shot at one time too many.

Josh had left the valley through a pass at the southeastern corner, the only easily traversed pass on that side of the valley, so he re-entered by climbing straight down Shoshone Ridge at the southern end of the valley.

He emerged from the pines onto the grassy plateau that was the valley floor, and a quarter mile ahead was a house built of pine logs, standing two floors high. Rising above its peaked roof was a wide chimney made of stones. To one side of the house, a small single-level addition was attached, its roof sloping downward. Josh knew behind the house was another such addition, which contained the kitchen.

Two hundred feet in front of the house and off a bit to one side was a barn, made of planks nailed into place upright. In a corral, a horse paced restlessly, and further back, where the grassy floor of the valley extended behind the house, a dozen head of mustangs grazed contentedly.

A man stepped from the barn, wearing coveralls and a wide-brimmed hat. Josh knew this to be the wrangler, Fred Mitchum. Fred raised one hand in a wave, which Josh returned.

As Josh approached the barn, he gave a tug of the reins to slow Rabbit to a walk.

"Didn't expect to see you so soon," Fred said.

"Didn't expect so, either," Josh said as he reined up before the pole fence of the corral, and swung out of the saddle.

"Have some trouble?"

Josh nodded as he gave the rein a couple turns about the fence, then turned his attention to a trough which was half filled with water. Here in the valley, a cool northwesterly breeze was drifting down from the mountains, but out in the grasslands to the east, the early summer sun had been harsh, and the wind hot. Josh's face was smeared with sweat and trail dust, his hair damp beneath his hat, and there was a streak of wetness down his back and along either side of his shirt.

He pulled his hat free, submerged it in the trough, filling it to the brim, and turned it over his head, letting out a groaning "Ahhhh!" as the water soaked his hair, and rushed down his face onto his shirt.

"What kind of trouble?" Fred asked, pursuing the matter.

Josh did not want to go into detail about the gunfight, as boasting was not the McCabe way. "Had some trouble with Reno and the boys. Had to fire 'em."

"Fire 'em?" Fred asked incredulously. "Reno was a top hand."

"Now he can be a top hand somewheres else."

Josh briefly detailed what he had found, the tracks of what looked to be a large body of riders, and they had helped themselves to some McCabe cows. "Reno wouldn't follow my orders when I told him and the boys to mount up and ride with me to get back the stolen cows. And they were drinking. You know how Pa feels about that. So I fired 'em."

"What're you gonna do now?:"

"Not much I can do, except ride into town tomorrow and see if I can hire a couple new hands, then ride back out to the line shack. Them riders will be long gone by then, but on the way back I discovered Reno had been letting his work slide for more than just one day. I found cattle roaming all over creation. We will have our work cut out for us."

Josh repeated his story for Aunt Ginny and Bree, again omitting the part about the gunfight. He also decided not to tell them about the riders stealing cows. No sense to worry them unnecessarily, he thought.

Aunt Ginny matched Josh in height, and at sixty-six, had somehow managed to avoid developing that matronly, portly figure that plagued so many women on the late side of middle age. Her hair was steel gray with a streak of white at each temple, and usually tied back in a bun. Her eyes were blue, with lines beginning at each corner and gently trailing away. Perched upon her nose were tiny, metal-rimmed spectacles.

She now gazed at Josh over the top of those spectacles. "I know you have a temper, Joshua. Are you absolutely certain you gave those men every chance to get onto their horses and join you in rounding up those strays?"

"Yes'm. I surely did. I gave them every chance. Firing 'em was the last thing I wanted to do. Reno is a top hand when he ain't drinkin'."

"Isn't drinking."

"Yes'm. Isn't drinkin'. It's gonna be almighty hard to replace him. Cowhands like him don't come along every day."

"Well, when your father comes back, he can figure out what to do."

"I don't mean no disrespect, ma'am, but by the time he comes home, I intend to have hired two or three new hands, and to have them cows all rounded up."

"Those cows."

"Yes'm."

The following afternoon was barely an hour old when Josh walked out to the meadow and dropped a loop over the head of a buckskin gelding. He had decided not to ride Rabbit into town, as the horse had covered a lot of miles the previous day, and Josh intended to be riding Rabbit when he returned to the line cabin in the morning. The mustang had two white stockings and a splash of white on its nose, and while it could not run as fast or as long as Rabbit – few horses could – it was a good cutting horse. Josh had used it before on round-ups, and thought this might be a good horse

to bring along as an extra mount when he returned to the line camp.

He had thought of giving the horse a name, like Buckskin, but then Bree might decide to override it with something cutesy, like she had with Rabbit. There was something perverse about his sister's sense of humor, he thought.

He led the horse back to the corral, where he slipped a bridle over the buckskin's head, then dropped a blanket onto its back, followed by his black leather saddle. Fred Mitchum walked up while Josh was tightening the cinch.

"Saddlin' up a little early, aren't you? The Saturday evenin' crowd isn't due for hours. You won't find anyone worth hiring until then."

Saturday night was the traditional night for a cowboy to howl. Cattle ranches paid once monthly, and on those nights, the town really caught fire. But even on these Saturday nights between paydays, many of the local cowhands would drift in, have a few drinks at Hunter's, play some faro, and some might wander down to Miss Summers' establishment.

Cowhands were a restless lot, especially the younger ones, never remaining with one employer long. Josh was sure he would be able to find a couple, maybe three, willing to sign onto the McCabe payroll and join him for a week of hard riding at the line shack, rounding up strays and patrolling the perimeter to make certain those riders didn't return.

"I thought I might ride in a little early," Josh said to Fred. "A cold beer just might hit the spot."

Mitchum gave a chuckle. "It does sound appetizin', I've got to admit."

At forty-five, Mitchum's face was lined beyond its years, like that of every man who had lived most of his life outdoors. Fred was thin, his shirt and coveralls bagging on him, but despite his spindly appearance, there was strength in his back, which became evident when he would heft a saddle to his shoulder with more ease than Josh could muster.

"Saddle up and ride in with me," Josh suggested.

Fred shook his head. "I'll be in later. Got me some things to finish up here, first."

Josh nodded. He pushed a foot into a stirrup and swung into the saddle. "See you in town, then."

With his Stetson resting atop his yellow hair and his Navy Colt at his side, Josh turned the cutting horse through the open corral door and down a wagon trail that led to town.

Josh admired Fred's dedication to his job. Here it was, Saturday afternoon, a time when most cowhands were having their weekly bath and shave, and thinking about beer or whiskey and possibly spending part of the evening with one of the girls who worked for Alisha Summers, the only businesswoman in town, and whose name when simply mentioned could cause Aunt Ginny to almost growl with anger. And yet he was thinking about work.

Pa had hired Fred specifically because he knew what kind of man Fred was, and Pa wanted a man with that kind of dedication to oversee the Circle M remuda. At most ranches, the wrangler was either a boy breaking into the cattle business but not yet experienced enough to earn his place alongside the cowpunchers, or an older cowhand no longer able to ride herd. Not so at the McCabe Ranch. Pa felt a cowhand was no better than the horse beneath him. In many parts of the west, the land was rugged and the civilization sparse, and a man's life often depended on the quality of his horse. Pa had scouted out the best man he could find to care for his horses, and offered him top pay. To be wrangler for the McCabes was one of the most sought-after jobs in the territory. And Fred took this job very seriously.

Josh rode across the valley to a trail that began in a small depression between two ridges. He followed it as it wound its way through a small canyon, then between two more ridges, through thick stands of pines, then out onto a gravelly plateau just beyond the valley. This plateau was where a small town was in the process of forming.

The town was nothing more than a scattering of buildings, roughly conforming to the shape of a street, near the mountain pass known as McCabe Gap. Pa had named it. He sort of liked the old-school terminology.

When Pa had been a child, his great-grandfather, the first John McCabe, had been a trailblazer and scout, back when the Pennsylvania mountains Pa hailed from had been a

frontier. He had dressed in buckskin and lived among Indians, and had many adventures to recount to his wide-eyed grandchildren. He had hunted and fought alongside frontiersmen with names like Daniel Boone and Simon Kenton. Some of these stories might have been exaggerations, for the sake of entertainment, but Pa and his brothers and cousins didn't care. The old man had been one of Pa's early heroes. And in the time of the first John McCabe, the term mountain pass hadn't yet developed. An opening between mountains large enough to ride a horse through was called a gap.

This little town, the only one within a five-day ride of the McCabe ranch, was not organized, and had no name, but was coming to be called by the name of the pass. McCabe Gap.

The saloon was a structure of upright planks nailed into place with a narrow strip of wood covering the gap between each plank. The roof was sloped, and swinging doors faced the street. A sign bearing the words HUNTER'S SALOON drawn in black paint, was nailed into place over the doorway. The establishment was owned by a burly, bearded man who had ridden for the McCabe Ranch until two years earlier, when he built this place and went into the saloon business.

"I'm getting too old for those long days in the saddle," he had told Pa and Josh one night. "I always wanted to run a barroom. Since there ain't one around here, I guess I'll have to build one."

At the time it was built, Hunter's was the only building on this little plateau. News of the existence of a saloon spread like proverbial wild fire, and very shortly there was standing-room-only in Hunter's on a Saturday night. It was also not long before an entrepreneur arrived by covered wagon and built a hotel fifty yards from the saloon. A stagecoach trail had been bringing travelers bound for Helena to within a couple miles of McCabe Gap for years, and the stage company contracted with the hotel owner, and soon was bringing customers directly to the hotel's front door. Many walked over to Hunter's for a cold beer after a day of sitting inside a stagecoach, swallowing trail dust.

Cold beer was a rarity on the frontier. Pa claimed to have tasted it once down El Paso way, in a saloon made of adobe where the barroom was cool even on the hottest days. At Hunter's, in a room behind the bar, which Hunter used as his living quarters, was a trap door leading down to a fifteen-foot deep cellar, which was where Hunter stored his beer kegs. A rope, which ran through a pulley driven into a timber overhead, was used to lower the kegs into the cellar once they arrived by stagecoach, and Hunter would climb down into the cellar to pour a draft when a customer ordered a cold one. Hunter also kept a keg tapped behind the bar, and charged the customary nickel for a mug of room-temperature beer. But for the labor of fetching a cold beer, he charged a full dime.

Not long after the hotel was in operation, with the stage line bringing customers to its front door, a general store was built, and then a livery stable went up beside Hunter's, and the street began to take shape. Now, two years after Hunter had opened for business, there was a handful of houses, and a seamstress's shop. There was talk of building a jail and maybe hiring a town marshal. And a bank would soon be going up, to serve the needs of the growing community and the ranchers and farmers in the surrounding area. There was also a small church that also served as a school house during the week.

Josh swung out of the saddle in front of Hunter's, and tethered the buckskin to a hitching post mounted by the front door, and pushed through the swinging doors to find three men sitting at a table. The three he had fired the day before. Tarley's shirt pulled tightly over a bandage at his right shoulder, and his arm was in a sling. Reno glared at him with eyes glazing over from too much whiskey, and Tarley turned painfully in his chair for a glance at Josh.

"You're a brave man, ridin' into town alone," Tarley said.

"I let you ride away the first time," Josh said. "You won't be so lucky a second time."

Tarley fixed his gaze on Josh for a moment, trying to muster some bravado, but then apparently decided to count himself lucky to still be breathing, and turned away.

Josh smiled to himself and continued on to the bar, which was nothing more than two long planks laid across upended beer kegs. He decided to let Tarley and his friends believe Josh had intended to wing Tarley, and not kill him. If they believed Josh had put the bullet exactly where he wanted it, they would be less likely to challenge him again. It also wouldn't hurt Josh's attempts to build a reputation of his own, and maybe step out from the shadow of Johnny McCabe.

Hunter stepped from the back room as Josh tipped his hat back on his head and leaned an elbow on the bar.

Hunter stood taller than Josh, with wide shoulders housing strength gained from a lifetime of hard work. He wore a pinstriped shirt, and an apron tied over a flat stomach. His hair was thick and black, with strands of silver sprinkled throughout, and his beard was long and bushy.

"Howdy, Hunter," Josh said. He had never known Hunter's first name.

Hunter had ridden onto the ranch thirteen years earlier, and asked for a job. He had given his name simply as Hunter. He offered no other, and none was ever asked. Such was the way on the frontier. Many a man was running from something, a noose or a woman in most cases, Josh figured, and you took his name as he gave it.

"Well, well," Hunter said with a smile. "You're in town a little early, aren't you?"

"I heard one of them cold beers callin' to me all the way from the ranch house. And I've got some hiring to do, and thought I might get an early start."

Hunter nodded. "I heard about what happened. It's all over town. All over half the territory by now, I reckon. Them three in the corner rode into town late yesterday claiming you run 'em off McCabe range, and outdrew Tarley and put a bullet in his shoulder."

"Couldn't be avoided. They were spending their time with a bottle instead of in the saddle, and wouldn't follow my orders. It was no less than Pa would have done. A group of riders cut across our range and helped themselves to a few head of cattle, and I couldn't get Reno and the boys to ride after them with me. And thanks to them, there's now cattle

straying probably as far as Crocker's spread. When I fired them and ordered them off our range, Tarley drew on me."

"Riders, huh? How many?"

"Hard to guess by their tracks. I didn't actually see any of 'em. They were long gone by the time I got there."

Hunter smiled, and nodded. "Well, it appears the name of Josh McCabe is going to become known in its own right, not just as his father's son."

Josh had long wanted to build a name for himself, not to simply be known as the son of a great man. But now that it appeared to be actually happening, he found himself surprisingly embarrassed to hear about it.

He thought he might change the subject. "Well, I got me ten cents here that I would gladly exchange for some cold brew."

"Do you really think I'm going to accept your money?" and Hunter started for the back room. "I'll be right back."

On the morning Hunter was to begin building his saloon, Pa, Josh and Zack Johnson had ridden in, and announced they were here to work. Pa said to him, "You put your sweat and blood into helping build our ranch. It's the least we can do to help you build your saloon."

Hunter had never allowed them to pay for their drinks. He never would.

Hunter had been gone only a few moments when Josh heard two sets of boot soles on the wooden floorboards behind him. He turned to find himself facing Reno and Whitey. Tarley remained seated.

"I'm gonna have a word with you, boy," Reno said. "Now that you're here, and not on your pappy's range."

"My father wasn't there yesterday. Tarley said his piece, and you're welcome to say yours."

"Listen, boy. I was workin' for your pappy when you was knee-high to a corn stalk. Been a top hand for him for a long time. We'll just see what he says about you swaggerin' out there and firin' me just because you think you're such a big man because you're the son of Johnny McCabe."

"It doesn't matter what he thinks, Reno. He left me in charge while he was gone, and it was my decision to fire you. He would have done the same thing in my place. You know how he feels about drinking on the job. Of course, if he

hadn't been away on business, you wouldn't have been out there drinking and letting the herd stray, anyway. You knew he left me in charge, and you wanted to push and see how hard I'd push back."

"You might feel like a mighty big man with that McCabe name, but it don't mean you're the man your daddy is. And I ain't gonna take your orders just because you got his name."

It was clear Reno wasn't listening to Josh, but was talking for his own benefit only, trying to work up a fighting anger.

The smell of Reno's whiskey-soaked breath reached Josh. He said, "Go sit down, Reno. You're full of whiskey."

"I ain't too full to break you in half."

This was it, Josh thought. Part Two of the test. Reno stood six inches taller than Josh, with fists like ham hocks. There was fat at his middle, the kind of fat too much drink can bring to a man, but there was solid muscle, too.

Reno was known as one of the best saloon brawlers in Montana, but Pa had beaten him. Now it looked like Josh was going to have his chance, whether he wanted it or not. Like with the gunfight, he would not be able to decline without creating a reputation for cowardice, a reputation which would dog him the rest of his life, or at least as long as he remained in the west. Not that Josh had any intention of backing down. Though, he was not as much interested in proving himself to anyone else, as he was to himself.

"Take your best shot," Josh said to Reno.

Reno balled one big fist and with surprising speed, considering how much whiskey he had consumed, and how large a man he was, drove the fist upward at Josh's head. Josh managed only to turn his head so the fist would strike his cheekbone a glancing blow. Rolling with the punch, Pa called it. Josh's hat tumbled to the floor.

Josh countered with a punch of his own, a right that glanced off of Reno's head, then he buried his left in Reno's whiskey-filled gut. Reno let loose a gush of air and sank to his knees.

Before Josh could turn his attention to Whitey, Whitey's fist struck Josh's temple, and staggered him. Josh

bounced into the bar behind him, which was all that kept him from falling.

Whitey stepped in and swung another fist, but Josh raised his arm and intercepted the punch, then swung a right hook catching Whitey at the side of the jaw. Josh's head was swimming from Whitey's punch, but he pressed on as he did not want to lose the sudden advantage he was gaining, and drove a left into Whitey's eye, then a right cross that caught him on the lip.

Reno was again on his feet, coming up quickly behind Josh and wrapping his arms about him and lifting him from the floor. Whitey was still a little too rocked from Josh's punches to move in, so Josh took advantage of this, raising both feet and planting them on Whitey's chest, and pushing away. Whitey fell backward, as did Reno, taking Josh down with him.

Josh rolled free of Reno's grasp, and sprang to his feet while he watched the heavier, less lithe Reno struggle more slowly to rise.

The dizziness from Whitey's punch had now cleared, and Josh found himself smiling as he readied himself for his opponents to make their next move.

Hunter had always claimed Josh enjoyed this sort of thing. Maybe he was right. Aunt Ginny did not approve, but at the moment, Josh did not really care.

Whitey came to his feet slowly, using the bar to help pull himself up. He then turned to face Josh with a revolver in his hand. Josh reached to his side to find his holster empty – his pistol must have fallen free when he and Reno tumbled on the floor.

"Now who's the big man?" Whitey asked.

Whitey suddenly felt a cold, thin blade pressed against his throat from behind, and shot his gaze downward to see a strong hand with thick fingers gripped around the handle of a Bowie knife.

"Drop that gun," Hunter said from behind, "or I'll cut you a new smile from ear-to-ear."

Whitey let the pistol fall to the floor.

"This is between Josh and Reno," Hunter said. "Stay out of it."

"That's the way I want it," Reno said to Josh.

Reno unbuckled his gunbelt and dropped it onto the bar. He then retrieved Josh's pistol and set it beside his own belt.

Reno said, "You might be better with a gun, but it's how good you are with your fists that shows your mark as a man. You daddy is one of the best I ever seen with his fists. Let's see how well you stand up."

Josh unbuckled his own gunbelt, and set it on the bar. "You're right about Pa, but you're wrong about being a man. It's not how good you are with your fists, or with a gun. It's what you are inside. Your loyalty, and your courage. And your self-respect."

The two men began circling each other. Any drunkenness in Reno had by now been knocked from him, and he moved like an animal stalking his prey. He was taller, and outweighed Josh by fifty pounds. The muscles of his arms filled out his sleeves, his shoulders made his shirt pull tightly, and he had a barrel chest. But he was more of a wrestler than a puncher, and if he got hold of Josh, the fight would be over.

Josh moved lightly on the balls of his feet, ready should Reno lunge at him, and to move in with his fists should Reno suddenly provide him an opening.

Reno suddenly leaped at him. Josh dove to one side, and Reno landed face first on the beer-stained floorboards. Hunter burst into a hearty laugh, and Josh heard a chuckle from the doorway; apparently others were drifting into town early as well.

Reno was slow getting to his feet. He had landed hard on the floor, and was a little unsteady as he stood, trying to regain his bearings. Josh, meanwhile had rolled to his feet, and now stepped in, and with his feet spread apart, and began planting punches into Reno's midsection. He turned his torso and rolling his shoulders into each blow, like Pa had taught him to do, like he had during countless hours of practice on the heavy bag hanging in the barn at home.

Reno grunted as each fist connected, but now that he was prepared, Josh found he was hitting a wall of solid muscle. He was not gaining any ground.

After four or five futile punches, Josh then changed tactics, before Reno could decide to ignore the punches

entirely and try to tackle him again, and brought a sharp uppercut into Reno's chin, then drove a left cross into his nose, which started blood streaming down over Reno's chin.

Reno staggered backward to the bar. Josh moved in to finish the fight, drawing back his right fist for one final punch. Reno suddenly stepped into him, not as badly hurt as he had let on, wrapping his arms around Josh again and lifting him from the floor.

Josh managed to pull his left arm free before Reno could fully tighten his grip, but his right was pinned to his side, and his feet were a few inches from the floor.

Josh fought to keep the air from being squeezed from him. The pressure increased against his ribs, and a couple of kinks he did not realize he had in his back snapped.

He drove his left fist into Reno's ear out of desperation. Reno winced, but continued to squeeze. However, Josh realized he was pursuing the proper course of action.

With his open hand he began to slap at the Reno's ear. Once. Twice. Reno's eyes were clamped shut at the pain. Josh managed a third slap, then Reno loosened his grip and Josh slipped free.

Josh dropped to one knee while Reno clasped a hand to his ear, blood from his nose now rolling down his neck and to his shirt.

Josh rose to his feet. With a roar of rage, Reno charged at him.

Josh ducked as Reno moved to tackle him, and Reno's momentum carried him over Josh's back. Josh straightened and Reno tumbled to the floor behind him.

Reno rose to his feet once again, unsteadily, almost falling once.

Josh ran toward him, leaped, and drove both heels into Reno's chest. Reno's legs went out from under him, and he landed hard on the floor again.

Josh scrambled to his feet. Reno rolled over into a sitting position, began to push himself upward, then his strength seemed to suddenly drain from him, and he collapsed to the floor to lie, huffing for breath.

Josh turned to face Whitey, who still stood at the bar with Hunter's knife to his throat.

Josh's chest was heaving for air, and sweat trickled down his cheekbones. "All right, Hunter. Turn him loose."

Hunter pulled back the knife, freeing Whitey.

"How about it?" Josh said. "You next?"

Whitey shook his head.

Hunter said, "Then I suggest you pick your friend off the floor, and get out of here."

Hunter looked to the table where Tarley still sat. "That goes for you, too."

Whitey grabbed Reno by one arm and helped him to his feet, and half-carrying his old friend, out the door. Tarley followed them, never once even tossing a glance toward Josh.

Josh retrieved his hat and gun, and leaned one elbow against the bar again.

"Here's that beer you asked for," Hunter said, reaching for a full mug he had placed on a shelf behind the bar.

His knuckles torn and bruised, Josh lifted the mug and tipped it, draining half of it. He then set the mug back to the bar, wiped the foam from his mouth with the back of his sleeve, and brought a hand gingerly to a lump rising on his temple where Whitey's fist had connected.

"That was mighty good fighting," a man said from behind him.

Josh turned to see a clean-shaven man of about his age. Probably the one who had chuckled from the doorway when Reno fell flat during the fight. His hair was cropped short, a flat-brimmed sombrero was tipped back on his head, and he wore a big bandanna folded in a triangle over a double-breasted shirt.

Josh said, "Don't believe I've made your acquaintance."

"Name's Long." The stranger extended his hand.

"McCabe. Josh McCabe." The grip of the stranger's handshake was a little tight on Josh's battered hand.

Hunter said, "He's new in these parts. Been in town a couple days, looking for work."

"Well," Josh said with a smile, "it turns out I'm hiring."

Long chuckled. "I kind'a figured you were. Word's been traveling pretty fast about how you fired those three, and one of 'em drew on you. I was hoping to bump into you in town sometime before the night was over."

"Where's the last outfit you worked for?"

"Russell Hall's spread, down in Wyoming."

"I'm looking for a couple of men to ride line with me. We got a few hundred steers to round up. Them three I fired were letting them roam free over half the territory, and letting strangers passing through help themselves to them. Pay's twelve dollars a month, and keep. The job's yours, if you want it. We ride at sun-up."

"You done hired yourself a hand."

PART THREE

McCABE GAP

SEVEN

Dusty sat in the saddle at the edge of a grove of alders and ash, and gazed toward a house almost a quarter mile away, across a grassy meadow. The building was two floors high and made of logs, with a front door shaded by a small sloping roof upheld by pine poles. Smoke drifted lazily from a chimney made of stones. Horses frolicked in the meadow behind the house. A ranch hand moved about the stable.

The McCabe Ranch. Home of Johnny McCabe. The man who was his father.

Dusty knew little of the family. He knew of the many exploits attributed to Johnny McCabe, like when he was with the Texas Rangers and took down five Comanche raiders with as many shots, before switching guns in a border shift, and bringing down five more. All the while with an arrowhead in his leg, and riding a galloping horse. Another story had McCabe squaring off against three opponents in a gunfight, drawing and fanning a shot into each of them before they could even clear leather. They claim he once took two men in one shot, firing a rifle through one and into another, during a skirmish between the Texas Rangers and some Mexican border raiders. Dusty was sure most of them were gross exaggerations, and others absolute bunk. News traveled quickly on the frontier, especially exciting news, but it tended to grow as it moved along. After a time, it scarcely resembled the actual event.

As for the man himself, Dusty knew little. He had learned a little from Lewis and Annie in Baker's Crossing, and had asked more questions at a couple cattle camps he had passed through on his long ride from Nevada. McCabe and two of his brothers had ridden with an outlaw gang for a

74

time when they were younger. Before that, McCabe had been a Texas Ranger. Eventually, he took a wife and started a ranch in California, near 'Frisco. His wife was shot—some folks claimed by a bounty hunter who was aiming for McCabe himself but got his wife by mistake. McCabe then took his young children and a few loyal hands to the Montana wilderness to start anew. Actually, much of this struck Dusty as a little farfetched, too.

As for the family, he had heard there were two sons who were fully grown, and a daughter. Their names, Dusty did not know. But they were his relatives. A couple of brothers and a sister.

Dusty watched as the ranch hand stepped into the stable, then emerged with a rope in his grip. The man ambled to the open meadow behind the house and dropped a loop on a palomino. The man led the horse to the corral, and then went back into the stable to emerge moments later with a saddle. Once the saddle was firmly strapped to the back of the palomino, the man led the horse to a hitching rail, then a dark-haired girl stepped out the front door of the house, flitted down the three steps from the porch to the ground, and nimbly climbed into the saddle. She exchanged a couple quick words with the ranch hand and then was off across the valley floor, her hair flying wildly behind her. His sister, Dusty figured.

He backed his horse further into the trees. He did not want to be caught watching the house. If even half of what he had heard about the man who was his father was true, to be caught spying on his home could have deadly results.

Dusty did not know quite how to feel, as he sat in the saddle, the home of his father before him. He felt a touch of anger at the thought that this home, quite impressive by frontier standards, should have been partly his, too. While McCabe and his other children were sitting at night under a dry roof and by a warm fire, Dusty had been in a bunkhouse in Arizona, unaware of even where he came from. And before that, he had spent many an evening with the Sam Patterson gang, making dry camp because the light of a fire might have alerted a pursuing posse as to their whereabouts. A little boy, huddled in a damp smelling woolen blanket, chewing on a

strip of jerky for his supper, and his actual family did not even know of his existence.

He was angry, but a tear darted its way down along his cheekbone, and he realized the anger was little more than a cover for the loneliness and the down-to-the-bone sadness had ridden with him for as long as he could remember. He reached up with the back of a fist to wipe away the tears, ashamed. Never allow weakness, Patterson had said. When you have a weakness, then your enemies have a way in which to strike at you. And every man is potentially your enemy.

A sad way of looking at life, maybe. But Patterson's lifestyle was such that trust in the wrong man could be fatal.

He wanted to ride over to the ranch house and announce who he was, and tell them he wanted to belong. It was his right to belong. McCabe and his children may have had no knowledge of Dusty's existence, and he supposed he could not really fault them for that, but he did exist, and he wanted to belong. He needed to, like anyone else.

But what could he actually do? Knock on the door and say, "Hi, Mister McCabe. I'm your son, from when you spent a night with a saloon woman named Rosie twenty years ago. What's for supper?"

Hardly.

He simply did not know what to do. But he knew he could not continue sitting here, staring at the house from this grove of trees.

"Come on, horse," he said. "Let's get out of here."

Dusty rode in the general direction of the pass, beyond which he had found was a small town. He had ridden past it two days earlier, skirting it widely as he figured that after all these weeks of traveling he probably looked more like a saddle bum than a drifting cowhand and vagrants tended to attract attention.

Where was he to go? What was he to do now that he was actually here? How could he approach his father? Should he approach his father? Or, should he simply leave well enough alone, and start for Oregon?

Maybe this made some sort of sense. Find Haley. Then find work and start saving money so he could maybe buy a few head of cattle.

Why remain here, confront McCabe and possibly open a can of worms better left closed? After all, maybe McCabe would not welcome him with open arms. Maybe McCabe wouldn't want a bastard son coming out of nowhere and disrupting his life. Maybe McCabe would tell him to get off his land and never come back.

Dusty had been on the trail for more than a month. His hair had been long to start with, but now he was beyond simply needing a shave. His beard was fine with youth, but was coming in fully and covering his chin, and streaking upward to form the beginning of sideburns. A fairly full mustache crawled along his upper lip. His trousers now sported a hole in one knee, and he needed a needle and thread to patch it up. Hell, he could have used a new pair of Levi's. A hot bath would be nice, and a bed and hot meal would be his first since leaving Nevada, except for the two cattle camps he had happened upon. Yet, he had spent his final five cents at Lewis's saloon.

What he needed was a job. From what he had seen since he had ridden into this area two days earlier, the only work available would be with horses and cattle, both of which he was quite experienced with. Of course, there was another line of work he knew much about, one Sam Patterson was very good at, but Dusty refused to even consider that.

Three years earlier, Patterson had said to him, "It's time for you to make a decision, Dusty. You're old enough now that if you're going to stay with us, you need to start pulling your own weight. I don't mean to sound harsh, boy, but some of the men have always objected to me keeping you with us, and now that you're practically full-grown, I can't have you stay with us any longer unless you start riding with us on jobs."

"What if I decide against it?" Dusty had asked.

"Then, you ride away. Free and clear. You'll be on your own, but keep in mind all I've taught you about survival. About people. And what I taught you about how to use those Remingtons in your belt, and you'll be all right."

Dusty did not have to wait to give his answer. He had already put much thought into this. "I can't be a part of stealing, Sam. I don't mean to sound like I'm judging you, because I surely wouldn't do that. You raised me and I'll always be beholdin' to you. But even though it might sound strange to anyone who doesn't know you, if I joined you and the boys, I'd be going against all you taught me."

"I was hoping that'd be your answer." Sam extended his hand and Dusty shook it. "You ride, boy. Roll up your bedroll, saddle your horse and ride. And don't look back. I love you like my own son, and I'll miss you. But it's the best thing for you."

And now, three years later, without a cent to his name and no food in his saddle bags, he still refused to take anything that did not belong to him, or which he had not earned.

The grassy floor of the valley stretched before him, and he allowed his horse an easy shambling trot, and eventually they climbed into a forest of hardwoods, aspen and birch mostly, as they neared the pass.

The afternoon sun was beginning to ride a little low in the sky, and his stomach was rumbling. A squirrel had made for a skimpy breakfast, and that had been many hours earlier. He thought he might ride into the small town and see if he could possibly find some work to do in exchange for a meal, and then possibly bed down in the livery. His blankets unrolled on a layer of straw would not be quite the bed he wanted, but at least he would be under a roof. Even though it was June and could be quite warm by day, the nights at this altitude still tended to be a little chilly.

Dusty wanted to lay low, to remain inconspicuous until he decided what approach, if any, he was going to take with his father. Maybe spending a few days in this town, working for his meals and sleeping at the livery, would be ideal. He had noticed a saloon earlier, and thought he might try it first. Chop some wood, maybe, or sweep a floor. Hell, maybe even serve beer. He had gained some experience with that in Nevada.

He followed the small pass between two wooded ridges, and fell into the shadows of early twilight. Beyond the pass, he came to a softly rounded grassy rise, and he guided his

horse up into it, which brought him back into sunshine. Down below, not two hundred yards away, a grizzly lumbered along.

The bear was keeping a roughly parallel course. Dusty's horse had not yet seen the animal, and as the wind was wrong, had not caught the bear's scent.

"Keep right on a-goin', big feller," Dusty said toward the bear, but loosened his pistol in his holster just to make himself feel a little more safe.

Of course, a pistol was not the ideal weapon to bring down a grizzly with. Sure, if the bear was close enough, and you were an incredible shot, you could place your bullet correctly in a vital place like an eye socket and kill the bear. But to have enough nerve to hold your pistol steady for a shot as a grizzly charged down on you would be quite a feat. You would not think because of a grizzly's tired, sloppy way of moving, with its head bobbing about as though the animal were simple-minded, that it could run quickly enough to be a threat to anyone. But a grizzly could be deceptively fast. If a grizzly was within pistol range and running toward you at full speed, you would have time to miss only once.

Dusty decided to add a rifle to his list of wants, to be filled once he found work. A Winchester, maybe. He intended not to begin the long ride to Oregon without one. As a cowpuncher, he did not really need one, and it might prove cumbersome, but for long distance riding, he decided a pistol simply did not provide enough fire power.

The bear lumbered on, going about its business. Dusty continued on his way toward the little town.

The late afternoon breeze was turning crisp and clear. Mountain air. Prior to this, he had spent little time in the mountains. For a time, the Patterson gang made a hide-out in a cabin on a ridge in Colorado, and once a posse had chased them clear to what was then the southwestern end of Montana Territory, which was now starting to be called Idaho. And the Cantrell Ranch stood before a backdrop of mountains; at times the mountain air would drift down— cool, crisp and clean. He could understand why his father would want to bring his children here.

Dusty descended onto a long grassy plain, and at its center was the small cluster of buildings that made up the

town. At the last cattle camp, which had been a week ago, one of the cowpokes had said the name of this little place was McCabe Gap.

This time, Dusty did not cut a wide circle. He rode onto the town's only street, his horse's head hanging with fatigue. The animal had been living on mountain grass, which can be rich in what a horse needs to maintain strength and stamina, but Dusty had been covering a lot of miles each day, and the animal was simply worn out. It needed a long rest in the town's livery stable.

However, before either he or his horse were to be granted rest, he needed to find work. The first order of business. Dusty reined up in front of a structure made of wooden planks, with a sign over the front door reading HUNTER'S SALOON. This was the place to start. Dusty swung out of the saddle, gave the rein a couple of turns about the hitching rail, then stepped up and onto the boardwalk, and through swinging batwing doors.

Hunter was idly pushing a broom, sweeping gravel and dust into a little pile at the center of the room, when he heard the doors swing inward and the scuff of boot soles. He glanced up at the young man in the doorway, and the first thing he noticed was the way the boy wore his pistol. Like it was a part of him.

Then he noticed there was something oddly familiar about him. About the set of his shoulders. About the strong, almost square jaw. And the look in his eyes.

"Howdy," Hunter said. "You're the first customer of the day, which I guess ain't too surprising, for a Monday."

The boy nodded.

Hunter shifted the broom to his left hand and stepped toward the boy, extending his right. "My name's Hunter."

"Most folks just call me Dusty."

Hunter's huge paw wrapped around Dusty's.

"You look like you been in the saddle a while," Hunter said. "Can I get you something to wash away the trail dust?"

"Actually, I smell coffee in here, and it sure smells good. I haven't had me a cup of coffee in a week."

"Well, the coffee does smell about ready." A kettle of coffee boiled away on a stove at the center of the room.

Hunter leaned the broom against a table, and poured Dusty a steaming cup.

"I got me a small problem," Dusty said. "I don't have any money. What I'm looking for is a job."

"A job, eh?" Hunter was not hiring. Though he was turning a profit, he was doing so barely. He would like to have had some hired help to relieve him of the long days he had to put in, but he simply could not afford it. This was cattle country, and ranchers and their hired hands usually lived on credit between drives to market. During the long stretches between cattle drives, Hunter rarely saw cash.

Yet, there was something about this boy he could not place—something oddly familiar about him.

"Tell you what," Hunter said. "First cup's free. Grab a chair, and I'll be right back."

"I don't want charity."

"Ain't charity. It's called hospitality. I'll never deny a man a cup of coffee or a drink of water. Grab yourself a chair, and one for me, too. I'll be right back."

Hunter stepped into the back room, and a few minutes later emerged with two tin cups. He filled them with hot, black coffee and handed one to Dusty.

"I'm much obliged," Dusty said.

"Think nothin' of it." Hunter dropped into a chair. "You been through here before?"

Dusty shook his head. "Never in my life. Not until today. Been sleeping on the trail. I happened onto this town, and I thought I might try to find some work."

Hunter took a sip of coffee. Thick, strong. Trail coffee. He had developed a taste for it during his years of working for the McCabes.

"So," he said. "What kind of work do you do?"

"Cowpunchin', mostly. And I've done some mustangin'. Worked a trail drive once, for the Cantrell spread down in Arizona. Rode shotgun for a freight outfit for a few weeks, before that."

"Arizona, huh? That's a long haul from there to here."

Dusty nodded. "Did it all on horseback."

Hunter's brows went up.

Dusty nodded. "Every mile of it. First to Nevada, then from there to here."

"You don't hear about that sort of thing anymore, but in the old days, long hauls like that were done more often. My daddy, he was a fur trapper back in the thirties, before he took up with a girl who was going west with her family, and settled in Oregon. He and those like him used to travel hundreds of miles at a time on horseback, with only their bedroll, a knife, and a good rifle."

Dusty nodded. "Got to get me a rifle."

"Today, it's all stagecoach, and soon there'll be a railroad spur swinging our way. About the only other man I hear about nowadays to travel overland is Johnny McCabe."

Hunter saw a slight reaction to the name. A brief, barely noticeable flicker in his eyes. Dusty had tried not to show it, but it had been there.

"You know the McCabes?" Hunter asked.

Dusty shook his head. A little too quickly, Hunter thought.

"No," Dusty said.

Hunter decided to let it pass, and continued. "I was a cowpuncher, myself. I rode for the McCabes for a lot of years, before I built this place. I don't know if Johnny McCabe ever even set foot on a stagecoach or a train. Everywhere he always went, it was by horseback. Even now, he's off to a cattle auction, and he went by horseback."

Hunter took a sip of coffee, his eyes on Dusty, trying to figure him. Dusty's eyes did not have the look of a man on the run, that sort of edginess known to the breed. He was calm, his brown eyes reminding Hunter of a still pond. Yet, what could bring a man all the way from Arizona? Especially by a round-about route that took him to Nevada? He must have logged a thousand miles. That's a lot of distance, especially with your backside in a saddle.

It was not the way of those who lived in the west to pry, so Hunter decided not to voice his questions. He would instead direct his attention to the Colt riding at Dusty's right side.

"I'll say one thing for you, Dusty. You carry that gun like you know how to use it. More than you'd expect from the average cowhand."

"Yeah. I've been trained by the best. But I ain't no outlaw. I've got no price on my head. And I don't go around looking for trouble."

"Didn't say you was, son."

"I'm just looking for work. If you ain't hiring, then I'm hoping you could direct me to someone who might be."

"You tried the McCabe place? There are about five ranches all within a day's ride of here, but the McCabe spread is the closest."

"Nope. I ain't looking for a cowpuncher job. Nothing that permanent. Just an odd job or two for a few days. Maybe a week or two, at best."

"Then what? Moving on?"

Dusty shrugged. "Next stop is Oregon."

Hunter chuckled. "Oregon?"

Dusty nodded, a little sheepishly. "There's a girl there, and..." he let it trail off.

Hunter nodded with a smile. "Many a man has done worse than riding a thousand miles on horseback for a girl."

Hunter took another sip of coffee. "Well, Dusty, I sure could use the help, but I can't afford it. Business is good, but it ain't been that good, yet."

"I ain't askin' for money. Just meals, and maybe a dry roof over my head for a few days."

Hunter gave him a long look. This was the slow time of the week. Monday afternoon. Just two evenings earlier, the barroom had been filled with cowpunchers, pouring down beer and whiskey, and playing cards. A couple of fights had broken out, resulting in overturned tables, and Hunter had to knock some heads together. And there had been the fight between Josh and Reno, one of the finest examples of fisticuffs Hunter had seen in a while. Josh was sure a chip off the old block.

Hunter could have used the help Saturday night, but at the moment, as far as odd jobs went, there was simply nothing that needed doing that Hunter could not do himself.

Yet, there was something he could not quite place about this boy, and he did not want him to leave until he figured it out.

"Tell you what," Hunter found himself saying. "Can you push a broom?"

"Yeah. Done it before."

"When your coffee's done, finish the floor. Then, there's some wood out back that could use splitting. I'm not much of a cook, but you're welcome to stay and have supper here."

"I'm beholding to you."

It was as Hunter watched Dusty push the broom, a swamper who wore his gun like a gunfighter, that it came to Hunter who this boy reminded him of. The way the boy walked, the set of his shoulders, and the way his gun seemed to be almost a part of him.

Now ain't that danged peculiar, he thought.

EIGHT

Dusty slept in the livery stable, his blankets unrolled on a layer of hay. He had made an arrangement with the man who operated the stable—he would be on hand at midday to act as hostler when the stage arrives, help change teams, and he could have a free place to sleep. Breakfasts were provided by Hunter, usually fried eggs and steak.

Hunter would often become distracted while the steaks were frying, and they would be sooty and flattened by the time they were served. Since Dusty had something of a knack for cooking, he volunteered to handle the breakfast duties one morning. First he tenderized the beef, hammering at it with the butt of an unloaded pistol, then he fried it, flipping it over regularly, which Hunter tended to forget to do. Dusty added salt occasionally. He served steaks that were juicy, excessively tasty, and not laborious to chew.

"You got a new job, Dusty," Hunter said. "You're the new breakfast cook."

"If you don't mind, I'd like to be the new supper cook, too."

Hunter winced. "My cooking's that bad?"

Dusty raised his brows and gave a quick nod.

Charlie Franklin, who owned the general store, was sitting at a table sipping coffee. Hunter did not officially open his saloon in the morning, but some of the locals liked to come in and drink some coffee and chat, so Hunter charged a penny a cup. Sometimes a newspaper that arrived on the stage the day before would be handed about.

"Hey, Hunter," Franklin said. "The way those steaks smell, you ought to consider opening for breakfast."

Franklin had a rounded stomach and thin, graying hair. Not the strong look of most of Hunter's customers, but unlike the others, he had not spent most of his life punching cows. But he was ambitious. Not only did he operate the general store, but he sold guns also, and dabbled in some gunsmithing.

"That's a fine looking pistol, Dusty. Could I see it?"

Dusty drew the gun and handed it to him. Franklin held it out a couple feet before his eyes, squinting as he examined the piece. "Ah, yes. Fine looking. Forty-five?"

"Forty-four-forty," Dusty said.

"You don't say. The Colt Peacemaker. The gun of the future. Walnut grip. Nice balance. In ten years, this will be about the only gun you'll ever see anyone carrying."

"It's a good gun," Dusty said, as Franklin handed it back to him. "But I'm looking at a long ride overland, on horseback. All the way to Oregon. What I really need is a rifle."

"Oregon? Your travels take you far, then."

Dusty nodded. "They sure do."

"Well, I have a fine selection of rifles."

"Nothin' I could afford, most likely. I don't have any money, and I don't plan on staying long enough to work and save any up."

"I'm sorry to hear you'll be leaving. The way you cook, it'd be a shame to lose you." He looked at Hunter. "Take my advice seriously. A good breakfast in the morning is worth paying for. And those guests down at the hotel, they have cash, a valuable commodity in this town between cattle drives."

Franklin also had a tub in the back room of his store, and sold a bath for a dime, and laundered clothes for fifty cents. Dusty had no money, but Hunter said for Franklin to add it to the saloon's tab. Dusty allowed himself to enjoy the luxury of hot water and soap, on the agreement that he work it off at the saloon. The mountain water he had washed in while on the trail was rich in minerals and got you tolerable clean, but there was nothing like steaming water and lathery soap.

While he was bathing, Franklin washed Dusty's clothes, and hung them on a line out back to dry.

"Don't know exactly what to do with that buckskin shirt, but your trousers and union suit are clean and dry. And I took the liberty of patching the hole that was in the knee."

Franklin also threw in a haircut and shave, though Dusty accepted the shave only. He had grown accustomed to longer hair during his years on the run with the Patterson gang. Once he was on his own, he paid for a short haircut, but after so many years of hair falling to his shoulders, he found he didn't like the feeling of a draft on his neck. While

Dusty sat in a wooden upright chair that served as a barber's chair, Franklin slid a straight razor through soapy foam he had applied to Dusty's face.

"I used to be a barber, back east," Franklin said, while he lathered Dusty's face and sharpened the razor on a leather strap. "What seems like a lifetime ago."

"A barber? How'd you find yourself running a general store? And doing gunsmithing?"

"Out here, a man does anything and everything to survive. Last summer, I earned a few dollars putting a new roof on Miss Summers'... shall we say...establishment. And I've helped Hunter move a shipment of freight, more than once."

"A jack of all trades, eh?"

Hunter had told Dusty to buy some clothes, too, so after the shave, Dusty did some shopping.

"The way things are going," Dusty had said to Hunter, "I'll have such a big debt to you that I'll be a whole year working it off."

"That's the idea," Hunter said with a smirk. "I'm thinkin' seriously about Franklin's breakfast idea. I want to keep you around as long as I can, considering what you can do to a steak."

Dusty had to admit, he needed the clothes. He walked out of Franklin's store in a new pair of Levi's, a white shirt, and with a second pair of Levi's and another shirt in boxes under one arm, and his buckskin shirt rolled under the other.

Before he left the store, his gaze had fallen upon a rack of rifles and shotguns standing behind the counter. Mostly weapons Franklin had acquired in trade, from customers who had no cash, and Franklin did not know them well enough to extend credit.

One weapon in particular caught Dusty's eye. A Spencer lever-action rifle.

Franklin handed it to Dusty, who brought it to his shoulder and sighted in on an imaginary target. A Spencer was loaded through a tubular magazine in the center of the stock, and the trigger guard acted as a lever that could be jacked, like a Winchester, to eject a spent cartridge and chamber a fresh one.

"This is a beauty," Dusty said. He also thought, but did not say, this would be the perfect rifle to have on his ride to Oregon. "What are you asking for it?"

Franklin shrugged. "I haven't put a price on it, yet. Spencers are out of production, and everyone is using Winchesters and Springfields these days. I doubt I could get much for it."

"It's in almost new condition. Not a scratch on it. I bet it hasn't been fired more'n a couple dozen times." Dusty jacked open the chamber, and was admiring the clean, slightly oiled steel.

"Don't matter. The market isn't defined by quality. It's defined by people's wants. It cost me three sacks of coffee and a can of beans. I didn't really want it, because I was afraid I wouldn't be able to get rid of it, but the customer really needed the coffee and the beans. What can you offer?"

"Not a thing. All I have is my horse, my saddle, my six-shooter, and my clothes. And most of my clothes were paid for by Hunter. I spent my last cent down in Nevada, many miles ago."

"Well, not to worry. This thing has been here a year already. I'm sure it's not going anywhere soon."

The idea of hiring a professional cook had never occurred to Hunter. But on Wednesday morning, a couple of hours before the noon stage was due to arrive, Hunter said, "Dusty, if I ran down to Franklin's and got us a couple big pots and a load of potatoes, how fast do you suppose you could put together potato and steak dinners for the passengers?"

"Are you thinking on getting into the restaurant business?"

"Why not? Them passengers, they have real cash, like Franklin said. Start with dinner today, and maybe tomorrow morning we'll open for breakfast."

"But I already have a noon job. Hostler, at the livery stable."

"I can take care of that. Old Arthur, who runs that stable, he owes me for so many beers he'll never be able to pay up."

Sam Patterson had said once folks just take naturally to some things more than others. With some it's business, like running a store. With others it's working with livestock. With some, it's painting or sculpting, or singing. With Dusty, it seemed to be two things—shooting a gun, and cooking.

Dusty had never considered himself to be more than a simple trail cook, throwing together whatever ingredients were available and trying not to poison anyone. But people did seem to rave about his cooking, so what the hell? A little time out of the saddle might make for a welcome change, he thought.

When Wednesday's customers boarded the stage, they did so with full, happy bellies. As the stage pulled out of town, Hunter sat in a back room counting his newly acquired cash, and Dusty found himself permanently relieved of his hostler duties.

"Hey, Hunter," Dusty called out, while he sat at a table enjoying a cold beer Hunter had told him to pour for himself. "How about we expand the menu a bit? Add Texas toast, maybe, and some homemade bread? And I can do a thing or two with a frijole, if I can find the ingredients."

Hunter called from the back room, "A frijole? Hell, I haven't tasted one in years. You can make those?"

"If I can find what I need. When this beer's gone, I'll take me a walk down to Franklin's."

Hunter stepped into the doorway. "How'd you learn to make 'em?"

"Just somethin' I picked up along the way."

Dusty did not want to tell him the actual way he had learned to make Mexican food. When he was nine, the Patterson gang had holed up in a canyon a few miles south of the Mexican border, and they would ride into a nearby town to whoop it up at a saloon, and with some of the women who worked the barroom. Dusty, much too young for such festivities, helped an older woman in the kitchen of a restaurant in the little town, and learned of the magic of cayenne and chili peppers.

Thursday's hotel customers found Hunter offering a traditional western breakfast of steak and eggs, all they could eat for a reasonable price. Hunter undercut the price charged at the hotel for breakfast, and he included two other items

the hotel did not have access to. A pig farmer a couple miles from town owed Hunter for some beers, so Hunter found himself able to include bacon on the menu. And it turned out, Dusty made the lightest, most wonderful homemade bread Hunter had tasted in a coon's age.

"Reminds me of the bread made by my momma," he said.

One cowhand in town for the morning, said, "Hunter, I didn't know you had a momma."

"I didn't. But if I did, her bread would have tasted like this."

The stage customers at noon found Texas toast on the menu, and slices of Dusty's bread were included with the steak dinner. The pig farmer also kept a small flock of chickens, so Dusty fried up a basket full of drumsticks and wings to offer the customers some variety.

Hunter was actually able to pay Franklin in cash for the items he had bought Wednesday, including Dusty's clothes. Franklin chuckled, almost giggled, with delight. "Prosperity is coming. Just around the corner. I know it."

Saturday morning, while Hunter was savoring a breakfast of steak and eggs, with a thick slice of toasted bread oozing with butter, he said to Dusty, "Tonight will be the start of what I originally hired you for. You ever tend bar before?"

"Yeah, for a short time, down in Nevada. Nothing fancy, just pouring beer and whiskey."

"That's all we do here. If someone asks for a beer, you fill a mug from the keg behind the bar. If they ask for a cold beer, you go to the keg in the root cellar. And the bottles of whiskey are all lined up behind the bar. Nothing to it at all."

Later in the afternoon, after the Saturday stage had departed and Dusty and Hunter had cleared away the dishes and cooking pots and kettles, Hunter suggested Dusty grab a little rest before the evening crowd started trickling in. Dusty carried a straight-backed chair out to the boardwalk and sat in the afternoon sun, rocking the chair back on its rear legs until the straight-back touched the wall. He lowered his hat over his eyes and reflected about what an unusual week this had been. It had been a good week, which he supposed was why it had been so unusual.

He had begun the week as an unemployed cowhand with a gunfighter's past that he preferred to keep hidden, riding on a fool's quest to find the father he had never known. A quest that had begun originally in Arizona, and had brought him clear to Montana Territory. He was ending the week with a job as a professional bartender and cook. Now, would you have cared to lay odds on that?

Working for Hunter was giving him a much needed distraction from his troubles. During the long ride from Arizona, he had had each entire day to think about first his mother, and then after he had left Nevada, his thoughts had turned to his father. What would he be like? How would he react when Dusty introduced himself? And there were evenings by a campfire, roasting rabbit, sometimes listening to coyotes howl from somewhere off in the darkness, and he would wonder what the flesh-and-blood Johnny McCabe would be like.

He had seen Wild Bill Hickok once, and remembered how oddly human he seemed, compared with the legendary figure developing in stories told in cattle camps and saloons. Hickok had been tall, with long flowing hair and a buckskin jacket, and a red sash tied about his middle, into which two revolvers were tucked. And he carried himself ramrod straight with his gaze fixed directly ahead, as people watched him ride by. He struck Dusty as being fully aware of his larger-than-life status. But he was just a man, not a god. And when he was putting on a shooting exhibition, which he charged admission for, he was accurate enough, but he was not particularly fast with his guns. Dusty could have easily equaled his shooting feats, and done so much more quickly. Dusty remembered feeling a little disappointed. He wondered how Johnny McCabe would compare to the stories told about him.

Hunter's job had given Dusty a week's worth of distractions from the original reason he was in Montana, and he thought he might indulge in these distractions a while longer, while he decided what to do. Whether he should ride out to the ranch and introduce himself, and risk the disappointment if things didn't go well. Or just head on out to Oregon.

His long trail had begun a year earlier, when he had written to the family of an elderly couple he had lived with for a short time, before he had gone to live with Patterson. He had written to learn if anything had ever been mentioned of his mother.

Actually, he mused, this had all begun twenty years earlier, with a saloon woman named Rosie giving birth to a bastard child. According to the bartender Lewis, Rosie had given the child to a family of traveling missionaries, who were returning east. It wasn't that she did not love her son, but rather it was that she loved him too much to see him grow up in a saloon. He had then been delivered to a family named Stowell—Methodist missionaries who were living in Missouri.

Sam Patterson had gone west and settled in Texas, and had spent a little time riding with the Rangers, fighting Comanches, who were master guerrilla raiders. So, when he volunteered to fight for the Union, with a feeling of loyalty for the country that was stronger than his loyalty for Texas, he was made commanding officer of a guerrilla unit. Their primary task was to attack and burn farms in Missouri that were owned by Confederate loyalists, and to burn bridges. Anything to hinder the Confederate Army.

The war ended, and while a former band of Union guerrilla raiders called the Red Legs were considered war heroes, and one member named Hickok went on to acquire almost legendary status, Confederate raiders like Jesse James and William Quantrill found themselves despised. Patterson found that, even though he and his men had fought on the side of the Union, they were somehow lumped together with Quantrill and the James brothers. Patterson figured it was because no other band of Union raiders acted with such methodical efficiency, and the Army and perhaps the country itself were afraid of them. They found they were unable to find work, as no one wanted one of Patterson's raiders on their payroll. So, they simply continued their exploits, now for personal gain rather than a war effort. Soon the group, renamed the Patterson Gang, found themselves on reward posters in Kansas, Colorado and Texas.

As Sam told it, he and his men had ridden onto a farm one night, intending to steal some stock and raid the house for supplies. They struck after dark, and after they had done

their damage, they took a torch to the house, as the chaos would better cover their getaway. However, one little boy had not screamed or cried. One dark eyed little boy, seven years old, had simply stood his ground with fists clenched and his jaw locked in determination as the house that had been his home erupted in flames, and riders swirled about, shooting and driving off horses and cattle.

Patterson reined up in front of the little boy and their gazes met. The boy would not break the eye contact. He would not give ground.

"Run!" Patterson shouted. "Get out of here!"

The boy would not move. Patterson aimed a pistol at him, intending to frighten him away lest he be accidentally trampled by one of the horses. The boy held his ground firmly.

Patterson never knew quite what it was about the boy—maybe the boy reminded him of himself, somehow. Finally, he scooped the boy up and sat him in front of the saddle, to keep him safe until the insanity ended. But when it was time to ride away, the building in flames and the man of the house lying dead with a bullet in him, and no other adult in sight, Patterson found he could not simply set the boy down in the middle of that kind of devastation and ride away.

Patterson asked the boy's name.

"Dusty," was all the boy would say.

Patterson had intended to deliver the boy to a church or some such place at the first opportunity, but somehow that opportunity never presented itself. The boy was wary of him at first, but as the family he had been with were dispassionate, never really knowing how to make a seven-year-old orphan boy feel welcome, and he did not even remember his mother, Patterson soon found himself becoming the boy's parental figure. A bond began to form between the two, Patterson often claiming Dusty was the son he never had.

Dusty grew, and he remained with the Patterson gang. Many of the men objected, but they were afraid of Patterson's temper and his skill with a gun, and so Dusty remained. Sam never allowed Dusty to participate in a raid or a robbery, and so his name was never included on any reward posters. At

fifteen, Dusty took the chance Sam offered, and rode away with his name clean.

Dusty made a life for himself, working on ranches in Texas, New Mexico and Arizona. First as a wrangler, then as a cowhand. Once he rode shotgun for a stagecoach company. But in the back of his mind were always the questions—where was he from? Who were his parents? Patterson had said once the farm where he found Dusty was the Stowell place, and that old man Stowell had been some sort of Methodist missionary, come west to save the heathen Indians. So, from a bunkhouse on the Cantrell spread, Dusty had written letters to Methodist organizations in Missouri giving them the name Stowell. They replied with names and addresses of the Stowell kin, who all still lived back east, and it was from them he obtained the name Rose Callahan, a saloon woman from Carson City who had given her poor, fatherless child away. And so Dusty's journey began, the long trail that eventually brought him here, to the chair he rocked back in, on a boardwalk in front of a saloon in Montana Territory.

He sometimes wondered what might have happened to Sam and the boys. About a year earlier, news of their exploits had stopped making the word-of-mouth circuit. Some said they thought Patterson might have been killed, but there was no official confirmation, and the reward posters remained up.

Dusty was brought out of his reflections by the sound of hoofbeats. He had dropped the brim of his hat over his eyes, and he now reached up with one hand to lift the hat enough to give him a view of the street, and the rider approaching. A thin man, forty-ish, in a wide brimmed hat, and a white shirt with suspenders strapped over his shoulders. He wore no gun, indicating he was probably not a cowhand—Dusty had yet to meet a cowhand who carried no gun at his side. The man rode easily, and swung out of the saddle with an ease and sureness that told Dusty that, even though he was not a cowhand, this man was an accomplished horseman. He gave the rein a couple turns about a hitching rail, then ambled onto the boardwalk, gave Dusty but a fleeting glance, and pushed his way through the swinging doors.

Dusty noticed the horse carried a brand that was a roughly drawn letter M, inside an equally roughly drawn circle. The Circle M. Dusty wondered if this man was a McCabe rider.

"Fred," he heard Hunter say from inside.

"You open for business?"

"Only for my best customers. How about a cold beer? Just got the keg tapped."

"Sounds good to me."

Inside, Fred bellied-up to the bar and waited while Hunter climbed the ladder down to his root cellar, and the keg of cold beer. Shortly, he returned with two mugs of foaming brew. Hunter set one on the bar before Fred, and the other he kept for himself.

"Looks to be a quiet night, for a Saturday," Fred said. "Josh won't be here to liven things up."

"When's he due back from the round-up?"

"Another week." Fred took a sip of beer. "And did he ever catch heck from Aunt Ginny the next mornin', after whuppin' Reno. His face was all bruised up, and on top of that, he and the new men he hired rode out the following morning, without even waiting until after church."

Hunter shook his head, his shoulders shaking with a silent chuckle. "Josh is braver than I am. I would never want to get that little woman all riled up at me."

"Say, Hunter. Who's that boy settin' out there on the boardwalk?"

"His name's Dusty. Works for me. I hired him Monday. He's my new cook and bartender."

"Cook and bartender, eh?" Fred took another sip. "Got gunhawk written all over him. And gunhawk means trouble."

"No, Dusty's no trouble. He's a good man. And besides, no man has gunhawk written all over him more than the man you work for. And you won't find a more stand-up man."

"That's the truth."

Fred took a sip of beer, and Hunter followed suit.

"Y'know," Fred said. "Strikes me as though I've seen him somewheres. Has he ever been through here before?"

Hunter shook his head. "Nope. Never been to Montana before."

"Strikes me as downright familiar."

Hunter raised his brows, his eyes dancing with amusement, as though he were privy to a great secret. "Don't he, though?"

Dusty, still listening outside, found that downright puzzling.

NINE

Dusty found tending bar was not a strenuous job, but there was a downside. You had to work danged fast. Back at Lewis's place in Nevada, Dusty had poured a few beers for travelers or miners, or some townsfolk drifting in looking for a respite from the hot, dusty day. But pouring beer in Baker's Crossing was nothing compared to a cattle-country town on a Saturday night. The bar was continually lined with cowpunchers, each wanting a mug of beer or a shot of whiskey, and wanting it immediately. Dusty found having only two hands to be inadequate. With an apron tied over his gunbelt, he scurried behind the bar, trying to meet the demands of Hunter's customers. One man wanted no head on his beer, another wanted an inch of foam. Hunter circulated about the room, greeting customers. When a cold beer was ordered, and many were, Dusty would call to Hunter, who would hurry down to the root cellar.

Dusty was always to remain behind the bar while Hunter was down in the cellar. Hunter suspected that, on previous Saturday nights, some cowhands had filled their mugs from the keg behind the bar while he hurried out back to fill an order for cold brew.

Many of the cowhands had no money. They were paid monthly, and some were paid only on credit, as their employers had little cash until their herd was ready to be driven to market, so Hunter kept a line of credit open to any cowhand who worked for one of the local ranches. If you were new to the area, and no local cowhand would vouch for you, then it was cash up front or no service. Dusty had a small ledger sheet in an apron pocket, and was tallying up the drinks as he went.

Somewhere before nine o'clock, one cowhand shoved another, who staggered backward a few steps, jostling another and spilling his beer. Soon fists were flying, and Hunter was in the middle of it, standing almost an entire head taller than most of his customers, calling for them to break it up, and grabbing men by the shirt collar and banging heads together. A punch glanced off his bearded chin, knocking him back a step, and he grabbed the man behind the belt with one hand dragged him to the door, and

threw him out into the street. Son-of-a-gun!, Dusty thought. Hunter is strong! All the while, Hunter had a smile on his face. Dusty, watching from behind the bar, realized Hunter was enjoying himself.

The fight had died away, barely, when a man stepped through the doorway, immediately attracting Dusty's attention. His clothes were dusty, which indicated he was fresh from the trail. But it wasn't the kind of dust that lands on a cowhand working long hours on the back of a horse. It looked like saddle-bum dust, dust that has built upon another day's dust, with more than a little sweat mixed in. He wore spurs, which indicated to Dusty he was not from these parts, as Dusty had noticed most of the cowhands in the northwest did not seem to wear spurs. Dusty himself did not wear them, despite living most of his years in the Southwest, because Patterson had taught him to always move quietly, and spurs tended to make a metallic jingling as you walked.

What caught Dusty's attention the most about this man were his guns. Remingtons. One riding low on his right side, the other equally low on his left.

The man stepped up to the bar. "I'll take a whiskey, boy."

"I'll take some indication you can pay for it, first."

"The only indication you'll get is this." The man reached for his right-hand gun, but before he could clear leather, he found himself staring into the barrel of Dusty's Peacemaker, not a foot from his left eye, the hammer cocked.

"Now, that ain't too neighborly," Dusty said.

The saloon, which had been rising from a murmur to a roar and then dying back down throughout the evening, was suddenly quiet.

"What're you gonna do, boy?" the man asked.

"Empty that eye socket if you don't set that gun down on the bar. Then pull the other, real slow and easy-like, and set it down, too."

"You think you got the nerve?"

"You want to try me?"

The man decided Dusty did not look like he was bluffing, and did as instructed. First one pistol, then the other.

"Time for you to leave," Hunter said suddenly from behind the man, and he delivered what Dusty was coming to realize was his customary way of helping a customer out the door when he had worn out his welcome. One hand gripped the man by the back of his belt, the other at his collar, then Hunter dragged him across the floor while the man kicked with his feet and cut loose with a long string of obscenities, mostly at what line of work he thought Hunter's mother might have been in, and Hunter tossed him out the door.

The room erupted in laughter, then the murmur of a dozen conversations being conducted at once resumed.

Some of the men eventually began to trickle out, their destination being the establishment owned by the woman named Alisha Summers.

"That man with the guns," Dusty said to Hunter. "He might be trouble."

"Him? I doubt it. Once his guns were gone, he wasn't such a big man."

"It's not that he was a big man. It's that he was a small man. That's what we've got to worry about." Then, Dusty added, "Besides, standing next to you, every man's a small man."

Hunter exploded into a belly laugh. The joke had not been funny enough to warrant such an enthusiastic a response, but Hunter had been helping himself to some of his own whiskey. Even though he was the proprietor of this place, it was clear to Dusty that Hunter was still a cowhand at heart, and it was Saturday night.

"Why don't you grab a beer and take a break?" Hunter said. "You've been workin' hard all night, and the crowd's starting to thin out. Must be past midnight."

That sounded good to Dusty. His feet were a little sore. He was accustomed to working long hours in the saddle, not on his feet. He untied his apron and dropped it in a heap at the edge of the bar. Grabbing a mug, he filled it from the keg behind the bar—he was too tired to climb all the way down for a cold one.

He stepped out the door, then to one side so he would not stand silhouetted by the light of the doorway. Something he had learned from Sam Patterson, which had become second nature.

The air was cool. A slight breeze touched his face, bringing with it a touch of balsam.

He glanced about quickly for any motion in the shadows that might be out of place. Another habit he had picked up from Patterson. Such ways might seem needless to some, Dusty thought, but they can mean the difference between surviving and not. Especially since the drifter Hunter had tossed out the door was out there, somewhere in the night. Even though Dusty had taken the man's pistols, he might have a rifle in his saddle.

Dusty tipped the mug for a sip of beer, and something caught his eye. A small glow, white but tiny and with a barely perceptible hint of orange, out beyond the edge of town, and up a bit. A campfire, on one of the ridge slopes beyond the gap.

He finished his beer, then returned to the barroom. A poker game was under way at a table near the stove. Hunter, the McCabe rider named Fred, and a couple cowhands were forming a small audience.

"Hunter," Dusty said.

Hunter looked over.

Dusty signaled with a nod for him to follow.

Hunter tailed Dusty to the doorway, and Dusty said, "Look up there, off in the hills."

Hunter did. "A fire. What about it? Drifters, probably."

"Yeah. Probably."

"It's a little odd, I suppose. You'd think they'd ride into town, see if there's a room available, and if not, or they couldn't afford it, they'd camp just outside of town. That's what most of 'em do."

Hunter backed out of the doorway and returned to the poker table.

Dusty, however, was not so sure. It was not simply the oddity of the location of the campfire, it was a feeling. Patterson had said, "Regardless of anything, no matter what anyone else says, always trust your gut-feelings."

The following day, Dusty fixed breakfast for himself and Hunter, and for Franklin and Fred and a few straggler cowhands who had slept off their whiskey in the livery stable or an alley, or a cot at Alisha Summers'. Then Hunter gave Dusty the day off.

From his chair on Hunter's porch, he watched the Sunday morning church crowd roll in. The church was a small, single-room building that also served as a local school. The preacher was a young Baptist man with hair that was receding into a jagged widow's peak, who pushed a plow when he was not going about his pastorly duties. He had an almost too gentle and sincere way when he spoke. Watch out for the ones who try to act too sincere, Patterson had once said. They will always be the ones who will greet you with one hand but with the other they will be reaching for your wallet. Sincerity should come naturally, not be something you have to attempt. But the preacher also visited Hunter's for coffee almost every morning, and laughed the loudest when the humor turned raucous. His wife was not much older than Dusty, and as they had no children, she spent her weekdays at the school-church serving as the school marm.

The school-church was maybe two hundred yards from the last building in town, which was Hunter's, probably to give the church-goers a feeling of separation from the more primal needs satisfied at Hunter's or Miss Alisha's. But from where Dusty sat on the boardwalk, he had a fair view of the building.

The young preacher stood by the steps, shaking hands and it seemed to Dusty, selling himself to the flock.

Dusty did not know how he felt about the concept of God. He believed, or rather, felt, that there was something to the concept. And when he was alone in the wilderness, he felt a serenity that seemed bigger than he was, especially in these Montana mountains.

"Do you believe in God?" Dusty had once asked Patterson.

Patterson shrugged. "I believe there is a God. I think everyone knows there is a God. They may try to talk themselves out of it, that such things are for superstitious fools, but deep down, in their heart, they know God exists. But I can't say I believe in God. I've killed too many people, done too many wrong things, for him to believe in me."

Dusty was not sure about that. It seemed to him a god who created the mountains, the streams, the pine woods covering these slopes, would be too optimistic to fully give up on anyone.

Dusty spent Sunday afternoon stretching out on the hay in the livery with a mug of Hunter's cold beer within reach. And as darkness settled in, he stood on the boardwalk in front of the saloon, looking off to where the campfire had glowed the night before. The hills were dark. No sign of any fire. But Dusty wasn't satisfied. He sat in his chair, rocking it back against the wall, and waited.

Hunter stepped out eventually for a breath of night air. "Dusty. I didn't know you were out here."

"Yeah. Just enjoying the night. I love the mountain air."

Hunter nodded. "Even after all the years I've lived in these mountains, I can never get used to how crisp and clear the air is."

Hunter brought Dusty a beer, then stepped in, and Dusty sat and looked off into the darkness. And to the hills outside of town.

No campfire at all. Still, something tugged at him.

He finished the beer, then rose to his feet and stepped into the barroom. Hunter had given him unlimited access to both kegs, part of the compensation for not being able to offer him pay. Dusty climbed the ladder down to the cool, damp root cellar, refilled the mug, and climbed back out. Hunter was leaning one elbow on the bar with a deck of cards in front of him, engaged in a game of solitaire. Hunter had a cigar going, and offered Dusty one. Dusty was not normally one to smoke, but what the hell? Good cigars did not come along every day.

With the cigar clenched in his teeth and the mug of beer in one hand, Dusty opened the front door a crack and looked off into the darkness toward where he knew the ridges to be, which he had crossed on his way into town from the McCabe Ranch a week earlier.

And there, high up on one of the ridges, was the glow of a campfire.

The following morning, he pulled on his buckskin shirt, rather than one of the shirts he had bought at Franklin's. As he poked at some strips of bacon sizzling in a skillet on Hunter's stove, he said to Hunter, "I need the morning off."

"Why?"

"I'm gonna saddle-up and take me a ride through the hills around town."

Hunter's brows dropped questioningly. "Can't it wait? The hills will be there after the noon stage leaves."

"What's in the hills may not wait. And I might be gone all day, and may not even be back until tomorrow."

Hunter's head rose a bit as understanding dawned on him. "You're still worried about that campfire, aren't you."

Dusty nodded, and he told Hunter of the one he had seen the night before.

"It's probably just some drifting cowhands," Hunter said. "Nothing to worry about."

"They didn't drift very far, did they?"

"Maybe they wanted to stay in the area a couple days. It was Sunday. Maybe they wanted to attend the church service."

"There weren't any drifters in the crowd yesterday. I sat outside here and watched them all ride in. And if you were right, then why'd they move their camp? The fire wasn't in the same place as it had been the night before."

Dusty turned from the stove to look at Hunter. "It may be nothing. Or it may be some Indians escaped from the reservation, on the run. It may be any one of a dozen things. But I've seen how dangerous men operate. I've got to check this out."

Hunter nodded. "I'll get by today. You take care of yourself, up there in them hills alone."

"I'll be all right. I've had a lot of training in how to be all right."

Before Dusty went to the livery to saddle up, he visited Franklin's. The time for that Spencer rifle was now. A pistol was worn by a cowhand for protection, but not from outlaws or hostile Indians, like many a dime-novelist wanted folks back east to believe. It was protection from being dragged to death by your horse. The primary cause of death for a cowhand was being thrown from the often half saddle-broke mustangs they rode, finding one boot caught in a stirrup, and being dragged to death while the horse ran, or being trampled by its hooves. With a pistol at your side, you had at least a chance to shoot the animal and save your life. The

pistol also gave you maneuverable shooting at close quarters, but generally, if accuracy was a requirement, you wanted a rifle.

"I'm here for that Spencer," Dusty said. He unbuckled his gunbelt, and set it on the counter. "I'll trade you this Peacemaker for it, straight-up."

"I might be willing to let you start up a tab, Dusty. No need to lose your pistol."

"Thank you kindly, but I don't know how much longer I'll be in the area." He still had not decided whether he was going to ride out to the McCabe house, bold as Boston brass, and introduce himself as Johnny McCabe's long lost bastard son, or simply ride on to Oregon.

Franklin slid the revolver from its holster to examine it.

"Careful," Dusty said. "It's loaded."

"It's a beauty, that's for certain. The Colt Peacemaker will set the standard for pistols for many years to come."

Franklin pulled the hammer half-way back then pulled the trigger, and with his free hand gave the cylinder a spin. "It's in great condition. Oiled like it just came from the factory."

"I was taught to always take care of my guns and my horses. You don't know when you might have to rely on one or the other to save your life."

Franklin looked up at Dusty curiously, almost as though he was trying to discern if Dusty was joking, but there was no sign of a smile on Dusty's face. "All right, Dusty. An even trade, it is."

"Can you throw in a box of cartridges? A rifle ain't much good without 'em."

"One box is all I have. I don't get much call for Spencer ammunition, anymore."

From a box behind the counter, Franklin grasped a box and handed it to Dusty.

"Before the deal is final," Dusty said, "I'd like to take it out back and try a few shots."

"By all means, please do."

A pine grew a hundred yards behind Franklin's store, reaching more than eighty feet to the sky, its trunk as straight as an arrow's shaft. The rifle was a fifty-two caliber.

Dusty loaded seven shots, then chambered a round. He drew a bead on a branch of the pine tree, and fired. The branch splintered. Dusty jacked in another cartridge, and with this shot, broke the branch cleanly.

Franklin was standing in the back doorway, watching Dusty select another branch and begin whittling away at it. Fine marksmanship. Franklin loved to watch a display of good shooting skills.

"Excuse me," came a woman's voice from behind him.

Franklin turned with a start. "Oh. Miss Ginny. I'm sorry. I didn't hear you."

"Obviously," Aunt Ginny said, her hands on her hips, one brow raised.

Aunt Ginny wore a bonnet, and dangling from one hand was a drawstring purse. Behind her stood a dark-haired girl, maybe two inches taller, and she also wore a bonnet.

"Miss Ginny," Franklin said. "Miss Bree."

"Hi, Mister Franklin," Bree said.

"I was just watching a pretty incredible example of marksmanship out back," he offered in explanation for not greeting his customers as they walked in the door, but knew it would be futile.

"I trust it was quite extraordinary," Aunt Ginny said curtly. "Meanwhile, we are here on our monthly visit for supplies."

From her purse she produced a list, and handed it to Franklin, who quickly tied an apron about his waist and set to filling the order. Two sacks of coffee...two sacks of flour...

The shooting out back ceased, and Dusty stepped in. "This gun's fine, Franklin. Shoots a little to the left, but nothing I can't compensate for."

He glanced at the women. With one hand he touched the brim of his hat. "Howdy, ma'am," he said to Aunt Ginny, then offered another "howdy" to Bree.

"Hi," Bree said, breaking into a smile that openly said she liked what she saw.

But Ginny simply stared.

"Well, Dusty," Franklin said. "It's good doing business with you. And that was some of the finest shooting I've seen since Johnny McCabe, himself. Oh, by the way, this is Miss

Virginia Brackston, and Mister McCabe-himself's daughter, Bree."

"Pleased to meet you both," Dusty said, realizing the girl with the smile must have been the one he had observed riding away from the McCabe ranch house a week earlier. His sister.

"Ladies," Franklin said, continuing the introductions, "this is Dusty. I never did get his last name."

Without a response, Dusty said, "I'll take the gun. It shoots just fine."

"Well, then, I guess we can call it a deal. Do you want a receipt?"

Dusty shook his head. "A handshake's always been good enough for me."

Franklin extended his hand and Dusty shook it. Franklin said, "Nice doing business with you."

"I'd best be goin'. Got a big day ahead of me." He glanced to Aunt Ginny and Bree, and touched the brim of his hat again. "Nice meetin' you ladies."

He crossed the floor, his gait light and easy, the rifle in one hand and the box of ammunition in the other, and he was out the door.

"Ma'am," Franklin said, "you got peaches on the list, but you don't say how many cans."

But Ginny did not hear him, her gaze fixed on the now empty doorway. "Gracious."

"Ma'am?"

She crossed the floor herself, to stand in the doorway as the young man called Dusty ambled down the street toward the livery stable.

Ginny turned, her gaze fixed straight ahead, but seeing nothing.

"Aunt Ginny?" Bree asked. "You look like you've just seen a ghost."

"Not a ghost. Not exactly." She returned to the counter. "Mister Franklin, tell me about that young man."

The question caught Franklin as odd, because it had nothing to do whatsoever with what he thought was the matter of hand, which was the number of cans of peaches Aunt Ginny wanted. But he dared not make her state her demand twice. Otherwise, she might fix him with the Gaze,

which always made Franklin feel like he wanted to crawl into his shoes and hide.

"Well, I don't know much about him, really. He rode in a week ago, has been working at Hunter's, doing whatever job there is to do. Even cooking. He's good with a gun. Stopped some trouble Saturday night with a draw that was in the class of Mister McCabe himself.

"I wasn't there, of course," he added quickly, "so I didn't see it."

"Of course," Aunt Ginny said.

"He just traded in his gun for that rifle he was shooting out back."

Bree said, "What is it, Aunt Ginny? Do you know him?"

"I don't know." She was openly puzzled, a sight that caused Bree to raise a brow of concern. Not much ever puzzled Aunt Ginny. "I really don't know."

"Why don't we go talk to Mister Hunter about him?" Bree suggested. "Since he's working there, it would stand to reason Mister Hunter would know more about him."

Aunt Ginny fixed her with the Gaze. "I can think of many places more suitable for a young lady than a saloon."

"He does look a little familiar, I guess," Franklin said. "Now that you mention it. I hadn't really noticed before."

Her gaze fixed on him, not sternly, but with agreement, and something that might have been wonder. "Indeed."

TEN

Zack Johnson rode along a trail that cut across the valley floor, a trail that had been made over the years by riders crossing from one end of the valley to the other. The trail was nothing more than a small dirt path with grass growing on either side.

Zack kept his horse to a shambling trot. The McCabes' home was his destination, and he still had a couple of miles of terrain ahead of him, but he was in no hurry. He was enjoying the morning. It was still early enough so the heat of the day had not yet descended upon the land and a light northwesterly breeze stirred the grass. The sky was a deep blue—he had never seen it more so—and an occasional heavy looking white cloud drifted low, near the horizon.

Zack Johnson was a year younger than Johnny McCabe's forty. He stood a little taller, with wide shoulders and well-muscled arms that filled the sleeves of a faded blue shirt. His hair was walnut colored, and was covered by a gray wide-brimmed Stetson. His jaw was square and clean-shaven, his upper lip covered by a mustache that was showing strands of silver.

At his side was holstered a single Remington. Unlike Johnny, who would not even consider going to the out-house without a pair of revolvers strapped to his sides, Zack carried only one. He had a second, which he kept home, and should need arise he could go and belt it on. A Winchester was tucked into a saddle boot beneath the pommel.

Zack was now a rancher, and before that, he had been a cowhand on the McCabe Ranch. But even before that, he had ridden with Johnny as a Texas Ranger, in the years immediately before the War Between the States, pursuing renegade Comanches, Mexican border raiders, and outlaws through the flatlands of southern Texas. They also pursued comely senoritas in the Texas border towns, drank too much whiskey and generally got into trouble.

Despite the tranquility of the morning, it was with the eye of a Ranger that Zack surveyed the trail ahead of him.

Zack did not really expect to find Johnny McCabe at home. Johnny had ridden out a few weeks earlier to attend a cattle auction, and Zack knew Johnny loved to meander

through the mountains, and would probably take his sweet time coming home, unless he found some choice stock. And Zack had some work waiting for him back at his own ranch, but he loved a morning ride, and this morning was simply too beautiful to pass up. Besides, he had not seen Aunt Ginny, Josh or Bree in weeks. Aunt Ginny was sort of a mother figure to him, as she was to all the cowhands who worked at the McCabe Ranch.

Zack knew Johnny had left Josh in charge of the ranch. Zack would never admit he was riding out to check on Josh. At least, not to Josh's face. He was just riding out to visit the family.

As he was riding along, lost in his musing while he clung to the saddle in that natural sort of way a horseman has that gives the impression he and the horse are one, he was not even fully conscious of the scouring his trained eye was giving the trail before him and the land about him, until he caught a quick flash of light, like the sun can make reflecting against glass or metal. It came from a low ridge maybe a half mile to his right.

It had been only for an instant, and then it was gone, like it had never been there. Had he been glancing in another direction, or simply not looking about as he rode, he would have missed it. He did nothing to alter his horse's gait, or even turn his head in the direction of the ridge for a better view. He did nothing to create an impression he had even noticed it.

Knowing a horse can many times sense a change in its rider's mood, as a horse can come to know a rider much like a rider comes to know his horse, he said, "Keep it steady, boy. Everything's all right."

Without turning his head, he rolled his eyes in the direction of the ridge as much as he could. It was simply a sharp grassy rise, with a few short pines decorating the summit. Too steep for even a mountain-bred horse to climb from this direction, but he knew about a mile further along, the ridge would flatten out a bit, and was more easily accessible.

He rode along casually. At one point, he stopped to let his gelding blow, then continued along. A mile melted away behind him as the gelding's gait ate up the distance. Then

another half mile. Ahead of him now was a flat meadow, and ahead, reduced to the size of an acorn by the distance, was the McCabe house, smoke rising from its chimney.

As he approached, the house growing in size, he could see movement in the corral, a head bobbing as a man walked. Probably Fred. As Zack drew closer, he could see that it was indeed the McCabe wrangler.

Zack liked Johnny McCabe's theory of making the wrangler a choice position, rather than the usual bottom-of-the-ladder job it was on most ranches. He was doing the same with his own ranch, with a young boy with the improbable name of Ramon Cormier, whose mother was from Mexico and father was French. Ramon was about Josh's age, and seemed to have a natural affinity with horses. Zack hoped Ramon would remain content as his wrangler, and not become lost in the romance of riding the range as a cowhand. He was paying Ramon better than any cowhand on his place, in an attempt to encourage him.

A small river cut across the valley maybe a quarter mile from the house, and years earlier Zack and Johnny had built a wooden bridge. Zack rode over the bridge now, the iron shod hooves of his horse drumming loudly on them. Fred Mitchum, about to step into the barn, looked up at the sound and saw Zack approaching.

"Zack!" he called out. "Nice mornin' for a ride."

Zack reined up in front of him. "Fred, is Johnny back yet?"

"No."

"Where's Josh?"

"Out ridin' line. He won't be back for a week. Why? Is somethin' wrong?"

"Maybe. I don't know." Zack swung out of the saddle. "Quick as you can, fetch me a fresh mount."

Fred asked no further questions. He had known Zack Johnson a long time, and Zack was perhaps Johnny's best friend in the world. It was common knowledge Zack had free access to anything that was Johnny's, and even though he now had his own home, this ranch would never stop being home to him. Fred grabbed a lariat he had coiled and dropped over a post in the corral fence and hurried out to the

meadow behind the house, where the McCabe remuda grazed and frolicked in the morning air.

Soon he was returning with a long-legged appaloosa. "Best runner we have, short of Rabbit. And Johnny's horse, Thunder."

Zack had already stripped the saddle from his own mount, and now went to work on the appaloosa. He then leaped into the saddle. "Take care of mine, will you?"

"Sure will. Do you need any help?"

"No. but if I'm not back in an hour, go into town and get Hunter. Tell him to follow my trail, and to be careful."

And he was off, bearing west.

Soon he was in the low hills that preceded the mountains that rimmed the valley. He found the access point to the low ridge he had observed earlier. He pulled his Winchester, and rode with it across the pommel.

He kept the appaloosa to a walk, its hooves landing with only a muffled thud on the pine needle strewn earth, or the soft sod of the occasional open grassy expanse.

As he neared the area from which he had seen the reflection, he dismounted, leaving the appaloosa with a rein trailing, ground-hitched they called it, and moved ahead, his rifle gripped in both hands.

He came upon the spot where the reflection had originated. It was now deserted, but plenty of tracks covered the ground. Two men, one with boots the size of Zack's. But a much heavier man, Zack judged by the depth of the track. The second man had a smaller foot, and narrower. Maybe the size of Josh. The ground was littered with cigarette butts, and nearby Zack found where a couple of horses had been tethered to a low hanging pine branch.

Two men had waited here, possibly watching the trail below. Maybe with field glasses, which might explain the reflected light.

Zack figured it had taken twenty minutes to reach the McCabe Ranch after he had seen the reflection. Fred was maybe five minutes rounding up the appaloosa for him, Zack was another few minutes saddling up, then he estimated it was forty-five minutes getting to this ridge, riding carefully and quietly. The total time, he figured, was a little shy of an

hour and a half. During that time, the two riders had mounted up and were gone.

It was probably nothing, he thought. But it just didn't look right. He decided to go fetch the appaloosa and follow their trail a short distance, just to be certain.

Civilization was slowly creeping its way westward, but still, in many parts of the West, these mountains included, the only law was your skill with a gun. McCabe Gap was the only settlement within a day's ride, and there was as yet no lawman there, and any community large enough for a town marshal would give him jurisdiction extending only to the town line. In the large tracts of land between such towns, sometimes hundreds of miles, the only law might be a Territorial Marshal, but there were simply not enough of them to adequately cover all the open range.

This was a rough land. Renegade Indians still occasionally raided, though increasingly more seldom, but they were being replaced with the even more dangerous white renegade.

Bands of outlaws, many of them guerrilla raiders from the late War Between the States who were now carrying on their own private war, roamed the remote corners of the west. Quantrill, the Jameses, the Youngers, and the Patterson gang. And other bands not so well known. They were seldom seen this far north, but with the Territory becoming more populated, and as a result more prosperous, with mining and cattle ranching bringing in other businesses, and with the law closing in on them down in Kansas, Missouri and Texas, it seemed inevitable some might drift northward.

Zack rode directly south, following the trail of the two riders, descending the hill and then directing his horse up slope heavily wooded with tall pines.

He had not ridden a mile further when at the summit of this ridge, the trail made by the two riders converged with another. Large scatterings of hoof prints, too many for Zack to even venture a guess as to the number of riders. Maybe ten, maybe more. One print seemed to obliterate another.

He dismounted, stepping down silently as he wore no spurs to jingle as he moved. Despite Zack's Texas roots, and that spurs rang almost musically at the heels of every cowboy who grew up in Texas, Johnny McCabe had convinced him of

the folly of them. You never know when you might need stealth to save your life, especially as a Texas Ranger, and the time required to unbuckle your spurs might be costly.

And at the moment, as he followed these riders through the mountains, he was no longer a ranch owner. He was once again, at least for the moment, a Texas Ranger.

The riders apparently milled about atop this ridge for a time. Cigarette butts littered the earth, some of them ground beneath boot heels, others had been left to smolder their way into oblivion. Then, they had ridden on, winding their way northwest, now moving in single file.

Riding single file was an old trick used when you didn't want anyone who might happen across your trail to be able to estimate how many of you there were. Many a Comanche raiding party had done this back in Texas in the old days, and Zack and Johnny and their band of Rangers had done the same. And there was only two reasons for a party this size not to want their number known. Either they were running from something, probably the law, or they were here to cause trouble.

Zack noticed some of the cigarette butts were still smoldering, but some were cold. Also, there were horse droppings not even a half hour old, yet others that had been made at least a day earlier, he would guess. These riders hadn't actually met the larger party and rode on with them. They had simply ridden along until they came to the trail made by the larger party, waited a few minutes while their horses blew, and then they continued on, probably following the larger party to an established camp.

Zack followed the trail up the slope of a small mountain. There were pines growing a few yards apart and standing tall, and in places there were openings and large outcroppings of rock. The trail then turned southwest as it descended the other side of the mountain. Zack's horse was mountain bred, like Josh's horse Rabbit, and it found its footing easily, but he could see tracks that were scuffed and kind of stretched out, indicating some of the riders were on horses that were slipping and sliding a bit.

On a small plateau atop a ridge, Zack found a deserted camp. The blackened remains of a campfire, a handful of empty cans of beans tossed about. An empty whiskey bottle.

The tracks were too confusing to decipher, as the ground was littered with too many boot prints, though Zack found where the horses had been staked out for the night and where the riders had apparently bedded down. Oddly, he found one clear boot print that was smaller than the others, and with a sharp, narrow heel. A woman, he realized.

From the looks of the charred chunks of firewood and the heap of more fully burned, powdered ash beneath them, they had not cared about keeping their presence a secret. From this ridge, a large enough fire would be clearly visible from town.

Zack had seen enough. To follow further might be dangerous, as he was only one man, and would be surely outgunned. He decided to return to the McCabe Ranch. If trouble was afoot, the safety of Aunt Ginny and Bree would be in question. With Johnny not yet returned, and Josh away with the line riders, Fred was the only hand at the house. He thought he might send Fred into town to bring Hunter back, and then Zack and Hunter would hold the ranch while Fred rode out to the line camp to get Josh and the boys and tell them to high-tail it back to the house.

Zack cut directly down the slope and emerged onto a trail that wound its way through the pine forest, the trail that led from the town, through the pass the town was named after, and into the valley. He rode through thick stands of birch and aspen. As he came out of the woods he saw, just ahead, a buckboard loaded with cargo, the seat protected from the sun by a small canopy. Two women were on the seat. One was Aunt Ginny, and the other, holding the reins, was Bree.

He touched his heels to the appaloosa's ribs, and the animal broke into a quick-stepping trot and caught up with the wagon.

"Ah, Zack," Ginny said. "It's good to see you on this fine, summer day."

He touched the brim of his hat. "Ladies. I was just heading back to your house."

"Now, that's odd. You came up behind us, but we didn't see you in town."

Leave it to Aunt Ginny to never miss a thing. Zack had often thought she would clean up at a poker table. "Well, ma'am, there could be trouble afoot."

"What kind of trouble?"

Zack told her about the tracks he had seen, and the camp he had found. "Have you seen any strangers around? Like, in town, maybe?"

"No," Ginny said.

Bree piped up. "Just the one, at Franklin's store. Looked like he could handle a gun. Mighty pleasing on the eyes, too."

Ginny cast Bree a sidelong glance. "Concentrate on your driving."

Bree returned her gaze to the trail ahead. "Yes'm."

"What stranger?" Zack asked.

"Oh, he has no connection with the riders you trailed," Ginny said. "Of that, I'm sure."

"How? Did you talk to him? Who is he?"

Without responding to his question, or maybe responding in a way he couldn't figure, she said, "I would be pleased if you could join us for lunch this afternoon."

Aunt Ginny served a lunch of fried chicken, potato salad and rolls. She also served a glass of white wine. Chablis, she called it. Whatever that was. Zack did not know wines. A cold beer at Hunter's, or a glass of whiskey or even maybe a brandy, was more his speed. Aunt Ginny came from money, down in San Francisco. Her father, grandfather to Johnny's late wife, had done well as a merchant seaman, at one time owning a small fleet of ships. Aunt Ginny had brought some reminders of her wealthy lifestyle in 'Frisco with her, including a collection of fine wines.

After lunch, Zack accepted a glass of brandy and one of Johnny's cigars, and he drifted over to the gun rack while Aunt Ginny and Bree cleared the table. A couple Winchesters were present, and an older Henry that was the predecessor of the modern Winchester. Also, there stood a muzzle-loading Hawken mountain rifle, which Johnny had carried with him as a young man. It was an old weapon, its bore now eaten by corrosive black powder to the point it was no longer safe to fire, and Johnny had long since started using a Sharps

buffalo rifle in its place. He kept the old gun for sentimental reasons. He said it was a connection to his younger days.

Zack had been present when Johnny won the old Hawken in a poker game down in Texas, years before Josh, Jack and Bree were even a twinkle in his eye. That rifle had ridden in his saddle boot back in '66, the year he and Zack had first found this valley. That winter, Johnny brought down an elk at one hundred-fifty yards with that gun, and kept them and a small band of Shoshones they were living with from starving.

Zack was standing in front of the rifle rack, the smoldering cigar in one hand and the brandy snifter in the other, as Aunt Ginny drifted from the kitchen.

"Would you take a walk with me?" she asked.

He followed Aunt Ginny out the front door. Bree had complained about being left to wash the dishes alone, but Aunt Ginny told her chores build character.

They strolled casually, commenting on the fine summer day and the refreshing north-westerly breeze that was keeping the flies away. Zack talked about his new home, and plans he might have for expanding the house should he ever find the right woman to take as his wife—he was older than most men when they start a family, but he did want children.

"Have you heard from Jack lately?" he took a sip of brandy.

"Yes. We received a letter three weeks ago. He's in his final year of college, two full years ahead of the others his age."

"I know he makes Johnny proud. But all his children do."

"Indeed. As they should. They come from fine stock, on both sides."

"They surely do." He took a sip of brandy. He knew Aunt Ginny had asked him to join her for a reason. She never did anything unless there was a reason. But he also knew he would have to wait for her to get to the point on her town time.

Their stroll brought them beyond the corral. They stood watching the horses of the McCabe remuda grazing in the meadow behind the house. One horse, a brown gelding,

galloped about, feeling frisky at the touch of the northwesterly.

"Zack," Ginny said. "You've known Johnny longer than anyone. Longer than even I have."

He nodded. "I suppose I have. Rode with him with the Rangers, when we were Josh's age. What seems like a lifetime ago."

"And you do know that he considers you his best friend." It was more of a statement than a question.

He nodded again. "I would have to say he is definitely the closest friend I've ever had, too. Sometimes more like brothers than friends."

"I think it might be safe to say that you know more about him than anyone else."

"I suppose so." He raised his brandy for another sip.

"Then you could tell me. Is it possible that he might have another child, a son, about Josh's age? Or maybe a little older?"

Zack choked on the brandy, a small spray escaping him and barely missing her. "No, ma'am. No chance of that at all. Excuse me for spittin', but you kind of caught me by surprise."

"Don't answer so quickly, Zack. Think about it. Any women, other than Lura?"

"Never. He would never have cheated on Lura."

"Of that, I have no doubt. But perhaps, before her?"

"Well, there was..." he did not know quite how to say this. These were times when bawdy or even suggestive language was never spoken by a man while in the presence of a woman. "I mean..."

"Say it, Zack. I'm not one of these prissy ladies who is going to pretend she has never heard foul word or that she has no clue where babies come from."

"Yes'm." He glanced toward his boots. He was not accustomed to hearing such words from a woman's mouth. But then, he should learn to let nothing about Aunt Ginny surprise him. "Well, ma'am, I mean, there were times when we were with the Rangers...well, we were just kids, really. And there were saloons there, and women who worked the saloons..."

"Whores, I believe they are called."

"Yes'm. Them kind of women. Well, there were times that...well, we were young and foolish. And drunk. Especially Johnny, sometimes. Drunk, that is."

He stopped, as though he had said something he should not have.

Ginny drew an impatient breath. "It's all right, Zack. I am well aware of his past battles with whiskey. Could any of those, shall we say, to ease your discomfort, encounters, have produced a child?"

He shook his head quickly. "No, ma'am. Of that I'm sure."

"How sure?"

"Very sure. We followed up with them ladies to make certain nothing came of it at all."

Then, his gaze suddenly darted off to a point somewhere ahead, but he was not seeing the horses or the trees beyond. He was seeing something in his memory. "Wait a minute. Maybe..."

Ginny was silent, letting him piece together the events time had dimmed in his mind.

He said, "It was a long time ago..."

"How long?"

"Well, I would guess about twenty years."

"Twenty years. Are you saying that he did cheat on Lura?"

His gaze shot to her. "No, ma'am. He would never have cheated on her. But well, it's kind of hard to explain."

"Try me. I have all afternoon."

Zack had not thought about this in years, but he told her about the events as best he could remember. "He had been working as a ramrod for a spread in California. That was when he met Lura. He was in love with her like with none other. Then, after he had spent a month with the line riders one time, when he went to see her, she was gone. Her parents told him she didn't want to see him again, and said she had told them not to tell him where she had gone."

Ginny nodded. "I remember that time well. She was four months pregnant with Joshua. Her parents had sent her away, and away was my house, in San Francisco. She was but my niece, but in many ways was more of a daughter to me than she ever was to my sister."

"Well, he went on a drunken spree like only he could do, and this was a bad one. It was almost like the spree was in equal proportion to his love for her, and the hurt he was feeling because he thought she had left him without even a good-bye."

Ginny nodded. "I don't know if I'll ever be able to forgive my sister for that."

"He quit his job and just headed east, over the mountains into what they called Utah Territory in them days, drinking himself stupid in every saloon along the way. His brother Josiah and me, we rode along to keep him out of trouble as best we could."

Zack explained Johnny had gone into one town alone, claiming he needed some time to himself, simply to think. "He had promised he wouldn't get himself drunk. But when Josiah and I woke up the following morning and he wasn't in camp, we went into town looking for him. Found him in the bed of a saloon woman, so drunk he could scarcely even see. She was a dark-haired woman, with dark eyes. Had some Indian in her, I thought.

"Back at camp, we filled him with coffee, and once he was ready, we rode on. All he could remember was he had gone into town and started pouring down whiskey. He remembered nothing after that."

"And this woman, she was never...followed up on, as you put it?"

"No, ma'am. We were young, and maybe a little stupid."

"Maybe is the operative word, there."

"Well, we rode north. It was how we found this valley, actually. Wintered here with a band of Shoshones. There was a girl, the daughter of one of the warriors, but as far as I know, a romance never really developed between them.

"He spent the winter mostly sobering up, and getting his head clear. He finally decided to find Lura and hear it from her directly that she didn't want to see him anymore. The letter didn't tell him where she had gone, but the first place he thought of was San Francisco. I guess she had told him about you."

Ginny said, "And when he arrived, he found Lura and their infant son. And they married."

"Yep. That's about the size of it, I guess."

"I'll never forget how he looked that day, standing on my doorstep. He's changed a bit, his face is a bit lined now, and he moves a bit more deliberately, as the impulsiveness of youth has finally fled him."

"Why do you ask all of this?"

"Because I've seen him again. Or, at least, the spitting image of him, as he looked when he first landed on my doorstep. And I think it's simply too much of a coincidence. Zack, I think the son of that dark-eyed saloon woman might be here, looking for his father."

ELEVEN

When dusk was starting to touch the land and Zack felt it was becoming apparent Johnny McCabe wouldn't be returning this day, he asked Fred to ride into town and fetch Hunter.

"I hope Johnny's all right," Zack said, standing on the porch and gazing off toward the darkening valley.

Aunt Ginny was in a rocker, a cup of tea in her hand. "I have told that man, time and again, that one day he will ride off and simply not come back. He will get himself killed, riding off alone like that. What does he think stagecoaches are for? And he seldom rides by the trails, but rather straight through the mountains."

Zack took a sip of the trail coffee he held in one hand. He said nothing. He knew when silence was the wiser choice.

She said, "Zack, if you would like to be on your way, I'm sure Sabrina and I will be fine until Fred returns with Hunter. You have a long ride ahead of you, and it's getting dark. And if those riders are indeed scouting possible targets to strike, if they are indeed outlaws at all, you might want to be home with your men, should they strike there."

"My ramrod is there, and a couple of the hands, and Ramon. And the tracks seemed to indicate the riders might be focusing on this side of the valley. They likely already scouted my place, and realized this is the bigger of the two ranches."

They were silent a moment. Then he said, "I still find it a little hard to believe that young gunhawk working for Hunter could be Johnny's son from that saloon woman, all those years ago."

"It's possible."

"Yeah, but is it really all that likely?"

"Do you think I might be jumping to conclusions?"

"Well, no disrespect intended, ma'am, but I do think it might be just a little bit of a stretch."

"Intellectually, yes. So do I. Possible, but not very probable. Yet, I've learned that the intellect can seldom be relied upon. It's the heart one must use, Zack. It is only with the heart that one can truly see. It is the feelings, more than the thoughts, that must be relied upon. Oh, we must all

employ judgment, but when we are confused, we need look no further than our own heart for the answers. And we will often find that we already knew the answer."

Zack shook his head, and took another sip of coffee. "Wise words, I guess. I don't know if I understand all of it, but wise words."

Ginny smiled. "I don't think anyone can truly understand how things really work. At least, not in this lifetime."

"Even so, this boy, he might look a little like Johnny, but ... "

She cut him off. "Not a little, Zack. And it's not just the way he looks. It's the way he moves. It's the look in his eye. But you will see for yourself."

His gaze had returned to the valley floor, but now he glanced back at her, his brows dropping with curiosity. "When?"

"In a short while. He'll be riding out with Fred and Hunter."

"And what makes you think that?"

"I don't believe a young man would remain idly in town when his family might be in danger."

Zack took a couple more sips of coffee, and drew in a deep lungful of early evening air. He and Aunt Ginny remained in silence, watching the shadows of twilight creep across the flat, grassy meadow that stretched into the distance.

Shortly, three riders appeared, emerging from the woods at the western edge of the valley. They had been on the horse trail Josh used a few days earlier, and the riders from the ranch often took when going to town. It was a full mile shorter than the trail that crossed the wooden bridge, but was far too rough for a wagon.

Zack watched as they approached in the dimming light. Zack couldn't see their faces, but he could easily recognize Fred by the relaxed set of his shoulders and the easy way he had with a horse. The other, larger and more heavily built, would be Hunter. The third Zack would recognize anywhere, in any light. The width of the shoulders, the narrowness of the hips. The way he moved with the horse as though he and the horse were one, as though he had been

born on the back of a horse. His left hand gently grasped the reins, his right gripped a rifle he held across the pommel. Zack had logged more miles alongside this rider than any other.

"Aunt Ginny, look. It's Johnny. He must have met them on the trail."

"Is it Johnny? Look more closely."

As they drew nearer, the realization that this was not Johnny McCabe struck him.

The riders reined up before the porch, and swung from the saddle.

"Howdy," Hunter said.

Ginny was on her feet now, standing beside Zack, teacup resting steadily in a saucer held in one hand.

"Good evening, Mister Hunter," she said, though her eyes were on Zack, obviously enjoying Zack's reaction.

Zack could see the young man clearly now at this short distance. The edges of his chin, the contours of his cheekbones. The resemblance was startling.

Hunter introduced them to Dusty.

"Yes," Ginny said. "We met earlier, in town."

"Pleased to make your acquaintance again, ma'am."

"Coffee is on, in the kitchen. Strong and foul, just the way you men like it. I'm sure you're no exception, young man. Zack and I will be right in."

Dusty followed Fred and Hunter through the door. Only once the door was closed did Zack look at Aunt Ginny.

He said, "I...I don't know what to say. It's like looking into the past."

"Isn't it, though? Of course, you'll find his eyes are darker. Like his mother's."

TWELVE

Dusty had not actually decided whether to let the McCabe family know who he really was, or simply light out to Oregon and leave well enough alone. And yet, here he was, standing on the front porch of the McCabe house, drinking coffee and enjoying the night air with Hunter, Miss Brackston, and the man introduced as Zack Johnson. Fred had taken the horses to the stable for tending.

Zack drained his cup and said, "I'm going to be hitting the road, now. Thanks for the coffee, Aunt Ginny, and the lunch."

"Take care," she said. "Have a safe ride home."

Zack cast one more glance at Dusty, then stepped down from the porch and headed for the stable.

Dusty had glanced about the house quickly while following Hunter and Fred to the kitchen immediately after arriving, taking in all he could of the home built by the man who was his father. He liked what he saw. The openness of the design, the stone hearth, the exposed timbers overhead. The first floor was entirely open, like some Spanish haciendas he had seen, yet the overall structure was more like that of a cape. The house had a sense of strength about it. If you could truly tell much about a man by the work he does, and the character of what he builds, and Dusty believed you could, then he was indirectly getting his first real glimpse of his father beyond the legends.

When Dusty and Hunter had finished their coffee on the porch, Miss Brackston invited them in for a refill. As Dusty followed her through the great open room to the kitchen beyond, his eye caught the rifle rack. Winchesters. And an old Hawken. You can also tell much about a man by the way he fights, and the tools he chooses for such a thing. Dusty again found himself pleased by what he saw.

This woman, Miss Brackston, her presence seemed to be everywhere, too. The fine furniture. The little white, spider-web sort of things on the arms of the chairs—doilies, he thought they were called. A brass candelabra on the dining room table. The delicate design of the shades on the lamps. If what he had heard was correct, his father's wife had

died years earlier, and Miss Brackston was apparently the woman of the house.

In the kitchen, Dusty found the pretty dark-haired girl he had met earlier in town. An apron was tied about her middle, and she wore a blue bandanna over her hair like a kerchief, a few loose strands of dark hair flying about. Her face was flushed from the heat of the stove. As they stepped into the kitchen, she was bending to open the oven door, a pot holder in one hand as she reached for the heated handle. She glanced over one shoulder toward the doorway, and gave a casual, "Hi, Mister Hunter."

Then she caught sight of Dusty and suddenly straightened, her eyes growing wide in a nervous rush of embarrassment. She reached one hand to her kerchief and found the loose hair, and sighed with resignation.

"Bree," Hunter said. "This is Dusty. He's been working for me at the saloon."

"We met earlier at Mister Franklin's," she said. Then, her voice bending with a touch of hesitant shyness, "Hello again, Mister Dusty."

Dusty chuckled. "It's just Dusty, Miss. Not 'mister.'"

Dusty found himself a little embarrassed himself, but not because he was caught with unsightly hair. This girl, apparently attracted to him, did not realize he was her brother.

"Sabrina," Miss Brackston said, "Get two more cups and saucers, please."

At Miss Brackston's request, they retired to the parlor while Bree continued to fix the evening's dinner. Dusty noticed Miss Brackston did not use the word supper. She seemed to be a woman of sophistication. And Dusty figured, some education.

She took the rocker by the hearth, and suggested Dusty help himself to one of the stuffed chairs.

"Thank you, ma'am."

Hunter volunteered to stir a fire to life in the hearth.

She said, "That would be nice, Mister Hunter. Thank you."

Miss Brackston was drinking tea, not coffee, and she took a sip.

She said, "I do feel a bit embarrassed about the two of you having to come all the way out from town, but Zack felt it was necessary. I'm sure we would have been all right."

Dusty spoke up. "Begging your pardon, ma'am, but I think he's right."

He told her of the campfires he had seen during the previous two nights. "This morning I rode out, found one of their campsites, and I followed their trail a few miles. They're covering a lot of territory, but they're riding in circles. Never roaming far from this valley, and apparently circling back to this area every evening."

"What might that indicate?" she asked.

Dusty glanced to Hunter, who was on one knee in front of the fireplace, stacking some wood for burning. He gave Dusty a quick nod, and Dusty returned his gaze to Miss Brackston. "It means they're scouting the area. They're raiders, ma'am."

"Raiders? What could they possibly want? There's no money in this valley, or in town. There's not even a bank."

"I doubt they expect to find money. They're most likely looking for horses—raiders are always looking for horses. And there's clothing, guns, ammunition. And there's... well..." he did not know quite how to voice this last thought.

"Women." She finished it for him.

"Yes'm."

She looked to Hunter. "So you abandoned your establishment in the face of a possible strike by raiders to come out here and protect us."

"I can always rebuild. But I agree with Dusty. They'll want horses, more than whiskey. This is the biggest ranch within a couple days' ride. There aren't many horses in town, and Zack's remuda is only about half the size of what you have here."

"There are women in town. That den of iniquity run by the illustrious Miss Summers might be a target."

Dusty answered, "I don't think that very likely. To a man on the run, a good horse, food and ammunition will be first in his thoughts. And clothing, too. It's not like he can just walk into a store and buy a new shirt. Not when there's a price on his head. Ammunition and clothing they can get at Franklin's, but for horses and food, especially horses, they'll

have to hit a place like this. And any women who might already be on a place where their other needs can be met could be targets."

"It's becoming apparent that you did a dangerous thing today, young man. Riding out there alone, trailing those men."

Hunter piped up, "You must be pretty good at it, too, because Zack never mentioned finding fresh tracks made by a single rider."

Dusty shrugged. "Just lucky, I guess."

Though, he knew that was not true at all. He had never considered himself lucky, other than that he had received good teaching along the way. He had simply ridden in the tracks of the riders he was trailing. His tracks would have appeared a little fresher than those made by the raiders, but not enough to stand out significantly.

To Miss Brackston, he said, "I don't know if it was all that dangerous, ma'am. I was all right. No one can find me if I don't want to be found."

He had not meant that to come out as arrogantly as it sounded. He thought of adding that he was trained by the best, but that might just create questions he did not want to answer. If it became known he had been raised by Sam Patterson, the folks in and around McCabe Gap would look at him as a potential outlaw, too. He seemed to be well liked by these folks, and didn't want to lose their respect. And he found, even though he had but met Miss Brackston today, it was somehow important to him to have her respect, too.

They ate dinner at the kitchen table. Fred paced about outside with a rifle in his arms while the others ate, then Hunter went out to relieve him.

"Mister McCabe has a fine collection of cigars," Miss Brackston said to Dusty, "and he enjoys one after a meal on occasion. I am sure he wouldn't mind if I offered you one."

"Thank you, Miss Brackston. That would be right nice."

"And it's not 'Miss Brackston,'" she said. "The boys always call me Aunt Ginny, and I don't see why you should be an exception."

"Thank you, Aunt Ginny."

Dusty found this cigar was one of the finest he had ever lit up, savoring the initial draught, and letting it out slowly.

"Mister McCabe has good taste in cigars," he said.

On the desk were three photographs, in three matching frames. A young man, about Josh's age, with light colored hair. Another, maybe a little younger, with darker hair. And a photograph of his sister.

"That would be Mister McCabe's children," Aunt Ginny said. "Joshua, who is off at the line camp right now. And Jackson, who is away at school. And you have met Sabrina."

She excused herself to the kitchen to help Bree with a few things, and Dusty stood by the desk, upon which the box of cigars set, and surveyed the room. The house of his father.

Out in the kitchen was his sister. Returning soon would be his brother. And no one at this ranch, nor in town for that matter, could possibly know Dusty to be anything but a cowhand drifting through, a cowhand who was a little too good with a gun.

He found himself feeling suddenly uneasy, like his being here was somehow wrong, that by interacting with these people as a stranger when he was so much more was somehow violating something.

He took another draw on the cigar and let himself pace, moving about the large, open room, noting the solidness of the floorboards underfoot, the strength of the timbers overhead. The fire Hunter had started crackled low in the hearth.

He stopped at the rifle rack. Guns were something Dusty knew well, and it was obvious his father did, too. Something they had in common.

Dusty wondered now, as he stood in the man's house, if they would ever meet. Or if they ever should. Maybe this would be enough, simply to see how his father lived, to learn a little about him. Maybe Dusty should simply ride out to Oregon, find Haley, and begin working toward the building of his own ranch. After all, what could he really expect from his father? Love? To be welcomed with open arms into the family? His father did not even know he existed. Regardless of blood ties, he and Dusty were strangers.

Dusty decided to ask himself a question. What did he really want out of this? Why did he really leave Arizona, riding all the way to Nevada, and then on to Montana? To get to know his father? Or, was it more than that? Family, he thought. He wanted family. Not just Sam Patterson and a band of outlaws, or a bunkhouse full of fellow cowhands, but a real family. A place where he could belong. And now that he stood in this house, he found he wanted it more than ever.

He suddenly became aware of a presence behind him. He glanced over one shoulder to find Aunt Ginny standing silently in the kitchen doorway, watching him.

"Oh, I'm sorry," Dusty said. "I was just looking at the guns."

"Yes. It's a fine collection. He has another rifle that he carries with him. I believe he calls it a 'Sharps,' though I am no expert in guns."

"A Sharps? I've seen a short-barreled carbine. The Union cavalry carried them in the late war, or so I've heard. And there's the longer Buffalo rifle."

"I wouldn't know one from another, but I believe I've heard the term 'buffalo rifle' or 'buffalo gun' applied to his rifle."

"A Sharps can hold only one shot." He knit his brow a little as a question formed. "I wonder why he would carry one when he has these fine Winchesters here that hold twelve shots each?"

She was looking at him curiously. Dusty thought he saw a twinkle in her eye, almost a suppressed smile, like she knew something she was not divulging. "You tell me."

"Well," he said, thinking aloud. "A Sharps is one of the best guns for accuracy and distance, and it isn't going to jam like a repeater. And if you're a good shot, one bullet is all you should need."

She gave a sort of half nod, half shrug. "It does seem I've heard him mention that line of thought one or twice."

Dusty turned to look back at the rifle rack. He didn't really think about it at first, but an old muzzle-loading mountain rifle like a Hawken was an odd thing to have, considering repeating rifles had been in existence for almost thirty years. But he also knew the answer.

He said, "That's why he has that old Hawken. He used that before he had the Sharps, even though there were more modern repeating rifles available."

"That was the rifle he carried when I first met him, twenty years ago. Mister Johnson claims to have seen him bring down an elk at two hundred yards with that rifle."

Dusty's brows rose skeptically. "That would be quite a shot."

"I've seen him do some pretty fantastic shooting."

"Do you think it would be all right if I looked at it? I mean, I've never actually seen a Hawken up close."

"I think it would be all right."

Dusty set his cigar in a small silver ash tray on a corner table, and gently lifted the muzzle-loader from the rack. The stock bore scratches, and the finish was now worn away in spots along the barrel. Dusty checked the percussion nipple quickly to make certain there was no cap in place and the gun wouldn't fire. Simple gun safety he had learned from Patterson. Then he brought the rifle to his shoulder and sighted in on an imaginary target.

Bree glanced out from the kitchen, then with alarm hurried into the dining room. "Aunt Ginny! That's one of Pa's favorite guns. He doesn't let just anyone touch it."

Aunt Ginny shot her a glance, gaze steely and firm, leveled at her from over the rims of her spectacles. It stopped Bree as abruptly as if she had been given a command. Then, Aunt Ginny said, conversationally, "I don't think he would mind this time."

Bree's mouth had dropped open, and she stared at her aunt with bewilderment. Not just anyone was allowed to touch Pa's guns without his say-so. Certainly not a stranger. You never know when you might have to depend on your gun to save your life, he would say. They need to be in perfect operating condition, and he felt he was the best judge of what perfect-operating-condition was when it came to a firearm. She doubted there were many who would disagree. The list of who could touch his guns was limited. Zack Johnson and her brothers were the only three she could think of at the moment. And maybe Hunter, but that was it. It was so unlike Aunt Ginny to step over boundaries.

Bree had to admit she liked Dusty, though she hardly knew him. He was cute. She could have almost died when he stepped into the kitchen and she was such a mess! There was a smoothness to Dusty, a fluidity in his manner, an ease in the way he moved. He stepped down lightly when he walked, reminding her of a cat, and though he wore hard-soled riding boots, he made hardly a sound as he walked along the floorboards. In fact, he even reminded her of Pa a little, but his eyes were darker. There was a certain quality she couldn't quite describe about the look in his eyes. Sometimes tranquil, like a still pond, other times smoldering.

But to let him touch Pa's guns?

She turned on her heel and returned to the kitchen, and busied herself at the dry sink, washing dishes.

Eventually, Aunt Ginny returned to the kitchen. "I was going to see if you needed any help out here, but you seem to have things under control."

Bree turned to face her, suds clinging to her hands and wrists. "Aunt Ginny, you know Pa would never want a stranger touching his guns."

Aunt Ginny seemed to draw herself up a bit, rising to full posture, her jaw firmly set, and she leveled he Gaze at Bree. "I believe we already covered this subject."

This time, Bree was not going to back down. She stood her ground, he gray eyes flashing with the temper she inherited from her father. "Well, it wasn't covered well enough. I want to know what's going on."

"Nothing that concerns you. Not at this moment, anyway."

"It seems to me anything that going on under this roof, the roof of my home, concerns me. Especially when it comes to letting a perfect stranger do something that would make Pa angry."

"I don't think it would. Not in this case."

"Well, we'll have to let Pa decide that, won't we?"

Aunt Ginny's gaze softened a bit. "Sabrina," she seldom called her niece Bree, "there are things afoot that I'm not quite ready to discuss yet. Do you trust me?"

Bree nodded. When it came down to the brass tacks, Aunt Ginny, Pa, and her brothers were the four she trusted most in the world.

"I know you're no longer a child," Aunt Ginny continued. "But there are things going on that I'm not quite ready to explain. I have to ask you to trust me, and to let it go for now."

Bree felt the anger draining away. She let out a sigh. "All right. I just hope you know what you're doing."

Aunt Ginny's left brow rose a notch. "As do I, child."

Dusty stepped onto the porch, his rifle held ready in his hands.

"Hunter?" he said into the darkness, no louder than he would have had Hunter been standing at his side. A call could carry on the night air, and he didn't want it to carry much beyond the ranch yard.

From off to the right of the porch, Hunter stepped from the darkness, seeming to almost materialize from nothingness. He held a Winchester, and a pistol was belted at his right hip. "All's quiet, so far."

"Where do you suppose Johnson is?"

Hunter shrugged. "Half-way between here and there, I reckon. Five miles lay between this house and his. Traveling by dark, and trying to move quietly, he'll be riding a good part of the night. But he'll be all right. There ain't too many better than Zack Johnson at staying alive."

"Why don't you go in and get some coffee? I'll spell you."

"You talked me into it." Hunter stepped up onto the porch.

"Leave the door ajar," Dusty said. "The sound of a door shutting can carry in the darkness, and I'd rather not let anyone who might be out there get a fix on our movements. And tell Miss Brackston—Aunt Ginny," he corrected himself, "to blow out the lamp in the front part of the house, and to let the fire burn down. Even from a distance, one of us passing by a lighted window could create what would look like a flicker in the light, and anyone watching the house would have a better idea of where we were."

"You sure know this business, don't you?"

"All too well." Dusty hadn't meant that to sound as cryptic as it had. "Why don't you go in and grab that coffee?"

Hunter laid a hand on Dusty's shoulder and stepped into the house.

Dusty waited, not moving from the porch, but standing motionlessly, allowing himself to blend into the darkness should anyone be watching the house. After a few moments the light from inside dimmed, as the lantern standing on the table by the gun rack was blown out. Good, Dusty thought. They were heeding his advice. Only then, with the window much darker, retaining only a faint glow from the kitchen at the back of the house, and from the fire crackling low in the hearth, did Dusty step down from the porch and into the night.

Dusty knew if the house was indeed being watched, it was probably from a distance. A rider could sit unobserved in the trees at the edge of the meadow, where Dusty had himself watched the house but a week earlier. The moon would be up in a few hours, and once your eyes adjusted to the dim light of the night, you would probably find a remarkably good view of the house. Even though you wouldn't be close enough to pick up the details, any motion would be quite visible.

Dusty walked past the barn, to stand beyond the edge of the ranch yard. In the early evening darkness he couldn't see it, but about a quarter mile dead ahead, the trail leading to McCabe gap would cross a wooden bridge that was mounted over a stream thirty feet wide, and maybe a foot or two deep. Riders would not want to chance cutting through the stream in the darkness, with slippery stones, and mud potentially deep enough for a horse's hoof to sink into. And it was unlikely they would want to cross the bridge, which would be all too visible from the front porch once the moon rose, and the clatter of horse hooves on the wooden planks would carry in the night air.

Dusty was trying to look at the situation from the point of view of a raider. An experienced raider would scout the area from one end to the other, and would know a surprise attack from the direction of the bridge would be impossible. He would then consider working his way around to the south, and come in from behind. So, the woods behind the house were Dusty's next destination.

He crossed behind the stable, then turned to follow the wall along to the back door of the house. He raised a fist and

gave the kitchen door three quick raps. After a moment, he heard Hunter's voice through the door. "That you, Dusty?"

"Yeah. Keep this door barred, and turn out the kitchen lamp."

Directly behind the house was a meadow in which the remuda grazed, and just beyond it was the tree line. However, the woods swung much closer to the house on the east side, coming within fifty yards. Dusty started for those woods, to learn how well he thought a group of riders might be able to maneuver through.

Where the woods covering the ridges were pine, with little underbrush and enough room between each tree for a horse to easily pass through, Dusty found those immediately east of the house to be a tangled bramble of alder and ash, with thorn bushes that caught his clothing and slapped him in the face, or scratched the back of each hand. Underfoot were dried leaves that crunched with each step. He had gone no more than ten yards into these tangled woods when he decided that for a man to pass through here, he would need to bring a stick to knock down a path. Bringing a horse through here would be impossible, especially after dark. Dusty was even more impressed by his father's choice of a location for his home.

Dusty returned to the house for a quick cup of coffee, and for some last minute instructions, should shooting start, though he doubted it would tonight. The house was too strategically located for a surprise attack to be mounted easily, and the raiders hadn't been in the area long enough for the advanced scouting that would be necessary.

He asked what instructions McCabe usually gave for Miss Brackston and Bree should trouble like this arise.

"There's a root cellar under the kitchen floor," Miss Brackston said. "With a trap door. He built the hinges on the underside, so the door wouldn't be visible from the top side."

A man after my own heart, Dusty thought. "Well, at the first sound of gunfire, I want the two of you down there. Don't come up until one of us comes to get you."

To Hunter and Fred, he said, "These riders will be carrying torches. It helps to scare folks, and adds to the confusion. They also need the torches to see by. Don't let the torches shake you. They'll also probably be firing guns as

they ride, and might be screaming, something like the old rebel yell. Don't let any of it get to you. Just stay calm, and aim just below the flare of the torches. The riders will be wide-open targets as they approach this place. You'll both be upstairs, one on the front side, the other toward the rear. I'll be outside. If I see them coming, I'll fire one shot. You both get to the windows, and as soon as they're in range, start picking them off."

Hunter chuckled. "You make it sound like it'll be easy."

"It will be, if we keep our heads about us."

With his rifle cradled under one arm and a cup of coffee in his hand, Dusty returned to the front porch. In the distance, in the ridges to the south, there was now the glow of a large campfire.

The rocking chair Aunt Ginny had used earlier on the porch was now empty, and the thought of it struck him as inviting. He had been awake since before sunrise, and he would guess it was now close to midnight, and he had many more hours to go before he could give in to sleep. But comfort can lull you, and he needed to have his senses sharp, so he remained on his feet, sipping coffee, and looking toward the orange glow on the ridge.

The door behind him, already hanging ajar, swung open a bit more, and Aunt Ginny stepped out, her steps falling lightly on the weathered boards of the porch. She stopped at his side, looking off toward the campfire. "We're in trouble, aren't we?"

He shook his head, but realized she would not be able to see the motion in the darkness, so he added, "No, ma'am. I don't think so. Not yet, anyway."

He took another sip of coffee. "As long as that campfire is going, that means they're probably up there, on the ridge. Once that campfire goes out, that's when we'll be in trouble."

THIRTEEN

Hunter stretched on the sofa in front of the hearth, his head sinking into a pillow, and a quilt pulled to his chin. A fire in the hearth would be nice, he thought, as the night air was a bit nippy, but Dusty had insisted they keep the house dark. Despite how cold he was, he knew the boy was right.

Hunter was too large for the sofa, his feet hanging awkwardly over one arm. He imagined Dusty would fit much more comfortably. Dusty was due to come off duty in a while. Dusty had begun the night, then Hunter spelled him, followed by Fred, and then Dusty again, each in two-hour increments. It would be Hunter's turn again, soon.

Dang, but it was cold. This reminded Hunter of riding herd on cold nights, or riding about with the line riders on bone chilling wintry days. Part of the reason why he now ran a saloon. Of course, while working with the line riders, you got to sleep in a line cabin with an iron stove that would keep the place comfortably warm.

An iron stove. Aunt Ginny had one in the kitchen. He could go in there and start a small fire in the stove, and Dusty would have nothing to complain about.

He knew he should stop thinking about lighting a fire and get to sleep. He was not a battle-hardened war veteran, but he had been in a few gun battles, enough to know you grab sleep when you can because you need your reflexes as sharp as possible. Yet, how could he sleep on this blasted sofa? With his legs elevated and his feet hanging out over the sofa arms, his toes were starting to go to sleep.

He kicked the quilt away with frustration, and swung his feet onto the floor. He would pace about and hopefully drive some life back into his toes. Then, he would give up on the idea of getting some sleep tonight and go into the kitchen and build a fire.

He then noticed it was no longer inky black outside with but a touch of pale moonlight, as it had been when he first tried to bed down on the sofa. It was now a deep gray, like it gets when dawn is approaching. What time was it, anyhow? And why hadn't Dusty come and gotten him when his shift was over? Was something wrong?

Hunter drew his revolver, checking by touch in the darkness of the room to make certain each percussion cap was in place. Then, he hurried across the floor to the door, which was still ajar.

He stepped out. "Dusty?"

"Riders approaching," Dusty said. He was standing on the porch in front of the railing, gripping his rifle with his right hand by the action, his finger curled about the trigger, and the forestock held in his left hand, barrel aiming upward, ready to be snapped downward for a shot.

Dusty didn't turn his head to face Hunter. Hunter realized Dusty was remaining motionless, because in the dim light of predawn, detail wouldn't be easily seen from a distance but motion might be briefly visible. Hunter remained in the doorway, following Dusty's example.

"They approached from across the valley," Dusty continued. "Odd, because the angle is all wrong if they were coming from that camp off in the hills."

Each man standing his turn on guard duty had observed the campfire burning steadily, then only after about four in the morning had it begun to grow a bit dim, though never going completely out. On a chilly night like this, whoever was up there was feeding the fire occasionally to keep it going.

"Your shift ended hours ago," Hunter said. "Why didn't you come and get me?"

"I figured you needed the sleep."

"I didn't realize I had fallen asleep at all, until I woke up and noticed how light the sky was getting."

"You were sure sawin' 'em off in there. I figured they must have heard you clear up to that camp."

"Very funny."

They heard a clatter of hooves on the wooden bridge. "A quarter mile away," Hunter said. "When did you first become aware of those riders coming? How far away were they?"

"Maybe a mile. I was staking out a perimeter, and was down near the bridge when I first became aware of something approaching. More of a feeling, than anything else. Then the crickets all stopped chirping, and then after a time, as the sky was growing lighter, I could see an occasional hint of

137

motion out there on the valley floor. So I ran back here to the porch."

"I'd swear, Dusty, you must be half Apache."

"Ute," Dusty said, seriously.

The riders seemed to be coming at a shambling trot, but not a gallop, as attacking raiders might. And they carried no torches. Hunter thought of going in to wake up Fred, who was upstairs in the front bedroom, when they heard Fred's Winchester action jack open and shut from above. The window was apparently open, and Fred was awake and ready. Probably heard the riders cross the bridge.

"Should I go get Aunt Ginny and Bree, and tell 'em to get down in the cellar?" Hunter asked.

"No," Dusty said. "I don't think these are raiders."

Then Dusty turned to him. "They're riding up to the house. You stand here and face 'em. I'll be off to the side. If they do mean trouble, with you here, me off at their side and Fred upstairs, we'll catch 'em in a three-way crossfire."

"You'll be wide open out there. In fact, I will be up here, too."

"Don't worry," Dusty was already vaulting over the porch railing to the ground below. "They won't see Fred and me until it's too late. They won't have a chance."

Dang, Hunter thought. Dusty was simply too good at this, and it was making Hunter feel a little unnerved. He had met few others who were this good at improvised warfare. Johnny McCabe and Zack Johnson were two of them. Yet, like them, Dusty didn't seem to be one who would enjoy killing.

Hunter could see the riders now, clearly in the growing light of dawn. All but the brightest stars had now disappeared overhead. Dusty had also disappeared, somehow melting into the grayness of the early morning light.

Four riders, Hunter could count, as they approached the front porch. They were now near enough for him to hear the drumming of their hooves on the sod.

Once they were maybe fifty yards from the porch, Hunter roared, "Rein up where you are, and identify yourselves!"

They reined up, and a deep voice with a sandpaper edge called back, "That you, Hunter?"

Hunter leaped from the porch. "Hold your fire! Fred! Dusty! Hold your fire!"

Fred had already left the upstairs window. Dusty emerged from somewhere to the side of the riders.

Dusty said, "Do you know them?"

The riders turned with a start—it was not until Dusty spoke that they realized there was a man off to one side.

Hunter would know the deep, rough voice of Josh McCabe anywhere. "Yeah. It's all right. Who's with you, Josh?"

Hunter was surprised to hear Zack Johnsons's voice. "Just me. And two of the hands Josh hired to replace Reno and the boys."

"Zack? I thought you had gone home."

Dusty was now standing before the porch, and Fred was emerging from the front door. Behind him was Aunt Ginny.

"I did. I told Ramon what the situation was. With him and the boys standing ready, I changed mounts and headed off to the line shack to get Josh."

Aunt Ginny stepped forward. A knitted shawl, looking gray in the early morning light, was pulled tightly about her shoulders. Spectacles were perched on her nose. "Zack, you rode all the way to the line shack after riding clear across the valley?"

"Yes'm. Johnny would have done the same for me."

He was correct, she knew. She had seldom seen brothers who were as close as Johnny and Zack. It was the warfare, Johnny had said. Fighting the Comanche, and pursuing border raiders across the Rio Grande into Mexico. Being shot at together, and even having to kill together. It creates a bond stronger than any other. Except, Johnny believed, the bond of parent to child.

"Why don't you all come in out of the cold?" she said. "I'll put some coffee on."

"What I would really like, ma'am," Zack said, "is to grab a little sleep before I head back. I've been riding hard all night."

"Of course. The bed in the guest room is made up. You know you're always welcome."

Fred took the horses to the stable to strip off the saddles and give the animals a good rub-down after the ride from the line shack. The two riders who had returned with Josh, one of whom was Long, stripped their bedrolls from their saddles and headed to the bunkhouse to stretch out.

Josh let his gaze linger on Dusty for a moment, then pushed past him to climb the steps to the porch.

"Who's the gunhawk?"

Aunt Ginny said, "Mind your manners."

After coffee, Hunter and the young gunhawk rode back to town. Aunt Ginny thanked them again, and told Dusty he was always welcome. Josh thought about that as he had a hot bath and pulled on some clean clothes. A white shirt and a neatly folded pair of Levi's taken from a dresser drawer. Dusty made him feel somehow uneasy.

Aunt Ginny had quickly fried up some chicken and served it with mashed potatoes and some of the previous night's biscuits. She didn't normally serve a lunch so elaborate, but she knew Josh would be hungry from his ride in from the line camp, and she also invited Josh's two new employees to join them. When Zack came downstairs, as the meal was commencing, she invited him to join them, too. She had been letting him sleep, figuring she would serve some left-overs to him if he slept through the meal.

As Zack cut into a piece of chicken, he said, "Where's Dusty?"

Aunt Ginny replied, "He and Hunter left for town shortly after you went upstairs."

Josh asked, "What is it with this Dusty? Just who is he, anyway?"

Aunt Ginny and Zack exchanged a quick glance. If Josh had blinked he would have missed it, but he did not blink and he did not miss it.

Aunt Ginny replied, "A young man Hunter hired to help at the saloon."

"Since when does Hunter hire gunhawks?"

"I wish you would not use that word. I have always loathed it."

"But that's what he is, isn't it?"

Zack changed the subject. "So, I wonder what Johnny found at that auction?"

"He should be home anytime," Ginny said.

After lunch, Fred gave Zack a fresh mount, and Zack was on his way home.

Josh stood on the porch watching as Zack grew tiny in the distance, until he was eventually swallowed entirely in it.

Josh always felt best when his belly was full, he was freshly bathed, and in clean clothes. Yet, he was not content. Something was gnawing away at him, and it was not that gunfighter working for Hunter.

Bree stepped out onto the porch. Her hair was falling loosely to her shoulders, and she wore a gray vest over a white blouse, and a matching gray split skirt and black riding boots.

Josh said, "I hope you're not thinking of going for a ride. It wouldn't be safe with them riders up there in the hills."

"Oh, I think I would be safe enough if I had my big brother with me."

"No, I don't think so."

"Come on, Josh. Or, is your backside too sore from that long ride this morning?" she asked playfully as she stepped down from the porch.

"I said, 'no,'" Josh snapped, his normally rough voice growing to a full roar. He had not meant to be that abrupt. He quickly softened his voice, as softened as it could get. "It's too dangerous to be out riding around, Bree. Even with one of us with you."

He was on edge, and tried to cover, but not well enough to fool her. She knew him too well. A lifetime of growing up alongside him. "All right, Josh. What's bothering you?"

"Nothing. I'm fine." He glanced away.

She climbed the steps back to the porch. "You've always been able to talk to me. Why not now?"

He reached out to the porch railing with both hands, and leaned his weight onto it, letting one foot drift forward. His gaze was fixed on the far side of the meadow, and his shoulders were bowed as though he was carrying a heavy

pack. Bree wanted to reach one hand to those shoulders in a show of concern and support, but didn't. You did not touch Josh. He was the most closed-up person she knew. She was the only one he would confide in at all, and then only in limited doses. If you touched him, he would just close up more.

Most of what she knew about him she had surmised from what little he had said over the years, combined with body language and a lot of reading between the lines. He carried a burden, a terrible one, of feeling inadequate compared to Pa. A man like Pa, with the legends that were growing about him, and the fact that most of the things said about him were based on truth, was mighty hard to live up to. Pa had always encouraged Josh to be his own man, and she knew Josh understood the wisdom of those words, but he was young and their father was almost a living legend, and when people looked at Josh, they saw the son of a living legend. They saw not Josh McCabe, but the son of Johnny McCabe. Can the boy shoot like his father? Can he fight like him, or ride like him? Is he the man his father is? No one had the brass to ask these questions directly to Josh, but he could see it in their eyes. He was a young man, with a young man's pride, and such things hurt. And so, Bree cut him a lot of slack. If he was rude or impatient, or cantankerous, she let it pass. She tried to take none of it personally.

She was about to let this pass, and was about to say, if he wanted to talk to let her know, when he drew a deep, almost shuddering breath, and said, "I've done a terrible thing, Bree."

Her brows dropped into a quick frown. But she remained silent, letting him continue at his own pace.

He drew another breath. Definitely a shudder. And his head was now hanging. "I knew about them riders, Bree. I knew about them all along. I found out about 'em the day I fired Reno and the others. I'd seen their tracks out there. It looked to me like they were bearing north, so I didn't say anything because I didn't want to worry you or Aunt Ginny unnecessarily. They were cutting some cows from our herd and taking them for beef. When I went to get the line riders to ride with me and face them, well, you know the rest. They wouldn't follow my orders and I fired them."

He turned to face her. "I didn't know them riders would turn around and head straight to the valley. I didn't know."

Bree decided to take a chance, and dropped one hand gently to his shoulder. "Josh..."

Wrong move. He shook free of her and bolted from the porch. "Just leave me alone."

He turned off toward the stable. He stood for a while by the fence, staring toward the grass at his feet, then he leaned against the top rail of the fence, folding his arms atop it and burying his face.

How was he going to look Pa in the eye when he returned home? And how could Pa ever trust him to look after the ranch again?

He had beat Whitey in a gunfight. He had defeated Reno with his fists in Hunter's saloon. With both situations he had enforced the authority Pa had bestowed upon him. He had hired some new men, and ridden with them rounding up the herd. Taking care of business, he had thought with pride. And yet, he had failed at the most important job of all— keeping Aunt Ginny and Bree safe. He was grateful for Zack, Hunter and even that gunhawk, Dusty, or whatever his name was.

Josh raised his eyes and looked off toward the meadow that opened up behind the house. The remuda grazed. One mustang pranced about in the late morning breeze.

A cup of coffee might taste good, he thought. Go into the kitchen, pour a cup, and then decide how he was going to tell Pa, and to prepare for the disappointment he would see in Pa's eye.

Josh walked around to the kitchen door, and found Aunt Ginny sitting at the table, a tea cup and saucer before her.

He nodded to her, then continued to the kettle resting on the stove.

"It's probably a little cold," she said. "I let the fire go out."

"That's all right." He opened a cupboard door for a cup, and filled it.

Ginny inwardly shuddered at the thought of what was in that pot. Cold, thick as sludge, and probably gritty with

grounds. How western men could drink it was something she could never fathom, but they seemed to almost crave it. Trail coffee, they called it. Mud would be the more appropriate name, she thought.

Josh started for the kitchen door, but Aunt Ginny stopped him in the doorway with one word. "Joshua."

"Yes'm?"

"Come and sit down, please."

"I'd really like to be alone right now, ma'am."

"Pardon me. I didn't mean to make it sound like a request. Come and sit down."

Josh reluctantly ambled to the table, slid out a chair, and dropped into it.

"Joshua, did I ever tell you that you've grown into a good man? A reliable man? One your father can be proud of?"

Oh, no, he thought. She must have overhead his conversation with Bree out on the porch. Or Bree ran in and detailed it to her. "No, I ain't, ma'am. Not by a long shot."

She did not correct his grammar. "Joshua, don't you think your father has ever made a mistake?"

He shrugged. "Everyone has, I reckon. But any mistakes he's made are only little ones. I beat him at checkers a few months ago because he missed one move. But he was tired that night."

"Oh, Joshua," she chuckled. "Your father has made some mistakes. Some very big mistakes. I've known him for a long time, and he's made some whoppers."

Josh found a sudden wave of defensiveness rise up. After all, she was talking about Pa. "Like what?"

"It's not for me to tell, but I think you might be finding out about one of them quite soon." She took a sip of tea.

Josh hated it when she did that, acting like she knew something you didn't, then not letting on any further. He knew it would be fruitless to prod her for any more information, though. She would reveal only what she wanted, and then, only in her own good time.

She continued. "One thing about your father's mistakes. He never fails to learn from them. You see, Joshua, a mistake is only a mistake if you don't learn from it. If you do learn, then it's not a mistake but a lesson. Now, you might have erred in judgment, but not in your responsibility. In

fact, it's your sense of responsibility that's causing you to be so unsettled about this."

"It's just that I was trying so hard. I wanted to do right so bad, to make Pa proud of me."

"And why do you think you might have made your mistake?"

He shrugged, was about to say, I don't know. Then it dawned on him. "I was trying too hard?"

She smiled. "Living in San Francisco, I had the good fortune to meet an occasional Chinese person. They have an interesting saying, 'More is less. Less is often more.'"

"More is less," Josh repeated. "That's just what I did, wasn't it?"

She took another sip of tea. "And Joshua, your father is proud of you. Very proud."

"How do you know?"

"I see it in his eyes whenever he looks at you, or talks about you."

Bree called from outside. "Aunt Ginny! Josh! Pa's home!"

Aunt Ginny returned her cup to the saucer, and rose from the table. "Come. Let's go say hello to your father."

Josh stood, sliding the chair back and away as he did so, still clutching his coffee. He felt so much better, like a heaviness was gone from him. He realized he was smiling.

THE MARAUDERS

FOURTEEN

Josh felt his chest swell with pride as he watched the rider approach. Tiny in the distance, not quite to the wooden bridge a quarter mile away, but still unmistakably Johnny McCabe. Josh supposed every boy felt that way about his father, but Josh might have felt it even more so.

It was not just any boy's father men talked about around campfires, or in saloons over a beer, telling of the time he took down five Comanches with as many shots. Some of the stories told were not true, or had been stretched so thin you could see through them, but the one about the Comanches was true. Pa and Zack Johnson had been with the Texas Rangers, and they had been ambushed by Comanches. Zack had taken a bullet, and still carried the lead to this day. Pa's horse had been shot out from under him. Pa then scrambled to his feet, drew a pistol as five Comanche horsemen bore down on them, and emptied his gun. Five shots, five Comanches. Two more Comanches were coming up behind the first five, so he did a border shift, and with a fresh pistol in his right hand stood waiting for them to come into range. But they reined up, sat in the saddle staring at him for a moment or two, then wheeled around and rode away.

Pa's horse was dead, and Zack's had ridden off. Zack had a bullet in his leg. Pa tied a bandanna about the leg to choke off the bleeding, then carried Zack the entire ten miles back to the fort.

"Just lucky shooting," Pa had said. But Josh knew luck had nothing to do with it. Practice, and raw nerve, were more like it.

Pa rode a chocolate colored stallion with a black mane. A tall animal, more than sixteen hands. Its legs were long, like a Kentucky bred race horse. It loped along casually, yet its long stride ate up the distance quickly.

Pa rode easily, as though sitting in a saddle were the most natural thing on earth. He rode more easily than most men walked. He didn't bounce in the saddle, and yet he didn't give the appearance of clinging tightly to the animal. He simply moved with the horse, as though they were one.

At this distance, Josh couldn't yet make out his blue eyes, his square jaw, or the deep lines under his chin or alongside each eye that came from a lifetime of riding into the sun and wind. But he could see the wide brimmed brown Stetson, the gray jacket. And the twin pistols, one at each hip.

Aunt Ginny stood at Josh's side. Bree was at the railing, the wind fluttering her hair.

As Pa drew within shouting distance of the house, Bree bounded from the porch, and ran to meet him. Pa reined up Thunder and swung out of the saddle, and Bree jumped into his arms with a squeal of, "Daddeee!"

She then took the trailing rein, and walked beside Pa, leading Thunder behind her.

Josh could hear her babbling. "We missed you so much. We've got so much to tell you. What took you so long? We expected you a couple weeks ago."

"Got me a little side-tracked in the mountains, that's all," he said. "You know how I am, out there alone in the hills."

He stepped up onto the porch. Aunt Ginny extended her hand graciously, like she was a Queen, Josh thought, meeting one of her subjects. But her face was alight with a smile. Johnny took the hand.

"Welcome home, John," she said.

Pa then turned his sky blue eyes to Josh. Pa stood taller by a couple inches, and Josh had to look upward a bit to meet his gaze. Josh shifted the coffee to his left hand and reached out with his right, which Pa grasped. His grip was strong, his hand rough.

"How were things while I was gone, son?"

Josh smiled. "I kept things together, I guess. Got a few things to tell you about, though."

Pa's hair had grown an inch or so since he had last been home, now falling past his shoulders. Sprouting from his jaw was nearly an inch of white whiskers. His clothes were covered with trail dust. But even so, Aunt Ginny violated her own rule of requiring you to be freshly bathed before you sit down at the table, and suggested they all come into the house for lunch.

Bree brewed a fresh pot of coffee while Josh filled Pa in on all that had happened since his absence. Reno and Whitey. The gunfight. The fist fight. Aunt Ginny was hearing some of this for the first time, and the way she leveled her gaze at Josh told him she wasn't happy about it. Not happy about the events themselves, and less happy that she hadn't been told.

And Josh told Pa about the raiders, first the trail he had happened upon outside the valley and the remains of a cow that indicated they were rustling McCabe stock, and then how Hunter and the young gunfighter working for him had ridden out here to protect Aunt Ginny and Bree. Pa didn't offer a comment as Josh told him about his error in judgment, didn't speak at all until Josh had finished.

"Yeah," he said. "When I was riding through mountains outside the valley, I saw signs of riders, and the remains of a camp. Once I've had a cup of hot coffee, why don't you and I saddle up and take a ride?"

After the coffee, Bree went outside to find Fred and have him saddle a couple geldings for Pa and Josh. Fred had already stripped the saddle from Thunder, and was commencing to give the horse a rub-down.

Josh buckled on his gunbelt, and then at Pa's recommendation grabbed a Winchester carbine, and thumbed cartridges into it until the magazine was loaded to its capacity of twelve.

"John, I'm concerned about you," Aunt Ginny said. "Here you've not been home an hour, and you're going to be back in the saddle."

"Think these old bones need a rest?" he asked, not smiling, but with the twinkle of amusement in his eye.

"Well, you're not a young man, anymore"

"I'm hardly ready for the rocking chair yet. Give me a couple more years."

"John, let Josh go into town and get Dusty, the young man working for Hunter. They can scout about and find the location of those riders. Dusty is very capable at that sort of thing."

Josh snapped, "And I'm not?"

"This is not the time for male pride," she leveled her gaze firmly at him from over the top of her spectacles. "You are more than a competent cattleman and horseman, Joshua, but Dusty has knowledge about this sort of thing. The kind that can only come from experience. Almost on the level of your father or Zack. And watch that tone of voice, young man."

"Yes'm."

She turned her attention back to Johnny. "Seriously, John. Let the boys handle this."

Josh looked at her curiously. Why was she so worried about Pa? When Ma died and Aunt Ginny moved in to help with Josh and Jack and Bree, they had struck an agreement. The household would be her domain, and the working of the ranch would be Pa's. Defending the place also fell into his territory. She had never, in Josh's memory, questioned him about such matters.

Pa looked at her squarely in the eye, and for a moment didn't speak. A sort of silent communication was happening between them. Josh frowned a bit, and placed his fists on his hips, wondering what this was about?

Then Pa said, "We'll be all right. We'll be back before dark."

And that was all that was said. Pa returned his dusty Stetson to his head, opened the door, and Josh followed him out to the porch and down to the gravelly yard, and out to the corral.

Tethered to the middle rail of the corral were two gray geldings, one with two white stockings, and one with three. Josh's saddle was on one, Pa's on the other. Pa's saddle bags were still strapped on, but his bedroll was now gone. And his Sharps was still in the boot.

Fred stood behind the fence, his foot up on one rail. He chewed a strand of hay. "I kind'a figured you'd be wanting

to check things out," he said, the strand of hay wobbling as he spoke. "I picked a couple of mounts that shouldn't stand out color-wise. I took the liberty of dumping the extra weight out of your saddle bags. Your stuff's in the tackle room. All I left in there were your moccasins and a couple boxes of ammo."

Pa nodded and swung into the saddle. One easy, smooth motion. Easier than most men half his age. Josh couldn't imagine what Aunt Ginny was concerned about.

He and Josh started away, Josh riding alongside Pa. Most riders held the rein in the right hand and any excess rein back and away with their left, using the excess as a quirt, slapping it against the rump of the horse if more speed was desired. Pa, however, had taught Josh to ride with the rein in his left, and with the excess simply hanging freely. If a horse couldn't pick up his pace with but a touch of the rider's heels to his ribs, he wasn't much of a horse. And this method allowed the rider to keep his gun hand free. Pa rode with his right hand usually resting lightly against the side of his holster, so if need should arise he could slide the hand upward and draw his pistol in one fluid motion.

"We'll make like we're riding to town," Pa said. "Head to the back horse trail, in case we're being watched. Then once we're in the woods, we'll cut north and up the ridge, and find last night's camp site."

At the far edge of the meadow, the horse trail began. It cut through the forest that covered the low ridges and hills between the ranch house and McCabe Gap, coming out behind Hunter's.

Once they were in the forest, with tall pines as straight as arrows closing in on them, Josh fell in behind Pa, assuming single file. He did so without being told.

Pa swung his horse to the right, Josh following, and they began the gradual ascent that would take them to the ridge where the campfire had been the night before. Pa slid his Sharps from the saddle boot and rode with it across the pommel. Josh slid free his Winchester and did the same.

The woods were now thick, pine trees no more than fifteen feet apart. These woods were different than those Pa had roamed as a boy in the hills of western Pennsylvania. Though Josh had never been east of the Missouri, Pa had

described the forests of the east, with maples and oaks and alders dropping leaves that grew dry and crunched underfoot, and that were tangled with underbrush you could never get a horse through. However, in these ridges and hills, the trees were mostly ponderosa pines and Douglas firs, some ranging more than fifty feet in height. There was little underbrush, and the forest floor consisted of brown, dry pine needles. This type of forest had its advantages, as Pa and Josh were now enjoying. They were riding their horses unencumbered up the slope, with iron shod hooves striking the pine needle laden earth almost silently.

When the slope leveled off, Pa swung from the saddle and reached into his saddle bags for his moccasins. Long, buckskin boots with soft soles, sewn together with rawhide strips. He had made them himself, based on the footwear the Shoshone used. His first pair had been given him by a war chief when he and Zack Johnson and Uncle Josiah had first wintered in this valley, nearly twenty years earlier.

Pa pulled off his riding boots, which took a moment because most cowhands preferred such boots to be skin-tight, clinging to the foot like they had been glued in place. Then he pulled on his moccasin boots, tying each with a rawhide thong just below the knee.

"I'm going to go cut for sign afoot," he said. "Stay with the horses."

Josh gave a nod. You can travel faster on a horse, but right now, secrecy was more important than speed. Pa would be able to move practically unobserved afoot.

Moving as silently as wind whispering through a pine bough, Pa slipped into the trees and was soon gone from sight. He could move through the wilderness as well as any Indian Josh had ever seen. Josh sometimes felt Pa was more at home in the wilderness than anywhere else. Josh thought, if things had been different and Pa had never met Ma, he might have been content to find a stretch of land deep in the mountains, far from any trace of civilization, and build himself a cabin and simply live out his days there.

Josh swung out of his saddle, keeping his Winchester in one hand. He felt he was too much of a target sitting up on his horse.

He waited for Pa. A gust of wind picked up, causing some pine boughs to sway a bit, then it died away. From somewhere off in the trees, a crow called out. Josh removed a canteen, took a sip, and he waited.

Sudden movement from off to his left caught his eye. It was Pa, silently materializing from the woods.

"I found a trail," he said. "Lots of riders. Looks like it might have been made this morning."

He and Josh mounted up, and Josh followed Pa for a couple hundred yards along the ridge until they came to the tracks. Then they back-trailed until they found the previous night's camp. The blackened remains of what had been a huge fire. Empty cans of beans. The stubs of cigars and cigarettes. A couple empty whiskey bottles.

Boot prints covered other boot prints. It was impossible to get a fix on what their number was, other than numerous. Josh could see some boot prints were larger than others. Some had a flatter heel. He could count at least eight different men. And he saw one set of prints that was smaller, narrower, with a sharper heel.

"Looks like they might have a kid with them," Josh said. "Or a woman."

"The fools," Pa said, stepping down lightly from the saddle and scooping up the bottles. "Don't they know sunlight through a bottle can start a fire?"

He dropped the bottles into a saddle bag. "Well, they're not trying to conceal themselves at all. Must be their number. Creates a feeling of safety."

"Why do you suppose they picked this spot?" Josh asked. "If they're not afraid of being seen, why not go down to a lower elevation? Flatter ground? Maybe closer to town, or to the ranch?"

Pa looked up at the trees overhead. Tall, straight ponderosas. "Can you still climb one of these, like I showed you?"

Josh let his gaze travel up along one trunk. The branches began a good thirty feet from the ground. To climb one of these, Josh would have to wrap his arms and legs around the trunk and wriggle his way up. Pa had seen the Shoshone do this to cut or break branches for a fire. But Josh hadn't even attempted this since he was ten, when he

was two full feet shorter, and about sixty pounds lighter. But Pa had asked the question, and Josh didn't want to admit to even a hesitation in front of this man.

"Yessir," he said boldly.

"Then, have at it."

Josh stepped down and handed Pa one rein. He slung his gunbelt over the pommel of his saddle, dropped his hat to the ground, and shouldered out of his vest and laid it beside the hat. "What is it I'm looking for?"

"You'll know it when you see it."

"How high do you want me to go?"

"You'll know when you get there."

Josh wrapped his arms around the pine's trunk, the roughness of the bark helping him maintain his grip, then let his legs follow suit. Hard-soled riding boots were not the best footwear for climbing, he realized immediately. He had usually been barefoot when doing this as a child. He decided he would ask Pa to help him make a pair of those Shoshone boots.

Up he went. Slowly, only a few inches with each wriggle. He was grateful the work he did kept him in good physical shape, because he needed to be for this stunt.

Sweat was soon rolling down each side of his face and under the back of his shirt, and he was sucking in air through his now open mouth. But he kept going.

He was soon on a level with the pointed tops of some of the shorter pines, and some of the taller ones rooted a little further down the slope.

"You see it, yet?" Pa called up.

"See what?" there was nothing significant as far as Josh could see.

"Keep going!"

Josh continued upward. Soon the pointed tops from down the slope were below him.

And then, he saw it. The open green expanse of the meadow at the valley floor. And the McCabe ranch house and its outbuildings, looking like small wooden boxes in the distance.

He had a perfect view of the house from here. He could even make out the remuda grazing behind the house, a couple mustangs running about, stretching their legs. A man

with a spy glass would be able to clearly see who was standing on the front porch or moving about in front of the stable or the bunkhouse. He would be able to see how many men there were, how well armed they were, and who was positioned where.

"Son-of-a-gun," he muttered.

Once Josh's feet were back on solid ground, he told Pa what he had seen.

Josh said, "How did you know there would be such a good view of the house from here?"

"It's where I would have chosen, if I was in their place. It's pretty obvious they were watching the house."

"Yes, sir."

"You ready to ride?" Pa asked.

Josh's hands were scraped, but not quite bleeding, from the roughness of the tree's bark, and his arms were aching and his legs quivering from the strain of the climb. But he would not let Pa be aware of this. He would not admit to weakness in front of this man.

"Yes, sir." Josh reached for his gunbelt.

FIFTEEN

Johnny McCabe and his son mounted up and continued following the trail, and confirmed it was swinging north and away from the ranch, and from McCabe Gap. The riders would likely be beyond the valley by now, but their exit route would have taken them near the Johnson spread.

"Think we ought to go check on Zack?"

Pa shook his head. "We'd never get there and back home again before sundown. We told Aunt Ginny we'd be home before dark. Zack and his men can take care of that place. And it would make no sense for these raiders, if that's what they are, to pass on a bigger spread for one so much smaller. But I might ride out and check on him come morning."

Josh and Pa were riding into the ranch yard as the last rays of sunset streaked the clouds overhead with shades of fiery red. First Pa had a hot bath, and then Josh drew a tub of hot water for himself. Once they were in clean clothes, they joined Aunt Ginny and Bree for supper. After the meal was finished, Pa stirred a little fire to life in the hearth, and took his favorite chair, and lit his pipe. Aunt Ginny was in her rocker, a cup of tea balancing in a saucer held in one hand. Bree sat on the hearth, her arms folded about her knees, looking genuinely happy to have Pa back. The firelight cast a dancing orange glow to one side of her face and plunged the other into darkness.

Josh stood, leaning with one hand against the mantel piece, trying to appear strong and just a little bit aloof, the way it struck him the strongest of men appeared to be. Pa, Zack and Hunter, for example. He was trying to measure up to the likes of men like these. Strength just seemed to radiate from them, but appearing strong this evening was difficult. Josh's backside hurt, from the base of his spine all the way down to the back of each thigh. He had done a lot of riding today. He had ridden hard this morning covering the distance from the line shack to the house, then he and Pa had traipsed all over the countryside trailing those riders. And he

had climbed a danged tree. The muscles of his arms and legs ached with fatigue, and his left shoulder was telling him maybe the climb had taxed it a little too much. But he wasn't about to admit to any of this with Pa in the room. Pa had been moving about comfortably, despite the fact that he had just returned from a long journey, all of it by horseback. You would think he had spent the day leisurely sitting about. So, Josh simply stood, trying to look confident and casual, and not move about too much for the sake of his soreness. And he definitely wouldn't be sitting any more than he had to.

"Son," Pa said. "Would you like a glass of scotch?"

Aunt Ginny shot him a glance over the rim of her spectacles. But Pa merely returned the gaze, meeting her squarely in the eye. Not too many people had the nerve to do that. In fact, Pa was the only one Josh had ever seen who was able to stand his ground and not even flinch when she was giving the Gaze. Compared to that, having the nerve to face a man who was drawing down on you did not seem like such an incredible accomplishment, after all.

"Ginny," Pa said. "He's a man, now. He did a man's job, taking care of this place while I was gone, and he rode with me as a man this afternoon. A man's entitled to a drink if he wants one."

It was not unusual for Josh to down a beer at Hunter's, but Aunt Ginny had never been there to see it. Not that he intentionally drank his beer in secret, it was just that he had never happened to mention it to her. And truth-to-tell, he did not like scotch, but he wasn't going to refuse an offer to share a glass with Pa.

Without a word, Aunt Ginny returned her gaze to the fire. Bree's eyes were gleaming, like she wanted to cheer. A victory for our side! But she held her silence, discretion being the better part of valor, and all.

"I'll get it," Josh said before Pa could rise from his chair. Partly out of simple courtesy, and partly because it would give him more of a reason to be on his feet and not sitting, without being obvious about it. He walked with an intentionally steady gait as he crossed the floor of the large, open room to Pa's desk, not allowing himself to hobble as he moved. Beside the desk was a small end table on which stood

a decanter and some glasses. By firelight, Josh poured two scotches, and brought one over to Pa.

Father and son shared their scotch in silence, Pa in his chair, firelight flickering over him, his pipe now resting in a small ash tray on a table beside him, and Josh standing beside his Pa, gazing into the crackling fire.

Josh took a sip, then another, the scotch burning its way down. For a moment, he found he couldn't breathe. How do men drink this? He didn't care for this at all. Pa, Zack and Hunter could drink it like it was water. But regardless of the taste of the stuff, Josh wouldn't trade this moment for the world.

After a time, Bree excused herself to bed. Once the scotch was gone, Josh did the same, setting his glass on the table beside Pa's chair. He gave Aunt Ginny a quick peck on the cheek and then climbed the stairs to the second floor, and his bedroom. He was glad the stairway was mostly hidden in darkness, so Pa wouldn't see Josh's grimace as his sore back and leg muscles complained about the climb.

Josh sat on the edge of his bed with intentions of pulling off his boots, but his bed looked so inviting that he simply dropped onto his side, and swung his booted feet up onto the bed.

Ah. Sweet relief. How could those tough old men like Pa and Zack do what they did, year after year, in the saddle? Twenty years earlier, when Pa and Zack had found this valley, they had done so by riding, on horseback mind you, all the way from California. Day after day in the saddle.

He stared at the dark ceiling. He wanted to sleep, but he found he was beyond sleepiness. When he got this way, his mind would work too fast, almost like it was spinning. He thought about those riders, and wondered if they would be back. Maybe, he thought. They had spent a lot of time watching the house, and if they were indeed raiders, they would be back. This was the biggest spread in the area, with the most to offer. Horses, ammunition, food.

His gunbelt was draped over a bed post. He hadn't worn it downstairs, because the weight of it had bothered his sore back muscles. He had come downstairs casually, and no one mentioned the fact that he was not armed.

He thought of the way Pa slept, with a wooden chair at his bedside, and one of his pistols on the chair. Just in case he had to get to his gun in a hurry. However, Josh thought about maybe doing something like that tonight, just in case those raiders decided to come back and try this ranch.

He heard a mantle clock above the hearth downstairs striking the hour. Josh counted ten. It was late, but sleep was eluding him. He thought, maybe if his aunt had turned in, he would go back downstairs, and have a second glass of scotch. As much as he hated the taste, it might help him unwind so he could sleep.

He sat up, and realized he felt a little better. His muscles, overly tensed from too much exertion, had relaxed a bit and some of the ache was now gone. He reached down and pulled off his boots, giving his pinched-up toes room to breathe, and then started across the floor in his socks.

He was part way down the stairway when he heard talking downstairs. Pa and Aunt Ginny. She had not yet gone to bed.

"You're proud of Josh, aren't you?" Josh heard her saying.

"He did a man's job."

"He also made an error in judgment. He was quite upset about that just before you rode in."

"But he owned up to it. I'm proud of him for that, too. And he learned from his mistake and won't make the same one again. That's also part of being a man."

"You were gone a long time, John. Longer than usual."

Then, they were quiet. Josh could visualize Aunt Ginny in her rocker, sipping on her tea. Pa in his chair, taking a draught of smoke from his pipe.

After a few moments, she said, "You're missing Lura, aren't you?"

"More than usual, for some reason."

"They say that when a loved one dies, you grieve for a while, then you put it behind you, and move on. But that's not how it works, not if you really love the person. You might get used to it, but you never seem to really move on."

"No, you never really do."

There was something different in Pa's voice, Josh thought, as he listened to Pa and Aunt Ginny talk.

Something Josh had never heard before. A sort of edge, but also a sort of wilting sound. If Josh didn't know better, he would think it sounded like pain. The kind that can slowly gnaw away at you. But surely not from Pa. He was not the kind of man who succumbed to anything. Pa wouldn't allow anything to eat away at him. He took a-hold of a problem with both hands, wrestled it down, and conquered it.

Pa had never talked much about Ma to Josh and Bree and Jack. He had told them stories about her, like how he had first met her and such, but he had never really talked much about how he felt about her. About her passing. He had heard from Zack and Hunter how Pa had ridden out in search of the man who killed her, and had never found him. He had been gone two months, and had come back empty handed. According to Zack, Aunt Ginny had a talk with him, and said she understood his desire for vengeance, but he had to let it go. The children needed him home. So, he gave up the search, and to Josh's knowledge, the killer had never been found.

All of this was before Josh was really old enough to remember. He did have a couple of fleeting images of Ma in his mind. One of a blond woman with a smile that made you feel all warm inside, and one of a woman singing him to sleep at night. He did not remember the song, but he could still hear the silky smoothness of her voice. And there was one photograph of her and Pa on their wedding day. Pa kept it on a stand in his room.

Pa and Aunt Ginny remained silent for a while. Josh lowered himself to sit on one of the steps, moving carefully so as not to make a sound. He winced a bit as his sore backside made contact with the wooden step.

Then, Pa spoke again. "It's been getting worse than usual, lately. It's like, I expect her to be there in bed with me at night. I roll over and find myself reaching for her, and she's not there. It startles me right out of my sleep. Sometimes more than once in a night. And sometimes she appears in my dreams, smiling. Reaching out for me. Taking my hand. That's why I was gone so long. Trying to come to grips with all of this."

Aunt Ginny said, "Does she say anything in those dreams?"

"Two nights ago, she said, I'll see you again, soon. I woke up shaking, all by myself, in the middle of the mountains. Tears running down my face, like a baby."

Josh's mouth was hanging open. Crying? Pa? Of course, Josh knew in theory that everyone cried at one time or another, but to hear this from Pa seemed somehow unsettling.

Aunt Ginny said, "Those are just dreams, John. Nothing more."

"I don't know. How do I know it's not something more?"

Josh knew Pa believed in spirits. During Pa's winter with the Shoshone, he had spent a lot of time with one of their shamans, and learned about the Indian view of life and death. That the body may die, but the spirit lives on. Pa spoke of that old Shoshone shaman as one of his most revered teachers.

Aunt Ginny was a little more traditional in her approach, keeping a Bible by her bedside and insisting the family give a traditional prayer of thanksgiving before each meal together, and she sometimes rode into town for church on Sunday.

Josh asked her about all of this once. Which belief was right? What was the actual way things worked?

"No belief is necessarily right or wrong," she said. "We each approach God in our own way. Or, more appropriately, God approaches each of us in whatever way we can understand him best."

"Then, why do so many have no toleration for the beliefs of others?"

"Of all the good qualities that can be found in mankind, sadly, open-mindedness is among the most rare."

"Then, why do you call Pa's beliefs silly Indian superstitions?"

She chuckled. "Your Pa and I have a unique way of communicating, that's all."

As Josh sat on the stairs listening, Pa said, "Sixteen years she's been gone. Sixteen years, eight months, and an odd number of days. I don't really know what the date is. Out in the mountains, it's easy to lose track."

"June twenty-fifth," Aunt Ginny said.

"June twenty-fifth. Sixteen years, eight months, and..." he was silent a moment as he did the arithmetic in his head, "fourteen days. The more time goes by, the more I find it hard to believe I've actually lived this long without her."

"You're a strong man."

"I'm not as strong as you might think."

Yeah, you are, Josh thought. You're one of the strongest men I've ever known. And yet, Josh often got so caught up in looking at Pa as a larger-than-life figure he could never measure up to, he sometimes forgot Pa was human. Hearing Pa talk like this brought it all home to him in an abrupt way. Like being slapped in the face.

Pa continued, "I've held on for the children, that's all. They were so young, and needed at least one of their parents with them. Without them needing me, I probably would have drunk myself to death by now. Or just ridden off into the mountains and not come back. When I'm out there in the mountains, I can almost feel her spirit on the wind. But now, Josh is grown and ready to take over the ranch. Jack will be out of school soon and starting his life as a doctor. And Bree is nearly grown."

"They still need you, John."

"I suppose."

He was quiet for a few moments, then said, "You know, I've been told that even though people think I'm brave and strong, the truth is I'm really too stupid to know when to quit."

She chuckled. "Whoever told you that?"

"Zack. One time with the Rangers, a long time ago."

"I'll have to speak to him about that. You have to be one of the most intelligent men I have ever met."

"No, don't say anything to him. He didn't mean anything bad. He was just commenting, that's all.

"You know, I've been in a lot of battles over the years, and I've seen some bravery. And I've seen some cowardice. And I don't really think there's much difference. Just extreme reactions to extreme situations. On one hand you have men who can just seem to rise up and do what has to be done, regardless of the danger or their own fear, to make sure as many of the men with them as possible can return home alive. And on the other hand you have men who are just

paralyzed by fear. Most men, though, fall somewhere in between. I guess, for some reason, I've always seemed to fall into the first category. Like that time I shot those five Comanches—I didn't even think about the danger. I just pulled my pistol and began shooting, like those Comanches were just tin cans setting on a fence rail and it was target practice."

"You know," Aunt Ginny said, "being able to look yourself in the face and see yourself objectively takes strength in itself. Especially when so much is made of your exploits, when you're talked about in saloons and around campfires. It would be so easy to form a larger-than-life image of yourself."

Pa said nothing. Josh imagined he was taking another draw on his pipe and staring into the fire.

Finally, Pa said, "I don't know. All I hope for is a summer without trouble. Then an uneventful fall round-up. Then, an easy winter. And then, in the spring, I'll be leaving Josh in charge, and riding to California. He's a man, now, and can handle things. I'll probably be back by first snow."

"You're going to visit Lura's grave?"

"Yeah. I've got to go."

There was then a long silence. Josh would normally have felt proud, very proud, to hear his father refer to him as a man, and saying he trusted him to run the ranch for an entire summer. But something about that silence, and a feeling in the air, made him uncomfortable. He was waiting for something more to be said, and he found he was holding his breath.

Finally, Aunt Ginny asked, "Will you really be coming back?"

Pa said quietly, "I don't know."

SIXTEEN

Johnny finally rose to his feet, held his pipe over the dying fire and tapped the mouth of the bowl with the flat of his free hand to empty the ashes, then returned the pipe to the glass ash tray on the arm of his chair. "Well, I guess I'll be turning in, Ginny."

"I think I might stay up a while longer, maybe have another cup of tea."

"Good night, then."

"Good night. Oh, and John?"

He had started for the stairs, but turned back to her.

She said, "It's good to have you home."

He nodded with a half-smile. "Good night."

She listened to his footfalls on the stairs as he climbed them. Remarkably soft, his footsteps were. Even in hard soled riding boots, he seemed to glide along rather than simply walk.

These were some of her favorite times, when she was the only one awake in the house. It seemed to somehow make the noises of the night come alive with more clarity. The ceiling creaked for a moment, the house settling. Even the rocking of her chair on the braided rug atop the wooden floor seemed more noticeable.

The dying fire crackled a little, just to let Ginny know a bit of life still remained. A tiny blaze danced atop the remains of one log. Ginny sipped her tea, watching the remaining lick of flame flicker, grow smaller, then come back a bit, flicker one more time, and then disappear entirely. She finished her tea, and went to the kitchen. The pot was still hot, and she poured another cup.

Rather than returning to her rocker, she walked the length of the parlor, and stepped out onto the porch. The air was refreshingly cooler now that night was upon the land and crickets chirped in the tall grass beyond the ranch yard. She heard an owl call in the distance.

She cast one nervous glance to the ridges at the far end of the valley, hoping not to see the glow of a campfire, and did not. Maybe the riders were finally gone.

She kept an old rocker on the porch, and it was this that she lowered herself into, not spilling a drop of tea. With

the saucer in once hand she lifted the cup with the other and took a sip.

This was not the usual blend of black tea that one expected to find in this country. Ginny bought her tea from a Chinese merchant in San Francisco. Green tea, it was called. Much more subtle in flavor, but it warmed you nicely from the inside out. Very meditative, the merchant had called it, and she found it was. Now that she no longer lived in San Francisco — the house she had inherited from her father had been closed up since Lura died — she had a friend purchase the tea and ship it to her. She kept a tin of black tea for guests, but when she was the only one indulging in a cup, she brewed green tea.

It was late. She and Johnny had stayed up much longer than usual. On a working ranch, the men are usually up before daybreak to fit as much work into the day as possible, and she was up with them. This ranch had no cook, which was unusual, as much so as Johnny's policy regarding the position of wrangler. Lura had originally done the cooking at the ranch in California as a cost-savings measure; it was a much smaller operation in those days. After her death, Ginny took over the cooking duties, and continued when Johnny moved them all here to the wilderness of Montana. So, when Johnny, Josh and the men were rising in the early morning, so was Ginny, cooking breakfast for them all.

Tonight, however, Johnny had been too restless, too filled with missing Lura, to sleep. And Ginny was worried about him.

She sat on the porch, her cup and saucer in hand replaying the conversation with him, listening to his words again in her head.

It was indeed true that when a loved one dies, you never truly recover. Ginny had never known her mother, who had died delivering Ginny's younger sister Sabrina, Lura's mother, when Ginny was but three. Ginny had been raised primarily by a nanny as her father was at sea much of the time, but she loved her father dearly and treasured her time with him, and when he died, it was a loss she bore to this day. And she had come to love her nanny as a mother, and mourned her passing as well.

Ginny believed death was not an end, but a transition, and so, she talked to the spirits of her father and her nanny sometimes, believing fully they could hear her. This was a practice she picked up, she supposed, from hanging about the docks when her father's ship was anchored in the harbor, and listening to Chinese elders talking about their beliefs.

Ginny also knew about loss from one other, though she talked of this to no one but her father and her nanny. Even her sister didn't know about the one man who had been the love of Ginny's life, but who had lost his life in a shipwreck.

Most people thought of Ginny as an old, eccentric spinster, without ever realizing, she was sure, that she had once been a young girl so hopelessly in love she could scarcely think straight. And when she thought of her young man, his body never even recovered from the wreck, to this day she could feel tears welling. No, you never really recovered.

There was one who didn't think of her only as an eccentric spinster, and he was the man Lura had taken to be her husband. Somehow, John was able to see her more three-dimensionally. When she fixed him with the Gaze for the first time, which she often used on people only because she found it amusing (her quirky sense of humor, her father used to say), John simply shot it right back at her.

And when Lura passed onward, so tragically young, and Ginny had told John she knew what he was going through, he didn't ask about how. He simply accepted it.

We each deal with loss in our own way. John would ride off into the mountains when the hurt became too unbearable, and scream to the heavens or whatever he did. Sometimes Ginny would lie in bed at night and think of her young man, seeing his face still so vividly when she closed her eyes, still seeing his shining eyes and his broad smile. And sometimes, this old woman so many were afraid of, would cry herself to sleep.

She took another sip of tea. Everyone had always been so afraid of her. Everyone except her father and her young man. And Lura and John.

Johnny McCabe had stepped into Ginny's life as a young cowboy who was too good with a gun, but who had

backbone and a heart of gold. Ginny remembered the first time she had turned the Gaze on him. She had learned how to do this from her father, a man with a deeply lined face from all of his years at sea, and a heavy, bushy brow. He would drop that brow into a fearsome looking frown and fix his almost gunmetal gray eyes on you, and you would feel the resolve just drain out of you.

John had met Lura in a cow town north of Stockton. Her father was the town doctor. John was working as a cowhand on a local ranch. He and Lura had fallen in love, much to the consternation of Sabrina and the good doctor. They had hoped to send Lura off to a finishing school, either in San Francisco or the doctor's native Boston. A dusty cowboy who used "ain't," didn't know the first thing about selecting wine, and wore his gun too low, was like a nightmare come true for Lura's parents.

When Lura found herself with child, Sabrina and her husband sent her east, to have the child with relatives of his, so as not to bring direct humiliation to them in front of their neighbors. Except, Lura hadn't gone to Boston, as instructed. At sixteen, she was willful, and decided if she was old enough to have a baby, she was old enough to make her own decisions. She headed instead to San Francisco, and her Aunt Ginny. Ginny's father was by then passed on, and Ginny still resided in the Brackston house.

John had been spending a month with the line riders when Lura discovered her pregnancy, and her parents sent her away. So, Lura waited for him at Aunt Ginny's, yet he never came for her. Lura swelled with pregnancy as she waited. One month rolled on into another, and eventually little Joshua was born.

It turned out that Lura's mother had written a note to John, copying Lura's handwriting as best she could, stating Lura no longer wished to see him, and she was going away and did not wish him to follow. The forged handwriting was good enough to fool the young boy. Johnny was heart sick, and went on a drinking spree, something he was known for in his youth, and it was a bad one. As Zack had said once, when Johnny goes on a bender, he really goes on a bender. It was on this bender that the boy called Dusty was apparently conceived.

Once John discovered alcohol can never truly remove your pain, he sobered up and he and Zack simply started riding. John wanted to get as far from that little cowtown in California as he could. Their ride brought them to this valley, where they wintered with the Shoshones. Then in the spring, he decided he wanted to find Lura and confront her about the letter. But he had no idea where she would have gone.

Zack said, "You know her, Johnny. Where would she have gone?"

Johnny thought about it, and said Lura had talked about an aunt in San Francisco who was more like a mother to her than her own mother. So, they saddled up and began the long ride from Montana Territory to San Francisco.

What Johnny found was Lura, with their child in her arms. When each told their respective side of the story, all was forgiven and the lovers were once again united.

Ginny decided to measure the backbone of this boy right off, and said to him, "Well, it took long enough for you to come looking for her, didn't it?" And she aimed the Gaze at him, shooting with both barrels.

And he fired it right back at her. Never flinching. Never looking away. It was then that Ginny was convinced Lura had found herself a good man.

Lura wanted to be married aboard ship, as her grandfather had been a sea captain and by then owned a small fleet of merchant vessels. Even though the old man had passed away long ago, the business was still in operation, with Ginny as the primary owner, so she had the small wedding party of Lura, John, Zack Johnson, John's brother Josiah, and herself rowed out to one of the ships. The captain, who had gotten his start working for Ginny's father as a deck hand, performed the ceremony.

The romance between John and Lura had been the stuff of storybooks. When they were in a room together, the bond of love was so strong between them you could almost taste it in the air.

And then she was gone, a bullet meant for John but cutting through her instead. John's wayward past from Texas had caught up with him. Lura was buried behind the little ranch house in California that had been their home.

Johnny had talked to Lura for years about the little valley in Montana, and he wanted to someday relocate there, but Lura hadn't wanted to move so far away from Ginny. Since her parents wanted nothing more to do with her, Ginny was now her only kin. Other than John and the children. And John loved Lura too much to ask her to make such a move.

After Lura's death, John decided maybe the time was right to take the family to that little valley. Along with them came Zack Johnson and a small number of cowhands, and they brought the herd with them. One long cattle drive. And Ginny boarded up the house in San Francisco and went along to help with the children. She had not seen San Francisco since.

John had seemed to feel drawn to this valley ever since his first winter here. He had often said if only he had listened to his heart and insisted they move here after they were first married, maybe that bounty hunter would not have been able to find them. Maybe Lura would still be alive.

Ginny respected him too much to offer such platitudes as, "you don't know that for certain," or "you shouldn't blame yourself," or "no one can know the future." Instead she remained silent.

And so, she and John raised the children here.

An agreement was made between them. The house would be hers to run, including the furnishing, and she would be responsible for the education of the children. He would oversee the operation of the ranch. The battle lines were not quite as clearly defined as that, and sometimes there was some overlap, but seldom.

There was no school in McCabe Gap at that time. In fact there was no town there at all until two years ago. So, Ginny served as teacher to the children. She taught Joshua, Jackson and Sabrina the basics of reading and writing and arithmetic. The so-called "three R's." Then she took them into higher learning. History. Literature. She had books sent from her house in San Francisco, and the children were educated in the classics. And they were taught etiquette. Joshua and Jackson, especially, had to know how to conduct themselves when in the presence of ladies and other gentlemen. In this time, girls generally didn't attend college, but Ginny firmly

intended the boys to go to a fine school. For Jackson, it was clear early on that he had a gift for science, and a strong sense of empathy. It was obvious medical school would be in his future. However, Ginny couldn't see Joshua as a doctor—his temperament wouldn't allow for good bedside manner. But maybe he would want to pursue law. The world would be open for him.

And Joshua and Jackson dressed like young gentlemen. A white shirt, a tie, a jacket. When they were very young, they wore the knickers and long stockings fashionable among boys his age in the more civilized regions, then grew into long trousers.

However, while Jackson seemed to embrace the concept of education, drinking in knowledge like the proverbial sponge, Joshua's heart was never in any of this. He didn't yearn for college. He yearned for working with horses and cattle. For open range, and branding season and drives to market.

He had been a reluctant student, preferring to day dream than to delve into the education she was trying to offer him. Poetry? He found it foppish. She tried to introduce him to Ivanhoe, one of the greatest adventures in literature, hoping to capture his restless heart and imagination. But he found it dull.

One day when he was twelve, she had left him at his father's desk with a volume of Hawthorne, which he was to do a book report on. She went to the kitchen to prepare dinner, and when she glanced into the room a half hour later to check on his progress, she found him gone. He was out back, leaning against the fence, watching a stallion his father had caught frolic in the corral.

She was about to reprimand him, when she had a sudden change of heart. Calmly, she said, "What is it about that horse that has you mesmerized so?"

"Someday, I want to catch horses just like him. I want to break 'em like Pa does, and I want to ride 'em."

She was silent for a moment, observing the look in his eye, the intensity with which he watched the horse, and realized she had seen the same in look in his father.

"Joshua, what do you want to do with your life? When you are grown?"

"I want to be just like Pa," he said without hesitation. "I want to ride like him. I want to know all there is about cattle and horses. I want to build a ranch like this. I want to work sunrise to sundown in the saddle, and when the day is done, to be able to look at my home and know I did a little more that day toward building it. I want to know any ache in my body from all that hard work counts for somethin'."

That night, after the children were in bed, Ginny sat with John by the fire, as they often did, and she told him of what the boy had said.

"He does not belong at law school or some such place," she said. "That was my dream for him, but it's not his dream for himself. What he wants is to be riding alongside you. His future is not law school. This land is his future. And so, I'm turning the responsibility for his education over to you. Teach him, John. He needs to know how to survive if he is to stand as a man among those who make their home out here. And there is no better teacher."

John said, "I wanted so much more for him than fifteen hours a day of back-breaking work in a saddle. I wanted him to make something of himself."

"I wouldn't say you have not made something of yourself. You're a good father, and you were a good husband to Lura. Your hair is at least a foot too long ..." she said this with a twinkle of fun in her eye, and he chuckled, "but you work hard to make a home for us out here. And you have to admit, though the work is hard, you like it. You find it fulfilling. There is no other work in the world for you."

He nodded with a smile. "I guess you're right. There probably isn't."

"So, teach him, John. I taught him to read literature. You teach him to read sign, to be a good judge of horseflesh. Teach him how to find water when there seems to be none about. Teach him to survive in this land."

Joshua's education, the only one he really needed or ever wanted, began the following morning, with Pa waking him up to tell him to get dressed and saddle-up. He was riding out with the men today. And he would be every day. He would be trading in his jacket and tie for Levi's and boots. And to Joshua's credit, he worked nights to finish that book

report, his last one, because his Pa had always taught him to finish a job he started.

In retrospect, Ginny could see why Joshua found Ivanhoe dull. The boy was in the presence of a real-life adventure hero. His father.

And now, Joshua was twenty, a top cowhand and well on his way to being his father's right-hand-man. Jackson was off in medical school in Boston. And Sabrina...oh, hell, Bree. Everyone called her that, why shouldn't Ginny? After all, Ginny was Ginny, not Virginia. My, but I'm getting pompous in my old age, she thought. Bree was fifteen, and turning into a lady. One with a rambunctious nature, but still a lady.

Actually, the girl's name was Virginia Sabrina, after the aunt who was like a mother to Lura, and after Lura's actual mother. John and Lura had called her Little Ginny when she was an infant. John still did sometimes. But after Lura died and Ginny moved in to help John with the children, having two *Ginnys* in the household might seem a little confusing, so they started encouraging the use of her middle name. And Sabrina eventually worked its way into Bree.

Now both Bree and Joshua, hardly children any longer, were upstairs asleep, and Ginny was sitting on the porch in a rocker, with a now empty tea cup.

Ginny thought Johnny McCabe must be the strongest man in spirit she had ever known. Even more so than her father. Yet, she found herself worried about him. Despite how fulfilling he found operating this ranch to be, it was always dampened a bit because he missed Lura so much. And now, though she had passed more than sixteen years earlier, it seemed to be getting worse for him. He had mentioned tonight that, come spring, he would be riding down to California to visit her grave, and she believed he really did not know if he would be coming back.

He had also said he hoped for an easy winter. Ginny let that roll about in her mind for a moment. She thought about the young man staying with Hunter, and how not so easy things were going to be around here, shortly.

SEVENTEEN

The following day, Fred Mitchum rode into town to indulge in a mug of cold beer at Hunter's, and he announced Johnny had returned the previous afternoon. And Johnny and Josh had taken a ride into the hills and determined the riders had cleared out.

And so, Dusty found he finally had to make a decision. He had been putting this off, because he had grown to sort of like this sleepy little town, and Hunter was a good man. But now he had to decide whether he was going to ride out to the ranch and introduce himself to the man who was his father, or simply saddle up and ride away.

Once the stage coach passengers had eaten and the dishes cleaned up, and there would be no more cooking chores for the rest of the day, Dusty poured a cold beer and took to the chair on the boardwalk out front, and leaned his Spencer rifle against the wall. He tipped the chair back, took a sip from his mug, and let the cool wind rushing down from the ridge wash over him, bringing with it a faint scent of balsam. He was wearing the white shirt he had bought at Franklin's, and a new pair of Levi's.

He would miss this place. He had liked Arizona, but it was not like this. The Cantrell ranch house was on a grassy plateau with the wooded foothills of the Sierra Nevadas as a back drop. The elevation was very high, the air crisp and clean, and he liked it. But not like this.

Yet, to stay would be to confront the man who was his father, and he found himself afraid. Afraid of being turned away. Afraid the emptiness he had endured as a child who belonged nowhere would come back.

He took another sip of beer, and noticed a man approaching, crossing the muddy street. It was Franklin, a small burlap sack bundled under one arm.

"Franklin," Dusty said, nodding his head in greeting.

"Dusty. Just the man I want to see." He stepped up onto the boardwalk, mud that had caked to his shoes dropping in clumps. And to think Dusty had swept this walk clean just this morning. Thank you, Franklin.

Dusty had never seen a town with a main street that wasn't muddy. No matter how hot and dry the climate might

172

be. Arizona, Texas, you name it. Between over-flowing water troughs, wash basins and chamber pots being emptied out side windows, horses using the very ground they walk on as an outhouse, and the occasional rain that would stir all of this to life in a foul smelling soup, the streets were generally muddy enough to slime up the soles of your boots. Give the street a full day of rain, and you would sink to your ankles in it.

Dusty said, "There's only one chair out here. I can fetch you another."

"No, that's all right," Franklin said. "I have to get back to the store. I can only be gone a minute."

Dusty nodded, waiting for whatever it was Franklin had to say. Dusty took a sip of beer.

Franklin said, "This is a small town, Dusty. Small, and still in its infancy. We can't afford a town marshal. We don't even have the funds to erect a jail. In fact, we don't have any funds at all. No town government to speak of. Just Hunter and me and a few others getting together once in a while to discuss civic matters. But well, with good citizens like you, Hunter, and the McCabes around, and Zack Johnson down the stretch, well, we all feel a little safer."

Down-the-stretch was the way locals referred to Zack Johnson's end of the valley, Dusty had learned. The McCabe Gap end was, in turn, up-the-stretch.

Dusty was not sure where Franklin was going with any of this, but he did not really care. After being on his feet all morning, in tight riding boots that pinched his toes, it felt danged good to sit and rock back, take an occasional mouthful of cold beer, and enjoy the breeze from the ridge.

He took another gulp while Franklin continued. "Especially the way you took care of things when those mysterious riders were about. Rode right out there, at your own risk and without even being asked, to make certain they posed no danger to the town, then riding out to the McCabe Ranch to make certain Miss Ginny and Miss Bree were safe until their men folk could return."

Okay. Enough. "Mister Franklin, what are you getting at?"

"Well, I'd like you to have this back." He opened the burlap sack and pulled out the gunbelt and Colt Peacemaker Dusty had traded in for the Spencer rifle.

"I can't pay you. And I don't want to trade back my rifle."

"I'm not asking for payment."

Dusty gave his head a single slow shake. "I can't accept charity."

"It's not charity, my boy. Think of it as payment. You took care of things the way a lawman would. And we'd all feel safer if you had the proper tools with you."

Dusty sighed. This bore the sound of commitment. "Look, I don't even know if I'm going to be staying on much longer."

"The gun's yours, Dusty. Take it." He held it out to him. "Take it as payment for services rendered. If you decide to stay—and I hope you do—then we'll work out something as far as lodging that will be a little more appealing than sleeping on a pile of hay at the livery. I'll make certain you have all of the ammunition and any other supplies you may need. And of course, hair-cuts and baths, all free of charge. At least consider it."

"I can't promise anything, but I'll think about it."

"That's all we ask."

Dusty took the gunbelt, and Franklin returned across the muddy street and down the boardwalk to his store.

Dang. These people were starting to look at him as some sort of benefactor. An unofficial town marshal. This created a feeling of being tied to the area. He already owed money to Hunter for all of the items he had put on credit at Franklin's. If he left now and headed off to Oregon, he would be sending money to Hunter for months. And now, this.

He sat, looking off at the ridge line visible from the front of the saloon. It looked almost velvety green from this distance. As he finished his beer, a thought sprang up and started to take shape. Maybe a ride in the hills was what he needed to clear his head.

He belted on his pistol, went inside and set the empty mug on the bar, then strode to the livery and saddled his horse.

The air was even crisper up on the ridge. A good ten degrees cooler, Dusty thought. Clean, and nourishing. The wind was stronger, causing pine boughs to sway as though the trees were waving at him. He removed his hat and slung it along his saddle horn to let his hair blow freely.

He rode along among the upright pines, letting his horse find its way. He rode with the Spencer across the pommel. It was not that he was expecting trouble, but his saddle had no scabbard, and he did not have the money to buy one, and he wasn't going to tack more onto the debt he already owed Hunter.

After a time, he topped out on a rocky ledge, and below and in the distance were the wooden structures making up the little town of McCabe Gap. A thin wisp of smoke was drifting from Hunter's stove pipe. A couple riders were moving along the structures, in Hunter's direction. Probably going for a beer.

He didn't know how, but in the short time he had been here, this little scattering of buildings that was not quite a town had made a claim on his heart. It had nothing to offer him, except a job cooking and serving beer at Hunter's and serving as the unofficial town marshal. But there would always be the specter of the truth just up the trail, in the ranch house the McCabes called home.

He didn't know if he could confront that truth, yet he didn't know how he could remain so close and not do it.

And there was Oregon, and a girl who was calling to his heart.

In a grassy section atop the ridge, he dismounted and loosened his horse's cinch. While the horse grazed, Dusty sat in the grass and watched some clouds drifting overhead, and an eagle gliding about in the winds.

He had ridden into the mountains hoping to clear his head and make a decision. However, he found no answer on the ridge or in the clouds or in watching the eagle. As he rode back down to McCabe Gap, he was still caught with stomach-tightening indecision. He was afraid to confront his father and risk being met with rejection, yet if he was to simply point his horse's nose west to Oregon, he would always wonder if he had made the right decision.

If only there was someone here he could talk it out with. Sometimes it is easier to sort things out if you have someone to bounce options off of. But there was no one, except maybe Hunter.

Dusty led his horse into the livery, stripped off the saddle and gave the animal a good brushing down, then headed into Hunter's.

Two horses were tethered at the hitching rail in front of Hunter's. McCabe brands. Dusty stepped up onto the board walk and gazed through the window.

Two men stood at the bar, a mug of beer in front of each. Hunter was standing behind the bar, grinning broadly, a third mug in his hand.

Dusty recognized one of the men. About his own height and age, long straw colored hair falling from under his hat to his shoulders. Josh McCabe. The man with him was maybe forty, with a weathered face and steel gray hair as long as Josh's. Though Dusty did not consider himself a gunfighter, he had been trained to think like one, and his eye immediately caught the man's twin Remingtons, one holstered at each side. Must be the man himself, Johnny McCabe.

A thought occurred to Dusty. He could just walk into the barroom and introduce himself, and get the matter over with. Then, if he was not welcome, he could just saddle up and ride on to Oregon.

He took a couple steps toward the swinging doors, then stopped. Uncertainty filled him, tightening his stomach almost like panic.

Forget this. He would be more comfortable simply not knowing.

He turned on his heel and strode to the livery. He was getting out of here.

He unbuttoned his shirt and shouldered out of it, and neatly folded it with his other clothing he had purchased from Franklin with Hunter's credit, and rolled them in his bedroll. Then he pulled on his buckskin shirt. It was of stronger material, and could better weather the rigors of the trail.

There was an old saddle lying in one corner of the livery. It had belonged to a drifter who had gotten himself

shot at Hunter's one Saturday night. No one had even gotten the man's name or knew where he was from, so there the saddle simply set. The finish on the leather had worn away in places, and the leather was cracking. The man who operated the livery had told Dusty he could take it. Dusty had no need, as his own saddle was in much better condition, but now he eyed the scabbard tied to the saddle.

It was a hand-made scabbard, cut from buckskin and sewn together with rawhide. Dusty slid his Spencer into it, and found it was a good fit. He drew a knife and cut the scabbard free, then tied it to his own saddle with the rifle's stock aiming forward and resting under the pommel, so he would have easy access to it.

Dusty saddled his horse, then tied the bedroll behind it. He filled both canteens at the water trough out front, then with his Stetson still hanging from the saddle horn along with the canteens, he led the horse outside and stepped into the saddle.

The sun had just dropped below the ridges to the west and gray twilight was settling upon the land, as Dusty gave the town a sweeping glance. What he figured would be his last. He would miss this little almost-town, but he needed to be riding on.

In the twilight, he noticed the two McCabe horses were no longer in front of Hunter's. Josh McCabe and his father must have ridden home. But he failed to notice Hunter himself standing on the boardwalk in the saloon doorway until he heard the deep baritone call out, "Goin' somewhere?"

Dang. Dusty had wanted to be long gone before anyone noticed he was missing. He turned his horse toward the saloon and walked it over.

Hunter stepped fully out onto the boardwalk. "You look like you're leaving."

"Yeah. It's time I was moving on."

"You weren't even going to say good-bye?"

Dusty shrugged. "Sorry. I just ain't very good at that sort of thing. I got business in Oregon I'd best be tending to. I'll be sending you the money I owe you."

"You don't owe me any money, Dusty."

"I don't accept charity." It seemed it this was the second time today he had said this.

"It's not charity. Come on inside, and have one last beer, and we'll talk about it." Dusty hesitated, so Hunter added, "You won't find cold beer anywhere between here and Oregon."

Dusty nodded. This was true. He dismounted and tied his horse to the hitching rail, where the McCabe horses had been tethered earlier.

Dusty rested one elbow onto the bar while he waited for Hunter to return from the cellar with the beer.

Dusty heard the heavy footfalls of Hunter's boots on the ladder, then Hunter stepped back into the room, and set one foaming mug on the bar before Dusty.

Hunter said, "You look like something's troubling you."

"I guess I just don't know what to do. Afraid to do something, but afraid not to do it."

Hunter took a sip of beer. "If you want to talk about it, I'm willing to listen."

Dusty did not know where to begin. He lifted the mug and took a deep pull of brew. "Okay, let's say you've never met your father."

"I've never met my father."

"I'm serious."

Hunter shrugged his massive shoulders. "So am I. I never have met my father."

"Do you know who he is?"

Hunter shook his head. "I take my name from an old mountain man who took me in, and raised me like his own son."

Dusty looked at him curiously. "You got a first name?"

Hunter shrugged. "Must have, at one time. I was too young to remember. And the old man, he never knew my name. A wagon train had been attacked and burned. Comanches. He came along and heard a baby crying. Found me. Any papers there might have been that would have identified me went up in flames with the wagons.

"At first he just called me 'boy,' but then, he discovered as I grew that I was good in the woods, good at tracking, and I could move through the woods like an Indian. By the time I was ten, I was already big enough to shoot his eight gauge scatter gun without it knocking me over, so I often put meat on the table while he tended his traps. So, he

took to calling me 'Hunter.' When I talk about my mother and her cooking, I'm really referring to his Indian wife. She was like a mother to me.

"And y'know, that's more than I've ever said to anyone else about my background. I like keeping things private."

"Well," Dusty said, "let's say only just a little while ago you found out who your father was. Would you go to meet him, and maybe be faced with him not wanting you in his life, or maybe even worse, not believing you were his at all? Or do you just ride on and never know?"

"And you rode all the way from Arizona to meet your father?"

"By way of Nevada. Pretty foolish, huh?"

"Dusty, your father would want to meet you. He wouldn't want you to just ride away."

"But how do you know for certain? I don't know if I could take being turned away."

"He would never turn you away."

It struck Dusty that Hunter wasn't speaking like he was guessing. He was saying it like he knew. Dusty said, "But how can you know for sure?"

"Look, Dusty, I've known your father a long time. He would never turn away a child of his. I know he never knew about you, because if he had, he would have gone looking for you. He would have wanted you in his life."

Dusty blinked with amazement. "Huh? What do you mean, you know my father? I never even told you who he is."

Hunter chuckled. "Dusty, you've got McCabe written all over you're face. The way you walk, the set of your shoulders. I knew there was something familiar about you when you first walked in. I couldn't quite put my finger on it at first, but after a few minutes, it became clear.

"That's why I offered you the job, to keep you here until you had the chance to meet him, and because I'd never turn away a child of his. I owe him my life a dozen times over. The fact that you can cook was a bonus.

"Your father gave me a job when I was having some hard times, a time when I just needed to lay low for a while and be left alone. He gave me that job, let his bunkhouse be home for me. And like I said, I owe him my life many times over. He took a bullet for me once. And even to this day, he

never asked any questions. Just took me in. Him and me, we've fought Indians and outlaws, droughts, blizzards and even a grizzly once. He and Josh helped me build this place.

"You owe me nothing for anything I've done for you. I'll never take money from him or one of his kids. This place will always be open to you, anytime you need it. Anything I can do, you just let me know.

"I think Aunt Ginny's pretty much figured out who you are, too. You can't slip much past her.

"Ride on out to the ranch. Tell him who you are. Go meet your father."

"You think I should?"

Hunter nodded. "Absolutely."

Dusty shrugged. "Well, I guess my horse is already saddled..."

"Would you like me to saddle up and ride out with you?"

Dusty took a deep breath and let it out slowly, as he tossed Hunter's offer about in his head. "No. I think this is something I've got to do for my own self. But thanks. Thanks for everything."

Dusty extended his hand. Hunter took it in a firm grasp and said, "Good luck,"

Dusty nodded, and headed for the door. He stepped out into the growing night. He felt a little uneasy with apprehension, but no longer afraid.

He swung into the saddle, and turned his horse toward the trail that led to the McCabe ranch.

PART FIVE

THE SIEGE

EIGHTEEN

Dusty reined up in front of the porch.

Well, this is it, he thought, finding the odd combination of anticipation, hesitance, and just a touch of fear that had filled him outside his mother's room back in Baker's Crossing filling him once again.

It was now fully dark. The parlor windows were alive with the low, undulating glow of a fire in the hearth. And he knew they knew he was out here, or at least that a rider was. A man like Johnny McCabe could hardly be unaware. He had taken the small horse trail behind Hunter's that came out at the woods a quarter mile or so from the house. Even so, the sound of an iron shod hoof on the sod makes a little sound, and Dusty had no doubt his father knew a rider had approached the house. Dusty would have known.

He sat in the saddle, looking at the house. The light of the quarter moon gave the log-built walls a kind of dark grayish color. He thought about calling out, "Hello, the house!" Then, thought better of it. Even though it was considered the accepted way to approach a stranger's house, he had met Miss Brackston, a civilized woman, and doubted she would consider such a greeting appropriate.

He decided the civilized thing to do would be to knock on the door.

He swung out of the saddle, gave the rein a couple turns about the hitching rail, then climbed the steps to the porch.

He felt suddenly so inadequately prepared. Here he was, still in his buckskin shirt, his Peacemaker riding low at his right side. Three days' worth of whiskers were on his jaw. He should have been freshly bathed and shaved, and in a

clean, broadcloth shirt. He looked like a scout, fresh from the mountains.

And he really had no idea what to say. Hello, I'm you're son? Or, hello, Mister McCabe. I bet you can't guess who I am. Or, I understand we have a mutual acquaintance, a certain Rose Callahan, from Nevada.

No, he decided he would just have to play-it-by-ear.

His knees felt a little weak. This is it, he thought. This was the home of the family he belonged to, yet didn't. This was the place he wanted to call home. What if they didn't believe him? What if they did, but didn't want him here? What if...?

He forced away the questions, clearing his mind before he talked himself into turning around, hopping on his horse and clearing out.

He raised a fist and knocked.

The door opened. It was the boy. His brother, Josh. Josh wasn't not wearing a hat, and his long yellow hair seemed to shine almost white in the firelight. He was still wearing his gunbelt.

"Good evening," Dusty said.

"Oh," Josh said with surprise. "The guy who works for Hunter. Dusty, right?"

"Yeah."

"Well, don't just stand out there in the night. Come on in."

Dusty stepped in, feeling suddenly very awkward, conscious of a sudden clumsiness in his feet as the heels of his boots clumped along on the floor. He pulled the hat from his head.

"Pa," Josh said, looking over to the hearth.

A man stood up and walked over. It was he. Johnny McCabe. Maybe two inches taller than Josh, his shoulders a bit wider. As he stepped forward, even though the lighting was dim, furnished only by the fire, Dusty could see the square jaw. And the way he moved, the set of his shoulders. It was how he himself might look at forty.

"Pa, this is Dusty. He helped Hunter out here that night, before I got back from the line shack."

"Dusty. Good to meet you." McCabe said, extending his hand. Firm grip. "Thanks for all you did.

"So, what brings you out?" Josh said.

"Uh..." Dusty wasn't sure where to begin. "I know it's late. I'm sorry about ridin' out here at this hour."

Then, Miss Brackston rose from a rocker by the hearth. The spectacles resting on her nose caught a shard of firelight like prisms. "Josh, for goodness sake, light a lamp, will you? We cannot entertain company in a darkened room like this."

"Yes'm." Josh returned to the hearth where two lamps stood on the mantel. He lifted the globe of each lamp and touched the match to the wick. Soon they were each glowing a pale yellow, sending shadows retreating to the far corners of the room.

Again, for the lack of nothing else to say in his sudden discomfort and awkwardness, but feeling compelled to say something, anything, Dusty said, "Sorry to be ridin' out at this hour."

"Think nothing of it," she said. "In fact, I was expecting you within the next few days."

Johnny McCabe looked at her questioningly, but she ignored him, refusing to meet his gaze. "Please, come and sit down."

Josh was standing by the hearth, his arms folded, watching as Dusty walked across the floor to the sofa. The dark-haired girl who was his sister, Bree, was sitting at the far end of the sofa.

"Good evening, Miss Bree," he said.

"Hi, Dusty."

Miss Brackston returned to her rocking chair. McCabe returned to the chair he had risen from, but he was now looking with curiosity from the woman to Dusty.

Aunt Ginny said, "Would you like some coffee? I'm sure some of that brackish mud you men call coffee remains from this evening's pot."

She knew, Dusty realized. Hunter was right. Somehow, she knew. He could tell by a certain look in her eye. A look that was knowing, and at the same time he saw a twinkle of amusement.

"Yes'm," he said uneasily, no longer as concerned about how he might say what he had to say, but feeling that the situation was somehow beyond his control.

"Josh, go get our guest a cup of coffee."

Josh gave a slow huffing sigh, obviously displeased at being suddenly reduced to an errand boy, and left for the kitchen.

"So," McCabe said. "Dusty, is it? Is there something we can do for you?"

"John," Miss Brackston said, before Dusty could answer. "Does he remind you of someone?"

"No, not really. Well, maybe. A little, I guess, now that you mention it."

"Who?"

"Dusty, I didn't really notice at first, but you look a lot like my brother, Josiah."

Miss Brackston let out a spontaneous cackle. John and his brother Josiah did indeed bear some resemblance to each other. "Well, I suppose he does, at that. But that's not who I meant."

McCabe continued. "I haven't seen Josiah in years. In fact, twelve years now, I suppose."

Then he realized what she had said, and looked at her. "Who'd you mean, then?"

Dusty was also looking at her in amazement. "How could you know? I mean, I didn't tell anyone. Hunter, he figured it out, but..."

"We all figured it out," she said. "You look something like your Uncle Josiah, yes, but you're the spitting image of your father."

McCabe's mouth fell open. "Wha..?" was all he could manage.

In the kitchen doorway, a coffee cup fell and shattered.

"Josh," Miss Brackston called out calmly. "Clean that up, will you?"

Johnny McCabe glanced from Ginny to the boy seated before him. Dusty did not know what to say. He had ridden out here not sure how to proceed once he got here, but he hadn't expected the news to be announced this way. And Miss Brackston—she was simply sitting staring back at McCabe, her eyes twinkling with amusement.

In the silence, every sound of the house was somehow magnified. A creak of an overhead timber. The monotonous clicking as a small ship's clock on the mantel ticked off

184

seconds to no one in particular. However, there were no sounds from the kitchen.

"Joshua," Miss Brackston called out. "I don't hear the sounds of things being cleaned up out there!"

Dusty then heard the clink of shards of glass being bumped together as they were swept up.

The woman in the rocker looked to McCabe. "I've got to say, John, I've never seen you speechless. I'll have to mark this down in my diary."

"How could this be?" he finally said. He glanced to Dusty, then back to her. "How?"

"You tell us. You're the only one in the room who was there."

She was enjoying herself. Dusty wasn't sure what he thought about this, but he found himself having to suppress a smile.

McCabe rose to his feet, and took a couple of paces toward the hearth. "It's impossible. I was never unfaithful to Lura. And there's been no one since."

"Think about Utah Territory," she said. "Maybe twenty years ago. Its called Nevada now. You were drunk out of your mind."

Dusty looked at her incredulously. How could she know the details? He wasn't surprised his father did not remember—it had been so long ago, and from what Dusty had been told by Lewis and Annie, McCabe had been about as drunk as a man can get. But Miss Brackston wasn't there.

She said to McCabe, "Think about a night a few weeks after you thought Lura had left you. Drunk out of your mind, in a little saloon, in a small mining town in Utah Territory."

McCabe shook his head. "I have no idea what you're talking about."

Miss Brackston looked at him firmly, but the twinkle was still in her eye. She was enjoying having the upper hand on Dusty's father, knowing something he did not.

Dusty had the impression of a sort of rivalry between the two, possibly each trying to get one up on the other. Good-natured, but intense. And even though the situation was in itself not funny and certainly not a game, she was taking advantage of it to see McCabe twist in discomfort. And

Dusty had the impression that, were the situation reversed, McCabe would be doing the same to her.

"Let me set the stage," she said, almost theatrically, "to jog your memory."

And she began to recount how his late wife, Lura, had been pregnant and whisked away by her parents, sent back east to have the child away from their friends and the patients and business associates of her father, the doctor, and that Lura's mother had left a farewell note to him, forging Lura's handwriting. "Not knowing she was in the family way, or where she was, you simply rode out."

Johnny drew a slow breath, and let his gaze drift upward to the darkened ceiling. "I hadn't thought about that in a long time. I got more drunk than I think I ever had before. I think I was hung over for a couple of days. It was my last bender. I was known for that sort of thing when I was younger, but that one was as bad as they got. It's amazing I didn't get myself killed.

"My brother Josiah came along, which is probably how I managed to survive. It was on that ride that we met up with Zack Johnson—I hadn't seen him since riding with the Texas Rangers, a couple years earlier. He rode along to help Josiah keep me out of trouble."

McCabe focused his gaze on Ginny. "I was so drunk, I wasn't sure where we picked him up, but when I sobered up, he was there."

"So, you don't remember her," Dusty said.

McCabe raised an index finger to point into the air, as if he were identifying a fragment of a memory that had just popped up. "Zack and Joe told me of a woman I spent a night with. It was in a little mining town. I don't remember what it was called."

"Her name was Rose," Dusty said. "Rose Callahan."

Josh charged from the kitchen. "Oh, come on, now!" his voice boomed. "Pa, we can't just stand here and listen to this nonsense. He's no more your son than, than...I don't know. But he's not your son."

"Joshua," Ginny said. "Is that mess in the kitchen cleaned up?"

But he ignored her, continuing, "I've never heard such a cock-and-bull story in my life."

Dusty rose to his feet, feeling a touch of anger now rising within himself, as well. "It ain't a lie. My Ma always believed he was my father. And those who knew her knew it to be true."

"Oh, come on, now! How could she know? She was a saloon woman! There's no way she could know."

"She did. Somehow, she knew."

"Don't give me that. There's no way she could have."

"Joshua," Ginny said. "Sometimes, a woman knows."

"Ginny," Johnny said to her. "You seem awfully ready to accept this."

"I've had some time to think about it. I met Dusty while you were away, and the resemblance struck me as too much to be coincidental. So I had a talk with Zack. He remembers this woman much more clearly than you, because he was not filling himself with enough whiskey to drown a horse. She was dark-haired, he said, and looked like she might have had some Indian heritage."

Dusty said, "She was part Ute."

"Pa!" Josh protested. "We can't just accept this. It's such a long shot. And who's to say he's even telling the truth?"

"What's his motivation?" Ginny asked. "It can't be money. While this family is comfortable, due to years of hard work on the part of your father, and some of my holdings in San Francisco, we are by no means living in opulence."

Dusty didn't know what opulence meant, but it sounded quite nice.

McCabe held his hands up. "It's too late to go any further with this. My head's spinning. I need some time to let all of this settle."

"Agreed," Ginny said.

"Dusty," McCabe said. "There are some empty bunks in the bunk house. Go grab one, and we'll continue this in the morning."

Josh was glaring at Dusty. "You bet we will."

Dusty tried to let sleep take him, but found it wouldn't cooperate. It was not that the bunkhouse was uncomfortable. It was fine, as bunks go. Dusty had slept in many a flea-ridden bunk house, and he had seen some so infested with

lice the men preferred to sleep outside even during the winter, huddled by a fire. But the only other he had seen as clean as this was Ben Cantrell's. The mattresses were free of bugs, and the floor neatly swept.

After he had stared at the shadowy rafters overhead for as long as he could tolerate, he climbed out of the bunk and pulled on his Levi's and buckskin shirt. He forced his feet into his riding boots, buckled on his gunbelt, and stepped down as quietly as possible on the sometimes squeaky floorboards so as not to awaken the other occupants. Fred Mitchum, a hand named Long, and another named Hardy. There were six other empty bunks.

Once outside, Dusty strolled about in the night, crossing the yard between the bunk house and the corral. He stood for a while, leaning against the fence and enjoying the brisk night wind whisking down from the ridges. Then he strolled on.

Before he really realized it, he was standing by the back door to the main house. The kitchen door. He tried the door knob and found it unlocked, which was no surprise. This was an age when the need to lock a door was a rarity. The knowledge that an uninvited guest might be shot on sight, with full approval of what little law actually existed on the frontier, was an effective deterrent.

Dusty found a lamp mounted on one wall over the stove. He struck a match, touched the flame to the wick, and a soft golden glow filled the room.

He found the stove warm, and a pot setting on it. He lifted the lid and found enough beef stew remaining to fill a couple of bowls. He hadn't eaten since noon at Hunter's, and found the sight and smell of the stew nearly set him to drooling.

A quick search of the cupboards turned up a wooden bowl and a ladle, and from one drawer he took a spoon.

He pulled a chair out from the table, dropped into it, set the bowl before him and commenced slurping.

The bowl was emptied quickly. He took it back to the stove for a second helping, and as he returned to the table, he took a moment to glance about the room a second time. The stove stood beside the inner wall, the stove pipe plugged into the back of the stone chimney. Across the room from it

was a row of cupboards and a long counter top. On the wall over the stove were two lamps, one of which was now burning. White curtains framed the windows.

An atmosphere of home seemed to glow from this house, and Dusty found himself envious of those who belonged here.

A voice spoke from the parlor doorway. A woman's. Low and a little throaty. "I thought I heard someone out here."

It was Miss Brackston.

"I'm sorry, ma'am," Dusty said quickly, rising to his feet. "I'm sure you ain't accustomed to folks rummaging around your kitchen at night. But I couldn't sleep, and I was hungry, and your stew smelled so good."

"I had a feeling you hadn't eaten, so I left a low fire in the stove to keep the left-over stew warm."

Dusty's brows knit with puzzlement. "You expected me to come sneaking in here?"

"This is the McCabe home, and you're a McCabe, aren't you? I could hardly call it sneaking."

"You definitely do believe me, then."

A brow rose. "And why shouldn't I?"

"Most folks wouldn't. The old man doesn't. Josh doesn't." Dusty shrugged. "I guess I wouldn't either, in their places."

"Sit, Dusty. Finish eating. I'll put on some water for coffee."

Ginny lifted a kettle and carried it to the iron pump mounted on a shelf on the same wall as the stove. She worked the handle until water gushed forth, and filled the kettle. She then set it on the stove and dumped in a proportionate amount of loose coffee.

She said to Dusty, "I normally crack an egg too, as the egg will catch most of the grounds, but you western men don't seem to mind the grounds."

Dusty shrugged. "Never really thought much about it. Just spit 'em out if I get 'em caught in my teeth."

Dusty was suddenly embarrassed, realizing what he had said might seem inappropriate in front of this civilized lady, but she burst out laughing.

"I'm sorry, ma'am," he said. "Sometimes I don't realize where I am. I'm used to sittin' with cowhands in bunk houses."

"Think nothing of it. I like your candor. I know most ladies like to pretend to be shocked and offended by the realities of the world, but I make no such pretense."

Dusty looked at her curiously. She was an odd one, but he found he liked her.

She settled into a chair across the table from him. "Where are you from, Dusty? I mean, you were born in that mining town, but were you raised there?"

He had begun to lift his spoon from the stew, then stopped in mid-motion. How to tell her? How to tell her he had been raised by Sam Patterson, whose notoriety wasn't quite on the level of Jesse James, but close enough. How would she react to learn the very survival tactics he had used to prepare this household for possible attack had been taught him by an outlaw? And she was now sharing her table with a product of that outlaw? Because, though Patterson had not fathered Dusty, he had raised him.

He did not like keeping his background secret, especially from this woman. For some reason, her opinion of him was becoming very important to him. And he also longed to be accepted simply for who he was, without hiding his background. However, he did not quite dare tell her.

It was more than he could have hoped for this evening to go as well as it had. After all, he hadn't been told to leave. Not yet, at least. Old man McCabe had taken the news better than Dusty would have thought. Josh wasn't overly pleased to learn he had a new brother, but Dusty did not really blame him. And here he was, sitting at the McCabe table. He didn't want to push his luck, and so he decided to keep his connections to Sam Patterson a secret. At least for now.

She had asked where he was from. He let the spoon continue its way to his mouth, slurped down the stew, and said casually, "Oh, I'm from everywhere, I guess." The standard lie. "I was raised by drifters, folks passin' through."

Ginny looked at him curiously. She had lived long enough and had learned enough about people to know when something was being held back. She wasn't accustomed to being lied to, and if anyone was foolish enough to try it on

her, she would quickly cut them down to size. But her instinct told her to go easy on this boy. At least for now.

She watched as he, without another word, drained his bowl, spoonful by spoonful.

She said, "You haven't eaten regularly for a while, have you?"

"Not until I took the job with Hunter. Between Nevada and Montana, well, that's a lot of miles. A lot of nights eating rabbit, or digging for roots. Or, a couple of times, I stopped by campfires and got a plate of beans and a cup of coffee. By the time I got to Montana, I had tightened my belt a couple of notches."

She served the coffee and they chatted about the weather, about how Hunter was doing and what business was like at the saloon, now that Dusty was doing the cooking and they were serving meals. Miss Brackston asked him where he learned to cook, and he said from folks here and there. Not entirely a lie. He was just leaving a lot of the truth out.

Finally, he pushed away from the table and rose to his feet. He felt the heaviness of sleep now creeping into his eyes, as though it were finally ready to take him. "Well, I guess I'd best be getting back to the bunkhouse."

"Nonsense. Family doesn't sleep in the bunkhouse."

"Well, that's where I was told to bed down for the night."

"Your father does not run this household. He operates the ranch, but the household is my territory."

"What will he say if he finds me sleeping under his roof?"

"He'd better say nothing, if he knows what's good for him. We made an agreement long ago. We never cross into each other's territory. We have a guest room upstairs, second door on your right. You can have it."

"I'm much obliged, Miss Brackston."

"A few things. First, no hats are worn in the house. Ever. I don't care about the cowboy rules of etiquette, that a cowboy wears his hat everywhere. Not in this house. Baths are taken regularly, and you wear clean clothes and are freshly shaven for meals. For Sunday dinners, a white shirt and tie are expected. You are allowed to wear a gun in the

house at any time, however, even for Sunday dinner. Your father long ago convinced me of the impracticality of not having a gun handy in this land. And what did I tell you about calling me 'Miss Brackston?' Any child of his calls me 'Aunt Ginny.' Any questions?"

"Yes'm. I'm wearing about all that I have. Hunter paid for a couple shirts and a new pair of Levi's for me, but nothing fit for Sunday dinner."

"You look to be about you father's size. I'll see that some of his are ready for you."

Dusty raised his brows with uncertainty. "I don't know. I think if I sleep upstairs, things are really gonna heat up here tomorrow."

"You let me take care of that."

NINETEEN

Ginny's room was not upstairs, but an addition to the first floor, off the parlor. She had always been a light sleeper, heard footsteps coming down the stairs shortly after the mantel clock chimed three times. She knew every sound in the house, and recognized the footfalls as belonging to John. It was not unusual for him to sleep but a few hours, then get up and pace about for a while. Smoke his pipe. Stand at the back porch, gazing off into the night. Zack Johnson had said once that Johnny's light sleeping came from having been shot at once too often, but it had become worse after Lura was shot.

She heard the tapping of John's riding boot heels on the pine wood floorboards as he crossed the parlor. She thought she heard a creak of leather, and figured he was probably wearing his guns. He did not even go to the outhouse without those things buckled about his hips. Again, from having been shot at once too often.

She heard the squeak of one hinge as he opened the front door and stepped out onto the porch. She remembered when the door first developed its squeak, and she had been about to ask one of the men to fetch a can of oil, but John dissuaded her. A squeaky door hinge tells you when the door is being opened, he said. Ginny wasn't known for her patience, and little things like a squeaky door hinge can drive her to distraction, but she had to admit he had a point so she let it go. The door had now been squeaking for more than seven years.

She also had no doubt John now knew Dusty was sleeping in the guest room. To get to the stairs, John would have had to pass the doorway to the guest room. Oh, well. Now Ginny didn't have to worry about how she would bring it to John's attention at breakfast in the morning.

Bree was slipping a spatula under a slab of sirloin from a skillet and dropping it onto a plate when her Pa stepped into the kitchen. She scooped some scrambled eggs onto the plate also and set it in front of him as he took his customary chair at the head of the table.

"Good morning, Pa," she said, and planted a quick kiss on his cheek.

"Good morning, Pumpkin," he said. An old nickname he reserved for her, and only Pa could get away with it. Josh would call her that sometimes, just to get her dander up. Worked every time.

She poured a cup of steaming black trail coffee and set it by his plate. Ginny was sitting at her chair across the table from him, a cup of golden tea before her.

"Bree," she said. "Could you please leave us?"

Bree looked at her curiously. Partly, she supposed from the odd request, but also because Ginny used the shortened version of her name. "But I haven't had breakfast, yet."

"You'll have your chance to eat. But your father and I have something to discuss."

She rolled her eyes, as if to say, okay, don't tell me what's going on. I don't care, and she strode away into the parlor.

John said nothing as he took a sip of that vile muck he called coffee. His graying hair was tied back in a tail, and he was cleanly shaven. He wore a brown range shirt under a worn leather vest, and his pistols were in place.

Ginny waited for him to say what he had to say. She lifted her cup for a sip, then returned it to its saucer. A waiting game. She knew he could wait her out, but he also knew she was capable of the same. She hoped it didn't go on too long, because Bree was hungry.

Finally he spoke. "You go too far sometimes, you know that?"

"I could say the same about you," she said calmly. "Telling your own son to sleep out in the bunkhouse."

Johnny sighed slowly, his gaze fixed on the plate before him. "I'm not in the mood for an argument. But we don't know for sure he's my son."

"John, the truth is obvious. Just look at him. I mean, Zack sees it. And so does Mister Hunter."

"Regardless, I'm not convinced. And I don't want him sleeping in this house until I am. If I ever am."

"And what are you looking for? Absolute, concrete proof?"

He looked up at her. His eyes were tired. He hadn't slept much the night before. "A birth certificate would be nice. Or some sort of legal document."

"Now, John. You know a child born like that would probably have no such record."

"I've already made my decision. He can stay until we figure this out, but not in the house."

"John, sometimes you just have to look into your heart, and see what your heart already knows."

He shook his head. "Now is not the time."

She was about to ask why now was not the time, but Josh stepped into the kitchen. "Mornin', everyone."

"Morning," John said.

Ginny said nothing.

Josh shrugged, and went to the coffee pot. He didn't know what the trouble was between Pa and Aunt Ginny. He had heard their voices as he came down the stairs but couldn't make out the words. Bree was sitting in the parlor and said, "I don't know what's going on, but you might not want to go in there." But Josh needed his first cup of coffee too badly to take her advice.

"Josh," Pa said. "Get your coffee and breakfast, and get ready to ride. We've got a day ahead of us."

Josh looked at him curiously. "We going to the line shack?"

"No."

But before he could say further, Dusty stepped into the doorway. He was freshly bathed, his hair still wet from the washing, and the scraggly beginnings of a beard that had begun at his chin and each side of his jaw were now gone. He wore a freshly laundered shirt that was a faded blue, and clean Levi's. Clothes he had bought at Franklin's, on Hunter's tab.

"Mornin'," Dusty said a little sheepishly. He had heard the sound of harsh words coming from the kitchen, and now was uncomfortably aware of the silence.

Josh looked from Aunt Ginny to his father, his own ire beginning to rise. "What's he doin' here? I thought he was sleeping in the bunkhouse. He should be eating with the men."

Johnny said, "Your aunt and I were just discussing this."

Dusty cast his gaze downward, hoping by not looking at anyone, his discomfort at being talked about would diminish. It didn't.

"He's a guest in this house, and he's here for breakfast," Aunt Ginny said. To John, she said, "You're forgetting something. You and I made an agreement long ago. This household is mine to run."

"Not in this house!" Josh roared.

"I don't recall you ever having a say about who stays in this house, and who doesn't," Ginny replied.

Johnny leveled his gaze at Josh. "And we don't shout at each other in this house."

Josh slammed his cup on the counter top, black coffee slopping over the rim, and he turned and stormed to the door.

"Joshua," Ginny said. "Where are you going?"

"I'll have my coffee elsewhere," and he was out the door.

Dusty said, "I'm really sorry. This is all my fault. I didn't mean to cause this kind of thing."

"It's not your fault," Ginny said. "Sit and have some breakfast."

"No, I'd better not."

Johnny nodded. "Yes, you should. Go ahead and have some breakfast. Regardless of how anyone feels, you were invited to stay in this house, and this family is not going to forget its manners."

Dusty didn't feel any more at ease. Regardless, he sat.

"Dusty," the old man said. "I have to admit, I don't know what to think. I mean, I can't find any holes in your story. But I need more than that. Some sort of real proof."

Dusty said, an idea occurring to him, "If you were to prove that you're your father's son, could you do it? I mean, if, say, in a court of law, could you actually prove it?"

Johnny cast a glance at Ginny. "What kind of nonsense is this?"

But Ginny was intrigued. "Could you, John? Answer the question."

"What kind of question is that?"

Dusty said, "If a judge ordered you to present real proof that you're your father's son, could you do it?"

Johnny's brows dropped questioningly, reflecting that he was not sure if he found this perplexing or simply absurd. He glanced to Ginny again, who was clearly enjoying this, then back to the boy who was claiming to be his son.

"Well," he said. "I had a birth certificate, back in Pennsylvania. It was in my mother's things. It was mailed to me when she died, but it got lost in the mail, which is not surprising, traveling all the way from Pennsylvania, most of the way by stagecoach. But my brothers know. If I had to prove I was my father's son, their testimonies would be enough."

"Where are your brothers now?"

"Well, two are in California. And one, Josiah, I haven't seen in years."

"If you had to prove to me, right now, as we sit here, that you're your father's son, could you do it?"

"Well..." he looked to Ginny, who was smirking. Then he looked back to the boy again. "All right. You've made your point. You can't really prove you're my son, but I can't prove you aren't. That doesn't make you my son, but it means maybe we should all take a harder look at all of this before we make a decision. But it'll have to wait for now. We have bigger problems on hand. You're welcome to stay for the time being, and you can have the guest room, like Aunt Ginny said. But you're to be considered a working member of the ranch. Working right alongside Josh and me, and the men."

Dusty said, "I'd have it no other way."

Aunt Ginny was looking at Johnny curiously, waiting for him to address the bigger problems he had mentioned.

He knew her well enough to know what she was thinking. In response to her unasked question, he said, "Last night, after you were all asleep, I suppose after Dusty had come back in and was given the guest room, I found myself awake and unable to get back to sleep, and I went down to the front porch to smoke my pipe."

"Yes," she said, "I heard you. I was having trouble sleeping."

"I don't wonder. Anyway, I saw in the distance, maybe eight miles away, a campfire. A big one."

"The raiders?" Dusty asked. "They're back?"

"I don't think they went too far away in the first place. They had ridden out beyond the valley for a while, probably scouting the area. Checking the size of each ranch and farm. They'll be after livestock, horses and cattle, and ammunition. They'll want to hit the biggest spread in the area."

"And that would be this place," Ginny said.

Dusty nodded. "With a place this size, a group of their number should be able to take all they need in one strike."

Johnny said, "I think our problems have just begun."

TWENTY

Josh went to the stable, grabbed a rope, then strode out to the remuda and dropped a loop over Rabbit's neck, and led the horse back to the stable. From there, his jaw set tightly, he dropped his saddle onto Rabbit's back, pulled the cinch tightly, and led the horse out into the ranch yard.

"Mornin', Josh," Fred called from the bunkhouse door. "Hey, where you off to in such a hurry? I could have fetched a horse for you."

Without a word, Josh curled the fingers of his left hand about the saddle horn, leaped into the saddle, and with a quick snap of his heels to Rabbit's ribs, tore out of the ranch yard in a gallop.

He had stormed out of the kitchen without even taking the time to fetch his hat. The wind caught his long hair, straightening it out behind him as he rode. Rabbit wasn't to balk at the opportunity to stretch his legs. He reached with his long stride into a mile eating gallop, and soon the meadow at the valley floor was behind them, and they were cutting through the back trail that began at the southwest corner of the valley, and would come out behind Hunter's saloon.

At first, Josh wasn't sure where he would go, as long as it was far from the McCabe kitchen. But then, as he rode, he felt a craving, a gnawing inside him, and realized he still had not yet had his morning coffee. Hunter's, he thought. Hunter could make good trail coffee and should have a pot going.

Dang, was he mad! He could not believe Aunt Ginny would not only invite a total stranger to sleep in the house, without even so much as consulting any of them. Sure, the house was her domain, which she was constantly throwing in everyone's face every time anyone disagreed with her. But there was such a thing as common courtesy.

Hell. If that gunhawk ain't going to sleep in the bunkhouse, Josh thought, then I am. I'm not going to sleep in that house until he is out of there.

He followed the narrow trail, at times no larger than a game trail, between two steep ridges, and then the land fell away at either side, and he found himself in McCabe Gap, the

back wall of Hunter's saloon two hundred yards before him. Josh rode around to the front of the building, dismounted, and tethered the animal to the front hitching rail.

He strode into the barroom, pushing aside the swinging doors with his shoulders, driving his heels into the floor. He found Hunter behind the bar, wiping the dust from dry glasses with a white cloth. He looked up at the sound of the swinging doors bursting open, then did a small double-take when he found it was Josh.

"Good morning, Josh," he said. "I don't usually see you or your father at this time of the morning."

"Any coffee left?" Josh asked.

Hunter nodded. "Let me get you a cup."

He set the glass and cloth down on the bar, grabbed a couple mugs, then stepped out and to the stove at the center of the room, where the coffee pot waited. He filled the cups, and handed one to Josh.

Josh knew Hunter realized something was wrong. Here Josh was, no hat. You almost never saw a cattleman with no hat. And the angry way he burst into the barroom. But far be it for Hunter to ask probing questions. He seemed to like approaching an issue from the side, and he did so now. "So, how'd it go, last night?"

"What do you mean?" Josh took a sip of coffee.

"You know what I mean."

"He came directly to our place from here, didn't he?"

Hunter nodded. "He's a good kid, Josh."

Josh leveled a gaze at him as though he wanted to bore holes through Hunter with his eyes. "How can you say that? He rides in here, out of nowhere, he's got 'gunhawk' written all over him, and he claims, out of the blue, to be Pa's son."

"He's also got 'McCabe' written all over him. Did you take a good look at him, Josh? He's the spitting image of your father. The way he walks, even the way he carries that gun at his side."

Josh winced as Hunter spoke. Why did this anger him so?

"I don't know," Josh said. "I guess so. Maybe. But you can find people who might resemble someone you know. Doesn't mean they're related."

Hunter shook his head. "No. Don't necessarily mean that. But too many coincidences, I guess. The way he talks. The look in his eye. The fact that your Pa could have conceived a child at about that time, in the very town, with the very kind of woman Dusty claims to be his mother. An awful lot of coincidences, don't you think?"

"No. He's just an opportunist, trying to cash in on a name. If Pa wasn't famous, and didn't have the biggest spread in the area, I doubt we'd ever have heard of this drifter. He would have gone somewheres else, and tried some other game."

"I don't think you really believe that. He didn't have to risk his life that night, helping Fred and me protect Aunt Ginny and Bree."

"And just where did he learn all that? From what I understand he seems to know an awful lot about that sort of thing."

"I never asked. Just like your Pa never asked me no questions." Hunter took a swig of coffee. "What's bothering you, Josh? Aunt Ginny's convinced, and so are Zack and me. Take a good look at him."

Josh leaned against the bar, his eyes aiming straight ahead, but not really seeing. He took a swallow of coffee.

"Even better, Josh, take a good look at yourself."

Now Josh turned his gaze to Hunter. "And what's that supposed to mean?"

"Is it that you don't believe him, or you don't want to believe him?"

"You don't know what you're talking about, Hunter."

"Don't I?"

Josh drained the cup, and set the cup down on the bar. "Thanks for the coffee."

"It's on the house, like always."

"Thanks for that, at least."

"Look, Josh. You're like a son to me. How could you not be, after all we've been through? Your family and me? I don't look lightly at any of this. I had a chance to work with him for a while, and I got to know him. Take the time to get to know him, yourself."

Josh wanted to inform Hunter just how wrong the big man was. But he found the words eluded him. Instead, he just turned, and walked out.

TWENTY-ONE

Johnny McCabe stood on the porch, his Stetson now· pulled tightly down over his temples. The chocolate colored stallion was tied to the front hitching rail. In the scabbard was Johnny's Sharps rifle.

Aunt Ginny and Dusty stood beside him.

"I still wish you'd let me ride with you, sir," Dusty said. "Two's better than one, considering the number of them raiders."

"Someone has to stay here with Aunt Ginny and Bree. Fred's a good man, but he's no gunhawk."

"And I am."

"It's no insult. That word applies to me, too. And to Zack."

Johnny stepped down from the porch, and swung into the saddle. "When Josh comes back, don't let him come riding after me. If I don't come back, don't come looking for me. Stay here, defend this place, and keep the women safe."

"I'll take care of things, sir."

Johnny sat in the saddle, looking at him. Really looking at him. It was unbelievable, but the way he stood, the way he wore his gun. Even the look on his face. The set of his jaw. And there was no denying he believed what he said, Johnny realized. He had been ready to defend this place with Hunter and Fred. If the raiders had struck, this place would have been transformed into a battlefield. No con man would risk his life like that, considering that Johnny had so little to offer him materially. This ranch was the largest in the immediate area, and they were comfortable, but they were by no means wealthy. There were cattle barons in Texas and California that made the McCabes look like pikers.

My son, Johnny thought. The son I never got a chance to know. And here I am, riding off into the mountains to scout those raiders. One man, one tired old man, against all of them. I may not come back.

"Don't call me 'sir,'" Johnny found himself saying. "Any son of mine calls me Pa."

"Yessir," Dusty said, then amended that. "Yes, Pa."

Ginny was smiling, and her eyes were glistening a bit. "Be safe, John. And do come back."

He said, "Keep tonight's coffee hot for me."

And he turned Thunder and was away.

On the return ride from Hunter's, Josh had found himself still not ready to confront anyone at the house. So, he had turned off the trail, and through the woods toward a little creek he knew of. Rabbit now grazed contentedly in the tall grass growing beside the water. Josh had picked a few handfuls of raspberries, as he had had no breakfast, and now, judging by the almost overhead position of the sun above, he was overdue for lunch. However, filling your belly with only wild fruit can have an unsettling effect. A few cramps just below his rib cage had told him to slow down, so he followed the berries with a couple mouthfuls of cold mountain water, then stretched out in the grass.

He had discovered this little creek when he was eleven years old, out riding about when he could escape from Aunt Ginny and her studies. Pa probably knew about it. Pa knew every square foot of this valley. But Josh had never mentioned it to anyone because he wanted it to be his secret place. Back then, he had sat in the grass overlooking the water and talked to Ma, and imagined in his mind maybe she could hear him. And who knew? Maybe it was like Pa said, the body can die away, but the spirit continues. Maybe she really did hear him.

As the years went by, and Aunt Ginny turned the responsibilities of his education over to Pa, Josh found less time to visit this little creek, and he began to dismiss his visits with Ma as little more than sentiment and imagination.

He had brought a girl here once, when he was seventeen. The daughter of one of the farmers who were plowing the earth on the other side of McCabe Gap. May Beth Harrington. She was fifteen, and knew how to ride a horse well, which surprised Josh. He had little respect for farming as a rule, or any work you couldn't do from the back of a horse, but she rode almost as well as Bree.

There had been other girls before May Beth, daughters of ranchers from the area who might attend a barn dance, and Josh would do-se-do with them, and then maybe receive a kiss before the night was over. But May Beth was his first he had taken things beyond a kiss with. He smiled at the

memory. They had spent the afternoon in this tall grass, two young lovers under the warmth of a late spring sun.

As they lay in each other's arms, Josh felt like the world was filled with wonder, and he had never felt more centered or calm inside. This business of carrying on his shoulders the weight of being Pa's son, for a while, seemed somehow kind of minimal. He could imagine maybe building a small cabin up here, he and May Beth, and giving Pa lots of grandchildren. And operating the ranch side-by-side with Pa, until Pa began to get on in years, then Josh would take over the operation, and this cabin he had built for May Beth and himself would become the ranch's headquarters.

But oddly, after that afternoon, he found his affections for May Beth began to oddly dissipate. He would think of that memorable afternoon, but he increasingly more seldom actually thought of May Beth herself. And at the next barn dance, he found her affections for him were less than might be expected, too. She was dancing with another cowboy, laughing, with eyes only for him, and Josh found he did not mind too much. He did manage one dance with her, but all she would do was smile with a hint of blush, talk about the price of corn and he talked about the price of beef, and then when the song ended, she was back with her new cowboy, and Josh's only concern was joining some of the other men in a ride to Hunter's for some cold beer.

There hadn't been a lot of girlfriends in Josh's life. After all, on the frontier, single women of marrying age were extremely few. There was one of Alicia Summers' girls, Jolene her name was. He had never learned her last name. They had taken something of a liking to each other, and a few times, when they were each a little too lonely, they had gotten together and she had never charged him. But he had taken no one else to this spot.

The creek was roughly circular, about fifty feet across, but fed by two small mountain streams, and it drained into the larger stream that cut across the valley, and eventually fed a small pond east of McCabe Gap some called McCabe Lake. A perimeter of grass surrounded the creek, and was sometimes used by deer to bed down at night. Three different game trails wound their way down through the woods to converge on this creek.

Josh sat up after a time, leaning back on one elbow, and let his gaze drift along the water of the creek. A humming bird zipped along, then darted away. A breeze kicked up, rippling through the grass and touching his hair.

"What do I do, Ma?" he said aloud, the first time he had actually spoken to her in years. "I'm so riled at the very thought of having him in the house. That gunhawk, claiming to be my brother."

He was replaying his conversation with Hunter in his mind. What it amounted to, what Hunter was trying to say by suggesting he look at himself, was that here was Josh, trying so hard to be like Pa, and then this stranger walks in, a son no one had known about, who actually is like Pa, without even trying.

And maybe Josh didn't like the idea of no longer being the only son of Johnny McCabe. Jack was Pa's son too, of course, but Jack was off in school, on his way to being a doctor. He would settle in some built-up place, probably, like San Francisco, or maybe he would stay east. Chicago, or Boston, or even New York. He would make his mark on the world through medicine. But it was Josh who would be riding the trails alongside Pa, and building the ranch alongside him, and eventually taking over for him. And it was Josh who lived forever in Pa's shadow. Maybe he didn't like the possibility of now being trapped in Dusty's shadow, too.

Josh did have to admit Dusty looked a lot more like Pa than Josh himself did. Josh took a lot after Ma, with the shape of his face and the color of his hair. Josh's bone structure was narrower than Pa's, more like Ma's, and as such, he would never have the physique of Pa. Dusty seemed to be built more like Pa, with wider shoulders, thicker forearms and wrists. And the square jaw, the firm nose. His hair color was even similar.

Maybe worst of all, Dusty carried his pistol as though he really knew how to use it.

Maybe Hunter was right. Hunter hadn't used the word jealous, but as Aunt Ginny had always said, if the shoe fits..?

"I don't know, Ma," he said aloud. "I try so hard to be like him. It's all I ever wanted. To be good enough to ride beside the man who men talk about over campfires and in saloons. And when I make a little progress, like the way I

handled Reno and the boys, I meet someone like Dusty who seems to be so easily what I try so hard to be."

Maybe you're trying too hard to be someone you're not, Josh. Try being yourself. You might find you, as your own man, are someone every bit as worth respecting as your father.

How about that, he thought with a smile. He could imagine he almost heard her voice.

He wanted to share Pa's belief in spirits, but he knew wanting to believe wasn't the same as actually believing.

"Well, Rabbit," he said to the horse, as if the horse could actually understand him, "time to mount up and ride back."

Josh had loosened the cinch, but now he tightened it again, pushed a foot into the stirrup, and swung into the saddle. He was twenty, and felt like a failure. He was afraid he would always be lost in the long shadow of a man whose greatness he could aspire to, but never fully achieve. Josh knew cattle and horses, and he knew he could one day take over the ranch when Pa was ready to hand its reins over to him, and he could gain respect among other ranchers. But men would never talk about him over campfires.

Why was that so important to him? Why did he even care what other people thought of him? Pa had often said, as long as he had the respect of Josh and Jack and Bree, he didn't care what anyone else thought about him. How do you gain that sort of confidence? That kind of independence?

Just another way he was failing to measure up to his Pa.

Josh turned Rabbit away from the creek, and as they moved toward the line of trees beyond the perimeter of grass, Josh cast a glance over his shoulder back to the water. "I love you, Ma."

TWENTY-TWO

Josh dismounted outside the stable. Fred had been stepping out of the tackle room at the side of the building, and seen him riding up. He reached for the rein. "I'll take him, Josh."

"Thanks, Fred. Oh, and I'm sorry I rode off so abruptly this morning. I had a lot on my mind."

"Think nothing of it."

Oh, well. Now to go apologize to Pa and Aunt Ginny. Pa was right. Manners had to be preserved. Josh had never stormed out of the house like that before, and he never intended to again. And after all, this was his home, too. He was not going to vacate it simply because of a tense situation. If anyone was going to bolt, it would have to be Dusty.

But Josh wasn't yet quite up to going in and facing the music. He wanted to take the edge off, first. He thought briefly of saddling another horse and riding back to Hunter's. Nothing took the edge off like a couple cold beers. However, he didn't feel like riding all the way back to town. Then, he thought of another good way to take the edge off, one that had always worked for him. Target practice. He and Pa kept a box of empty cans in the tackle room just for that purpose.

Josh carried the box out to the corral fence. He stood six cans on the top rail of the fence, then took thirty paces back. Beyond the corral was an empty expense of meadow, as the remuda was grazing off to the other side at the moment. He drew his gun, and with powder and ball and a percussion cap he took from his vest, he loaded the sixth chamber, then returned the gun to his holster.

Josh readied himself, letting his hand hang above his pistol. He kept his fingers loose, relaxed but not limp. He drew a deep breath, then whipped his gun free of the holster, brought his arm to full extension, and fired at each can, trying to pull back the hammer and pull the trigger all in one smooth continuous motion. Like Pa had taught him.

From the kitchen doorway, Aunt Ginny and Bree were watching. Six shots. Four cans flew from the rail. They watched as Josh shook his head with disgust at himself, then

produced a second, loaded cylinder from his vest, and began removing the spent cylinder from his pistol.

"I don't know what we will do with that boy," Aunt Ginny said. "Always trying to be like his Pa. There is nothing necessarily wrong with that, and Josh is like his Pa in more ways than he realizes, but he's like your mother in some ways, too. The blend of the two is part of what makes a unique individual. If only someone could tell him that."

"No time like the present," Bree said, and started for the corral.

"Bree," Aunt Ginny said. "I've tried. He's never listened to me."

"He'll listen to me if he knows what's good for him."

Josh lined up six more cans, then took thirty paces back, and saw Bree striding toward him. Her dark hair was tied into a tail that swung behind her as she strode, and she wore a white blouse and tan split skirt, and black riding boots. She would have lived in Levi's had Aunt Ginny allowed her, but her aunt was adamantly against that. A lady does not wear britches! Today's outfit was one of Bree's compromises.

"I noticed you missed two," Bree said.

"I'm not very good company right now," he said, turning to face the cans as though they were an enemy gunfighter ready to draw down on him.

"I didn't notice any difference," she said with a smirk.

He gave her a sidelong glance. He didn't really appreciate the sarcasm. He squared away against the cans.

"When are you going to stop this nonsense?" she asked.

"Bree, just leave me alone, all right?"

"Do you like this? Do you really like feeling sorry for yourself because you're not enough like Pa?"

He let out a slow sigh, and his teeth came together tightly. "Look, don't push it. Stay out of my head."

"You can never be exactly like Pa. You're not supposed to be, any more than I can be exactly like Ma, or Aunt Ginny. We have to each be ourselves."

"That gunhawk who rode in here last night doesn't seem to have much trouble being like Pa."

"How do you know? We haven't even got to know him. He might look a little more like Pa, but you have a lot of Ma in you, too. Is that so bad?"

Josh squared away against the cans again, and drew. Six shots. Four cans, and one of them had not been a direct hit. Rather than leaping off like the other three had, it spun a bit, then toppled to the grass.

"Bree, you're distracting me."

Bree was about to say, you'll never be able to shoot like Pa, because that's not your strength. Your strength is in livestock. Pa said to her once that he'd seen very few who have the natural way with horses that Josh does, and that he envied that.

But before she could say it, Dusty spoke from behind them. "Not bad shootin'."

She looked over her shoulder to see the boy who claimed to be their brother strolling up. She didn't see where he had come from. She knew Aunt Ginny had accepted him, and it looked like Pa was beginning to, but Bree wasn't sure how she felt.

"I don't recall asking your opinion," Josh said. "And I don't need an audience. I wish you both would go away."

Dusty stopped beside Josh. "Can't leave two standing."

Dusty's pistol leaped into his hand. He held it at hip level, and with the palm of his left hand working the hammer, fanned four shots so rapidly they blended together into a single roar. Both cans leaped away from the fence.

"Pretty fancy." Pa said, from behind them. Bree jumped. None of the them had been aware of Pa riding up behind them until he spoke. Thunder's hooves had landed quietly in the soft sod, and the roar of the gunfire drowned out any noise that was anything less than loud.

Pa was sitting atop Thunder, his wide brimmed Stetson in place, and his pistols buckled about his hips.

"Fancy enough," Dusty said, flipping open the loading gate and dropping the two empties to the grass.

"Fancy. And fast. But fast isn't always what you want."

"Oh? And what do you want?"

Josh answered for Pa. "You want smoothness. Smoothness creates accuracy."

Dusty glanced at him with annoyance. "I got both cans."

"Yes," Pa said. "But it cost you four shots."

Pa swung from the saddle and handed the rein to Bree. "That kind of accuracy can get you killed. A man with a slower draw can still drop you with one shot while you're scattering bullets all around him."

"They say you're the fastest there is. Care to prove it?"

Pa shook his head. "I'm not the fastest there is. My brother Josiah was always faster, and Zack Johnson is no slouch. And from what I just saw, you're much faster than I ever was. What I am is smooth and accurate."

Dusty didn't know what to make of this. "I've heard lots of stories..."

"And they're just that. Stories. Josh, set up ten cans, and I'll demonstrate the way an old Texas Ranger shoots."

"Ten cans?" Dusty asked.

Josh was smiling. He knew what was coming. He hurried to the fence and stood ten more cans along the top rail.

Johnny McCabe's right hand fell to his side, hovering above the Remington waiting in the holster. His fingers were relaxed but not limp, as he had taught Josh. "Say when."

Dusty said, "When."

The pistol sprang into his hand and he brought his arm to full extension—all in one smooth, continuous motion—and he began squeezing off shots. His thumb reached for the hammer after each shot, and his finger squeezed the trigger so quickly Dusty did not see how the hammer had time to even lock into place. Each can jumped away, with the roar of the previous shot still ringing in Dusty's ears.

When the pistol was empty, McCabe drew the left gun, and tossed both pistols across his chest. He caught the left-hand gun with his right, and the empty pistol with his left, and he continued firing with his right while he slid the empty gun into his left holster. The exchange had been so fast the roar of his final shot with his right-hand gun had barely faded when he resumed shooting.

When the second pistol was empty, smoke rising from its muzzle and dissipating over Dusty's head, none of the cans remained on the fence.

Dusty's mouth was hanging open. "That has to be the smoothest border shift I've ever seen."

"You bet it is," Bree said.

Pa said, "That's the way to shoot. Smooth, not fast. Fast is great for putting on a show. But it's smoothness and accuracy that'll allow you to walk away from a gunfight, while your opponent is carried away feet first. I've had to face more than one man who's faster than I am. A couple years ago, down in Cheyenne, I had to face a punk who wanted to say he beat Johnny McCabe in a gunfight. Thought it would make him famous, I guess. He was either too young or too stupid, or both, to realize killing a man is never a good thing. In the time it took me to pull a pistol, he drew and fanned three shots. Two into the ground by my feet, and one that whizzed by my ear. I placed one shot dead center into his chest."

As Johnny spoke, he removed the cylinder from each pistol, and took a loaded cylinder from a vest pocket and snapped it into place. "Cock the pistol as you draw. Make your draw, your aim and your first shot all in one motion. And make the first shot count. You're good, Dusty, and there are few who could beat you now, but it would take only one of 'em to put you in the ground. No matter how good you are, there's always room for improvement."

McCabe took the rein from Bree. "I'm going to take Thunder to the stable and rub him down. Josh, are the line riders still here?"

"Yeah. They're riding back out tomorrow morning. I was thinking of going with 'em."

"Go tell 'em to hold tight. And then join me in the kitchen for a cup of coffee. We've got to talk."

Dusty and Bree watched as Josh started for the bunk house, and Pa took the rein from Bree and began leading Thunder toward the stable.

"What do you suppose they're going to talk about?" Dusty asked.

"Whatever it is," she said, "it's between them only. Pa has always been one to keep his business private. Whatever

you say to him in private, will stay in private. And whatever he says, he expects likewise."

"It's a good way to be." Dusty leaned on the fence. "Tell me something. I know how Aunt Ginny feels about me. And it ain't no secret how Josh feels. Pa—he's coming around, but I think he's reserving full judgment, I guess, until after this thing with those riders is taken care of. But how do you feel?"

"Dusty, just what do you want here?" she asked, answering a question with a question.

"Well, I guess I just want to belong. Most of my life, I didn't really feel like I belonged. Then, when I found out my mother's name, I went to find my past. I didn't really expect to find out who my father was, but when I did, I just had to go find him. And seeing what you all have here, I guess I just want to be part of it. To be a part of the family."

"Well, I'd say your first day hasn't gotten off to such a good start."

"No, ma'am. I'd say it hasn't. I guess I don't know much about belonging to a family."

Bree was silent a moment, collecting her thoughts. "You know, Dusty, you don't want to push too hard. This may be hard on you, but it's hard on all of us, too. You can't just step into a family, announce, 'Hi, I'm your brother,' and expect to be welcomed in with open arms right from the start.

"Now, Josh and me, we were born into the family, and our whole lives have been spent defining not only who we are, but where we fit into it. It may not have been fair that you weren't born into the family like we were, but now that you're here, you're going to have to take the time to find your own way, and where you fit into the family. And I guess it's our job to give you that time."

"So, you do believe me, then?"

"At first, I wasn't so sure. But the more I think about it, the more I suppose I guess I agree with Aunt Ginny that it's obvious."

Dusty nodded. "All right. I'll promise not to push too hard."

She gave a little grin. "And I promise to give you some time."

"I might also need a little help. I don't know much about what it means to be a part of a family."

"I think this might be a learning experience for all of us. What we might need to do is help each other out. That's what families are for."

TWENTY-THREE

Johnny McCabe stepped into the kitchen to the smell of freshly brewing coffee. Josh was by the stove.

Josh said, "Coffee's on. Want a cup?"

"Always," Johnny said.

Josh poured two cups, set one at Pa's customary place at the head of the table, then pulled a chair to one side and dropped into it.

Pa sat and took a sip of coffee. "You sure got mad this morning."

"Yeah," Josh said. "I owe everyone an apology for storming out like that. Aunt Ginny, especially. But I just don't know about Dusty. I just don't like him. And I don't understand why Aunt Ginny accepts him so easily."

"Well, there are a lot of things about your aunt that I'll never fully understand. But I'm coming to think she's right. I think he is who he says he is."

"Pa," Josh started, raising his voice, but Pa held up a hand to silence him, and continued.

"I don't think he can expect us all to accept him as family overnight. That wouldn't be fair to us. But it wasn't fair to him to be deprived of a family all of his life, either. You know, it could easily have been you born in that mining town, and him born and raised here amongst the family. You were both born about the same time."

"I wonder which one of us is older?"

Johnny chuckled. As one who was born second, Johnny didn't quite understand what it meant to be the first-born, but his older brother Matthew had told him once it was something special, a sort of extra responsibility you have when you 're the oldest child. Sort of like the unofficial leader of your parents' offspring.

"Let's see," Johnny said, trying to remember things he had all but forgotten over time. "If my memory serves me right, if I'm remembering the time frame right, I'd say he's about two months younger than you. Maybe three. So, you're still the first-born."

"Well, at least there's that."

"It's going to take time, Josh," Johnny said. "This sort of thing is new to us—we don't get a new family member every day—but it's new to him, too. We've got to allow some settling-in time, for us and for him. Then, we'll see what happens. But we've got more pressing problems right now."

He told Josh of seeing the fire the night before. "I spent most of the day riding the ridges, picking up their trail."

"Dang it. I should have been there with you, not storming off, having a temper tantrum."

Johnny shook his head. "No. At first, I did think I would have wanted you with me, but there are times when the fewer the riders, the better. I left Dusty here to take care of Aunt Ginny and Bree, and I knew you'd be back soon.

"Anyway, I rode through the hills cutting for sign and I found it, and it surely is the same riders. I followed them to the site of last night's camp. They had pulled out by sunrise or thereabouts, and I followed their trail, which wound its way first south, then southwest, then north, then northwest. Kind of snake-like, through the mountains."

"What do you think they want?"

"I think they're raiders, just like we've been speculating. And I think we should all go with that assumption until we know otherwise for sure. These men are good. Better than most. I think they knew I was there. They had left behind guards to watch their back trail, and I only knew because I was downwind from them and Thunder caught their scent before they saw or heard me."

"What'd you do?"

"I turned Thunder, then dismounted and led him quietly to a place maybe a quarter mile back, changed into my moccasins, and doubled back on foot. But the wind had shifted, favoring them, and I couldn't get too close."

He took a sip of coffee and continued. "I figure there were two of them, and their horses either heard me, or caught my scent, which alerted the scouts that something was out there. I waited close to an hour, playing cat-and-mouse. A couple times, one of 'em would throw a rock into bushes, trying to get me to jump at the sound, but I wouldn't fall for that. After a while, they mounted up and rode on."

"So, what do we do now?"

"We prepare for an attack."

McCabe took another sip of coffee while Josh sat silently, letting those words settle in. He had helped defend the ranch against an attack by Sioux renegades five years earlier. He had been fifteen, perched on the roof, using the peak for cover and firing a Winchester. They had been in serious danger; the renegades had outnumbered them by three to one. But Josh had been filled with the thrill of adventure, and the thought of losing the battle had never occurred to him. The years between fifteen and twenty, however, can be big years, and Josh now saw the world more as a man than a boy, and he realized just how much he had to lose—the family had to lose—should the raiders overrun this place. And he found himself afraid.

"There's one more thing," Pa said. "I believe Dusty is who he says he is. But I'd like you to keep an eye on him."

Josh looked at him curiously.

"When I was out riding today, I noticed a trail made by a single rider. It came from our ranch, and the rider went all the way out to that camp last night, then returned here, but taking a different route."

An old trick, Josh knew. It had been taught to him by Pa, himself. Don't use the same exact trail when coming and going, in case you're being watched.

"You think it might be Dusty?" he asked.

"I don't know. I will admit, I don't want it to be. But keep an eye on him. At least for now."

They heard the front door burst open, and the sharp click of hard-soled shoes moving at a running pace across the parlor floor, and Bree charged into the kitchen doorway. "Pa! Josh! Dusty says to come quick!"

They followed her back across the parlor, past the dark and silent hearth, and to the front porch. Dusty was standing by a railing. "There," he said, pointing with the index finger of his right hand. "Off on that ridge, about half way down."

Josh followed his gaze. "I don't see anything."

"Wait a minute."

Then, it reappeared. A flash of light that held steady for a few moments, then faded.

"Light, reflecting off metal," Pa said. "Someone in that tree you climbed, Josh, or one just like it. Using a spy glass."

"Using a spy glass?" Bree asked.

"Yeah," Josh said. "Watching us."

TWENTY-FOUR

The McCabes had an uneasy dinner. When conversation arose, it centered on the party of riders up on the ridge. How many in number, what they could be after. Who they might actually be. Bree knew little of guerrilla raiders, so Pa told her about William Quantrill, the James brothers, Sam Patterson. He told of how, during the late War Between the States, both the Union and the Confederacy had employed raiders to strike at each other's supply routes, burning bridges and such. Knowledge of Confederate raiders was quite common, but few knew the Union had used them, also. Wild Bill Hickok had ridden with a group called the Red Legs.

Pa said, "Often history is written by whoever wins any given war. Had England won the Revolutionary War, then today we would be looking at George Washington and John Adams and the others as traitors, not patriots. They would have been hanged, and that would have been the end of it. Likely, history books would not even refer to it as the 'Revolutionary War.' It would be looked at as little more than an uprising by a faction of anti-British rebels. And we would all today be loyal British subjects."

Pa went on to explain that after the War Between the States, the raiders, like all other soldiers, tried to integrate themselves back into civilian life, but some were unsuccessful. Many of the soldiers went west, and the raiders who couldn't readjust to peacetime living continued to raid, but now doing so for profit.

"In their own way, men like Jesse James and Sam Patterson are victims of the War, as much so as the men they killed during the conflict."

Josh said little during dinner, but he occasionally stole a glance at Dusty, and thought about what Pa had said. The trail of a single rider leaving the ranch and then returning by a different route. Now, Josh felt he had a better understanding of his feelings of reservation toward Dusty. It wasn't because he was jealous of any resemblance Dusty might have toward Pa, as Bree and Hunter had thought. He had known something wasn't quite right with Dusty—his

instinct told him Dusty had been holding back information from the start.

Was Dusty indeed his brother? Josh reluctantly accepted that. Aunt Ginny, Hunter and Bree were right. Just looking at him, you could see he was indeed a McCabe, or it was one whale of a coincidence. Bree was more McCabe in her looks than was Josh, who looked more like their mother's side, but Dusty was more McCabe even than Bree. But he hadn't been raised a McCabe. Pa had said once the Shoshone believed your spirit grew from those of your parents, but Josh didn't think so. Josh believed you were a product of your environment. Dusty hadn't been raised by Pa and Aunt Ginny, so he wouldn't necessarily have their values.

After dinner, Pa posted guards. He took the first watch himself, then Dusty the second, and Josh the third, then Fred, Long, and the other two men would finish off the final shifts before sunrise. But as Pa had said to keep an eye on Dusty, Josh wasn't going to trust him to take the watch unobserved. Rather than sleep through Dusty's watch, Josh would listen carefully from his open window.

Finally, after an hour, he thought he might sneak downstairs and make certain Dusty hadn't ridden off to inform the raiders of the situation at the ranch. As Josh didn't have moccasins, he simply went in sock feet to the top of the stairs. He had pulled on his jeans over his long-handled underwear, and buckled on his gunbelt.

He moved down the stairs carefully, the only sound of his passing being an occasional creak of a board underfoot.

It was as he stepped down onto the parlor floor that he caught a smell of tobacco smoke, a quick subtle indication he was not alone, and which was all that kept his heart from stopping when Pa suddenly spoke from the darkness. "Going somewhere?"

Josh let out a curse. "Pa, you almost jumped me out of my skin."

"When you're moving about in the darkness, never assume you're alone. Always be prepared, even for the unexpected. Because when your guard is down, even an opponent who's not as fast or strong as you are, or as experienced a fighting man, will have the advantage."

"I'll remember," Josh said. "I was coming down to check on Dusty."

"You didn't think I'd let a man I'm not sure about stand watch alone, did you?"

"I should have known better."

In the darkness, the room was a void of blackness. But Josh had grown up in this house, so he was able to work his way over to the hearth without bumping into anything, and sat down on the stone step.

"You're wearing your gun," Pa said. "I can tell by the creak of the leather of your holster and belt. And a man walks a little differently when he's carrying a pistol at his side. And you're not wearing your boots."

"You're good, I'll give you that."

"No. I'm smart. An old scout told me once, you gotta learn by observing. Not only watch what's going on around you, but listen and even sniff the air. Here in the darkness, using my eyes was useless, so I just closed my eyes and listened."

"You know, I think I understand that. Just before you spoke, I caught a whiff of your pipe smoke."

"Good. Now, how about you taking a walk out to the front porch and see if you can locate Dusty?"

"What am I going to tell him if he sees me? That I don't trust him?"

"Might not be a good idea. Just make up a lie. Tell him you couldn't sleep, or something."

Josh rose to his feet. He flashed Pa a quick grin, even though he knew Pa could not see it in the darkness. "Aunt Ginny wouldn't approve of telling a lie."

Josh could tell by the way Pa spoke he was grinning, too. "Aunt Ginny is asleep."

Josh padded his way across the wooden floor. At the doorway, which was ajar, he drew his pistol so the weight of it in his holster wouldn't make the leather creak.

He wondered briefly why the door wasn't closed tightly, then pulled it more open so he could step out, the hinge rubbing gently and letting out a low-level squeal.

He stepped onto the porch and glanced about. The moon had risen, and its pale light gave a silver glow to the expanse of meadow before the house. Beyond, dark shadowy

ridges rose to meet a starry sky above. On one ridge was a fluttering point of orange. A campfire.

Josh approached the railing and leaned onto it with his elbows. His revolver was still in his right hand.

"You know," came Dusty's voice from the darkness, "if I had been one of them raiders sneaking up on this place, you might be dead now. Sound always travels better at night, and I heard the hinge of that door clearly. And the metal of your gun shines clear enough in the moonlight, once your eyes adjust to the darkness."

Dang. Josh hated to admit it, but Dusty was good.

"So, what brings you out here?" Dusty asked.

"Oh, I found I couldn't sleep," Josh lied. "Thought I might catch a little night air."

Dusty stepped from the darkness to stand in the moonlight by the porch. Cradled in the crook of one arm was his Spencer rifle, and his revolver rode low at his right side. "I guess I could believe that. I could, but I don't. I've been circling the house every-so-often, and as I came by the porch, I caught an occasional draft of Pa's pipe smoke. My guess is you two don't really trust me much, yet."

"Well..." Josh fought hard to find some clever way of denying this and coming up with a plausible lie, but the words were not to be found. He guessed he was not a very clever liar.

Dusty continued, "I suppose, in your place, I wouldn't have a lot of trust in me, either. Someone like me comes riding in here with an outlandish story, I guess I'd have a lot of questions, too."

All right, Josh thought. Maybe honesty was the best policy, as Aunt Ginny had always said. At least, to a point. "I do have a lot of questions. I gotta admit that. And I was out here checking on you. But I see you have things under control, and my questions can wait until this thing with the raiders is taken care of."

"Go get some sleep," Dusty said. "You take over for me in less than an hour."

Josh nodded, feeling a little foolish that not only would Dusty have been able to get the drop on him so easily, but had seen through his lie. He turned, and started back for the door.

"And leave the door open," Dusty said. "The sound of a door shutting might carry all the way to the woods in the night air."

He sure was good, Josh thought, as he stepped past the open door. Maybe a little too good.

TWENTY-FIVE

Josh had slept little, but come morning he was out of bed and downstairs for his morning coffee at his usual time. This was a working ranch, and despite the threat of the raiders camping off in the ridges, work still had to be done. Fred had commented the pasture out back they were currently using for the horses had been pretty much grazed out, and Pa had said maybe it was time to move the remuda to another, fresher pasture they sometimes used, toward the center of the valley. Josh wanted to first ride over and make certain the fence posts and rails were all in good shape. If he found any in otherwise condition, he would be having to commence repairs.

Pa normally would be coordinating such things, but the night before, as Josh went back into the house after talking with Dusty, Pa had said he would be riding out first thing in the morning to scout. Josh would be in charge until he got back.

Josh usually stood by the counter as he had his coffee, because he usually had a long day in the saddle waiting for him and didn't want to tax his backside any more than necessary in a chair. However, as he poured a cup, he found fatigue a little too demanding this morning and the chairs at the table looking a little too inviting, so he allowed himself to drop into one of them.

Aunt Ginny stepped into the kitchen, an apron tied about her waist and her spectacles perched on the end of her nose. "Oh. Good morning, Joshua. You don't usually sit down for coffee in the morning."

He nodded. "Rough night, that's all."

"I don't think any of us slept much, considering the threat up in the ridges." She fixed herself a cup of amber tea, and took a chair to one side of the table. She didn't drop into a chair. She descended gracefully. "I'm baking muffins for the men. Would you like one?"

Josh shook his head. When he was this tired, his appetite usually fled him. "No thank you, ma'am."

"Now, I know you're tired. Refusing food."

"Especially your muffins. They're the best around."

She smiled. "Joshua, you are not without charm. It's not many who can refuse a woman's cooking and still make her feel good about it."

Not only was he not hungry, he found he had a small headache, too. He took a sip of coffee, then reached with one hand to rub his eyes.

The night before, during what little sleep he had managed to gain, he had dreamt fitfully of riders descending on the ranch, with torches blazing into the night. He had dreamt of gunfire, and seeing the roof in blazes, and Pa and Fred lying dead, their shirts soaking with blood. And Dusty laughing, raising his rifle into the air, shouting, "You trusted me! You fools!"

It was a good thing he didn't believe in premonitions.

Josh's coffee was gone before he knew it. He knew it was going to be a long day when he scarcely remembered the first cup. He lurched to his feet, finding it more effort than usual, and poured a second cup.

"I'll take my second cup outside," he said. "I've got to find Fred."

Aunt Ginny looked like she was about to say something, but then didn't. Josh thought briefly about asking her what she was going to say, then decided against it and started for the door. He had enough to be concerned about. For one thing, lack of sleep. If he should have another night like the last one, he might not be alert enough to be of any use should those raiders actually attack.

He stepped outside, finding the sky overhead a steel gray and the eastern horizon beginning to come alive with the fiery rays of sunrise. Pa was at the corral fence, the stallion Thunder tethered to the top rail. Pa was tightening the cinch. Or the girth, as Pa called it. That seemed to be a Texas thing, calling the cinch the girth. Pa had spent many years in Texas, and the influence showed. As Josh approached, coffee in one hand, Pa unwrapped the rein from the fence, pushed a foot into the stirrup and swung into the saddle.

"Pa," Josh said. "What're you doing still here? I figured you'd be gone by now."

"So did I. I couldn't find Fred. I went to the bunkhouse, and one of the men said he saw Fred riding out an hour ago."

"Riding out? To where?"

"Keep an eye out, will you? I expect to be back by mid-afternoon, maybe sooner. But same instructions as yesterday. If I don't come back, don't come looking for me."

And with that, Pa turned Thunder west, and rode away. To anyone who might be watching, like with a spyglass from a tree, it would look like Pa was heading toward the small horse trail that would lead to town. But once in the mountains, Pa would turn his horse north and approach the raiders' camp.

Josh raised one arm, crooked at the elbow, and rested it against the fence. He was so very tired. Going to the tack room himself for a rope and fetching a horse and then saddling it, all seemed like so much work this morning. He took a sip of coffee. Where in tarnation had Fred ridden off to?

The kitchen door closed, and Josh glanced in that direction to see Dusty approaching, cup of coffee in hand.

"Good morning," Dusty said.

Josh nodded. "You wouldn't have any idea where Fred rode off to this morning, would you?"

Dusty raised his brows and shrugged. "No idea at all. Is it normal for him to do that?"

"Not for him. He never just rides off like that. In fact, getting him to just take a day off at all is like pulling teeth."

They finished their coffee, then Josh had Dusty ride with him to check out the condition of the corral at the center of the valley. Two posts and a handful of rails would indeed need replacing.

"Where do you get your fencing?" Dusty asked.

"This ain't a very big outfit," Josh replied. "You do a lot of the work yourself. We ride out to the ridges and cut what we need."

Dusty shook his head, looking at the fence. "Can't you get one of the men to do this?"

"I know what you're thinking," Josh said. "No self-respecting cowhand likes to work out of the saddle. But when you're trying to operate a ranch yourself, you do what has to be done."

"Do I dare ask who digs out the outhouse?"

"The new man," Josh said with grin, and they rode back to the house.

"I'm going in for another coffee," Josh said. "You coming?"

"No, I'll be out here."

Josh nodded, and headed for the house.

He found the coffee pot still hot, and poured one more cup. He had noticed Bree sitting in Aunt Ginny's rocker on the front porch when he and Dusty rode back, and when he heard the front door open and then close again, he figured it was Bree. He was right.

"Josh," she said, stepping into the kitchen. "Where's Dusty riding off to?"

Josh snapped a gaze to her, his brows dropping questioningly. "I didn't know he was riding off anywhere."

He set the coffee cup down on the table and strode across the parlor to the front door, Bree at his heels.

From the porch, he could see Dusty in the distance, riding west. The same direction Pa had taken hours earlier.

"What do you suppose is going on?" Bree asked. "I heard the men saying Fred had ridden out this morning, and no one knows where he was going. And now Dusty rides off."

"When he comes back, if he comes back, I plan on getting some answers."

The sun was trailing toward mid-afternoon height as Dusty returned. His horse was lathered, and he was thirsty. He had ridden out without a canteen, and was grateful for the small stream he had happened upon in the ridges, but that had been too many miles ago.

He dismounted in front of the stable, plunged his hat into the water trough, and held it high and dumped it into his eagerly waiting mouth, most of the water splashing down over his shirt. He was so thirsty he did not at the moment care that he was drinking after horses.

He let the horse drink a little, then led it into the stable so he could peel off its saddle, and give it a rubdown.

Josh spoke from behind him. "Where have you been?"

"Looking for Fred," Dusty said, hefting the saddle and setting across the side of the stall.

"Why didn't you tell me where you were going?"

Dusty turned to face him. "Because Pa left you in charge, and I didn't think you'd let me go."

"So you just took it on yourself to go and do what you wanted anyway? We don't do things that way here."

"Josh, those aren't just local boys out there in those ridges, looking for trouble. They have all the ear-marks of professional raiders. If something happened to Fred, we've got to find out what, and when. If they somehow lured him away, then they've got us one man short. We're already outnumbered, as it is. I didn't want to take the time to argue with you about it. I'll tell Pa about it when he gets back."

"And I don't like you calling him 'Pa.'"

"Sorry. He told me to." Dusty returned to his horse, pulling a brush off a nail in one wall.

"Drop your gun," Josh said.

Dusty glanced over at Josh curiously. Josh had pulled his revolver, and it was aimed toward Dusty.

"What's this all about?" Dusty said.

"I said, drop your gun."

Dusty shook his head.

Josh said, "I know you're fast. Faster'n me. But you're not so fast you can draw that gun before I can cock mine and fire."

Dusty dropped the brush to the floor. "All right. But not because I think I couldn't beat you, but because a man doesn't draw on his own brother."

"You might be my brother, and you might not be. But regardless, I know why you're here. Now, drop that gun if you want to go on breathing."

Dusty reached for the grip of his pistol.

"Slowly," Josh said, "and with the finger tips."

"Whatever you say. You've got the drop on me." Dusty gripped his Colt Peacemaker with the tips of his fingers, slid it from the holster, and let it drop to the stable floor.

"You're lucky I don't shoot you where you stand," Josh said. "but just on the off chance that you might actually be my brother, I'm going to let you ride out of here with your hide intact. I want you to go out to the remuda and drop a loop on the horse you rode in on, saddle it, and ride out of here. And I don't want to ever lay eyes on you again, because I won't be so generous next time."

228

"Not till you tell me why."

"You're riding with them. The men who've been camping in the ridges."

"Now, how did you ever come up with such a notion like that?"

"I weighed it all in my mind. That story of yours is so far-fetched, I wouldn't be surprised if it was just an attempt to work your way into our confidence. And if that story's true, then you're all that much more despicable, to think you could steal from your own family. You weren't out looking for Fred just now. You were reporting to those men, on our strengths and weaknesses."

"You know what I think the situation really is? I think you've got more than your share of pride. And my existence, which is because your father spent a night with my mother, is a slap to that pride. But if pride is all a man has, then he must be a pretty empty man."

Josh's face was starting to redden. "Get off this property now, or I'll finish this where you stand."

"Shooting down an unarmed man? Is that the McCabe way?"

"I don't need my gun to finish this."

Dusty's temper had never been a volatile one, but when he got mad, he really got mad, and he was at that point now. He held his hands palm upward, his fingers waving toward himself in a beckoning motion. "Come on, brother. Let's see what you've got."

Josh tossed his gun aside, and charged at Dusty.

Dusty ducked, and Josh fell forward onto Dusty's back. Dusty straightened, and dumped Josh head first to the floor behind him. Josh landed in a somersault, his Stetson tumbling away. Josh had executed a similar maneuver on Reno.

Dusty turned to drop onto Josh and go to work with his fists, but Josh brought both feet upward and thrust them into Dusty's chest, pushing him away. Dusty lost his footing and fell to the hay strewn floor.

Both scrambled to their feet, then went toe to toe, Dusty landing a punch to Josh's ribs, and Josh returning one to Dusty's stomach.

Dusty stood at least an inch taller, with broader shoulders and arms that packed more muscle, but Josh was lighter and quicker, ducking a roundhouse punch thrown by Dusty, then with his feet planted far apart for balance, sent an uppercut to Dusty's jaw.

Dusty's feet went out from under him and he landed on his back.

Josh dove at him, but it was Dusty's turn to bring both feet up, and he sent Josh flying over his head and to the floor.

Both again scrambled to their feet. Dusty's hat had fallen and lay against his back from the chin strap.

Josh lunged at Dusty, who stepped aside, and wrapped an arm around Josh's neck to hold him pinned at his side. With his free fist, Dusty punched at Josh's face. Once. Twice.

Josh managed to get one hand on Dusty's collar and another behind one leg, and lifted him from his feet. Both fell to the floor, and Dusty's grip on him was broken.

Each, now huffing for breath, lurched to his feet and charged at the other.

Josh raised his fists and snapped his left out for a jab that landed on Dusty's cheekbone. Dusty then swung a roundhouse punch, his fist glancing against the side of Josh's jaw. Josh sent another jab to Dusty's face, mashing his upper lip, then a right cross to an eye, and Dusty's feet again went out from under him, and he was again on the floor.

Dusty propped himself up on one elbow, blood trickling from his lip, but he rose no further. His chest heaving for air, he brought up a hand to wipe the blood from his lip, and a gash on his cheekbone.

Josh stood over him. He was also sucking in air, and a red welt had started to rise above one eye, and another at his cheek. He was shaking his right hand, the knuckles of which had taken a beating against Dusty's face.

"I can't help it if you didn't have a family when you were growing up," Josh said, "and maybe you are my brother. I don't know. But I want you off this ranch. And tell your partners out there we're ready for 'em if they decide to ride on us."

Dusty rose to his feet, and staggered past Josh to the stall. He backed out the horse, leaped onto its back, and with only the halter to turn the horse with, he nudged its ribs with his heels and the horse burst into a gallop, carrying him out the stable door.

Bree stepped from the porch to see Dusty riding away with no saddle, and with his hat still dangling behind him.

"Dusty!" she called out.

"Forget him," Josh said, approaching the porch. His hat was once again in place, and his revolver in his holster. Tucked into the front of his gunbelt was Dusty's Peacemaker, which he had picked up from the stable floor.

"You've been fighting," Bree said.

Josh nodded. "But he knows I know the truth about him, now. He won't be back."

TWENTY-SIX

Dusty kept his horse to a walk as he rode onto the single street of McCabe Gap. Ahead of him was Hunter's Saloon.

The bleeding had stopped from the pounding he had taken from Josh's fists, but his lip was swelling and one eye had swollen shut.

Dusty had no money, but was hoping to exchange some labor for a glass of whiskey. Maybe two. He knew money wouldn't be an issue for Hunter, but Dusty had his pride. Maybe he could resume his cooking and bartending duties. Or, he could just put this town and the McCabe family behind him, and head out for Oregon.

His quest was over, he decided. He had met the McCabes, told them who he was, learned a little about who they were and where he was from.

Dusty reined up beside a horse that was already tethered in front of Hunter's. He swung from the saddle, feeling a tightness at one side of his ribcage. Not only were his ribs bruised, but maybe he had pulled some muscles, too.

As Dusty gave the rein a couple turns about the hitching rail, Hunter hurried out onto the porch, hastily slamming and locking an outer door over the swinging doors. It was as he turned from the door, starting toward the horse tethered beside Dusty's, that Hunter noticed him.

"A little early to be closing up, ain't it?" Dusty asked.

"Actually, I was heading out to your Pa's place. Fred rode into town this morning and told me those raiders might be back. I was going to see if you boys needed any help."

"Actually, I was hoping for one of your cold beers. Or maybe even a glass of whiskey."

"Judging by the look of you, I'd say you needed one. Come on, we got time for one."

Hunter unlocked the outer door, and Dusty eased himself into a chair in the barroom as Hunter fetched a bottle and a couple shot glasses from behind the bar. He took a chair across the table from Dusty.

"You hiring?" Dusty asked. "I've gotta pay for this whiskey somehow."

"I'll take your help any time you want to offer it. But I'll never take your money. You drink and eat here for free."

Dusty tasted a little blood, and realized his lip was bleeding again. He reached up to wipe it away with the back of his hand and then knocked back a mouthful of whiskey.

"You look like you got run over by a horse," Hunter said.

"That's about the size of it."

"Can I assume it's safe to say things aren't going so well with the family?"

"With Josh in particular."

Hunter nodded. "The boy can be quite a scrapper. He's held his own in here on a Saturday night more than once."

"Well, he's made it clear I'm not welcome. He thinks I'm scouting for them raiders."

"He doesn't believe your story?"

"I think he does, or at least he's leaning that way. But he thinks I'm a spy for the raiders, anyhow."

"Josh tends to think with his temper. Sometimes it benefits him, but sometimes it can be a dangerous thing, and he ends up having to work twice as hard to pick up the pieces later."

"I guess I was a fool."

"For what?"

"For thinking...whatever it was I was thinking. You can't just ride into a place, a grown man, and announce you're a long lost son or brother, and expect to be welcomed with open arms."

"You're not a fool for wanting to meet your family. In fact, I think you're entitled to it. And to have the chance to get to know them. To learn about where you come from."

"That's just it. I was hoping to find my roots. But my roots aren't there in that house. I thought I'd find them there, but I didn't. I found a man's home, his family, but not mine. Not really."

He knocked back some more whiskey, and continued. "I did a lot of thinking about that on the ride out from the ranch. Josh, he was raised by the old man. That house is his home, and has been for as long as he can probably remember. Me, I'm not even from Montana. When I think of where I'm from, it's Arizona, New Mexico, Texas. I wasn't

raised by the old man. I was raised by..." he had been about to say Sam Patterson, but caught himself before the words could escape. "By someone else."

"You share blood with those people. Except for Aunt Ginny, but that won't matter to her."

"Yeah. She was the first to accept me. She believed my story before I even had a chance to tell it. She had it figured out before you and I even arrived that night."

"Yep. She's quite a woman. The glue that holds the family together, really."

"And you're right, I do share blood with the old man, and Josh and Bree. But family ain't about blood. It's about love. It's about being part of each other's lives. Me, I'm just a stranger, an outsider, who happens to also have McCabe blood. They didn't ask for me to come crashing in on their lives."

Hunter nodded, and there was a smile in his eyes. "So, what are you gonna do now?"

Dusty shrugged. "I don't really know. Maybe head on out to Oregon. There's a girl waiting for me there, and I don't want to keep her waiting too long. Or maybe try to seriously talk you into that job as bartender and cook."

Hunter knocked back his drink, emptying his glass, and refilled it. "Well, whatever you decide, you don't strike me as the kind who would leave a job unfinished. Them riders are still out there in the mountains, and if they decide to hit the McCabe ranch, I plan to be right there shooting back at 'em. And maybe you can't call those people family, but they are blood, even Josh, and you know more about tactical warfare than anyone I ever met. Except for maybe the old man himself. You ain't said much about your background, but I bet you've quite a story to tell, and I hope to hear it someday. Maybe on a cold winter night, sitting around a wood stove with a bottle of whiskey. But in the meantime, we've got a job to do. Let's ride back, and hold off any long-term decisions until them raiders are taken care of."

Dusty nodded. "All right. I'm with you."

Johnny McCabe swung out of the saddle in front of the stable, and was giving the rein a couple wraps about the

hitching rail as Josh approached from the house, Dusty's Peacemaker tucked into the front of his gunbelt.

"Is Fred back yet?" Pa asked. "Thunder needs a good rubdown. We covered a lot of miles today."

Josh shook his head. "I'll take care of him. Why don't you go in and have supper. I just finished."

"Doesn't the family eat together anymore?"

"Aunt Ginny said there's too much going on for us to worry about that."

Pa nodded. "We're going to have tight security every night, like this was a military camp. I'm going to want guards posted all night to warn us should riders approach, and I want them posted by day, too. In the morning, I'll ride out again. We've got to keep an eye on them. Try to guess their number and maybe even figure when they plan to strike, by their movements throughout the ridges, camp placement and such things."

"No," Josh said. "I think I should go. You'll be needed here, if they should decide to attack during the day. You're our leader. I'm more expendable than you are."

Johnny was about to protest—Josh was not in any way expendable. Yet, he couldn't deny his son was right. The leader should be in camp should the raiders strike.

It was then that Johnny allowed himself to fully notice the pistol tucked into Josh's belt. "That's Dusty's gun, isn't it?"

Josh nodded.

"Where is he?"

"He's gone, Pa, and he ain't coming back." Josh told his father about the fight.

"Did he actually admit to riding with them?"

"No, but he didn't deny it, either."

"Well," Johnny scratched his chin. "If that's the situation, then I guess you took care of it. I will say I'm a little disappointed, though."

"Why? I say, good riddance to him."

"That's because he's not your son. I should have been there for him, the way I was for you. I'm no less his father than I am yours or Bree's or Jack's. I was kind of hoping that, well, maybe I could get to know him, and maybe undo some of the damage."

Pa turned and started for the house. "You're a good man, Josh. It's good to know I can count on you."

Josh couldn't help but smile. And yet, he also couldn't help but notice a weariness in Pa's step, like each foot was unusually heavy.

Josh realized he had been thinking entirely about how Dusty's sudden appearance affected him, but he had never given any thought to Pa's feelings. After all, Josh thought, how would he himself feel if he was in Pa's place?

He reached for Thunder's rein, to lead the stallion into the stable, when one of the men called out, "Riders comin'!"

Josh looked out toward the meadow that stretched away northward across the valley floor. Pa had stopped in midstride between the stable and the house, and was also looking. Josh found he had to squint against the sun, which was drifting low above the ridge line to the west, and could see a group of riders. Six, maybe seven.

Josh walked toward Pa.

"It can't be the raiders. There aren't enough of them," Josh said.

"I think you're right," Pa said. "The horses move like they've been ridden a lot of miles. Raiders would want to use fresh mounts."

Josh hated to admit he had not noticed this, but now that Pa had mentioned it, he saw that each horse indeed held its head down a little as it stepped, and the riders were keeping their horses to a slow trot. Even so, Josh loosened the pistol in his holster.

As the riders pulled to within two hundred yards, Josh still couldn't make out their faces because the sun was drifting low and their faces lost in deep shadows. But he knew the two riders at the head of the group by the way they carried themselves in the saddle. One had wide shoulders that sloped a little as though the rider were always tired, and he moved with a slow deliberation that belied the quickness he could command with a gun or a fist. Zack Johnson. And the man who sat beside him, with a narrow build but who rode a horse like he had been born to it, was Fred Mitchum.

The riders reigned up before Johnny and Josh.

"You're a long way from home, aren't you?" Johnny asked Zack through a wide grin.

With one hand Zack pushed back his hat back, taking the shadow of the wide brim away from eyes that always seemed to dance with mirth, and the scar a Kiowa knife had made on his left cheekbone.

"I heard an old friend of mine was in trouble," Zack said, flashing a smile that was always quick to surface. "He's a no-good son-of-a-biscuit, but I thought I'd see if we could lend a hand anyway."

Fred said, "Aunt Ginny sent me to ride on down the stretch and bring in some reinforcements."

"Thank you, Fred," Aunt Ginny said from the porch.

Johnny glanced over his shoulder toward her; he hadn't heard her step out from the house. "You could have told me where he was."

"You never asked me," she said with a smug smile. "And you never would have agreed to it, because you're too stubborn to ask for help."

Johnny gave her a long look, smiling with his eyes, then turned back to the riders. "Zack, what about your place?"

Zack shrugged. "Well, I owe you my life a few times over."

Johnny nodded. "That goes both ways."

"And I figure," Zack said, as he swung out of the saddle, "you got more here to offer any raiders than I do, and more to lose. I got no family. It's just me, the small crew that works for me, and my few hundred head of cattle. It wouldn't take me as long to rebuild."

Johnny clasped a hand to his old friend's shoulder. "I appreciate it."

"Aunt Ginny," Zack called out to her. "I hope you cooked enough for all of us. We been ridin' all afternoon, and Fred, here, has been in the saddle all day. We're each of us hungry as a b'ar."

"I've prepared a huge pot of stew for you all. Come on in."

"Josh and I'll take care of the horses," Johnny said. "You boys go on in."

"No, Pa," Josh said. "You've been in the saddle all day, too. Go on in. I can take care of the horses."

Johnny clasped a hand to his son's shoulder, as he just had with Zack, and turned to follow the others to the house.

Josh grabbed Thunder's rein again and led the stallion along with the other mounts to the stable. He led each horse into a stall, where he tied a rein to an iron ring imbedded in a wall, and began to strip off the saddles. Thunder was antsy. As tired as the stallion was, he didn't like walls and wanted to be outdoors as soon as possible.

"Easy, big fella," Josh said.

The man outside called out again. "More riders comin'!"

This time, Josh felt alarm. Who else would be coming? He drew his pistol, quickly checked the loads, and then ran outside.

Pa and Zack were standing on the porch. Zack's foreman, Ramon, who had ridden with them, stepped out of the house with a Winchester ready in his hands. Zack gripped a revolver in his right hand. Pa's pistols were still holstered, but they were never far from his hands.

Long shadows now stretched across the valley floor. A vague hint of motion and the faint drum of shod hooves on sod were the only indications that something was out there.

"I only see two," Zack said.

Johnny shook his head. "You're eyes are better'n mine. I can't make out one from the other."

"Must be age catching up with you."

Johnny shot a glance to Zack, whose smile was back. The old joke still persisted. Zack was younger than Johnny, though by only a year and some odd months, and was forever reminding him of it.

Josh could see there were only two, also, as the riders drew nearer. "I wonder who it could be?" he called back to the porch.

Johnny looked to Zack. "More of your riders?"

"Shouldn't be," he said. "I left a skeleton crew to watch the herd, and told them not to follow. I don't want to ride back and find my cows wandering all over the countryside."

The riders approached the buildings, keeping their horses to a shambling trot, and reined up before the porch. One wore a heavy beard, his eyes hidden under a dark hat.

"Hunter," Johnny said. "It's starting to look like old home week around here."

"I couldn't let you boys have all the fun for yourself."

Beside him was a rider whose hat was suspended at his shoulder blades from a rawhide chinstrap, and he wore a faded blue shirt.

"Dusty," Johnny said. "I thought Josh told you to ride on."

Josh said, "I did, Pa. I guess I didn't tell him good enough."

Dusty swung from the horse's back, and stood to face Josh. "You may not want to accept me as family, and maybe it's unfair of me to ask. But I'm your brother, like it or not, and nothing can change that. And here, defending this place, is where I belong. After this is over, I'll ride on if you want, but not until then."

"How do we know you can be trusted?" Josh said. "How do we know you wouldn't shoot us all in the back if the raiders attack?"

"Because if I was scouting for the raiders, I wouldn't have been here with Hunter and Fred, ready to defend the place before you got back. I would have ridden out to the raiders' camp, told them the situation, and they would have struck that night."

"Why's that?"

"Because of how shorthanded we were that night. Raiders aren't fools, and they're not in this for the thrill of a contest. Their goal is to take as much as they can, with as little harm to themselves as possible."

Josh was silent. He stared at Dusty for a moment, then turned to the porch, and to Pa.

Pa and Zack were both looking at Dusty silently. They both knew more about warfare and raiding than Josh would ever know. They had seen more men killed, some of them by their own hand, than they would ever be able to count. Josh saw it in their eyes sometimes, when they were sitting by a fire, sharing a glass of whiskey. There would be a mention of the old days, and their gazes would meet for an instant, and then they would be silent and there would be a sort of heaviness in the air, and the lines on Pa's face would seem deeper than ever, and the dance in Zack's eyes would fade.

Josh saw it now, and felt that strange heaviness in the air, as Pa and Zack looked at Dusty. They were seeing him as if for the first time, seeing something in him that they understood. They were seeing a kindred spirit, Josh knew, and realizing he was no outlaw. Suddenly, Josh felt small and impossibly young.

Pa nodded at Dusty with understanding, and said, "I was wrong, Dusty. I was short-sighted. Welcome back. We'll be pleased to have you fight alongside us, if it comes to that."

Josh nodded, and turned back to his brother. "Pa speaks for me too."

And he pulled the Peacemaker from his belt and handed it to Dusty.

Dusty gave his brother a small grin, and tucked the pistol into his holster. "Come on. Let's see if Aunt Ginny can rustle us up some grub. It's gonna be a long night."

TWENTY-SEVEN

That evening, preparations began for the defense of the McCabe house, because Johnny was starting to feel this might be the night the raiders would strike. Dusty felt it, too.

"How do you know?" Bree asked.

"They came back for a reason," Johnny said. "And now that they're back, they're not going to wait any longer than they need to. The longer they're out there in the mountains, the longer we'll have to prepare."

"Not only that," Dusty said. "There's a feeling in the air."

Josh nodded. Though he didn't have the experience at this sort of thing Pa and Zack had, and apparently Dusty had too, and maybe he would never be able to fully wear the label of gunhawk himself, he had to agree. There was some sort of intangible feeling in the air. Almost an eerie sort of stillness. A sort of hush had fallen on the land.

Johnny McCabe went to the porch, looking off toward the darkness of the valley floor before him. The sun had now fully set, but the moon had not yet risen, though he knew it would soon. And that would be when they could expect trouble. It would take a foolhardy rider to try to cross the valley floor in darkness this thick. A horse could trip over an uneven clump of grass and send its rider sprawling. The sky was heavily laden with stars, which cast off their own meager light. Johnny could make out a dark formless mass to his left, which he knew was the barn. But you wouldn't want to ride a horse in this.

He had positioned Zack and some men in a small stand of trees in a low spot, off beyond the corral. A small stream that trickled in from the ridges caused a small pond to form there, and a stand of alders stood at its rim. The night was cold, so Johnny had told Zack to dig a fire pit and build a small fire for warmth, but to make certain the flames didn't rise above the edge of the pit. Otherwise they would be visible from a distance.

Johnny stepped down from the porch, his pipe smoldering in his right hand, his pistols riding at his hips. He walked to the edge of the ranch yard, which by day gave you the best view of that stand of alders. He could catch an

occasional draft of wood smoke as the breeze turned his way, but he could see no sign of fire. Good.

He returned to the house, hearing the hinges squeak a bit as he did so, and found Aunt Ginny waiting for him on the porch. He climbed the steps to stand beside her in the cold.

"It's cold tonight," she said. "I have a shawl wrapped about me, and I'm still cold."

In the darkness Johnny could barely make out her form. He had known it was her because of her height, and the scent of her perfume. A sort of lilac fragrance she had shipped in from 'Frisco every spring, once the snows had receded and the stage routes were again passable.

Johnny stood in his shirt and vest only. He wore no jacket. The cold was indeed penetrating his shirt, sending its biting fingers into his flesh, but he did not shiver. He forced himself to simply relax, and experience the cold of the evening as it reached out to him. He sometimes did this, even on a mid-winter day, stepping onto the porch with no coat for a few minutes, simply to better experience the power of nature. It somehow made him feel a little more connected to it.

"Back where I grew up," he said, "in Pennsylvania, the summer air is heavy with humidity, so on a day as warm as this was, sweat would be dripping from you after even the easiest of chores. And the heat would last into the night. You'd be more than comfortable in shirtsleeves only, and the humidity would give a dampness to the night that would even be felt on your bedsheets or pillow."

"I have never been east. Do you miss Pennsylvania? Your parents' farm?"

His shoulders rose in a shrug, though he knew she would not be able to see the motion in the darkness. "I do to an extent, I suppose. We had a good family, a lot of love in that little farm house. But at seventeen, my father had advised me to join either the Army or the Navy, and see some of the world before I made any decisions that might affect my future. He told me that he would have been more than satisfied for his four sons to settle nearby and farm, but we had to each do what was right for us. And such a decision couldn't be made objectively when all we had ever seen of the

world was our seven-hundred acre farm, and maybe a twenty-mile area beyond it."

"A wise man."

"Indeed he was. And since I was already a good horseman, and I had an uncle who was at one time a Texas Ranger and had given me my first set of pistols, and I had become fairly good with them, I decided to go west and join the Army. One thing led to another, and I wound up with the Texas Rangers. And I fell in love with this land. That little farm in Pennsylvania was where my roots are, but I knew this land was where my heart would always belong.

"When I first saw the Rockies, it was like I had really come home for the first time. And that first winter I spent in this valley, even more so. When Lura and I started building our first ranch, I would stand outside the door at night, and I could almost feel these mountains calling to me."

Ginny actually already knew most of this story, but she was silent, letting Johnny tell it, as though he needed to say the words again. Besides, she never got tired of hearing it.

His three brothers were, she knew, Matthew, Josiah and Nathan. Matthew was two years older than John, and had married and was ranching about a day's ride south of Stockton. Ginny had met him, and found him to be surprisingly sophisticated for a Pennsylvania farm boy. He had an almost theatrical way of moving, and was well-versed in the classics. He read Shakespeare for relaxation. Unlike John, he managed his ranch from a desk, generally was more comfortable in a white shirt and tie, and he knew his wines. A man of thought, and a good man, but not a man of action. Josiah was often called the silent one because he was a man of such few words. He was two years younger than John. He resembled John strongly, though his chestnut hair was devoid of the hint of amber John's had had when he was younger, and he stood maybe an inch taller and had a slightly heavier frame. Josiah, who seemed to have an even stronger affinity for the wilderness than did John, and whose eyes had always seemed distant. A year after Lura's death, after helping John and Zack Johnson bring the entire family and all of the livestock north to this valley, Josiah had simply announced it was time to move on, and rode out. John had

said he always expected that day would come sooner or later, as Josiah was a wandering spirit. He was surprised Josiah had remained as long as he had. But what surprised him even more was Josiah had never been heard from again. A lot of things can happen to a man riding alone in this land. Many a man died alone in the mountains, or the desert. His bones might be happened upon in later years, but his identity would never be known. And there was Nathan, the youngest, who had joined the Navy in following his father's advice, but was the only one of his four sons to return to Pennsylvania. Though he and John corresponded by mail, they had not seen each other in more than twenty years, and he was the one brother Ginny had never met.

"I sometimes wonder," Johnny said, "if I was right to bring you and the children here. I mean, with the riders up there in the ridges, and that party of renegade Sioux that attacked a few years ago. Life out here can be so cheap, sometimes. Some of the men are hard, so empty of compassion. They can cut a throat as easily as you might cut up a chicken for frying. I wonder if maybe I should have taken the children back to Pennsylvania, and made a living farming."

"I cannot even imagine you behind a plow. Or even worse," she said with a chuckle, "you actually working afoot."

He smiled. Cowboy machismo made a man of the west shudder with revulsion at the thought of working afoot. Setting up fence poles, or digging potatoes out of the earth.

"Not that I haven't done that kind of work with my father and brothers," he said. "And we have to lay fence here on the ranch once in a while. But maybe you're right. Maybe such a life wouldn't be right for me. But maybe it would have been safer for the children."

"Maybe so," she said, "but consider this. Jackson is where he would have been, anyway. In school. And Joshua would never have been happy on a farm back east." It felt unnatural to call him Josh, but she was trying to be a little less stuffy. "He would have wound up heading west and falling in love with the land much as you did, and could very well have found himself in a situation like this, anyway. But he would have been much less prepared for it. And think

about Dusty. He would still have been conceived, but he would have had even less opportunity to find his father."

"What about Bree? My own daughter is in a life-and-death situation she wouldn't have been in, had it not been for my decision to raise her here, and not back east."

"John, how did you father die?" She knew fully well the answer. He had been killed by a desperate man, who had robbed a store at gunpoint and was attempting to escape.

Johnny and his brothers had been in the Pennsylvania forest cutting fire wood with their father, when the robber happened upon them by chance. He had just robbed a store in the nearby town, and in his desperation, fired a pistol into the elder McCabe's chest. The robber fled while the life blood of Thomas McCabe drained onto the earth in front of his sons. And all of this had happened in the woods of Pennsylvania, not a mile from the McCabe farm house.

"Point taken," Johnny said.

"Even if we all die here tonight, I would still have no regrets. It's not the quantity of years, it's the quality of them."

They stood in silence for a while. Johnny took another draw from his pipe, discovered it had gone out, as pipes do frequently, but decided not to strike a match out here in the open. The glow of the match might be visible from a distance.

The breeze kicked up, and Ginny shuddered at its coldness, and pulled her shawl more tightly about her.

"To revert back to a conversation of a few nights ago," she said. "are you still thinking of riding to California in the spring?"

"I don't know," he said.

"You know, John, she isn't actually there. Only her earthly remains are."

He nodded, though again knowing she could not see the motion in the darkness. "Ever since my first winter in this valley, with the Shoshones, I have believed the body dies away, but the spirit continues. Kind of similar in some ways to the teachings I got in my mother's Methodist church, when I was growing up. Really, I guess all religions are pointing in the same direction. The words may be different, from one culture to another, but the goal is always the same."

"Heaven? Eternal reward?"

"No. There is no reward. And no punishment either, for that matter. Except in our own hearts. It's all about the spirit, Ginny. The old shaman I talked a lot with, the 'medicine man' I guess most white men would call him, said that heaven and hell begin here on earth, in a person's heart, and continue onward even after the body dies. He said two men can be standing side-by-side, but one can be in hell and the other in heaven."

"For a supposedly ignorant people, their beliefs and philosophies run quite deeply."

"That night you and I talked, I was feeling the loss of Lura so strong. But now, as we stand here on the porch, I don't really feel the loss much at all. I feel almost like she's standing here beside us."

"Maybe she is."

"And I think maybe my place is here, not riding clear across the country just to visit a grave."

"Loss is like that. One day you feel it so profoundly it's all you can do to even climb out of bed in the morning, and the next you don't feel the loss at all, like the one you lost is not really gone. Like, as you said, the spirit continues, so there is no real loss, just a transition. A change. And life is forever changing."

"You're speaking of the loss of your father?"

"No. Well, him too. I don't speak much of a young man who was in my life when I was about Josh's age. And Dusty's."

"Yes, that sailor. You've mentioned him."

"What I never have told you is that I was deeply in love with him. We were going to be married once he had saved enough money. But he was lost at sea on one of my father's ships. I have never loved again. And there are times when I feel the loss so profoundly, even to this day," her voice almost broke, and she paused, steadying herself, "and yet there are other times, when I, too, feel as though he is standing right here beside me."

"It isn't fair, is it, to love so strongly, to want to build your whole life with someone, then to have that someone for only a short time, and have to go on the rest of your life alone?"

"I don't know, John. But I do know that I'm freezing to death out here. I'm going to go in and make a hot cup of tea, and put some coffee on for you men." She gave his arm a squeeze, and stepped through the doorway.

Johnny stood on the porch, not feeling alone. Feeling almost like Lura was beside him. Like he could reach out to touch her. Like he could almost smell her scent, a sort of peach-blossom cologne she used to wear. He realized he was half-consciously reaching out with one hand toward where he felt she might be standing.

He smiled to himself. He didn't know if her spirit was really there or not. But at least for the moment, he was having an easier time believing what the old Shoshone shaman had told him.

The smell of coffee eventually lured Johnny to the kitchen, so Josh took his place on the front porch. The porch gave the best view of the valley floor, and the probable direction the raiders would be approaching from. The moon was now peeking over the horizon, and Josh knew within a short time, the meadow that stretched away across the valley would be alight with the sort of pale, eerie light the moon cast. And then, they would begin expecting the raiders.

There was one concern nagging at Josh. It was actually kind of obvious, and he did not know if Pa had overlooked it, or was just waiting to address it at a more opportune time. Yet, the concern continued to hammer at him—if Dusty didn't create that lone set of tracks leading away from the ranch toward the mountains, then who did?

As the tossed this over in his mind, he saw a long, angular frame ambling toward the porch in the moonlight. "Fred," he said.

"Hey, Josh. Is your Pa still awake?"

"He's inside having a cup of coffee. Why?"

"Maybe it's nothing. But..."

"At a time like this, nothing should be overlooked. What's wrong?"

"It's Long. You know, that cowpoke you hired after you fired Reno and the boys?"

"Yeah. What about him?"

"Well, he's missing. I know your Pa told us to grab sleep while we can, but to keep our rifles close. But I couldn't seem to fall asleep, and I wanted to see if any of the boys were still awake to maybe play a round of cards. I found his bunk empty. I looked around, and I can't find him anywhere."

Just maybe, Josh thought, he had found the answer to the question he was just thinking about. And boy did he feel like a fool.

Josh decided to conduct a quick search himself for Long, and he thought it might be a good idea not to do this alone. Especially if Long was one of the raiders, then he might be good with a gun. Not that Josh was necessarily reluctant to face a gunman on his own, as he had done well against Whitey, but he did not want to take a chance on getting shot and causing Pa to have to face the raiders one man down. Josh didn't want to bother Pa with this, as Pa had enough on his mind. And whether he wanted to admit it or not, one of the best gun hands he had ever seen was upstairs in the guest room, which overlooked the ranch yard.

Josh needed to get Dusty's attention without going into the house. He stepped down from the porch, and in the darkness, grasped along the earth in front of the hitching rail until he found a pebble large enough to travel, but small enough not to break a pane of glass, and let it fly toward the guest room window.

The window latch turned, and the window swung open.

"Dusty," Josh called up. "Get down here. But make it seem like you're just coming down on your own to get some air."

A few minutes later, Dusty stepped onto the porch. His hat was missing, and his shirt tails were flying free, but his gun was belted about his hips. "What's going on?"

Josh quickly explained. "I feel like such a danged fool. I was the one who hired him."

"Don't feel bad," Dusty said. "We're all danged fools more often than we'd like to admit."

Josh allowed himself a small grin. "Thanks, but I seem to be playing the part a lot lately."

"Let's go check the stable. See if any of the saddles are missing."

Josh, Dusty and Fred headed for the stable. Josh struck a match and lighted a lantern, lighting the windows regardless of caution, and they indeed found Long's saddle missing.

"Y'know," Dusty said, "this might be for the best. Now, they'll know for certain how many armed men we have. It might discourage them."

Josh said, "If he comes back, he's gonna have to answer to me. And he ain't going to like it."

"He won't be back," Dusty said. "At least, not alone."

After the cup of tea, Ginny had gone to her room to lie down and see if sleep would take her, but it proved elusive. After a half hour, she gave up and went into the kitchen for maybe another cup of tea. She found Johnny sitting at the table. He had taken his pistols apart and was tamping a load into the sixth chamber of each cylinder. With one cylinder now completely loaded, he locked it in place, then with his finger hooking the trigger guard, twirled the pistol almost absently and slapped it into the holster at his right side. This had developed into a habit with him throughout the years— the easier you can juggle your pistols, he felt, the lighter and more natural they will seem in your hands. Your life can depend on that.

Ginny said, "Zack, Hunter, your brother Josiah, they all have said that you were the best they have ever seen with one of those things. I am grateful for your skills with a gun, because they have protected us more than once. But somehow, the way you carry them about, as naturally as though they are a part of your body, has always struck me as a little unnerving."

Johnny nodded, locking the cylinder of his second pistol into place. "Lura used to say the same thing."

"All the men out here walk about with those things strapped to their belts. Even Josh, now. It's a necessary evil, I suppose."

"We live on the frontier. About as close to living with nature as you can get. In nature, there are animals who will kill to eat, and others that will kill to protect themselves. A

mountain lion will kill to eat, because it's a predator. It knows no other way. An elk won't kill to eat, because that's not its way. But if a mountain lion tries to catch it, then it'll use its antlers to protect itself. The antlers aren't evil, they just help the elk to take its part in a cycle that has existed long before men arrived on the face of this earth."

"I still think killing is wrong."

"Is the mountain lion wrong for being what God made it to be? A predator? For that matter, you could compare the mountain lion to those men up in the ridges."

"A mountain lion is a dumb animal. Those raiders are responsible for their actions. God did not make them to kill."

"Circumstances did, or they wouldn't be doing it. Whatever they once were, they're now predators and they no longer know any other way. To us, they're evil, like the mountain lion is to the elk. The elk has what the lion can only gain through force. The raiders probably look at us in the same way."

"I find that hard to fathom."

"I've known many an outlaw in my time. Men who would be considered evil by most standards. But each of them was a human being, like you or me, with dreams and hopes and who felt love and sadness, given the situation. But somewhere along the way, something happened to turn them into predators. And you know what I always found interesting? Not one of them ever looked at himself as evil."

Johnny rose to his feet, and was about to spin his second pistol as he had the first before shifting it to his left hand and holstering it, but with the disconcerting effect it had had on Aunt Ginny fresh in his mind, he simply transferred the gun to his left and slid it into his holster.

"Are you telling me," she said, "that you don't feel some sort of animosity toward those men out there? Those men who might ride in here and try to burn and kill everything in your life?"

"I understand them, Ginny. That does not mean that I feel sorry for them. If they should come riding down here, I'll do everything I can to stop them. They might be the mountain lion, but they will find that this elk has mighty sharp antlers, and knows how to use them."

She shook her head slowly, and when she spoke it was barely above a whisper. "It is a savage world we live in sometimes, isn't it?"

"A man I once knew said everyone kills. And not just on the frontier, and not just in the direct, more obvious way. Bankers kill, when they foreclose on a home because the family's not able to pay the debt. A business owner who successfully drives out a competitor is, in a sense, trying to destroy someone. People kill, Ginny. Some kill to take what they don't have, others kill to keep it. And some, just because they enjoy it."

"You make it sound so cold. Like life is so empty. It's not. Living is so much more than that. Much more than simply killing."

"Yes, it is. But you have to be willing to take the bad with the good. The wilderness can be a mighty beautiful place, as long as you can tolerate its savage side. Life can be mighty fulfilling, but you sometimes have to be willing to kill to keep from being killed, or your family from being killed."

There was suddenly a thump at the back door, like it had been struck with a fist, and Josh called from outside, "Here they come!"

TWENTY-EIGHT

Ginny felt the breath catch in her lungs, and her heart leap into her throat. Bree had been in the parlor, lying down on the sofa, but she now ran into the kitchen. Johnny grabbed one corner of the table with both hands and gave it a shove, sending it sliding and overturning, then grabbed a loop of rawhide nailed into place on one floorboard and pulled upward, and a trap door opened. "Into the root cellar, both of you."

Johnny's sudden burst of action caused some of the fear to drain from Ginny. It's harder to be afraid when you're in motion, dealing with a situation. She said hurriedly, "You first, Sabrina. Go!"

Bree climbed down a ladder into the darkness below, then struck a match and brought a lantern to life.

"Do you have the gun?" Johnny asked.

Bree glanced at a shelf built against the earthen wall, and the bundle wrapped in burlap. She quickly unwrapped it. A small caliber Colt Navy revolver. She looked up at her father, and nodded.

"You know what to do with it," he said, more of a statement than a question.

She nodded, her eyes wide with fear, yet with a steadiness he admired. After all, she was a McCabe. "They won't take us alive, Daddy."

Bree's instructions hadn't been to use the gun to shoot at attackers. The gun was to make certain she and Aunt Ginny were not alive to be taken. Sometimes death is not the worst alternative.

"Can you do it?"

She nodded. "If I have to."

He could see it in her eyes. The gunhawk spirit. He knew she could do what had to be done.

"Wait until the last possible moment, and use your judgment." He then looked to Aunt Ginny. "Get going. I'll close the door behind you."

Despite her entry into middle age, she handled the ladder quite nimbly, and Johnny allowed himself one final glance to the women in his life, the daughter he loved dearly and the woman who was like a mother to him, who had left

behind her life in San Francisco to help with the children when his precious Lura had been killed. Then, he dropped the trap door shut, and with his foot on the door to hold it shut, he grabbed the rawhide loop and pulled it free. He wanted nothing to indicate to any raiders that this was a trap door. He then up-righted the table and set it back in place over the door.

He had not heard the back door open, but Josh was now standing in the doorway. "They all set?"

Johnny nodded. "How many?"

"Eight, at least" Josh spoke quickly, urgently. "Maybe ten. They got the jump on us. Rode in quietly, and didn't light torches until they were half across the valley. They're crossing the bridge now, and moving at a full gallop. They'll be here in minutes."

"All right," Johnny said. "Get everyone into position."

And Josh was out the door, his gravelly voice roaring into the night as he called out orders.

Fred Mitchum grabbed the Sharps rifle and a Winchester, and charged up the stairs to the guest room window which overlooked the ranch yard. Josh, as agile as the best Shoshone warrior Johnny had ever seen, climbed onto the front porch roof and leaped upward, curling his fingers around the roof edge, and pulled himself up. From the guest room window, Fred handed the Sharps out and up to him. Josh then positioned himself behind the peak of the roof.

Dusty took his designated place at one parlor window, Johnny at the other, both looking out at the front yard. Hunter went into the extension that served as Aunt Ginny's bedroom, and a window that faced out toward the corral. Others took to the windows of the bunkhouse.

From the rooftop, Josh could make out eight dancing, flickering lights from the direction of the wooden bridge. The riders were advancing. Almost within rifle range. But he could also see seven more approaching from the woods to the west. They were attacking from two directions. Josh called out, "Riders to the west, also! Seven of them!"

"I see 'em!" Fred called back, then ran out to the corridor, and the top of the stairs. "Riders to the west, too.

Josh counts seven torches. Eight coming straight on from the bridge."

"Seven to the west," Johnny relayed the call to the others on the ground floor, and those outside who could hear him. "Eight coming straight on."

One of the men in the bunkhouse echoed the call. "Seven to the west, eight straight on!"

The riders were still not close enough for Josh to make them out as anything more than globs of darkness beneath each flickering torch. At their speed, he figured they wouldn't be in range of Fred's Winchester for maybe another ten seconds. However, a Sharps had more range than any other rifle Josh knew of.

Josh used the peak of the roof to steady his left arm as he held the forestock of the Sharps, and he pushed the butt of the rifle into his right shoulder and drew a bead on a spot of darkness beneath one of the dancing points of flame. Pa was better than any man alive with a pistol, but with a shoulder arm, Josh had developed skills that stood on Pa's level. A fleeting thought occurred to him as he tightened his finger on the trigger—if they all lived through this, Josh would have to challenge Dusty to a marksmanship contest with rifles, and see if the show-off could keep up with him then.

The Sharps thundered and bucked against Josh's shoulder. The tiny dancing flame dropped and became stationary, then disappeared as it was extinguished beneath the hooves of other riders.

The rider had either fallen from the saddle, or was at least wounded and had dropped the torch. Either way, Josh could spare no time wondering about it. He swung the trigger guard down, which dropped the block and exposed the chamber. He pulled the empty metallic cartridge from the chamber and tossed it away, then pushed in a fresh round and pulled the trigger guard back into position again, closing the breach. The rifle had been originally designed for use with paper cartridges and a percussion cap, but Pa had taken it to a gunsmith in Wichita who retooled it so it could fire metallic cartridges.

Josh now shifted his attention to riders coming from the west. They were now close enough so the low rumble of

their hooves on the sod could be heard. With the chilly mountain wind striking his right cheekbone and ear, he drew aim on the lead rider, and fired.

He saw no reaction. He must have missed. He reloaded the rifle to try again. Guns now started firing from both groups of riders, tiny spots of flame that erupted and then were followed by the report, as sound traveled more slowly than light.

He could now make out the dark silhouette of each rider. He fired at the one at the head of the pack approaching from the bridge. The heavy caliber bullet took the rider squarely in the chest. The man fell backward and out of his saddle, and was trampled by the riders who were behind him.

Josh reloaded again, as the riders descended onto the ranch.

Zack Johnson had been standing by the fire pit, holding his hands out toward it, palms out, to catch some of the heat. Three other men stood by him, doing the same. One muttered, "Dang, it's cold."

"Won't be long," Zack said. "Another hour or so, and Johnny will be out with Hunter and a couple others for the second shift."

Zack and Hunter had been sharing a cigar with Johnny earlier in the evening when Johnny told them of his idea about posting some men out here by this stand of alders.

"Actually," Johnny had said, "the idea wasn't mine. It was Dusty's. He has a good mind for guerrilla warfare."

Hunter said, "Like father, like son."

Ramon was taking a stroll to where the horses were tethered by the alders, while Zack stood by the small fire.

"Zack," Ramon said, "here they come, I think."

Zack hurried over. He could see the pinpoints of firelight dancing atop torches as riders approached the house. He could also see another set of torches, off to another side.

"Two groups of riders," he said. "One coming straight at the house from the north, and the other from the west. Mount up!"

They swung into the saddles and turned their horses toward the ranch, riding hard. A rifle would be useless from

the back of a galloping horse, so Zack and the men were armed with pistols only, and they would not be shooting until they were within close range. Zack held one in his right hand and at his left was holstered another.

"Hold your fire," he called out, "until I say so."

As they rode, they could hear the report of the Sharps cutting through the night. Josh, from the rooftop, Zack figured. Then another. It looked like one rider fell.

The two groups of raiders converged one hundred yards from the ranch house and charged in as one large mass, and the night exploded with gunfire, from the raiders and the house and bunkhouse.

"Fire!" Zack called out, and with pistols blazing, he and his men charged into the right flank of the raiders.

Fred had repositioned himself at the kitchen doorway, with orders to open fire on any riders who managed to escape Zack and his men. Of course, once the raiders lost their torches, distinguishing them from the others would be impossible in the darkness, so Fred had orders to simply shoot anyone approaching the kitchen doorway. Johnny had instructed everyone to avoid the back of the house, so Fred would know anyone he saw would be a raider.

Johnny and his men were returning fire as bullets from the raiders struck the front wall of the house and the porch, and a couple parlor windows shattered, scattering glass across the floor. Johnny was crouching behind a window beside the door, from which he could see Zack and his men charging into the raiders. The night was alight with dancing torches, the flashing of guns discharging, and he could hear the gunfire, and the screams of men dying.

Dusty was at a window to the other side of the door, and Johnny called over to him, "Don't scatter your shots. Make each one count. Save your ammo."

Raiders who had escaped the attack from Zack and his men charged into the ranch yard between the bunkhouse and the main house. Johnny had positioned a couple of Zack's men in the bunkhouse windows, along with the hand who had ridden to the line camp with Josh and Long. In the main house, Johnny and Dusty were firing from the parlor windows, and Hunter from Ginny's bedroom. They all caught the raiders in a crossfire. Johnny held a Winchester in his

hands, firing rapidly and jacking away the empties, and Dusty had his Spencer.

One man's horse reared out of panic, but he stood to full height in the stirrups regardless and brought his torch back to throw it onto the house roof. Josh already had the Sharps to his shoulder with the hammer cocked back, searching for a target in the melee below, and found the man with the torch. Josh fired, and the man fell backward, rolling over the rump of his horse and to the ground.

A bullet burned the side of Josh's left shoulder—he was not sure which direction it had come from. He turned quickly, then realized he was over-compensating and tried to adjust, but was too late to keep from toppling over the front of the peak. He reached out wildly for a handhold, but to no avail. The rifle clattered away from him along the roof and disappeared below. Josh rolled onto his back and scrambled madly with his feet, trying to dig his heels into the shingles and slow his descent. But he managed to slow it only slightly.

He went over the edge of the roof, and landed with bone-jarring severity on the hard packed earth below, rolling in an attempt to break his fall, but still finding the wind knocked from him.

He lay still for a moment, trying to force air back into his lungs. He had a mouthful of dust, and his hat was gone. It apparently had separated itself from him somewhere between the roof's peak and the ground. His ears were filled with the roar of gunfire, and a riderless horse raced past him.

He could feel both arms and legs, and there seemed to be no real pain—he had broken an arm once and knew how an injury like that felt. He decided any further checking for injuries would have to wait, and forced himself to his feet and moved at a limping sprint for the corner of the house by Aunt Ginny's bedroom, discovering sharp pain in his left knee as he ran.

Once behind corner of the house, he flattened his back against the wall and drew his pistol. He peered back from around the corner at the battle. A rider had apparently seen him afoot and was riding toward the corner of the house. Josh brought his arm to full extension, and with one shot from his Colt Navy dislodged the man from the saddle.

From his window, Dusty had seen Josh fall, but could do nothing to help without charging face-first into the raiders. One rider charged after Josh, but then was knocked from his saddle from a bullet that came from Josh's direction, so Dusty figured Josh must have survived the fall.

Three riders galloped off to the right beyond Dusty's sight, and Dusty thought they might be trying for the east side of the house to see if it was unprotected, which it was.

"The east side!" Johnny called out, showing his thinking was moving along the same path as Dusty's. "Cover it while I cover the front!"

Dusty went to the window nearest Pa's desk at the wall to his right. He had no time to open it. Raising his rifle like a club, he drove the stock through the glass, then readied the gun for firing as the three riders outside completed their ride along the east side of the house, whirled their horses around, and charged at the windows.

One raised a torch, and Dusty knew the intention was to throw it through a window and start the house burning. Dusty squeezed off a shot from his Spencer, and caught the rider in the stomach. The man folded and fell from the saddle, the torch going with him.

A second rider fired a shot toward Dusty's window, which sent Dusty ducking.

The bullet caught Johnny in the ribcage, spinning him around. Before he could fully regain his footing, another bullet from the ranch yard caught him in the chest, and he dropped to his knees.

"Pa!" Dusty called out, and ran to his father's side.

Zack fired until his pistol was empty. He tossed it aside and pulled his second hand gun, when his horse was shot out from under him. He managed to roll free as the horse hit the ground. Had one foot been caught in a stirrup, he might have been trapped beneath the animal. He scrambled to his feet, surrounded by chaos, men swinging empty rifles like clubs. One man standing beside Ramon caught a bullet in the chest. The bullet exited through his back and took a spurt of blood with it. Zack fired at the man he thought had done the shooting, though in this bedlam, he couldn't be sure.

A bullet caught Zack behind the left shoulder. It felt like a club had struck him, and it spun him around so he faced the rider who had shot him. Zack squeezed the trigger of his pistol and emptied the man's saddle.

Ginny stood with Bree in the flickering light of a lantern that stood on a small table in the root cellar. She could not possibly hear Dusty's shout over the roar of the gunfire, but somehow—she could not explain how—she had.

"Wait here," she said to Bree, and climbed the ladder.

Ginny Brackston had never been a physically strong woman, but she put her back against the trap door and pushed. It lifted slowly, and she felt her knees wobble, but she did not relent. She forced the door upward. The table slid away as the door rose. She climbed out and into the kitchen, and let the door slam down behind her.

Fred was at the back door, firing. He did not see her, and could not even hear the slam of the trap door over the deafening gunfire.

She hurried into parlor. Johnny was lying on his back, with Dusty kneeling at his side.

Dusty had forgotten about the third rider, who was now at the window by Johnny's desk, a pistol in his hand.

"Dusty!" Ginny called. "Behind you!"

Dusty wheeled, gripping his rifle at hip level, and the rifle barked, and the man's head snapped back, his head split as though it had been struck with an ax.

A man leaped from his horse onto Zack, pulling him to the ground. Zack's pistol came free of his grip, and his left arm would no longer move from the bullet it had taken, but he raised a foot and kicked the man away.

The man leaped to his feet and faced Zack with a Bowie knife in his hand. And the man was smiling, his big white teeth catching the moonlight. His hat had fallen away and long shaggy hair tossed about in the mountain winds. He was smiling! To him, this battle was nothing more than sport. One of the most dangerous men, Johnny had always said, was the man who killed simply because he enjoyed it.

The man lunged at Zack, who could do nothing more than jump back to avoid the blade.

Then, a man called out, "Let's get out of here!"

The man with the knife turned and ran, until he was met by another rider who gripped his hand and swung him up and behind him on the horse, and they galloped away with the other fleeing riders. Of the fifteen who had attacked the house, Zack counted only six riding away.

Zack groped along the ground in the darkness until he found his pistol, which contained only two more shots. He let both go in the direction of the retreating raiders, and hoped at least one found its mark, but did not think it had.

Of the men who had been positioned at the stand of alders with Zack, one had been shot in the head and was lying on his back in the grass, with unseeing eyes staring toward the stars. Another was down with a leg he had sprained when his horse had been shot out from under him. A third had been shot clean through the chest and was dead. Only Zack and Ramon were on their feet.

The nine raiders who had not ridden away were lying in the grass, some twisted as though they had gone writhing and kicking into death, others lying as though they were merely asleep.

Zack remembered a trick he had seen a Comanche warrior pull back in Texas. The warrior had hidden among the bodies of his fellow warriors who had been shot in battle. He remained still and pretended to be dead so he could escape later. Zack wanted to make sure all of these raiders were dead and not playing possum. His gun was empty, and with his left arm now losing all sensation, he knew he wouldn't be able to reload the gun, so he looked to one of the men from his ranch, who was walking over. A man he knew only as Koller.

Zack said, "Do you have any shots left?"

"Yeah. I just reloaded."

"Give me your gun."

Koller handed over a Colt forty-four, and with it in his right hand, Zack went to the downed raiders, driving the toe of a boot firmly into the ribs of each man.

"Boss," Ramon said. "You're bleeding all down your back."

"Yeah. I'll tend to it."

When Zack was satisfied all the raiders were dead, he handed the pistol back to Koller.

Ramon said, "Hey, Zack. There's someone running out from the house."

Zack looked toward the house to see the running man, a Winchester in his hand. His face was darkened by the night, but his white shirt was clearly visible, and a vertical stripe at each shoulder indicated suspenders.

"Fred?" Zack asked.

"Zack! Johnny's been hit. Bad."

Zack felt the breath catch in his chest. He had always known the moment would come for him and Johnny, when one of them would have to look down on the dead body of the other. He found himself suddenly almost weak-kneed at the question he had to ask. "Is he still alive?"

Fred nodded gravely. "But I don't think he'll live the night."

Despite the weariness that was now creeping into Zack's muscles and bones, and the weakness he was starting to feel as blood leaked from the bullet wound in his shoulder and soaked his shirt down his back, he burst into a sprint for the house.

TWENTY-NINE

"We've got to get him upstairs to his bedroom," Aunt Ginny said, and instructed Josh to take his father by the shoulders and Dusty to take the feet, and they lifted him and started up the stairs.

"Gently, boys," she said.

Once he was in bed, Hunter managed to work Johnny's shirt free while Ginny pushed a handkerchief against the two wounds in an attempt to suppress the bleeding. Zack stood by the bed, unable to help because his left arm was now entirely useless.

Bree stood beside him, pleading. "Zack, you've got to come downstairs and let someone look at your shoulder. You're bleeding all down your shirt."

"I'm all right," he said.

"Listen," she said firmly, letting the sound of her voice make it known she was a McCabe, "we can't have you keeling over from a loss of blood. We got too much to handle right now."

Her gray eyes were glaring at him. He couldn't help but let a snicker escape. He said, "You're your father's daughter, all right. Okay, I'll go downstairs and get my shoulder looked at. But keep me posted."

She nodded.

"He's shot badly," Ginny muttered, more to herself than anyone else. "I've seen him take a bullet before, more than once, but never like this."

Bree's fussing at Zack had given her a distraction, but now she simply stood and looked at her father lying in the bed. His eyes were shut, and his face had taken on a grayish color.

Bree said, "Has he woken up at all?"

Ginny shook her head. "Dusty was at his side first. He said his eyes fluttered a couple of times, then he was out."

Ginny tossed the blood soaked cloth to the floor, then untied her apron and began using it to push against the bullet hole in the front of his chest. It was low, just below the ribs. This seemed to be the one bleeding the most profusely. The front of her dress was streaked with blood. Bree was pushing a cloth into the bullet hole in the side of her father's

ribcage. Her sleeve was soaked with blood from the wrist to the elbow.

Dusty and Josh were standing at the doorway. One of Josh's shoulders was spotted with blood and his shirt sleeve had been cut by a bullet, but the bleeding had stopped. His face was smeared with dust.

"This isn't working," Ginny said. "He's bleeding too danged fast."

"We're going to need a doctor," Hunter said.

Dusty asked, "Is there one in town?"

"No," Josh said. "There's one in Helena, I guess, but it's too far away. We won't be able to get him back here in time."

"There is Granny Tate," Ginny said.

"I'll go get her," and Josh left the doorway.

"Sabrina, I'll need you to tear up some sheets for use as bandages. We have to control this bleeding."

Bree hesitated a moment, staring at her father, then in a quiet voice said, "Yes, ma'am," and headed for the linen closet at the end of the corridor.

Josh strode for the stairway, the knee he had injured now feeling numb and strangely afloat. He had also wrenched his right shoulder. Must have been in the fall, he figured. He could barely lift his hand above his gunbelt. And his shoulder smarted from where the bullet had grazed it. But none of this mattered. He had a job to do, to ride into town and bring Granny Tate back. Any son of Johnny McCabe should be able to do what was needed, regardless of any personal pain. It was no less than Pa himself would have done.

But as he started down the stairs, his knee buckled. He could not bring his right hand up to grasp the railing and keep himself from falling and he went down, driving his cheekbone into the railing.

Dusty was at his side. "Josh, are you all right?"

"Yes. Leave me alone."

Josh tried to push himself to his feet, but his knee wouldn't support any weight.

"You can't go after that granny woman," Dusty said. "You can't even stand up."

"I have to," Josh growled.

"You fell off the roof, Josh. Stay here and rest up. I'll go."

"No!"

"There ain't no choice. We have to get that granny woman here, before Pa bleeds to death. And you can't even get into a saddle."

Josh hated to admit it, but Dusty was right. Josh nearly trembled with fury at himself for not being able to get the job done.

"All right," he said. "Go. Her son-in-law does some blacksmithing in town, and some farming. They have a small cabin not a half mile north of town."

"Let me help you down the stairs," Dusty said, hooking an arm around Josh's back.

"No. I'll be all right. Go get Granny Tate."

Dusty hurried down the stairs out through the kitchen, and found Fred and the men were carrying off the bodies of the fallen raiders.

Fred said, "Don't really know what to do with 'em right now, but we can't leave 'em laying around in the front yard."

"Maybe in the morning, we can search the bodies for any identification," Dusty said. "And if there ain't none, McCabe gap must have some sort of boot hill."

"How's your Pa?" Fred asked.

"Not well. They've sent me to go get Granny Tate."

"Want me to round up a mount?"

"No. I can do it. But thanks."

Dusty found a rope in the stable, and went out to the edge of the woods beyond the meadow where a horse was standing in the moonlight. The entire remuda was awake, having been scattered by the noise of the battle. Fred and the men would probably be days rounding them all up, but this animal hadn't roamed far.

"Easy, boy," Dusty said as he approached, not knowing if this horse was indeed a gelding, as in the darkness he could make out only its rough silhouette. It could very well have been a mare, but most men rode geldings.

The horse was skittish, raising its head as Dusty approached. Dusty stopped moving, but continued to speak

in the most soothing voice he could muster. "Easy, boy. Easy. Ain't gonna hurt you, boy."

The horse lowered its head again, and Dusty started forward. He began spinning the rope in a wide, slow loop. At the sound of the rope whispering in the night air, the horse raised its head again.

"Easy, boy, easy."

The horse turned suddenly. After all of the noise earlier in the night, he wasn't going to stick around, but Dusty threw the loop and dropped it over its head.

The horse pulled a bit, then reared back, clawing at the air with its fore hooves.

Dusty pulled the rope tightly. "Easy, boy."

The horse dropped back to all fours, and Dusty walked over and stroked its nose with one hand. "See, boy? Ain't no one going to hurt you."

He led the horse back to the stable, where in the light of an oil lamp he discovered it to be a buckskin with one white stocking and a white mane, and it was indeed a gelding. He quickly strapped his own saddle to its back, and with the bridle in place, led it back outside where he stepped into the saddle and was gone into the night.

Ginny was no stranger to treating bullet wounds. One time, Johnny had been in a skirmish with rustlers who had attempted to take some of the herd at night, and the men had found him lying in the grass with a bullet crease at one temple. Another time, she had dug a bullet from his shoulder. But it had not been buried very deeply. Nothing like now.

She sat in a rocker, her eyes fixed on him. A lamp on a stand by the bed was casting a yellow glow to the room, and in this lighting she thought he seemed so gaunt. His cheeks looked hollow, his eyes sunken in. His color was taking on a grayish hue. She had taken a needle and thread to both wounds to close them, and the bleeding had almost entirely stopped. Tied into place were bed sheets she and Bree had ripped into makeshift bandages. But she knew he was far from out of the proverbial woods. She had not said anything with Bree present, but there was a good chance he was still

bleeding internally, and stopping something like that was beyond her expertise.

The first bullet had struck his ribcage, cracking one rib and probably fragmenting in the process. She was certain none of the fragments had pierced a lung, because his breathing was even and nothing bubbled from the wound. The second bullet had actually entered at the base of his chest, just below the rib cage, where she knew the esophagus, stomach and the tail end of the liver came together in a sort of three-corners country. For the bullet to have not torn through at least one of them would probably be hoping for too much.

Bree materialized at the doorway. Dark circles had formed beneath her eyes and the color had drained from her face. A combination of fear and weariness. But she had not wavered. Had not broken into tears. Her father's strength was in her.

"Aunt Ginny, why don't you go down to the kitchen and have something to eat? I can sit with Pa."

Ginny shook her head. "No, I'm fine. I'll stay here."

Bree stepped into the room. "Aunt Ginny, we're going to need you to be strong, and you have to take care of yourself in order to be strong. I'll sit with Pa."

"Where's Josh?"

"He went outside to help the men."

"In his condition? He can barely walk."

"He needed to be doing something. He thought he would go crazy just sitting downstairs, waiting."

Ginny nodded, then sat in silence for a moment. Bree stood her ground at the doorway. She was not moving, not giving an inch. Maybe she had a little of her maternal grandfather in her, too.

With a sigh, Ginny decided to concede, and rose to her feet. As she passed Bree, she stopped and gave her niece a kiss on the cheek. "If anything happens, anything at all, you call for me."

"I won't hesitate."

Aunt Ginny stepped from the room, weariness more present in her sagging shoulders than she realized was visible, and a certain authority normally in her step was now missing.

266

Bree was going to sit down in the rocker, but then saw Pa's pistol belt was lying in one corner.

"Well, we can't have that," she said aloud. "If you wake up and your guns aren't within reach, you'll raise the roof."

She fetched the belt, marveling at the weight of it and how her father not only carried it effortlessly, but seemed to feel more natural with this cumbersome thing buckled about his hips than not.

She buckled the belt together, then slung it over a bedpost at the head of the bed. Then she sat at the bed's edge, and brought one hand to Pa's face. He did not flinch as she touched him, and she noticed how warm he was. Fever. Infection from the wounds.

"Oh, Pa," she said softly, and felt a tear making its way down her cheek. She quickly reached up to wipe it away. Can't have any of that. Not now. We all have to be strong for each other.

She stood and walked to the open doorway, and looked across the corridor and through another open doorway. The guest room, which Dusty was using. Through the doorway, she could see the window that looked down onto the front yard.

"Dusty," she said, as though her brother could hear her. "Hurry."

Downstairs in the kitchen, Ginny went to the wooden bread box John had made for her, and took a muffin left over from that morning's breakfast. As she did so, she found herself thinking that while she was proud of the strength Bree was showing, she hoped Bree was not too independent and strong. Ginny felt she herself took those qualities to excess, and often thought they were part of the reason she had never married. Many a man is afraid of those qualities in a woman. In fact, she had met only one who was able to love her in spite of them, and maybe even because of them. Most men, she was convinced, would rather have a woman they could believe is a little helpless so they can take care of her, and be continually reassured of their masculinity. Ginny thought a man with such insecurities would not be the kind of man she would want to spend her life with, but there were times at night when loneliness would creep in on her, and

she would start longing for the husband and family she would never have.

True, John and Lura's children were as her own now, as she had helped raise them, but only because sadistic fate had deprived the children of their mother.

She was tired. Her mind was racing as it often did when she was fighting exhaustion. To look at Josh and Bree, and Dusty, who were seeing their father possibly mortally wounded, made her wonder about a conversation she had had earlier with John on the front porch. If he had taken the children to Pennsylvania to farm, rather than to this valley in Montana, he would not be lying upstairs near death.

She had tried to discourage such regrets in him, but she now wondered herself. The sleepy little farming towns of Pennsylvania never saw guerrilla raiders descending upon them, or saw women hiding in a root cellar, ready to kill themselves rather than be taken captive. They never saw men swaggering about with death buckled about their hips because failure to do so might be to invite violence, an odd sort of paradox in which the ability and willingness to commit violence actually prevented the threat of it. Usually.

She realized she was standing at the bread box, stale muffin in hand. But she did not move.

Oh, John. Why did you have to go and get yourself shot? When you get better, am I going to give you a tongue lashing! All those times you rode off into the mountains, and I thought you were going to get yourself killed and never return. But then, you go and get yourself shot under your own roof.

Who was she kidding? Was he going to get better? Could even Granny Tate, that mysterious little woman who had learned a mixture of home remedies, practical medicines and even a little voodoo on a plantation in Georgia save him now? Even her skill had its limits.

She sat at the table, and thought maybe she should go out to John's desk, and grab some paper and a pen. Jackson would need to be informed of what had happened. This might seem an odd time to be writing a letter, but she needed to keep herself busy. Simply sitting and waiting might drive her mad.

And yet, what was she to tell in the letter? She decided she might want to wait a day or two. To see if John was going to live. Which, she had to admit, was looking doubtful.

Pessimism was something Ginny did not believe in. Her dear father had preached against it endlessly, and she had always resisted it. Yet now, she found her strength withering, felt herself caving in. Tears began rolling down her cheekbones, and her shoulders shook with sobs, and she did not fight them.

Josh, Hunter and Zack sat on the front porch. Josh was in Aunt Ginny's rocker, and Zack and Fred simply sat on the floor of the porch with their backs against the wall. Zack's left arm was now in a bed sheet Hunter had fashioned into a sling, and another bed sheet had been wrapped about his shoulder, under his shirt. The bleeding seemed to have stopped.

Hunter had seen bullet wounds in the War Between the States, and in his years working for Johnny. No need to bother Aunt Ginny with this, he thought. She and Bree were busy working on Johnny. Hunter would see if he could do something about Zack's wound. To his surprise, the wound wasn't deep at all. Sometimes, an older model gun that took a lead ball rather than a bullet didn't do the damage you would think. Apparently, it had been one of these Zack had been shot with. The bullet, or ball, had torn him up, but bruised him more than anything, and had seemed to bounce away. He was cut up fairly bad, but Hunter did not think any bones had been broken.

With Ramon and Koller holding Zack down on the floor, Hunter had poured whiskey into the wound to clean it. The old Texas Ranger captain Zack and Johnny had served under had always kept a bottle for specifically this purpose, and Johnny followed suit. The science of infections was still largely unknown, but trial-and-error had shown that if you clean a wound with alcohol, the chances of infection seemed to be cut down considerably.

Zack's shoulder had gone numb from being hit by the bullet, but the whiskey drove the numbness away dang quick, and Zack had screamed and kicked as the fluid worked its way into the torn skin of his shoulder.

The bleeding had pretty much stopped, but should it start again, Zack knew of another remedy. One time with the Rangers, he had caught an arrowhead in one thigh. After it was cut out, a gaping gash remained, and it was sealed shut with a hot iron. It hurt no worse than the whiskey. If he needed, Hunter could hold him down again, and Josh was pretty good with a branding iron.

Zack had gone upstairs to check on Johnny. Bree was there, and Ginny came in with the bottle of whiskey, and she and Bree cleaned Johnny's wounds with it. Johnny hadn't even flinched once. That was an indication of just how bad Johnny was hurt.

Zack sat outside in silence, along with Josh and Hunter. Crickets were chirping away in the night. A whippoorwill gave a call from somewhere out in the dark woods. The smell of gunsmoke was still in the air. Soon, Zack knew, the eastern sky would begin to lighten to a sort of gray glow with predawn.

"Do you think he's going to make it, Zack?" Josh asked.

Zack drew a deep breath and let it out slowly. "If he was any other man, I'd say no. I've seen other men die from wounds that aren't so bad. But I've seen your father do some mighty impossible stunts. If anyone has a fighting chance of living through being shot up like that, it's your Pa."

Josh nodded, trying to feel convinced, yet not succeeding.

THIRTY

Dusty's horse was running hard. It was almost as though the animal understood the gravity of the situation. It knew the terrain, and Dusty let it have its head. It had not slowed as it neared the wooden bridge, but rather charged across it, its iron shoes rapping loudly like gunshots against the wooden planks.

The horse ran until it was winded. Dusty reined up, and dismounted and loosened the cinch for a few minutes while he let the horse blow, then he tightened the cinch, stepped back into the saddle, and they were off again.

The horse was starting to show fatigue as they approached the end of the third mile. It slowed to a shambling trot as it carried Dusty up a low hill, and onto a plateau in a gap between two ridges that rimmed this corner of the valley. It was on that plateau that the little town stood.

By using the position of the constellations as a gauge, Dusty figured the time to be somewhere between two and three in the morning. He was not surprised to find the all of the windows in town dark.

He followed along the street, and then left the buildings behind, heading north. A half mile north beyond town, Josh had told him. The trouble was, he had never ridden over this particular stretch of land and in the darkness, he may not be able to see something like a building and might ride on past it.

He rode along, the horse now slowing its pace a bit more. Its coat was lathered from running so hard. He gave the rein a little tug to slow it to a fast walk. It wouldn't do for the horse to exhaust itself before they could return to the ranch.

They had been gone from the town's lone street maybe five minutes when he caught a scent of smoke mixed in with the balsam-rich mountain air. Wood smoke. Maybe a stove. The house must be near. And at the brisk walking pace the horse was keeping, Dusty estimated they had covered maybe a half mile. Then, a dog began barking, off to the right of the trail. A watch dog, which meant a house. Thank you, Lord.

Dusty rode until the barking of the dog grew louder. Then, at a point where the barking seemed to be no more

than maybe fifty yards away, and off to the dead right, he reined up, and called out, "Hello, the house!"

There was no response, so he called out again.

A window glowed to life, flickering at first, then becoming a steady, pale yellow. Someone had lighted a lamp. He nudged the buckskin forward, aiming at what he thought must be the front yard.

The gelding turned to their left, stepping around something Dusty couldn't see in the darkness, but he decided to trust the animal's eyesight over his own.

A second window lighted, then a long, thin vertical shaft of light appeared as a door opened.

"Hello, the house!" Dusty repeated again.

"Who's there?" a voice called out. A man.

"My name's Dusty," he said. He wasn't accustomed to having a full name to give when people asked that question, but then decided he now had one, so he was going to use it. "Dusty McCabe. Johnny's son. We've had a shooting out at the ranch, and he's been hurt bad."

"Ah didn't know Johnny had a son named Dusty." It was a man's voice, rich with a Georgian drawl.

"It's a long story. Aunt Ginny fetched me to bring back someone named Granny Tate."

A woman spoke. A voice that was old, like cracked leather. "Land sakes, Henry, step aside. Invite the poor boy in."

"Come on in," the man said.

Dusty stepped down from the saddle, leaving the rein trailing, or ground-hitched, and approached the house.

The door opened wide, and Dusty stepped into a small kitchen. A stove pipe protruded from one wall, and connected to it was a cast iron stove. A dry sink was built into a cupboard at another wall. The floor was earthen.

The old woman rose only to Dusty's shoulder in height. She wore a kerchief over white, wiry hair. Her face, a chestnut brown, was deeply lined with years. She squinted up at him through a pair of metal rimmed spectacles, and rested her weight on a cane.

She said, "You say you're Johnny's boy?"

"Yes'm." He had no hat to remove, as he had left it at the ranch.

She gave him a long look, then nodded. "I can see him in you. And you say, he's been shot?"

Dusty nodded quickly. "Twice."

"It must be quite bad if Ginny can't handle it herself."

She looked to the man. "Henry, go harness up a buckboard. Be quick about it."

Within five minutes, a team was hitched to the wagon, and Dusty was on his way to the McCabe ranch, with Granny Tate at his side. Dusty sat on the hard, wooden seat, holding the reins between the middle and ring fingers of each hand as the wagon creaked and bumped its way along the trail. Henry had offered Dusty some stable space for the buckskin, and to tend it while it rested up. The old woman looked like she had the durability of a dried and brittle leaf shaking in a autumn wind, but she held to the seat with a steadiness that belied her years, the number of which Dusty would not even dare venture a guess at.

"You folks live here long, Mrs. Tate?"

"Ain't no need to call me Mrs. I'm Granny to everyone. Been so since I was about your age. Been a granny doctor most of my life. But in answer to your question, we been here about two years, now."

"What's a granny doctor?"

"Someone who treats the ills of folks what can't afford some college-trained white man to come and do the same thing and charge 'em money for it. Why, I've birthed more babies than I could ever count. Set broken bones, fed medicine to the sick. Even dug out a bullet or two. And never charged a cent for it."

"What brought you folks here? This is pretty good cattle country, but you folks don't look like ranchers. And the gold fields are east of here, and you don't see too many farmers in these parts."

She chuckled. "You young folks always think of gold as though it can move mountains or change the weather. It's nothing more than a rock, and neither Henry nor I are going to waste our time digging it out of the ground, where the Good Lord put it."

"But why here? Why McCabe gap?"

273

"Because I'm needed here. A granny doctor goes where she's needed. Henry, he's my grandson. We was born into slavery, working for Mas'sa Tate until the war ended and Mista' Lincoln set us all free. That's when Henry changed his name to Freeman, 'cause that's what he be. A free man. He's proud, and wanted me to change mine, too, but I been Granny Tate for too long. Granny Tate's who I still be.

"We come west to get away from the white sheets. Henry thought we could start over here, where they ain't a lot of folks, and everyone is too concerned with just surviving too care much about who's colored and who's white.

"Your Pa, he's a good man. He does a lot of good for Henry. Brings him a lot of business. Henry does all the smithy work for your Pa's ranch. But you know what means more to Henry than all the work?"

Dusty shook his head.

"Your Pa looks him square in the eye, and never calls him 'boy.' And when your Pa looks at him, he doesn't see color. He just sees a man."

Josh stood on the porch alone, one hand resting on the railing. The eastern sky was awash with a gray glow, obliterating the stars. The night birds had stopped their calling, but the birds of morning hadn't yet taken flight. A silence fell upon the land as though all were waiting with a hushed reverence for the rising of the sun.

This was Josh's favorite time of day. And yet, this morning, he was unable to appreciate it. Upstairs, his father was unconscious, two bullet holes in his chest. Despite Josh's best attempts at optimism, he had to admit to himself that his father was dying.

Josh felt cold. The mountain air bore a chill, but that was not the cold he was thinking of. He felt cold inside.

He thought of Jack, for the first time tonight. Jack, back east, in medical school. Jack was a year younger, and though his life was taking him in a different direction than Josh's, they had been raised in this house, alongside Bree. Raised by Pa and Aunt Ginny. Jack usually managed to return home every year, for a few weeks every summer. But otherwise, Josh seldom saw him anymore.

Josh figured he had the responsibility of writing the letter to Jack. The letter telling him that their father was dead. Of course, he was putting the proverbial cart before the horse, as Aunt Ginny would have said, and right now, optimistic thinking was necessary. And yet, he couldn't keep his mind from drifting down a path he didn't want it to go. How do you even write such a letter?

Josh didn't know how this family would survive without Pa. He didn't know how he would survive without Pa.

Just yesterday, the most important problems in Josh's life had been that he seriously doubted his ability to live up to Pa's growing legend. And he was having trouble trying to choke down the thought that a drifter riding onto the ranch, bearing a resemblance to Pa and claiming to be the son of a woman Pa could not even remember being with, could live up to Pa's legend so much more easily than Josh could. Today, those problems seemed so insignificant.

The mountain breeze brought to him a sound, a distant rattling, like iron shaking against wood in a staccato rhythm. He looked off toward the wooden bridge and saw motion. A dark shape. A wagon, crossing the bridge. It was Dusty, hopefully returning with Granny Tate.

Josh pushed away from the railing, and went to the doorway, and called out, "Dusty's back!"

Josh then hobbled down from the porch, his knee-cap feeling afloat, and a strange numbness present immediately below it. Dusty pulled the team to a stop, and Josh hurried to the side of the wagon to help Granny Tate down.

"Must have been quite a fracas here," she said. "I can still smell the powder smoke in the air."

Bree appeared at the doorway. She had been busying herself dusting, which had been done just two days earlier, and would not need to be for another week, but she had to do something while she waited. Aunt Ginny had returned to Pa's bedside.

Josh escorted Granny Tate to the porch, looping one arm so Granny could hang onto it like a handle, and she climbed the steps slowly, lifting one foot gingerly to the next step, and bringing the other up behind her. She steadied herself all the way using a hand-cut hickory stick as a cane.

She climbed the stairs to the second floor as such, and Aunt Ginny stepped aside as the old woman examined Johnny.

"Has he woken up at all?" the granny doctor asked.

"No," Ginny said. "He hasn't even stirred."

"He's bleedin' inside, is what he's doing. You have a good tight bandage here, but he's still bleedin' inside."

Bree asked, "What can be done?"

Granny shook her head slowly. "Not much, child. Oh, them big-city doctors back east, in places like New York or Boston, they could cut him open, find the blood vessels that are torn, and maybe sew them up. And if he didn't die from infection or the blood loss he's already suffered, he would be all right. But out here, there ain't much you can do. I'm awful sorry."

Ginny stood silently, looking at the hollow-cheeked form of Johnny McCabe.

"Can you do the operation?" Josh asked.

"No, child," Granny said. "There's a lot I can do that them big-city doctors can't. I can look at a patch of woods and see all sorts of roots and herbs that can ease pain, or do other things. I doubt there's all that many who know as much about bringin' a child into the world as I do. And I can set a broken bone with the best of them. But to cut into a person, that's beyond me. The nearest doctor is in Helena, and I doubt even he could do anything, in these conditions.

"No, I'm afraid all we can do is wait. With injuries like this, you never know. I've seen some hurt much worse pull through, and I've seen others hurt much less suddenly die."

"Well," Aunt Ginny said. "I appreciate you coming all the way out here."

"No trouble at all. I just wish there was something I could do. Johnny McCabe is one of the finest men I've ever met."

"I'll have Dusty take you home."

"No, I'd rather stay with you. Until this is over, whichever way it goes."

Aunt Ginny managed a smile of gratitude, despite her weariness and her worry.

Granny said, "You're all exhausted. You get some rest. I'll set with him for a while."

THIRTY-ONE

Ginny went down to her room to lie down, and sleep took her quickly. But it was a light, restless sleep.

She was in the past, watching the young gunhawk who wore his guns too naturally stepping through her doorway for the first time, to be reunited with Lura and meet his infant son Joshua.

Then she was sitting in the parlor at the little ranch house he, his brother Josiah, and Zack Johnson had built. He was standing in front of a casket, looking down at the pretty face, with the classic bone structure about her cheekbones and the straw colored hair gathering in almost ethereal ringlets about her shoulders. John's hair, pure auburn with no traces of gray yet, was pulled back in a tail falling between his shoulder blades, Indian-style, and he was wearing his Sunday-best broad cloth jacket and trousers, and a white shirt and tie. And about his waist were those infernal, ever-present guns. She watched him stand strong, no shudder that might betray internal sobs. Just standing stoically. But when she looked closer, she saw a tiny tear streaming its way down the side of his nose.

The dream shifted, and she was on the seat of a conestoga wagon, holding the reins in her hands. The four-year-old Joshua and his brother Jackson, barely three, ran alongside the wagon, bouncing a ball against the side as it moved slowly along, the team of oxen moving at the speed a man could walk. Sleeping on a pallet of blankets in the wagon behind her was Sabrina, eighteen-months old. John pulled up beside her, his wide Stetson covered with a layer of dust, his chin and jaw sprouting two months' worth of an auburn beard. And there were the guns, riding at his hips. Behind them was another wagon, driven by Fred Mitchum, which served as the chuck wagon. Behind them all was the herd. Five thousand head of cattle, with Josiah, Zack and Hunter serving as drovers. A mile to her left was a spectacular ridge line, carpeted with dark green pines toward the base, and reaching to the sky with craggy, rocky fingers. To her right the land fell away into the distance in waving ripples of grass. Absolutely breathtaking, no matter which direction she looked in.

The scene faded, and she found herself in the root cellar, standing alongside Sabrina, now nearly fully grown. Their ears were ringing with the roar of the gun battle raging above. She was suddenly struck with the feeling she should be upstairs. Something dreadful had happened. She had somehow heard Dusty's cry, above the gunfire. And she knew in her heart it had finally happened to John. After all these years of living so dangerously but somehow evading death, it had finally caught up with him.

She relived her climb up the stairs, pushing open that danged heavy trap door, and running into the parlor doorway, where she saw John on the floor, Dusty at his side.

And she was startled awake to find herself in her room.

The window was alight with the grayness of early morning. Still fully dressed, she swung her feet to the floor and walked out to the kitchen, where she found Bree sitting with a cup of tea.

"That's just what I had in mind," Ginny said. "It turns out sleep was not such a good idea, after all."

The day wore on, and somehow, John didn't die. He didn't improve, either. He simply lay there, gray, his cheeks hollow and his eyes sunken in. His breathing was even, but Ginny thought it was growing a little more shallow.

"Could be building fluid in his lungs," Granny said. "Hard to tell."

Granny checked his pulse, found it rather high at eight-four per minute, and he was a bit warmer than normal. "Running a fever. The heartbeat picks up its speed when your body temperature goes up."

"What could that mean?" Ginny asked. She and Granny Tate were standing alone in the room, so she said, "Be truthful with me."

"Infection," Granny said. "The fever's because his body's fighting it. But the shallow breathing might mean his lungs are filling with fluid."

"He's losing the fight."

Granny nodded. "It does look that way, child."

Ginny turned, and paced absently toward the window. "How do I tell the children?"

"I wouldn't. At least, not just yet. Like I said, I've seen some strange things. Men hurt worse than this who have full recoveries. Others hurt much less who die anyway."

Ginny nodded. "Then, we will simply have to wait."

The men tried to go about their work. Fred tended to the remuda. The horses had mostly scattered during the gun fight, so with the help of Dusty and Josh, he spent most of the day rounding them up. Every hour or so, Dusty and Josh would ride back to the house and check on their father. A bandage was tied about Josh's shoulder under his shirt where the bullet had grazed him, and he had difficulty climbing into the saddle with his injured knee, but he refused to spend any time resting, despite Aunt Ginny's and Granny Tate's recommendations. He simply needed to work. To keep busy.

Bree, Aunt Ginny and Granny took turns sitting with Johnny. Staring, praying, but all the time feeling helpless as he waged his war against death.

"Lord, don't take him now," Ginny found herself saying, as she sat by his bedside. "Lord, don't take him now."

From the doorway, Granny Tate said, "Child, the Lord will take him when the time is right, and not a moment sooner or later."

"But he's still a young man. He's got so many years ahead of him. His children may be mostly grown up, but they still need him. And Dusty has barely met him. A boy should have the chance to get to know his own father. To have finally found out who his father is, and to have ridden all this way to find him, just to have him snatched away like this..."

"Life and death are two parts of a greater whole, child. Praying to change the way things are is a waste of your breath, and the Lord's time. Everything is born, it grows, it lives, then it passes on to a higher existence. The trees, the grass, the animals of the woods, and us. We all take the same path. If it's your time to pass, the greatest doctors in all the world won't be able to stop it. And if it's not your time, then all the bullets in the world won't be able to change it.

"Don't pray for more years, child. Pray for better years. Don't pray for good times, or easy times. Pray for strength."

Ginny nodded. She understood what Granny was saying. She would have given that same advice were she in Granny's place. But sitting here, watching this man wage what appeared to be a losing battle, she found her faith and philosophies seemed a bit abstract, maybe not strong enough to stand when struck with hard reality.

"And pray for guidance," Granny said. "From the Good Lord, and from those who have gone before you. No matter how old we may get, or how smart we think we've become, we're all still in need of it."

Once the horses were rounded up, Josh and Dusty busied themselves helping Zack load the bodies of the dead raiders into a buckboard. Fred hitched a team, and Josh and Dusty drove the wagon into town.

One of the dead men was Long.

"Poetic justice," Josh said.

A short distance beyond the single street of McCabe gap was a cemetery with seven graves, each marked with a wooden plank standing upright. One read: UNKNOWN. SHOT TO DEATH AT HUNTER'S SALOON. 1877.

"This is our boot hill," Josh said. "That one there died in a gunfight in Hunter's, one Saturday night last fall."

Another read: UNKNOWN. FOUND FROZE ON McCABE MTN 1872.

"Pa found that one in the spring of seventy-two. Every-so-often, Pa rides through the mountains that line our section of the valley, or he sends a rider to do it. To make certain no squatters are settling in. That spring, Pa found an old man dressed in buckskins lying dead on the side of the mountain. He had a broken leg. Pa figured he got caught in a snow slide, broke the leg, and froze to death. Couldn't get back to camp. Pa found a few beaver traps. He must have been an old trapper."

Another read: THREE FINGER JACK. HANGED BY MOB 1873.

"Lynched," Josh said. "from the branch of a big old maple, just outside of town. We call it the hangin' tree, now."

"Who lynched him?"

"Some of the town folks, and a few cowhands from ranches in the area. He was accused of shooting a cowhand

over a card game on the Watson spread. He was brought into town and was supposed to be held in Hunter's tool shed for a territorial marshal, but the crowd got liquored-up one night, and hanged him."

"Did he actually do the shooting?"

Josh nodded. "He claimed the man he shot was reaching for his gun. But the man he shot was well known and liked, and Three-finger was a stranger. We never even knew his full name. But what do you expect in a town with no law?"

"The town's too small," Dusty said. "They wouldn't be able to pay a marshal. A lot of little communities are in the same fix."

Josh grabbed two shovels from the buckboard, and handed one to Dusty. "Come on, let's bury them and get back to the ranch. I want to check on Pa."

He stepped onto the blade of the shovel, and pushed it into the sod, beginning a grave. After a few shovelfuls, he looked to Dusty, who was digging away beside him.

Josh said, "Do you think Pa will make it?"

Dusty looked at him, was about to say something, then thought better of it, and continued digging.

They returned to the ranch as the afternoon was progressing into dusk. Josh asked if he or Dusty could take a turn sitting with Pa while the women got some rest, but Granny Tate scoffed. "Men-folk don't know anything about tending the sick. You wouldn't know what to do if anything happened. Never did know a man who was any use when it came to tending the sick."

Bree had prepared a supper of steak, green beans and potatoes. She had not much felt like cooking, but Granny Tate had said they needed to eat to keep up their strength. The McCabes sat at the kitchen table with Zack, while Granny sat upstairs with Pa. But they found their appetites lacking, and simply stared at their food, or occasionally nibbled.

Zack built a small fire in the hearth, using only his right hand as his left shoulder was tightly bandaged and his arm was still in a sling. Once the fire was crackling away, he paced about impatiently as the windows darkened with

nightfall. The fire cast orange light that flickered against the walls, and shadows danced and contorted. Josh sat in the chair usually reserved for Pa. Bree sat in Aunt Ginny's rocker, and Dusty on the sofa.

Granny Tate and Aunt Ginny were with Johnny. Ginny had instructed Zack and the kids to remain downstairs. Even though they all wanted to be at Johnny's bedside, she thought a crowded room would do no good for the patient.

Granny Tate leaned over the bed, pressing a finger against the inside of Johnny's wrist while she watched the second hand on her pocket watch wind its way slowly around the face. "Ninety-one. And he's warmer to the touch."

"And" Ginny added from the wooden straight-back chair in which she sat, "his breathing's more shallow."

Granny put an ear to his chest. Oh, but for a stethoscope, she thought, but those things cost money she did not have. Yet, with only her unaided ear, she thought she could hear a rumbling as he inhaled. "Not good."

"Will he live the night?"

Granny looked at her gravely. "I wouldn't bet on it, child."

The night wore on. Josh nodded off in his father's chair. Dusty stretched out on the sofa. Zack went outside to take a walk, but gave instructions to call to him if anything happened.

Bree went upstairs to bring a cup of tea to Aunt Ginny, and she leaned over her father to give a light kiss to his forehead. "Good night, Daddy. See you in the morning," and she went to her room to lie down. She didn't want to sleep, but her body was forcing her to give in to the demand.

Granny Tate was in Dusty's room sleeping lightly. Ginny was alone with Johnny.

She sipped her tea. "Oh, John. How could you have let this happen? You just have to pull through this. You just have to."

She set the empty cup and saucer on a stand by the bed. The clock downstairs chimed ten. Her shift was over, and Bree's was about to begin. But she did not want to leave his bedside.

Sleep, however, soon won its way with her, and her head began to drop forward, and she drifted away.

Johnny McCabe realized he was standing. He was in the middle of his bedroom, and Aunt Ginny was sitting in a chair before him. Her back was to him, and she was slumped forward. He could tell by her slow, rhythmic breathing that she was asleep.

His hair was tied behind his head, and he was fully dressed, in a gray shirt and trousers. Though, he didn't remember owning clothes of exactly this color.

Odd, he thought. And he felt a little groggy. He couldn't quite remember how he came to be standing in his room, or why Aunt Ginny was sitting in here, sleeping.

The window was dark. It must be late. Then, the clock downstairs chimed eleven, confirming this.

He realized his bed wasn't empty. There was a man in it. Gaunt, his skin a sort of gray color in the pale light of the lamp mounted on the wall.

He realized with a start the man was himself. He was lying in the bed.

"What the hell?" he muttered aloud.

He approached the bed, and pulled back a cover to see the man—himself, bare chested, and with a bandage wrapped about his ribs and upper stomach.

Yes, he thought. He remembered. Gunshot wound. Two, in fact. One from the side, another from the front. Downstairs. The raiders attacked the house.

What was going on here?

It did not look like the sick, wounded version of himself lying in the bed was breathing much at all.

Must be a nightmare, he thought. He had grown accustomed to them, since Lura died. Even though years had passed since she was shot, he still relived it in his dreams. Returning to the ranch house after a long day in the saddle, swinging out of the saddle, Lura waiting for him by the front door, the bullet seeming to come out of nowhere and striking her just below the collar bone. He catches her as she falls, and she looks at him with puzzlement and surprise, then with one final exhale she's gone. The love of his life is gone,

and he looks up at the heavens to scream, and jumps suddenly awake, finding himself in bed.

And yet, those nightmares had never been anything like this. Here, he was reliving nothing. It was as if he were witnessing a scene, a scene in which he himself was a participant.

He was quickly reminded of a book Ginny had brought with her from San Francisco, and which he had read during a series of cold December evenings a couple of years ago, written by some Englishman by the name of Dickens. He felt like Scrooge, looking at himself while escorted by the ghost of Christmas Present.

It had been a stupid book, he thought. Ginny, of course, disagreed. It was destined to be a classic. Johnny couldn't see how. He thought the whole concept was preposterous. Real life is not like that.

And yet, here he was, looking down on himself like in that book.

A dream. It had to be a dream. He hoped it would end soon. He was starting to find the whole thing unnerving.

He became faintly aware of the scent of peach blossoms in the air. And then, a presence at his side. He turned to see the most beautiful woman he had ever laid eyes on in his life.

She stood five-one, with hair falling to her shoulders in ringlets the color of straw. She was in her early twenties, the age when she had been shot.

His mouth fell open, his eyes filling with tears. "Lura."

She smiled, her head leaning gently to one side as it always did when she smiled. She was dressed in a flowing gown, of the same gray he wore.

"My love," she said.

"This is a dream. It has to be a dream. Or, am I going mad?"

She stepped toward him. "It's no dream, my love. And you're not going mad. I'm here, and you're here."

She let her fingertips gently slide down one cheekbone, and he took her by the shoulders. She was real. Flesh and blood.

He said, "But you're dead. I saw you die."

"No one ever dies, Johnny. I was shot, and my body died away, but I have never been far from your side. I have been with you all the way, as you and Aunt Ginny raised the children."

He was going to ask how, but somehow, in his heart, he knew. It was like the old Shoshone shaman had said.

He pulled her closer, wrapping her in his arms, and her lips were on his, her arms reaching around to his back and pulling him to her. His fingers were stroking her hair, and he was drowning in the scent of peach blossom she so frequently wore.

After all these years, he could at last be with her. After all this waiting.

"It's just the same as when we first met," he said. "I said it then, and I say it now. A man could drown in you."

"And I want you to drown in me for all eternity."

She then pulled away, taking a deep breath. "But Johnny, we can't. I know we've been apart for a lot of years, but we can't."

He found his brows dropping into a sort of half-frown out of puzzlement. "What? Why? Why can't we..?"

"Because, it's just not your time. You still have so much to do."

He felt tears welling. "But I can't lose you again. It's just not fair."

"Nothing's fair in life, my love."

"Then, why is all this happening? Why are you here now?"

"Because," she reached with a hand to the side of his face. "I have a message for you, and it had to be delivered personally."

"What message?"

"It's okay to live, Johnny. I died, younger than most, and you've been living with so much guilt because you weren't able to keep that from happening."

"I should have protected you. I should have kept you safe."

Her face glowed with a smile. "You did everything humanly possible to protect me. But to live is to take risks."

"But..." he looked away, sucking in a lungful of air. It was suddenly hard to breathe. He felt a lump welling in his throat, and his vision was swimming with sudden tears.

"I know, Johnny. You've been with living with a terrible guilt. The gunman was aiming for you, because of the reward that was on you and your brothers from years ago. But he hit me instead."

"That bullet was meant for me."

"No, my love." With her hand still on his face, she gently turned his head until their eyes again met. "It was meant for me."

His brows knit again with puzzlement. "How..?"

"It was my time. It wasn't your time. It's as simple as that. When it's not our time to go, not all the bullets or all illness in the world can take us. But when it is our time, nothing can prevent it."

"I don't know..." he found this confusing. He wanted to believe what she was saying, yet...

A voice spoke from behind him. A deep baritone that sounded as old as time itself. "John-nee."

He knew it instantly. He turned to find himself staring into eyes that seemed to reflect an almost bottomless pool of wisdom. The face was weathered and lined, the nose bent like a hawk's. The man's hair was white like a newly fallen snow. He wore a buckskin shirt and trousers made of the same. The Shoshone shaman, Many Lives.

Johnny found himself smiling. "My old teacher."

"Let yourself believe, my son. Too often we try too hard not to believe what we, at the core of our spirit, already know. We are born knowing, and then spend a lifetime forgetting and then trying to re-learn. Or turning away from what we knew and trying to convince ourselves that what our eyes see and our ears hear is all there is."

Lura stepped around to stand beside the shaman, facing Johnny. "It's time you started letting yourself live. Instead of grieving my early death, celebrate our love every day, in the way you live. And let yourself love. Life is too short to deny yourself love. Another may come along, and denying her will not in any way protect me, or belittle what we have."

"I don't want anyone else. I want you."

"And you still have me, in your heart. You always will. I will always be here, waiting for you, for when it's your time. But until then, let yourself live life to its fullest, as it was meant to be lived. Let yourself love. We all have enough love to give to more than one. You're still a young man, with many years ahead of you."

"But my son," the shaman said with a smile, placing a hand on Johnny's shoulder much as Johnny had with Josh a few days earlier, "try a little harder to stay out of the way of bullets."

Johnny burst out laughing. Lura was, too. Johnny found his stomach hurting as the laughter rocked him. Tears flowed again and he couldn't stop them, but they were no longer tears of grief. He felt like all the years of pain that had settled deeply into his bones, the pain of believing he had not protected the woman he loved, and she had caught a death intended for him, seemed to drain away with the laughter, like a sponge being squeezed.

He struggled for a few gasping breaths, and finally straightened to find his wife and the old shaman still there.

The old man had a deep smile. "Live your life, my son. And when it is indeed your time one day, we will meet again."

And the Shoshone turned, and stepped away into a wall of mist Johnny had somehow not even noticed until that very moment.

Lura again brought her hand to Johnny's face. He hadn't thought about it in a long time, but that was a trait of hers and she would do many times in a day.

She said, "I have to go too, my love."

Johnny nodded. "I figured as much."

"Do one thing for me?" she asked, glancing to Ginny, who was still sleeping in the chair by the bed. "Tell her and the children that I love them?"

He nodded. "I'll do that."

"I will be seeing you, when your time comes. And then we can be together forever. Until then, always remember, I love you dearly. And even though I am gone, I am never really far away. I never have been."

She turned, and Johnny watched her step away and into the mist, but he found that he wasn't crying. The pain he had lived with so continually, and had actually grown

accustomed to, was no longer there. For the first time in years, he actually felt young. He realized he was smiling.

Johnny suddenly realized he was no longer standing, but was lying in bed. His head was on his pillow. And he was still smiling.

He took a deep breath, and winced with sudden pain. The two bullets. He had almost forgotten. And dang, they hurt. Yet, he felt so light, so free, so...young. The guilt, and the weariness that came with it, were indeed gone.

He opened his eyes, and found himself staring at the roughhewn timbers of the ceiling in his bedroom. Ginny was sleeping gently in the chair beside the bed.

He pulled one arm up to the covers. He was going to pull them down and climb out of bed. He felt wonderful. He felt alive. And yet, his arm felt like it was made of lead. He was as weak as a kitten. He was sticky with old perspiration. Fever, he figured. He had been wracked with infection from the wounds, and he had lost a lot of blood. He had seen a lot of men on various battlefields die of infection from less serious wounds.

Good old Zack, he thought. Must have used their old battlefield treatment. Dumping raw corn squeezings into the wound. Johnny had done the same to Zack once when Zack had caught an arrow head in his leg, before sealing the wound shut with a hot iron. The old army doctor stationed at the fort was amazed that not only did Zack live, but he kept his leg.

Johnny glanced to the bedpost to find his guns hanging. Good. He didn't like them far away.

"Ginny," he said, his voice not much more than a whisper despite his best effort.

But she heard it, awaking with a start. Her mouth fell open, and her eyes widened.

"John. You're awake. Thank the Good Lord!"

He and Ginny never missed an opportunity to needle each other, and he was not going to start now. "Here I am, layin' here dyin', and you fall asleep."

"Thank the Good Lord," she said again, her eyes welling. "Granny Tate. I've got to get Granny Tate."

She rose from the chair, and hurried to the door. "Granny Tate!" she called out quickly. "Come quickly! He's awake!"

In the parlor, Dusty awoke with such a start at Aunt Ginny's cry that he rolled from the sofa onto the floor. Josh sprang out of the chair and found his injured knee had stiffened considerably as he dozed, and it was all he could manage to hobble across the floor.

Granny hurried into Johnny's room, her cane tapping along as she moved, and looked down at Johnny, her nose wrinkling with a smile. "Glory be. Welcome back."

"Granny Tate," Johnny said. "I hope I haven't been much trouble."

She chuckled. "Not at all, child," and she glanced to Ginny. "Like I said, child, sometimes you just don't know."

Bree was suddenly at the doorway, squealing, "Daddy!"

"I'm all right," he managed to say, with a voice he found exasperatingly weak.

Ginny said, "He's going to be all right. Now, all of you, off to bed. Leave him some room to breathe."

Bree had to drop a kiss onto her father's cheek before she scurried back to her own bed. Josh and Dusty gave a final goodnight and then were gone, Josh saying, "We've got to go tell Zack."

"Now that things have calmed down a little in here," Granny Tate said, "how are you feeling?"

"Tired. My chest hurts when I breathe. But I feel alive. Really alive," and he realized he was smiling again.

Ginny looked at him curiously, but Granny simply said, "Is there anything you'd like?"

"Yeah. I'd kill for a cup of coffee."

He was alive. He was going to live. Ginny was grateful, but now the game was on, once again. The game between them.

"Coffee?" she said. "At a time like this? And do you want real coffee, do I dare ask, or that dreadful sludge you men call trail coffee?"

"Don't make me laugh, Ginny. It hurts too much."

With a smile, Ginny said, "I'll go down and heat the water."

Johnny found himself yawning. "I may not be awake when you get back. I feel awfully tired all of a sudden."

"Between the fever and the blood you lost," Granny said, "you're going to need a lot of sleep. If you're asleep when she gets back, we'll keep the water hot for you."

"Oh, and Ginny?"

She was already at the doorway, but she turned and said, "Yes?"

"Lura says to tell you she loves you."

PART SIX

THE LONG TRAIL

THIRTY-TWO

Three years earlier, Johnny and Ginny had been sitting before the hearth. The hour had been late, and Josh and Bree had long since gone upstairs to bed. John had one of his roaring fires going, and as usual, none of the lamps in the parlor were burning, so the room was illuminated only by the leaping, dancing firelight.

Somehow, the conversation turned to death.

"If I should go before you," John said, sitting in his usual chair with his pipe in his hand, "I don't want my body to lay in state for days while everyone and his brother comes to stare at it and say what a great man I was, even if they felt I was really a sum'bitch. It's always that way when someone dies. More than one man becomes a saint just by dying. Me, I'd rather be a sum'bitch and get to live to ride through the mountains one more time."

Ginny had been sitting with a glass of wine, and she found herself laughing. "John, you kill me sometimes. So, what are we supposed to do with you? Just plop you in the ground without a proper send-off?"

"I want a Shoshone funeral."

"And what, pray-tell, is that?"

"A funeral pyre. A big one. You wrap the body in buffalo robes, along with some of the deceased's most sacred possessions, then light a big fire."

"You'd probably still have those infernal guns around your hips."

John chuckled. "Probably."

Ginny wasn't usually this glib, but she had followed her usual glass of wine at dinner with two more. "So, if you should drop dead tomorrow, what am I supposed to do? Send

Joshua buffalo hunting so we can have some robes to wrap you in?"

"I suppose blankets would do."

"Ah, a concession on your part. Minor, though it is. There's no chance, I suppose, that we could get a bigger concession out of you, and have your consent just to be buried in the ground like everyone else?"

"Not a chance."

"I was afraid of that."

Now, three years later, she was in a wooden upright chair by Johnny's bed, watching while he sat, supported by two pillows, sipping chicken broth from a spoon. He was now shaven and freshly bathed, his hair tied back in a Shoshone tail, and he was wearing a long-handled union suit.

"Not bad soup, Ginny," he said between sips.

He was balancing the bowl in his lap. She had wanted to hold it, but he had said he wasn't a baby who needed to be spoon-fed, and he wouldn't spill the soup. And he surely didn't, as he took one spoonful after another.

She said, "Remember a few years ago, that conversation we had one night by the fire about that Indian funeral you wanted?"

"Came pretty danged close to getting it, didn't I?"

"I have to ask, how did you really expect us to pull that off? Did you really expect us to cart you all the way into the mountains, build a huge bonfire and throw you into the middle of it, and just stand there and watch you burn up? We'd be lucky if we didn't start a forest fire."

Johnny chuckled. "I'm sure you all would have managed it."

She shook her head. They were sitting here, good-naturedly harassing each other as though he wasn't just back from the brink of death.

Three days had passed since he had first awakened from the fever she thought was going to claim him. She had gone downstairs to heat water for coffee, and when she returned to his room with a steaming cup of it, he was indeed asleep again. But he was sleeping peacefully, breathing deeply and evenly. His heart rate was still a little fast, but Granny figured it would be until he could build back the body fluids he had lost.

Ginny brought the cup back to the kitchen, thinking she might see if one of the men wanted it, rather than simply dump it, but when she sat at the table, the tears overtook her. She buried her face in her hands and simply cried, her shoulder's shaking as she drew shuddering breaths, and said over and over again, "Thank you, Lord. Thank you, Lord."

Granny returned home the following afternoon. "He's out of the woods, now. I can go. I'll be back tomorrow afternoon to check on him. But if anything happens, anything at all, send one of the boys to fetch me, and I'll come a-running."

Before she left, she prescribed lots of water for him, as much as he could take. But don't force it on him. She didn't want any of it coming back up, because the strain could further injure the bullet wounds. If he wanted something hot, tea was what she thought he should have. No coffee, even though she knew he wouldn't listen to her and would demand it, anyway. When he started feeling hungry, he was to have chicken and beef broth only at first.

Johnny slept most of that first day, waking occasionally, and on the morning of the second day, he seemed stronger. Some of the usual resonance had returned to his voice, and his eyes no longer seemed to be sinking into his skull. He was still a ghostly pale, and she thought he seemed a little feverish again, but the improvement was noticeable. She helped get him bathed, though he surprisingly could handle most of the job himself, and got him dressed and shaved. That was when he said, "I've got to have a cup of coffee, Ginny."

What the hell, she thought. One wouldn't kill him. He had already survived two bullets, so what harm would a cup of coffee do? She went downstairs and brewed some of that black mud he called coffee. With a little good-natured pleading, one cup led to another, but he himself stopped it at two.

"Coffee makes you lose water," he said, "and that's not what we want right now. I need to build my fluids back."

Ginny was amazed at how this man took charge of his own recuperation. Almost like he was his own doctor, and she the nurse. She supposed she shouldn't be surprised, because this was how he handled everything.

Josh stood looking down through his bedroom window to the yard below. From his window he had a view of the barn, and if it had been daylight, he would have been looking directly at the corral. At the moment, the yard was lost in almost pitch blackness, as the moon was covered by a rolling sea of clouds. Going to rain tomorrow, he thought. Yet, even though he couldn't really see the yard, he did not have to. He knew every nook and cranny, every rock. Every strand of grass. This was his home.

And as he stood in the window of his bedroom, he knew, after this night, he might never see his home again.

The clock downstairs bonged twelve times. Midnight. Not generally the best time to be hitting the trail, but if you wanted to leave without being seen, it was perhaps the best time.

He was fully dressed. A gray range shirt and tan pants. His Navy Colt was buckled about his hips. On his bed behind him were his bedroll, his saddle bags, and a Winchester.

He didn't want to leave. He felt a pang of sadness strike deep within him that he might never see this place again. But he was the son of Johnny McCabe. A job needed doing, and intended to see it got done.

He draped his saddle bags over his shoulder, and tucked his bedroll under one arm. He snagged his hat from the peg it had been hanging on, and placed it on his head. He then snatched his rifle from the bed, and stepped out into the hallway, placing his feet down lightly so his boot soles would make no sound on the wooden floorboards. He gently shut his door, and then made his way to the hallway.

The house was quiet. Pa was gently sleeping in his room. The door to the guest room, which was now Dusty's, was closed. As was Bree's.

He made it down the stairway, keeping to the edge of the stairs so the boards underfoot would not bow and creak too much. He held the rifle in his left hand, and with his right, he gripped the banister tightly. It wouldn't do for his bad knee to give way, and cause him to stumble on the steps, and attract attention to himself.

The door at the far wall of the large open room was shut. He hoped she was asleep. He didn't want to talk to anyone. He knew they would just try to talk him out of what had to be done.

The large room was dark, but he knew it like he knew the yard outside. Every nook and cranny. He walked past the sofa, and then toward the door. He opened it slowly, and only a couple of feet. He knew about the squealing hinge, and didn't want it to awaken anyone. But he knew this house, and knew the hinge sounded when the door was open about three feet.

With the door open only a couple of feet, he slid sideways out the door, and then gently shut it.

A horse was waiting for him in the stable. Rabbit. Earlier in the evening, he had led Rabbit into a stall, and left him there. He was hoping neither Fred nor Dusty would notice, and neither seemed to.

He struck a match and brought a lantern to life, but kept the light turned down so only a faint, gray light filled this corner of the stable. In the near darkness, he saddled Rabbit. He tied his saddle bags and bedroll to the back of his saddle, tucked the Winchester into the saddle boot, then he blew out the lantern and led Rabbit out into the darkened yard.

He allowed himself one final look at the house. The moon overhead was peaking briefly through an opening in the clouds, allowing him a view of the structure. A large, rectangular house shaped like a cape. Pa had said this was a common design back east, but it was one Josh saw seldom in the west. The walls were made of pine logs, and a stone chimney stood tall.

He then swung into the saddle, and started Rabbit away at a quick walk. He left the ranch behind him.

The following morning, Aunt Ginny took her customary place at the table, with her back to the stove. This had become her chair for practical reasons, so she could jump up and tend to things on the stove as need arose. Bree sat at Ginny's side. Dusty, freshly shaven and wearing a white shirt, and with his Colt Peacemaker holstered at his

side, poured a cup of coffee and walked around the table to take the chair opposite Aunt Ginny.

"I just noticed something," Aunt Ginny said. "I haven't seen Josh this morning. Would someone go upstairs and ask him if he is going to grace us with his presence for breakfast?"

"I'll go," Bree said, and hurried from the kitchen. Dusty and Aunt Ginny could hear her light footsteps as she scurried up the stairs.

"It's not like him to sleep in," Ginny said. "He's usually the first to rise."

"He might need a little more rest. He's still banged up from that fall he took from the roof." Dusty took a sip of coffee. "I think it's going to be a while before life settles back to something close to normal around here."

"It's too bad you and Josh gave each other such bad first impressions. He can be headstrong, but when you get to know him, I think you'll find your brother's a good sort. And right now, we're all going to have to be strong for each other, and there will be no place for dissension."

Dusty didn't want to admit he did not quite know what dissension meant. Patterson had taught him to read and write, but his education never went much past the basics. But he thought he got the general drift of what she was saying. "Yes'm. I'll do my part."

"You know, Dusty, the impression I get is that you generally do."

Bree ran down the stairs, and into the kitchen, eyes wide. "Aunt Ginny! Dusty! Josh is gone."

"What do you mean, gone?" Aunt Ginny asked.

"He's not in his room. His bed hasn't been slept in. and his bedroll and saddle bags are gone."

Dusty glanced to Aunt Ginny. "I'll go to the stable and see if his saddle is still here."

Ginny and Bree followed him out the back door. Beyond them was the meadow where the herd of horses that made up the McCabe remuda lounged, some grazing contentedly, others running about. None of them gave any indication that, just a few nights earlier, the night had exploded in gunfire and death.

At the sight of Dusty and the McCabe women, Pa's chocolate colored stallion reared up with his front hooves kicking at the wind, then he was down on all fours, pacing about, kicking at imaginary targets, letting everyone know he was king. What a magnificent animal, Dusty thought. Pa and Josh were the only two who could ride him, Dusty had been told.

But one horse was not there. Dusty said, "Rabbit's gone."

Aunt Ginny said, "Where could that boy have gone to?"

"I have an idea," Dusty muttered to himself. Indeed he did. He had been having similar thoughts himself.

"What's going on?" Bree asked. "He didn't go after those raiders, did he?"

Dusty nodded. "I think he did."

Aunt Ginny brought a hand to her mouth to stifle the alarm she felt. "He'll be killed."

"No he won't," Dusty said. "I'll go after him."

"But he has a head start," Bree pointed out. "A good one. Maybe six or eight hours."

"Doesn't matter. His trail will be fresh, and easy to follow."

"What if he catches up to the raiders before you catch up to him?"

"He won't. I'll catch up to him first. There are very few men who could leave a trail I couldn't follow. Pa might be one of them, and Zack another. But Josh isn't. I'll catch up to him."

"Dusty," Aunt Ginny said. "You may know more about that sort of man than Josh does, but one of their bullets could kill you just as easily as him. Be careful. I want both of you to return safely."

Dusty gave her a half smile, not knowing quite how to react to concern about his well-being. "I'd best saddle up."

That night, Josh picketed his horse toward the edge of the circle of light cast by his small fire. A kettle rested in the coals, and inside was brewing some trail coffee. He had laid his saddle bags and bedroll near the fire, and from one saddle bag had produced a skillet and a can of beans, and a can opener. He had hoped to have roasted rabbit for supper,

but had seen only two during his day of riding. He had fired at one with his revolver, and missed. When he saw the second one a few hours later, it was maybe five hundred feet away. He decided to go with the rifle as it would be more accurate at that distance, but when he reached for it, the rabbit darted away.

Josh dumped the beans into the skillet. His horse had been grazing quietly, but then suddenly looked up toward the darkness beyond the glow of the fire. Josh had lived on the frontier long enough to know not to ignore a warning sign like that from a horse. Josh casually loosened the pistol in its holster, while continuing to work on his supper.

"Hello, the fire!" a man's voice called from the darkness, in the accepted manner of approaching another's campfire.

Josh recognized the voice. But what would he be doing out here? Josh figured he had put eighteen miles between himself and the ranch today.

"Come on in," Josh called back.

The man stepped forward and into the glow of the fire. It was indeed Dusty, clad once again in his buckskin shirt, with his hat hanging against his back from its chin strap, and his Peacemaker at his side. He was afoot, leading his horse. Dusty's Spencer rifle was in a scabbard, tied to the saddle.

"That coffee smells good," Dusty said with a smile. "Mind sharin' some?"

"Do you mind telling me what you're doing here?"

Dusty shrugged. "Probably the same thing you are."

And he turned his back to Josh and began stripping the gear from his horse.

Josh said, "What I'm doing here is none of your business. You might as well climb back into that saddle and ride back the way you come."

Dusty dropped his saddle to the ground, then approached the fire, holding his hands out to its warmth. "It's gonna be cold tonight. Summer's sure taking its time getting to these mountains."

Josh gave Dusty a sidelong glance, and put the skillet on the fire. He drew his Bowie knife and began stirring the

beans to keep them from burning or sticking to the bottom of the skillet.

"The coffee smells good," Dusty said again.

"Yeah, I heard you the first time. It's almost ready."

Dusty pulled a tin cup from his saddle bags. "You're wrong, you know."

"It's not almost ready?"

"No, I mean you're wrong about it not being any of my business."

"Look, Dusty, I appreciate the help you gave back at the ranch. Not only your gun, but your knowledge too. And maybe you are my brother. I don't know. But..."

Dusty cut him off. "It's not every day you have someone ride up and claim to be your brother. I don't blame anyone for being skeptical, I guess. If you weren't, it would mean you're touched in the head."

"Aunt Ginny's not skeptical."

"But Aunt Ginny's not the one who I'm claiming is my father. And I'm not claiming to be her brother. She might be able to see the situation a little more clearly because she's not as close to it."

Josh let out a sigh, his shoulders sagging a little. "I have to admit, I didn't want to believe you at first. Maybe I still don't. I don't know. A brother I never knew about, because Pa got drunk in a saloon one night."

"How do you think I feel?"

Josh looked from the skillet to Dusty. He had never considered that.

Dusty said, "I never thought I'd find either of my parents. But when I learned my mother was a saloon woman," Dusty could never quite get himself to say saloon woman, not when talking about his mother, "I felt anger at my father even though I didn't know who he was. Anger that he could just ride in, whelp a child, and ride on without ever looking back. But then, I found out he never knew about me. And after I got to know him a little, I've come to really believe he would have come back for me, had he known about me."

"That's the kind of man Pa is."

They were silent for a few moments. Josh continued to stir the beans. Dusty thought the coffee smelled ready, and poured a cup.

"Y'know," Josh said, "I never really knew my mother, either. She was killed when I was only four. Pa said she was a good woman, though. A good mother, and a good wife."

"I can't imagine Pa with any other kind of woman."

"Pa has grieved over her loss every day since. I guess he's never really gotten over it."

"Josh, Aunt Ginny asked me to ride out after you. She wanted me to bring you back."

"You're wasting your time."

"She asked me to bring you back, but that's not what I'm going to try to do. I've been having similar ideas about going after them raiders. This ain't only your problem, Josh. It's ours. I mean to ride with you."

Josh supposed it wouldn't hurt to have a second gun along. And Dusty had proven his loyalty. "All right. As long as you don't get in the way."

"Thanks. I'll try not to," Dusty said, with a little sarcasm and a half-grin. He took another sip of his coffee. "There's one more thing I've got to tell you. Something that's been eating at me since the day after that gunfight. Something about them raiders I haven't told anyone yet."

Josh's brows knit out of curiosity. "Like what?"

"I recognized three of them that we buried. They used to ride with the Sam Patterson gang."

Josh asked slowly, "Just how do you know any members of the Patterson gang?"

"It's a long story."

"We've got a lot of time." The beans were starting to burn, but Josh no longer cared.

And so, Dusty told him the story of how Sam Patterson had taken a small boy from a farm house he and his men had attacked and set on fire. Patterson had intention to deliver him somewhere, anywhere, that a child could be cared for, but never found the opportune moment. Maybe out of circumstance, and maybe out of choice. Maybe the old raider had always wanted a normal life, a family, and knew Dusty was the closest he would ever come to any of that. Either way, he raised the orphan boy, teaching him how to survive, how to shoot. How to trail a man when there was no outwardly visible sign. How to make a fire that would not be seen from a distance. How to find water. And most

importantly, Patterson taught him values he himself had not been able to adhere to.

And now, Dusty had found some of the men who had ridden on the McCabe Ranch were Patterson's men.

"Why didn't you mention any of this earlier?" Josh asked.

"I was trying to win the trust of the family. I didn't think it would be possible if you all knew I had been raised by an outlaw."

"And you don't think the best place to begin earning trust is by telling the whole truth?"

"I guess I was wrong."

Josh nodded. This might explain the nagging feeling he had that there was more to Dusty than was readily apparent. He returned to stirring the beans. "The word making the rounds was that Sam Patterson has disappeared, maybe been killed, and that his gang had broken up. Does this mean they're back together?"

"I don't know what it means," Dusty said. "But I intend to find out."

"If Patterson is still alive, and has reformed his gang, where do you stand?"

"I stand where I am, alongside my brother."

"You claimed that man raised you. You don't feel any loyalty to him?"

"He didn't really raise me. I raised myself. He fed me when I was too young to hunt my own supper, and gave me the tools I need to survive in life, and to live a better life than he did. But I was always aware I had come to be with him because he killed the family I had been living with, and burned their home, and he could have given me to a family to be raised properly, but had chosen not to. I never really considered him my father. A friend, maybe, who I am grateful to because of all he taught me, but never quite a father. When it came time to ride away, I was able to do it without looking back."

"So, even if you had known that was Patterson up in the ridges, you still would have stood by us?"

Dusty nodded. "I might have ridden out to them to try and talk him out of hitting the ranch, but if push came to shove, I would have stood by my family, just like I did."

301

"If Patterson was riding with them, then that means he was one of the ones who escaped. He may have been one of the ones who shot Pa. If that's true, then I aim to shoot him. Where do you stand on that?"

"The reason I was planning to ride after them is because I've got to know if Patterson was indeed with them. And if he was, I'll be the one to take care of him."

THIRTY-THREE

"They didn't put much care in hiding their tracks," Josh said as he and Dusty rode along the side of a lazily sloping ridge, ponderosa pines standing tall about them. "These tracks are almost a week old, but still so easy to read you could almost do it with your eyes closed."

"They had no reason to believe anyone would follow them," Dusty said, his Stetson pulled low to shade his eyes from the sunlight slipping through the bows overhead. "When they rode away from the ranch, we didn't make any immediate attempts to come after them, so they probably figured we were hurt too bad."

"This trail has been going south since I first picked it up, and they've been keeping a steady pace. Almost like they're heading to someplace in particular."

Dusty nodded. "It seems that way, doesn't it?"

The trail took Dusty and Josh to a small rocky ravine, probably a stream bed in the spring, Dusty figured, and then onto a second ridge. The trail continued down from the ridge and into a small valley of tall mountain grass, with scattered birch and aspen.

They reined up at the rim of the valley, and Josh said, "Beautiful, ain't it?"

Dusty nodded.

"There's places like this all through the mountains. I figure I'll one day take over the ranch from Pa, when he's older. But there are times I've thought I might want to find me a good woman someday, white or Injun, it doesn't matter as long as she's got a lot of sand, and build me a cabin in a place like this little valley, and raise young'uns. I would pick a place deep enough into the mountains so the white man will be a long time in bringing his rules and laws that can tie a man down."

Dusty said, "You'd be a long haul from any town."

"That'd be fine. You wouldn't need many supplies, because you could live off the land. There's deer, elk, moose and bear that could last you a lifetime. And fish in the streams. You could put in a small patch of corn.

"A good woman to stand by me, and raise a family with me. Sometimes I think if I got me that and a place like this, I'd never look back."

"Y'know, Josh? I'm starting to suspect there's more to you than meets the eye."

Josh snorted with disgust at his own sudden burst of sentimentalism, and started his horse down a game trail that led into the valley.

They found the remains of a camp near a small spring. The leaves that had fallen from the aspens in previous years and now covered the earth in a layer of mulch had been cleared away, and in their place were the charred remains of a campfire.

"They don't seem worried about being followed at all," Josh said.

Dusty shook his head. "It's like I said. And yet, they're not wandering aimlessly. They're definitely riding somewhere in particular."

They dismounted to rest the horses, and filled their canteens from the spring.

"You'd think," Josh said, "that they would ride north for Canada. Get beyond the reach of the law, in case a territorial marshal went after them."

"It was never Patterson's way. When I was with him, he kept his activities mostly to Texas and New Mexico Territory, and kept a hide-out in the Rockies. Patterson found a small canyon, with only a narrow pass for an entrance, and with steep rock walls all round it, and he built a cabin. The canyon was easy enough to find if you knew where to look, but it was high up in the mountains, and you needed a mountain horse to get there. Patterson kept a remuda of mountain horses only, just for that reason.

"He and his men would sit back drinking whiskey and eating steak taken from rustled steers while the law ran itself ragged trying to find him. He even invited a photographer to the hideout once to take a picture of him and the men, he was so cock-sure the law would never find him. One time he found out a journalist had come west from New York City to do a write-up on the Patterson Gang, and Sam met him in Denver and escorted him blind-folded to the hide-out, so he and the men could be interviewed.

"More than one outlaw rode south into Mexico for safety, just like up in this territory they ride north to Canada, but Patterson told me that kind of safety is never a sure thing. A U.S. Marshal would have no jurisdiction in Mexico or Canada, but an imaginary line like a border would never stop a bounty hunter, and the Texas Rangers have crossed into Mexico illegally more than once to bring back outlaws.

"If Patterson is the leader of this group we're chasing, then I'd bet the law eventually forced him out of his hide-out, and he's come north to set up his operations here. I'd bet he's found another canyon or a small valley somewhere in these mountains."

As Dusty spoke, his eye caught sudden motion in the tall grass of a meadow that began at the edge of the spring and stretched away for a couple hundred yards.

"What's wrong?" Josh asked, kneeling by the spring, filling his final canteen.

"I saw something."

Josh rose to his feet. "What?"

"I don't know."

Blades of grass suddenly moved, and a gray furry head with long ears popped suddenly into view.

Dusty smiled. "How would you like something other than beans tonight? Not that the beans were bad, but they ain't my first choice."

"Good luck," Josh said. "I had two chances to avoid eating beans, and missed both of 'em."

"How far away do you think he is?"

Josh shrugged. "Maybe a hundred feet. You'd better get the rifle. He's close enough for a good head shot."

"Nope. He's looking right at me. If I move, he's gonna skitter away."

"You're gonna try a pistol shot?"

Dusty nodded.

Josh snorted a chuckle. "Like I said, good luck."

Dusty drew a breath and slowly let it out, trying to remember everything Pa had told him a few days ago about pistol shooting. To try for a smooth motion more than speed, cocking the pistol as you grab it, to bring your arm to full extension, to use one well-placed shot rather than scattering three or four.

Dusty's pistol leaped into his hand. The rabbit bolted. With his arm at full extension, he fired. The rabbit dropped.

"I don't believe it!" Josh exclaimed with a grin.

Dusty holstered the smoking pistol, and he and Josh ran into the grass beyond the spring. They found the bullet had shattered the rabbit's skull, but spared all of the meat.

"What a shot!" Josh said.

"Not many men can say they outdrew a rabbit."

They camped in a wooded ravine ten miles southwest of the valley where Dusty had shot the rabbit. The horses were picketed where they could graze, but still be within the glow of firelight. Josh reclined against an old lightning struck trunk, chewing a roasted rabbit leg to the bone. Dusty rested back on his rolled out bedding, his saddle used as a pillow.

"Roasted rabbit," Josh said with relish, "does indeed beat a can of beans."

"Pretty good shooting, eh?"

Josh tossed the rabbit bone over his shoulder. That was the last of the rabbit meat, and his belly, like Dusty's, was full. "I've got to admit, you're faster'n I'll ever be."

"You've got to be fast," Dusty said, suddenly serious, "if you plan on shooting Patterson. I don't believe bushwacking a man is your style, which means you'll have to face him if you're going to shoot him. I've seen him draw on a man before, and he's mighty fast."

"Faster'n you?"

Dusty shook his head. "No." He said it not like he was bragging, but simply stating a fact. "I've met only one man faster'n me, and that's Pa. Even though Pa doesn't want to admit it. That shooting he did when we were target practicing, that border shift he pulled off, it was the best I've ever seen."

"Is Patterson faster than me?" Josh asked.

Dusty nodded. "I ain't seen him in a few years, and a lot can happen in that time, but he was really fast with a gun."

Josh shrugged. "Well, I've still got'ta face him. No matter how fast he is."

"No, you don't. Let me face him. I want to take him down for this as much as you do. Maybe even more."

Josh shook his head. "Nope. He's mine. It's something I've gotta do. I understand how you feel, but this goes deeper than just being mad at him."

Dusty sat up. "What is it, then?"

"You don't know what it was like growing up in that man's shadow. I'm not just anyone's son, I'm Johnny McCabe's. The man was as well known as Wild Bill Hickok even before I was old enough to walk. How can I ever expect to match up to a legend that's even bigger than the man himself?"

"Why do you feel you have to?"

"Because if I'm ever going to be anything in this life, if I'm ever going to be my own man, then I've got to come out from the shadow. And he casts a mighty big one."

"How about our other brother? Jack? Does he feel the same way?"

Josh shook his head. "I don't think so. Jack always had a sort of independent streak in him. He took to book learning like a natural. His world will be back east, in a big city. Boston, or somewhere. He'll be a doctor. He'll marry, and raise kids in a town house, or somewhere like that. Nothing that happens out here will probably seem all that relevant to him."

"I hope to meet him too, someday."

"You'll probably get your chance this summer. That is, presuming you and I live through this to return home. He usually visits for two or three weeks in July or August, before the new semester starts."

Dusty was silent a moment. Then he said, "You know, in trying to get out from Pa's shadow, you might get yourself killed."

"Then, I'll die like a man."

"You'll still be just as dead."

Dusty lay back down on the bedroll, his head resting on the saddle. "It seems to me a man has enough to do in life just trying to be himself, without trying to compare himself to anyone else."

"Sometimes, I guess I feel like I can't be myself, like just having the name means so much more is expected of me. Sometimes, I wonder if I'm up to it."

"Maybe it's time to stop trying to be what everyone expects, and start being what you want."

Josh sighed. "Maybe I just don't know what that is."

Shortly after sunrise, they rode down a rocky barren slope, following the trail left by the raiders. Dusty's hat hung from the chin strap, bouncing against his shoulder blades.

He asked, "What's it like growing up in the McCabe household? Last night you made it sound like it wasn't very pleasant. Like you had a lot of pressure on you as a child."

"No. At least, not from Pa and Aunt Ginny. I'll never forget the look of dread on her face the first time I strapped on a gun. She knows Pa has ridden a rough trail, and knows it's only natural for his son to do the same, but I think she was still hoping for something different for me. Like maybe school back east, like Jack. She used to talk about me maybe studying law."

A chuckle burst from Dusty. "You? Law?"

Josh was smiling. He nodded.

"With your temper? I could just see you in court, pounding the stuffing out of the opposing lawyer."

"No kidding, huh? But no, the pressure was there, but it didn't come from them. It came from others. I don't think Pa or Aunt Ginny were even all that aware of it. But every time I stepped into a saddle, the boys on the ranch expected me to handle the horse like I was an expert horseman, because Pa was. When I was ten and was thrown by a horse, I remember Reno, one of the men who used to work for us, saying, 'he ain't like his old man, is he?'"

"I think it's a dang lot to expect a ten-year-old to ride like a full-grown man who's been in the saddle all his life."

Josh nodded. "But at ten years old, I didn't think that way. I felt I was less than Pa, and it made me feel bad. One day, when I was twelve or thirteen, and missed a rabbit with my squirrel gun, Hunter said, 'I guess you're not quite the shot your old man is.' He didn't mean anything bad by it. Hunter is one of the finest men I've ever known. But still, the words stung. They hurt down deep. Even now, I find myself pushing, always trying to go the extra step, trying to be worthy of being called Johnny McCabe's son."

"Is that why you lit out after these raiders alone?"

Josh nodded. "I guess that's part of it."

Josh looked to Dusty. "I ain't never talked about any of this to anyone before. I'd appreciate it if it didn't go any further."

"It won't."

They rode in silence for a half mile. The ridge bottomed out onto a flat, grassy expanse. The tracks were very plain here, as the earth was dry. In places, entire chunks of sod had been kicked up by the pounding of hooves.

Dusty said, "What was it like when you were growing up? What was the family life like?"

Josh went on to paint him a picture of life in the McCabe household. Despite the pressure he felt from the outside world, the home itself was filled with the glow of love, and of the rock-solid feeling of peace that comes with knowing your mother and father, or in this case, Pa and Aunt Ginny, are there to protect you, to pick you up when you fall, to keep out the evil of the world. And most importantly, to know that they love you, not for what you do or don't do, or say or don't say, but simply for who you are. That might be the most important thing a parent can do for a child.

Josh had a few faint memories of the ranch house in California. It had outer walls of adobe. He remembered a parlor, off of which was a kitchen and a bedroom which was Ma and Pa's. A loft was built over the parlor, which served as a bedroom for Josh and Jack. A small bunkhouse outside was built, and was where Zack Johnson, Uncle Josiah and Hunter slept.

"The house itself was an old hacienda, part of an old Spanish land grant that had been abandoned back in the forties, when Mexico lost California in the war, and a lot of the Spanish deeds were ruled null and void. Ma and Pa fixed it up, and added the outbuildings."

"How did she die?" Dusty asked.

"Shot in the ranch yard one afternoon. The way it was told to me, she was walking toward Pa with a basket of eggs on her arm. The shot was fired from atop a small hill beyond the barn. A large caliber rifle, like Pa's Sharps. Or that old Hawken. She died in his arms, while whoever shot her just rode away, scott-free.

"Pa, Zack and Uncle Joe rode after him after Ma was buried, sort of like we are now, but when they were a few days out, there was a hard rain that washed the trail clean away. They never found him.

"It was shortly after that when Pa moved us all north, to the valley we now call home. I don't know if we were the first white settlers in that part of Montana, but we were firmly settled in by the time of the big gold strikes at Grasshopper Creek and Alder Gulch."

Josh gave a sort of sad sigh. "Pa was saddened by the news of the gold strikes, and the towns of Bannock and Virginia City and Miles Town that boomed to life as settlers flooded in to pan for gold, and to dig for it. The town of Helena, which used to be Last Chance Gulch, is only a few days ride from the ranch. A couple years ago, the town at McCabe Gap began to spring to life. Only a stage stop for now, but it's growing, and it's only three miles from the house. Pa, he always liked the feeling of total freedom that comes with living in a stretch of wilderness far from any white settlement. He doesn't even like McCabe Gap being so close to the house. Even that little town is too big for him. He finds civilization makes him feel hemmed in. That's where I get it, I guess.

"One night, sitting in front of the fire, Pa said that with every settler who rides north along the Bozeman Trail into Montana, or who rides the river boats north along the Missouri up from St. Lou', a little more of that freedom slips away. One day, he said, even here in Montana, barbed wire fences and no-trespassing signs will divide the land. People will cut the land up into sections, and the freedom to just ride through the mountains and camp where you had a mind to will be gone."

The trail came out onto a well-worn wagon road, where the tracks mixed with those of many others.

"This is a stage route," Josh said. "I've been through here once, with Pa. We're about a day and a half north of Bozeman. But last I knew, there was a mining camp between here and there."

The tracks of the raiders seemed to disappear on the stage road, because the dirt was so hard packed.

"I guess we can ride along the trail a ways," Dusty said. "See if they turned off anywhere."

They rode in silence for a stretch. Dusty tossed a glance toward Josh, wondering at the depth of this newly revealed side of his brother. He would have guessed, by Josh's bravado and posturing, that his interests ran no deeper than gulping mugs of beer at Hunter's, getting into a brawl, and occasionally having a night with one of Alisha Summers' girls.

Dusty said, "You know, you're not an easy guy to like, but maybe Aunt Ginny was right. You are worth getting to know."

Josh frowned a bit. "I don't know if that was a compliment, or if I should be offended."

Dusty gave a half smirk. "Maybe a little bit of both. Come on, let's ride."

THIRTY-FOUR

The town was called Midas, after the name of a local mine, the shafts of which spider-webbed their through a nearby ridge. Josh and Dusty let their horses move along at a loping walk. Either side of the street was lined with canvas tents, each serving as a house for a miner and his family. Children ran and played, splashing through the muddy streets. Women worked scrubbing laundry against washboards or hanging wet clothes on a line, the face of each woman lined beyond her years from a life of too much hard work.

"Don't matter where you are," Josh said. "California, Colorado, or here. Mining towns all look the same."

"I didn't get to see too many down in Arizona and New Mexico Territory," Dusty said. "Mostly ranching and farming down there. After seeing this, I count myself lucky."

"Maybe we should stop and ask some questions. The riders didn't seem to turn off the trail at all, which means they must have ridden through here. Maybe someone saw them. Hell, maybe they're here right now."

"There must be a saloon in this town."

"There is in most towns."

"Maybe we could stop there and ask some questions. Saloons are always the best clearing house for information. And I could use a beer to wash down some of this trail dust."

Josh and Dusty reined up before the only building made of wood, though it appeared to have been slapped together hastily, with an uneven roof line, a door jamb that was a full inch lower on one side than the other, and gaps between some of the boards on the wall large enough for a man to push a finger through. Painted above the doorway in black letters was PICK & SHOVEL SALOON.

Compared to the brightness of the cloudless sky outside, they found the barroom dim, lighted only by two windows at the front wall and a coal lamp mounted behind the bar. The lamp emitted a foul smelling smoke, more so than most such lamps. A man with a long, snarled beard falling over the front of a dirty undershirt stood behind the bar. Suspenders were strapped over each of his shoulders,

and a soot and grease stained apron was tied about his round belly.

"What can I get for you gents?" he asked in a thin and raspy voice, through a toothless smile.

"Beer's fine for me," Josh said, and looked to Dusty.

"Make that two," Dusty said.

"Got no beer. Waiting for the afternoon stage."

"Then, make it whiskey, I guess."

"Two whiskeys it is," the barkeep said. He placed two glasses on a plank that stood on two upended beer kegs, which passed for a bar, and dumped brownish liquid into them from an unlabeled bottle.

Josh counted eight empty tables filling the small barroom floor. The only other occupant of the place was a saloon woman standing at the bar. She looked like she was about Josh's age, maybe a little older. It was difficult to gauge because of the war paint caked on her face. Her lips were an unnatural red, her face a chalky white, and her cheekbones were painted a rosy hue. Her brows were dark and plucked pencil thin, and some sort of shade of blue had been plastered over her eyelids. Her hair was an odd artificial sort of platinum color. Not the kind of woman Aunt Ginny would invite to a quilting bee.

Dusty sampled his drink, and held back a grimace. If he should ask, the barkeep would probably claim this was sour mash, but Dusty would have bet it was rubbing alcohol, with a touch of kerosene to give it a kick. He decided not to ask, because he and Josh were here to pursue more important questions, and a man standing accused of selling rubbing alcohol for whiskey would not be as willing to volunteer answers.

It was Josh who spoke first. "I suppose you see just about everybody who passes through."

The snarled beard bobbed up and down. "Yessir. Thet I do."

"You didn't happen to see a group of riders come through town three or four days ago, did you?"

The barkeep's glance darted to the girl, then back again. So quick, Dusty would have missed it if he had but blinked. But he did not miss it.

"What kind of riders?" the old man asked casually. He was trying very hard to seem casual.

"They weren't drifters," Dusty said. "They would have been wearing guns like they knew how to use them. And they would have looked like they've been on the trail a few days."

"Sort of like you boys."

Josh glanced at Dusty. He was not sure what to make of the comparison.

Josh took a sip of the whiskey. Dusty could see he was doing his best to hold back a grimace, also.

"These boys might have had a woman with them, too," Josh said, thinking of the smallish shoe print that had been found among the tracks made by the raiders. "Any chance they could have stopped here?"

The barkeep shook his head. "Ore wagons and stage coaches have been all that's come through in weeks. You boys are the first strangers."

Dusty looked down to his drink. There was no way he would be able to finish it. No matter. The need for politics was over. The barkeep had told them nothing—and yet, he had told them everything.

The saloon girl was leaning back with her elbows propped against the bar behind her. This caused her shoulders to curve forward a bit, and her dress fell from them, adding to the inviting look she was trying to muster for Josh. She let a smile drift his way, and he returned it with a grin of his own.

"How about you?" he asked. "You see any riders come through here? Maybe in the last day or two?"

She shrugged. "None that I can remember."

"Try to remember."

"Buy me a drink?" she asked.

Josh shook his head. "I don't think so. Nothing against you, but this stuff could pass for rat poison."

"Hey," the barkeep said. "This is some of the best moonshine available. I paid top dollar for it."

"You got cheated." Josh returned his gaze to the girl. Despite the heavy make-up, which Josh usually found less than inviting, there was something almost pretty about her.

"My name's Felicia."

"Pleased to meet you, Felicia," Josh said. "Maybe I'll buy you that drink some other time. We have a lot of miles to cross, and not a lot of daylight left."

Josh and Dusty made camp at the base of a wooded hill a mile or so from town. Dusty sat with his back against the trunk of a large cedar, a tin cup filled with coffee in one hand.

"Josh," Dusty said, "I have me an idea our search is about to end. I think those raiders have a camp somewhere within riding distance of this town."

"And what makes you think that?" Josh was stirring some life into the fire. Looked like another night of beans. They were down to their final can.

"Partly a gut feeling. I've learned not to ignore a gut feeling. But also, I think that old barkeep lied."

"And why would you think that?"

"Because anyone who would try to sell that concoction as drinkable moonshine is a born liar. And because I don't believe a man on the trail is going to pass up a saloon woman he can buy a drink for. And since I know the way outlaws live, or at least Sam Patterson and his boys, they would never pass up a situation like that."

"Would men on the run take the time to dally around at a saloon?"

"They would have no way of knowing we are following them, so there's no reason for them not to take their time."

Dusty took a sip of his coffee and continued. "I have to wonder if somewhere in those ridges west of town there might be a canyon that would suit their purposes, like that old one Patterson used back when I was a kid. If I'm right, then they're at their hideout now, nursing their wounds. Maybe riding into town once in a while to visit the saloon, and the women that work there. One thing Sam taught me, you have to get to know your enemy, learn the way he thinks. And part of that is learning his habits. And a man doesn't often change his habits. "

Josh nodded. "Of course, if they do have a hideout somewhere in these hills, and they're frequent patrons of that saloon, and that barkeep would lie for them, and presumably

the saloon girl did too, then you can bet Patterson and the boys know we are following them, now."

Dusty nodded. "That means we're going to have to be more careful."

"I have to admit," Josh said, "and this ain't easy for me, I'm glad you came along. I ain't had a lot experience at trailing a man. I would be out of my league, here."

"I haven't had much experience with it, either, really. But I've been on the other end of the hunt a lot."

"Well, now is the time to put to use all you learned from Patterson." Josh pulled the can of beans from his saddle bags. "This is it. The last can. Either we shoot us a rabbit tomorrow, or we'll be sleeping on empty stomachs."

"We could always eat at that saloon," Dusty said with a grin.

Josh returned the grin. "I don't think so. He'd be likely to serve us rat, and try to pass it off as chicken."

"I wonder what kind of wine Aunt Ginny would want to serve with that?"

Josh chuckled. "So, you think we should figure Patterson knows we're following him, and who we are?"

"I think it would be best to err on the side of caution, as Patterson used to say. But he may not know exactly who we are. For all they know, we might be lawmen, or bounty hunters. Of course, you can bet Patterson knew which ranch he was hitting, and who it belonged to. He's gotta expect anyone trailing him could be gunhawks from that ranch."

Dusty took another sip of coffee. "You know something that bothers me? Patterson was always so careful in everything he did. He seemed brazen to some, but there was always a shrewd caution in his brazenness. He never took unnecessary chances, especially with his own life, or the lives of the men riding with him. He took his responsibility to them seriously."

Josh nodded. "Any good leader would have to." He stirred the beans around the skillet with his Bowie knife.

"And part of that caution always involved advanced scouting."

"He sure scouted the ranch extensively. Watching us from the ridges using a spyglass. He took his time, probably

making sure he had all the information he needed. Even sent a man in as a spy."

"That's my point. He had to know this was the ranch of Johnny McCabe. He has to know what Pa is capable of. And anyone who knows anything about Johnny McCabe knows that where he is, Zack Johnson is never far away. And even if he didn't know I was there, he had to know you are there. And despite what you might think, you are very much the son of our father. No one is going to take you lightly."

Josh let those words sink in. He had to admit, they felt mighty good.

"So, my question is," Dusty continued, "why would he even bother to attack the ranch the way he did? He must have known Pa and Zack would have a small army put together, waiting for the attack. He had to have seen Zack and Fred and the others crossing the valley, from Zack's place to ours. Yet he rode in anyway."

"Got caught in a crossfire. Half of his men got killed."

"In the time I was with them, they never had a casualty count that high. Once, a man got killed when a shotgun rider on a stagecoach cut loose with a load of buckshot, and tore him apart. A couple other times, men got wounded. But Patterson planned so far in advance, planning for all the contingencies, as he called it. The element of surprise was your biggest strength, he always said. And yet, he had to know we'd be waiting for him."

Josh shrugged. "Getting careless in his old age?"

"We're going to find out. And I think we're going to find out soon." Dusty got to his feet, and went over to the fire to refill his cup. "Come morning, we're going to ride in a wide circle around that little mud hole of a town, and cut for sign. I'll bet we're going to find the tracks we're looking for, leading into the mountains."

"And what happens when we find their hideout?"

"Then, things will get really interesting."

They ate their beans. Dusty from an old, battered tin plate, and Josh directly from the skillet.

As darkness settled upon the land Dusty stretched out on his unrolled bedding with his saddle under his head. Josh sat on a fallen log he had rolled near the fire. He held a twig

in the flames until its end caught fire, then removed it and watched the tiny flame flicker until it died away.

"You know," Josh said, "if we're as close to the raiders' hideout as you think we might be, we should be more careful riding tomorrow. Especially after we find their trail."

Dusty nodded. "And this should probably be our last campfire. These foothills are a lot more open than the mountains the ranch is in. A fire could be visible for quite a distance."

Dusty was about to kick off his boots and crawl into his bedroll when a horse whickered from somewhere in the darkness beyond the rim of firelight.

"Sioux?" Josh asked.

"If they were, we wouldn't have heard them."

Dusty slowly, casually, slid his pistol from the holster, moving so as not to let on to whoever was out there that he and Josh were aware of their presence. Josh just as casually rose to his feet and strolled to his saddle.

"I think I might turn in," Josh said as he moved. "Morning's going to come mighty early."

"That it is," Dusty replied. "I was thinking the same thing myself."

Josh slid the Winchester from his saddle, then dove behind the cover of a cedar, landing in a shoulder roll and coming to a kneeling position behind the trunk of the tree, his hat skittering away somewhere in the darkness behind him. Dusty sprang to his feet and leaped behind the log Josh had been sitting on. Lying prone, Dusty raised his head until his eyes were above the edge of the log, and he held his pistol ready for use.

Josh jacked a cartridge into the rifle's chamber. He called out in a gravelly roar, "Whoever you are, we know you're out there!"

A female voice, sounding vulnerable and a little scared out in the darkness, called back, "Don't shoot. I'm coming in."

She rode forward. Platinum hair caught the dim firelight and almost glowed, telling Dusty and Josh it was the girl from the Pick and Shovel, before she was close enough for them to even see her face. Her saloon-woman dress had been replaced with a simple blouse and a skirt, and she sat

astride the saddle. She held the reins in one hand like an experienced rider.

"It's okay," she said. "I'm alone."

"What are you doing out here?" Josh asked as he stepped out from behind the tree. Dusty stood also, and holstered his pistol.

"I had to see you both," she said. "It's really important."

Josh leaned his rifle against his saddle, and took one of her hands as she swung down from the saddle.

"You set a horse like you know how to ride," Josh said.

"I was raised at an Army post. My father was a cavalry sergeant."

Josh looked at her incredulously. "Then, what are you doing in that town?"

Dusty said, "We have time for her life story later. What I want to know is, what's so important it'll send a girl riding a mile out into the darkness alone?"

"I had to come alone. There was no other way. If anyone knew I had come out here, all three of us would be killed."

As she spoke, she folded her arms tightly about her, rubbing each shoulder with the opposite hand.

"Are you cold?" Josh asked.

"The night is turning off a little chilly," she replied. "I guess I didn't dress properly for it."

Josh pulled a faded blue jean jacket from his saddle bags. He motioned for her to sit on the log, and then draped the jacket about her shoulders.

"Dusty," he said. "Why don't you see if we have any coffee left? And toss some more wood on the fire. Get it burning big and warm."

Dusty dropped a piece of a dead branch into the fire, dropping it hard enough so sparks would fly. Josh glanced at Dusty with surprise at the sudden shower of sparks, and Dusty gave Josh a look that said he did not appreciate being a go-fer.

As Dusty was draining the last of the coffee into Josh's cup, the girl said, "Felicia's not my real name. It just sounds like the kind of woman who would be able to get men a-wantin'. My real name is Sarah-Ann."

"You don't need a fancy name to get men a-wantin'," Josh said.

She gave him a pleased smile.

Dusty rolled his eyes with disbelief, and handed her the coffee.

"Do you mind if we call you Sarah-Ann?" Josh asked.

"I think I'd like that. It's been so long since anyone called me that," she said a little sadly.

"Look," Dusty said. "I don't mean to seem rude, but I have to wonder what you're doing out here, alone, at this time of night."

"I came here to warn you. Go back where you come from," she said gently. "There'll only be trouble if you stay in this area. Real trouble."

"You don't even know us. And yet you're risking your life to ride out here?"

"It's just that, I know what those men are capable of. You two seem like good sorts. I just don't want to see them hurt anyone else." She took a sip of coffee. "I can't stay long. If they even suspect I rode out to talk to you, they'll shoot me."

"Who would?" Josh asked.

"Flossy Knight, the woman I work for. And her beau, Victor Falcone."

"Vic Falcone?" Dusty asked.

She gave him her full attention now. "You know him?"

Dusty was careful with his reply. "I know the name. He rides with..." he hesitated a moment while he appeared to search his memory for a name, "...Sam Patterson, doesn't he?"

She nodded. "That's him. Only now, he's got his own gang together. I've never met Sam Patterson. Vic and the boys have a hideout somewhere in these hills."

"How do you know that?"

"Flossy has them bring us girls to the hideout sometimes for...for..." she stopped as if she could not bear to speak the word, and lowered her head in shame.

"Those-sons-of-a-," Josh visibly erupted, and almost made a show of keeping his temper in check.

Dusty had to hold back a grin. He had already seen Josh's temper enough to know when it was real. Just be careful, he thought. Don't over-act.

Josh said, "Could you lead us to their hide-out?"

She shook her head. "Whenever they take us there, they always blind-fold us."

"How do they take you? Wagon or horseback?"

"By horseback. A wagon couldn't make it over the trail."

"How long does it take you to get there from town?"

She shrugged. "Three hours, maybe."

Dusty stepped away to think for a moment, one hand rubbing his bristly chin unconsciously.

"They're afraid of you boys," she said.

"Why?" Josh asked.

"Because of the way you carry those guns, and the fact that you asked about them as soon as you rode into town."

Josh shrugged. "Well, we'll make sure and be careful."

"Please do." She gave him a smile.

She handed him the coffee cup. "I really should be heading back to town."

"You took a risk coming out here," Josh said.

"Not really. I often ride alone at night, when business is slow, to clear my mind."

She climbed back into the saddle, and handed him back his jacket.

"You ride careful, now," Josh said. "Take care of yourself."

"I always do."

She turned the horse out of the ring of firelight, and once her hoofbeats had disappeared into the distance, Josh said, "Well, now. We've met a vamp named Felicia, and a shy farm girl named Sarah-Ann. Two for the price of one."

Dusty said, "If she's telling the truth, then that might explain why they were careless when they attacked the ranch. Vic has leadership skills, but never was as thorough as Sam in his thinking."

"Even if this Vic Falcone is the one in charge now, and he's as careless as you remember, would he be stupid enough to have sent a girl out riding into the night alone just

to pry information out of us? It seems like kind of an elaborate thing to do."

"Yeah. He might. The thing about being on the run, it makes you wary. Maybe overly so. And you sometimes take foolish chances. The interest you seemed to show in the girl, back at the saloon, might have made Vic think sending her out here would be a good idea. What he did, though, was tip his hand. Because, now we know for sure he and the boys are in the area. It was a mistake I don't think Sam would have made. Underestimating your opponent can get you killed."

"So, what's next?"

Dusty grabbed his bedroll and began to roll it. "Grab your gear. We're getting out of here. We'll ride a while, then set up another camp."

"Why?"

"Precaution. And we'll make cold camp tonight. We'll bank this fire good so it will burn long into the night and give anyone out there something to look at while we ride away. In the morning, before we start cutting for sign, we'll take us a little ride back this way. You might find it educational."

By sun-up, they were already saddled up and riding, heading back to their first camp of the night before. The earth in and around their camp was littered with a scattered collection of hoofprints and bootprints.

"You can see they tried to pay us a visit last night," Dusty said. "They waited out there in the darkness, giving us time to go to sleep. Then they charged the campfire."

"That's a second time they underestimated us."

"We can't keep banking on them doing that, though. We can't afford the luxury of underestimating them."

Josh could seem, among the boot prints made by the men, was a set of smaller tracks. They matched the smallish bootprints he and Pa had seen at the raider's camp, back in the ridges that rimmed their valley.

Josh said, "These tracks look like they were made by maybe a woman. Must have been Felicia."

Dusty nodded. "She probably didn't ride out alone. These men held back, maybe a half mile out, while she rode into our camp alone. Then they held back and waited."

"Come on," Josh said. "Let's go find their hide-out."

THIRTY-FIVE

The trail created by the woman who called herself both Felicia and Sarah-Ann, and the men who rode with her, moved its way into town. Josh and Dusty followed the trail until they reined up on a low grassy hill overlooking the tents and ramshackle buildings that were Midas.

"So," Josh said. "Looks like those riders might have spent the night right down there in town. And they might be there now. Maybe we should check it out."

"No, you're not riding down there," Dusty said.

Josh looked at him. "Why not?"

"Because, here's where we part company. You're turning back for the ranch."

"Not likely."

Dusty twisted in the saddle to face him. "Josh, this is pointless. You've got too much to lose. Those men down there are professionals. You're good with a gun, better than most, but you're not a professional killer. They all are. Go back home. Aunt Ginny and Bree need you. Go back. Run the ranch with Pa. Live the life you're meant to live."

"And what are you going to do?"

"I'm going do what I have to."

"And why is it all right for you?"

"Because, it's my fight."

"Wait a minute." Josh's shoulders sagged a bit with exasperation. One thing Dusty had noticed about him—very expressive body language. You knew where you stood with him, what he was thinking, but he would never survive in a poker game. "How is this your fight, and not mine?"

"Because, I know those men. I have to make certain Patterson really wasn't with them when they hit the ranch. It looks like he wasn't, but I have to make sure. And even so, they have to know I was there at the ranch. They were watching it closely enough to have seen me. This gives us a score we have to settle."

Josh looked down toward the town, and sat in silence for a few moments. Then he looked back to Dusty. "It means a lot to me to measure up to being his son. Maybe too much. I don't know. But I could never call myself his son if I let my brother ride down there alone. Face it, Dusty. You rode onto

324

the ranch to find your family, and you succeeded. I'm not the only one who has to make some adjustments. You have to learn you're not just a lone wolf anymore. We're McCabes, and we ride together."

"It's going to be rough. We may not get out alive."

Josh shrugged. "Life can be like that."

"What about Aunt Ginny and Bree?"

"They have Pa. He'll take care of them when he's recuperated. And they have Zack, and Hunter, and Fred. And they have Jack. They'll be all right."

Dusty smiled and nodded. "All right, brother. But we're not riding into town. I think staying with our first plan is the better idea. Follow me."

They cut a wide circle around town, searching for tracks that would have been made by the three riders who had been with the girl. Tracks made by the riders on their way to town from the ridges.

In a set of low grassy hills south of town, they found a line of hoof prints pressed into the dry earth. The riders had been holding to single-file, which made it impossible to guess their number.

Josh and Dusty reined up and sat alongside each other, examining the tracks from the saddle.

"What do you think?" Josh asked.

"It's them."

"Probably. But how can you tell for certain? There might be more than one group of riders moving about these hills. I'd hate to spend all morning following the wrong set of tracks."

"It's them," Dusty said. "Why else would they ride single-file?"

"That doesn't necessarily mean anything. Pa always had us ride single-file. Just to be on the safe side. So anyone coming on our trail wouldn't be able to tell it was just two riders and think we might be easy prey."

"You don't think that way unless you have a reason to. Pa probably learned that with the Texas Rangers. But most folks wouldn't think to do that. A group of cowhands leaving town and returning to their ranch probably wouldn't. Besides," Dusty said, turning from the trail to look Josh in

the eye, "manhunting isn't all that different from hunting a deer. A lot of it's instinct. And mine tells me this is the trail."

Josh nodded. "All right. Lead the way."

The trail swung southward, away from town. Dusty and Josh followed it for a mile, where it turned southwest, then directly west, and led them deeper into the foothills. The low grassy hills soon gave way to steeper slopes scattered with junipers and an occasional pine or cedar. About noon, the trail turned north and followed a line of ridges, then after a mile, swung west again.

Josh and Dusty stopped in a grassy ravine to let their horses blow. They dismounted and each loosened the cinch.

"You wouldn't think they knew where they were going at all," Josh said. "The way the trail winds around through these hills. It almost seems aimless."

"Oh yeah, they know where they're going." Dusty was removing the canteen he had slung over the saddle horn. "They're cutting back and forth, zig-zagging, so there won't be a clear direction toward where they're going."

Josh took his own a canteen from his saddle and took a sip. "So, tell me about this Vic Falcone."

"He was Sam's right-hand-man for the last couple of years I was with them. Falcone wasn't the worst of the lot, but he had nothing against shooting a man in the back during a robbery to prevent that man from pointing a finger at him later. But Patterson wouldn't allow that sort of thing. They didn't come much harder than Falcone, but he was afraid of Patterson."

"But you said he wasn't the worst of the bunch?"

Dusty shook his head. "That honor would go to a cutthroat named Kiowa Haynes.

"Can't say I've ever heard of him."

"That's because you grew up here in Montana. If you had been in Texas or New Mexico, you would have heard the name. He got it from what a Kiowa did to his face with a knife, years ago. He was the most dangerous man I've ever known. They say he'd skin a man alive just to hear him scream, and I believe it. And he was even worse to a woman. He's actually part Apache, and rode with 'em for a few years when he was younger. But to an Apache warrior, honor is

everything, even more precious than life itself. There was no honor in Kiowa Haynes, and they say he was banished from the tribe."

"Why'd Patterson ever let him ride with him?"

"Because he's a top notch scout, and a good man to have on your side in a fight, and one of the worst when he's not. You can bet Pa has heard of him."

"How did Patterson keep him in line?"

"As dangerous as Haynes is, he's no match for Patterson with a gun. And when it comes to fighting with fists or a knife, Haynes was more savage, but he never dared challenge Sam. Old Sam always had this sort of quiet confidence about him. I think Haynes just wasn't sure, and didn't want to take the chance."

Dusty tipped his canteen for a sip. "Kiowa Haynes is the second reason I'm out here, trailing these men. I have a personal score to settle with him. Haynes was opposed to having me along from the start. I was too young to be of any good to them, and he said they couldn't afford to have one more mouth to feed when I couldn't pull my own weight, but he didn't dare buck Patterson.

"Then, one night when we were all feasting off an elk one of the men had brought down, Haynes gabbed a steak I was fixing to eat. He came up behind me and with his knife, and speared it right off my plate, and told me if I gave him any grief, he'd carve me up like that elk. He loved to hear children scream, he said, and he knew how to make a person live for days while he was working on him."

"I'll bet you were scared."

"Absolutely. I was barely eight years old. Well, Patterson came walking by, as Haynes was saying what he said to me. Patterson whipped out a pistol. So fast I could barely follow the motion of his hand, and he snapped a shot into the ground between Haynes' feet. Haynes jumped back and looked at Patterson wide-eyed. Patterson told him if he ever hurt me in any way, the next shot would be between his eyes. Patterson said he would shoot him as soon as he would shoot a rabid dog, because he didn't see much difference. He said to Haynes, 'You have a job with us, and you do it well. But if you ever cross me, and you're dead.'

"That was when I realized Haynes was really afraid of Sam. Haynes never bothered me again. He'd glare at me whenever he had the chance, just to let me know the hate was still in him, and that he would never forget. But he didn't dare take a chance on crossing Sam.

"I rode away when I was fifteen. I've never seen any of them again."

Josh put the cork back in his canteen and slung it on the saddle horn. "Looks like you'll at least be seeing Falcone, once we find their camp. What will you do if that Haynes hombre is there?"

"I'd like to shoot him. I know I'm faster now than he's ever been. I've seen him in action, and he's good, but I know how good I am. I'd like to goad him into a gunfight, and then rid the world of him."

"But that wouldn't be right."

"Why not?" Dusty returned the canteen to his saddle, and then began tightening the cinch. "Especially after they attacked the ranch, and almost killed Pa. The thought of what Haynes would do to Bree and Aunt Ginny if we had lost the battle, using his knife on them, makes me mad enough to kill."

"The reason you can't is because you're Pa's son. If you did that, you'd be no better than they are. You got something to live up to, now."

Dusty nodded. "I always had my own conscience to live up to. Patterson said your own conscience is your hardest judge. But now, it's almost like the family is looking over my shoulder. I find myself feeling like I don't want to let any of them down."

Josh nodded. "That's part of what belonging to a family is about. You're not alone, anymore. You have people who will be there for you when you need them, and you'll be there for them. And your actions reflect on them, and theirs on you."

A scent caught Josh's nose, a faint touch of peach blossom was on the breeze. How odd, he thought, glancing about. Peach trees don't grow in these hills.

They mounted up and rode on.

The trail led them further into the mountains, westward for a while, then turned north once again.

They camped the night at the base of a steep slope, in a grove of tall pines. Josh drew his knife and dug a hole three feet deep, in which they built a low fire. The walls of the hole would block most of the firelight. Kind of like what Zack and his men did in the small grove of trees at the edge of the ranch yard, before the raiders attacked. No need to let Falcone and his men know someone was on their back trail.

Dusty and Josh had finished their last can of beans the night before. They had seen three or four rabbits during the day, but didn't dare chance a shot that might let raiders know they were out here. In the mountains, a gunshot can echo and carry a fair distance. However, Dusty had dug some roots they could chew on, and Josh had brought along some jerky from the ranch.

"I didn't know these were edible," Josh said. "They taste almost like sweet potatoes. Let me guess—you learned this from Sam Patterson."

"I learned almost everything I know from him."

"I'm kind of glad he isn't with that group anymore. I'm glad you don't have to face him. Considering all he taught you, and that at one time he was the closest thing to a father you had."

Dusty nodded. "Me, too."

"How far ahead of us do you think they are?"

Dusty shrugged. "They had a couple hours lead on us when we found their trail this morning. We've been keeping a steady pace, but they were taking their time. Probably no more than forty-five minutes, now."

"So, when we find their camp, what next? Try to get the drop on them, and take them to a territorial marshal? There's one in Helena. Keeps his office there."

"That's the plan, I guess," Dusty said, cradling a tin cup filled with hot coffee in both hands. The night was turning off cool, and his fingers were feeling a chill. "That's what Pa would expect, isn't it?"

"And from what you tell me of these men, what do you think the chances are of us pulling it off?"

Dusty shook his head. "Not very good."

"We're not riding out of there, are we?"

"You had to figure, when you first lit out on their trail, that you probably wouldn't be going home again."

Josh sighed thoughtfully. "I have to admit, I really didn't give it much thought. I was just filled with hate, and intended to go after 'em. And being Pa's son, I figured it was my job. I never gave much thought to what would actually happen if I found 'em."

"You've got to always think things through to the end result. Learned that from Patterson, too. Every time you do something, you set a series of events in motion."

"What was he? A gunfighter or a philosopher?"

"He was a man who lived hard and saw a little too much, but learned from all of it. Maybe, in his own way, like Pa."

"They might have ridden a similar trail in some ways, been shot at a few times too many, and had to do a lot of killing. But Pa learned different lessons from it all."

"That's what sets Pa apart from a lot of the others." Dusty took a sip of his steaming coffee. "One thing Patterson was, though, was a good teacher. You don't just ride into a situation blind, he would say, and we're not going to just ride into their hideout when we find it, either. They must have found a place they could defend easy. If they hadn't, they wouldn't be staying in this area at all. We'll have to ride careful, and when we find it, we're going to sit and watch a while, scout the area so we know what we're riding into.

"Again, it's a lot like hunting deer. We'll have to be patient. There will be a lot of waiting. Maybe even a couple days worth. And most likely guards will be posted, so we'll have to be watching for them."

"You ever play chess?" Josh asked.

Dusty shook his head. "I was a fair hand at checkers, though."

"I have a feeling you'd be pretty good at it. Remind me to teach it to you when we get back home."

"So, you think we'll live to ride back?"

"At first, I have to admit, I wasn't too pleased that you invited yourself along. But I'm realizing more and more my odds of getting out of this alive have probably tripled with you being here."

"I hope you're right," Dusty said, and took another sip of coffee.

The sun was not even a half hour into the morning sky and Josh and Dusty were following the trail made by the raiders. Following it deeper into the mountains, through a rocky pass, then up a steep slope heavily wooded with pines. The trail meandered its way down through a small ravine, then to the top of another ridge, then along its crest where it opened into a small canyon.

The walls of the canyon were rocky and steep, but the canyon floor was thickly wooded with maple and aspen. A chimney made of stones was visible behind the bushy branches of one maple, and smoke drifted skyward.

"I think we've hit paydirt," Dusty said.

"So you have, boys," came a voice from behind them, along with the sound of two Winchesters being jacked. "Don't make a move for them guns, or we'll blow you clean out'a them saddles."

The man stepped into view. He wore no hat, and black hair fell to his shoulders. A strip of cloth, stained dark from campfire smoke and sweat, was tied about his temples. Black hair fell to his shoulders. A lightning bolt scar trailed down one cheekbone and into the side of his mouth, lifting it into a leering half-smile.

"Howdy, Kiowa," Dusty said.

THIRTY-SIX

Kiowa Haynes broke into a smile, though there was no smile in his eyes. "Well. Look who's come back. I'll bet you never thought you'd ever see me again."

"I never thought I'd be that lucky."

Haynes snickered. It seemed to Josh this man liked being disliked.

"You always did think you were too smart for the rest of us," Kiowa said.

"Kiowa," Dusty said, keeping his voice conversational, "I came looking for Sam, but I've been told he no longer rides with you."

However, Kiowa continued as though he hadn't heard him. "But I got the drop on you, and I did it easy. You just remember that the next time you're feeling so danged smart."

"I said, I came looking for Sam."

"He ain't here."

"That's what I heard. Who's in charge now? Vic??"

Kiowa simply stood his ground, his mouth twisted into a smirk, his eyes squinting. Josh had observed that men who were dangerous, or at least thought they were, often held their eyes in a perpetual squint.

"All right, boy," he finally said. "I'll take you down to the cabin. But first, I want you both to shuck them guns."

"Kiowa," Dusty said with surprise that sounded so real Josh would have thought it was genuine, if he did not know better. "After all the years I rode with you and the boys, you don't think you can trust me?"

"I never thought I could trust you. And you never rode with us. You just tagged along because Sam kept you as some sort of pet. We allowed it because he was boss. But he ain't here to protect you no more." Kiowa Haynes held a Winchester in his hands, the barrel aimed toward Dusty. "Now, toss down them guns, or the new boss will be seein' you with a bullet in your head."

Josh turned his head a couple of inches, to allow himself a glance behind him and Dusty with his peripheral vision. A man was standing a few yards behind the horses, a Winchester also in his hands.

"Turn that head anymore," Kiowa said, "and I'll blow it clean off your shoulders."

Dusty reached toward the buckle of his gunbelt, and Haynes said, "with your left hand only, boy. I seen how fast you are with a gun."

Dusty raised his right hand into the air, and unbuckled the belt with his left and let it fall to the earth. Josh did the same.

"And the saddle guns."

Josh and Dusty slid their rifles free, and let them drop.

Kiowa instructed the man behind Josh and Dusty to go fetch their horses. With Kiowa in the lead and the other man behind them, they rode along a narrow trail that led down and into the canyon.

At the canyon floor, Kiowa directed them through a stand of birches and into a large meadow Josh guessed to be thirty acres, in which a small herd of horses grazed. Josh counted maybe twenty. He guessed them to be the remuda. They were strong looking horses, and long-legged. You can tell a lot about a man by his horse, Pa had once said, and these horses were built for running. At the center of the meadow was the log cabin. It was made of crudely cut logs. The stone chimney rose along one wall.

A man not much older than Josh and Dusty was sitting on a bench outside the cabin. He wore a flat-brimmed sombrero that had seen a lot of wear. His face was reddened, but whether from the sun or too much whiskey, Josh couldn't tell.

"I see you have a new man," Dusty said, so casually it was almost conversational.

"You ain't met Loggins," Kiowa said. "He joined up after you rode out. He ain't much with a six-gun, but he's the best you'll ever see with a rifle. Even better than Patterson was."

"Not better than me," Dusty said. "And definitely not better than my friend Josh, here."

"Still cocky, are you, boy? That's gonna get you killed sooner or later. And I'd bet on sooner."

Josh noticed Dusty referred to him as friend. He decided to say nothing, and follow along with whatever plan Dusty was cooking up.

The man called Loggins said, "Who are these two?"

"Found 'em up on the rim of the canyon," Haynes said. "The runt here," he indicated Dusty with a nod of his head, "used to ride along with Patterson. I don't know who the other one is. As soon as Falcone gives the word, I'll turn 'em both into wolf bait."

Haynes dismounted and rapped on the cabin door. "Hey, boss. It's me. Found me a couple riders up at the canyon rim. Brought 'em down."

A man called from inside. "They law?"

Dusty immediately recognized the voice as belonging to Falcone.

Haynes glanced at Josh and Dusty. "Them two? Nah."

"Then shoot them both."

"You know one of 'em. That kid who used to tag along with Patterson."

There was a hesitation. Then, "Bring 'em on in."

"Get down from the horses, boys," Haynes said to them. To the other man who had been with him on the canyon rim, he said, "Take care of the horses."

With Haynes in the lead and Loggins behind them with a pistol in his hand, Dusty and Josh stepped into the cabin. A fireplace built of stones and held together with mud plaster decorated one wall. There were two doorways flanking the fireplace, and each was blocked off with a blanket hanging from nails driven into a timber overhead. Bedrooms, Dusty supposed. A table was positioned at the center of the main room.

A dark haired woman with hollow cheeks and deep crevices about her eyes sat at the table. She wore a white petticoat and fish-net stockings, and in one hand was a glass. Standing behind her was a man with a drooping mustache that needed trimming. His hair was dark but with silver strands, and it fell shaggily below each ear. He wore a gray, long-handled undershirt, and a suspender over each shoulder. Buckled about his hips was a gunbelt which held a Colt Peacemaker, very similar to Dusty's. In one hand was a

half full bottle of whiskey, and in the other, a glass that matched the one the woman was holding.

Dusty stepped forward boldly, as though he were more guest than prisoner. "Howdy, Vic."

"Dusty," he said. "It's been a long time."

Dusty nodded. "I hear you're still in business."

Falcone nodded. "Thought about retiring, shortly after you left. But this is the only life I know."

"What about Sam?"

Falcone shrugged. "About a year after you rode out, he did the same. Haven't heard from him since."

"Prob'ly dead," Haynes put in.

Without looking at him, Dusty said, "You'd like that, wouldn't you, Kiowa? One less man for you to be afraid of."

Kiowas's lips pulled back, like a wild animal about to strike, and he reached for his knife. Falcone's right hand shot up, palm outward, in a stopping motion, and it had the desired affect on Kiowa. Then Falcone said to Dusty, "I see you two aren't getting along any better than you ever did."

Dusty shrugged. "I don't get along with any man who gets his fun by scaring children. Threatening to carve them up with a knife."

"It ain't too late," Kiowa hissed. "All I need is the word from Vic."

Dusty turned to face him. "You'll need a lot more than that. I'm not a kid anymore, and you're nowhere near man enough to do the job without a lot of help."

"Enough, you two," Falcone sad.

Dusty turned back to Falcone. Kiowa let his gaze linger on Dusty a moment longer, then looked back to his boss.

"Who's this one?" Falcone asked, indicating Josh.

"Josh," Dusty said, thinking quickly, grasping for a name. "Josh Brackston. A gunhawk I've been riding with a while."

"Never heard of him," Falcone said.

Josh decided to enter the play. After all, he was finding this was not unlike poker. "You hang around Montana Territory a while, you'll hear of me."

Dusty looked to him, not knowing whether he wanted to laugh, or kick him. Shut up, he wanted to say. Leave this to me.

The outside door then opened, and a woman stepped in. The saloon girl from Midas.

"I so love a bath in this mountain water," she was saying, before she saw who was standing with Falcone.

Her hair fell in dripping wet strings down her back, and she wore only a petticoat and a slip. Her eyes met Josh's for a moment, then turned away, but the moment was long enough for Falcone to notice.

"So," he said, "I see you two have met?"

Dang, Josh thought. I'd love to get him to a poker table. He's good.

"Yes," the girl said. "They stopped at the Midas saloon a couple days ago."

"Yeah," Dusty said, thinking quickly. "We were asking for you."

"Tempy," Falcone said, addressing the girl Dusty and Josh knew also as Felicia and Sarah-Ann. "Are these also the two you met at the campfire?"

She had moved to Loggin's side, and he swung an arm about her shoulders proprietarily, as though he were trying to make a statement to Josh and dusty. His pistol was in his other hand.

She said, "They surely are, Vic."

"I say we kill 'em both now," Kiowa said.

"It wouldn't make good sense," Dusty said, "to kill two men who've come looking for a job."

Here we are, Josh thought, in more danger than he had ever been in. With but one word from Falcone, this Kiowa Haynes would probably give them worse deaths than they could imagine. But dang, he was enjoying this.

"What kind of job?" Falcone asked.

"Hopefully, the kind that can pay better than working for two-bit cattle outfits. I told Josh, here, I knew Sam Patterson and Vic Falcone, and maybe they could hire us on. We've been looking for you since."

"Boss," Kiowa said, "I never did trust this kid. And I don't now."

Falcone set the bottle and glass down, and rested his hands on his hips. "I have to admit, Dusty, I never did consider you the type for a life like this. When Sam gave you the choice to either ride with us or ride away, I was not surprised when you chose the second of the two."

Dusty shrugged. "I tried to take Sam's advice, and ride the straight and narrow. But there's just no money in it. Sure, I could homestead, maybe run a few head of cattle. But I want more than that out of life."

"I don't know. I always liked you, Dusty, but liking you and trusting you are two different things."

"I say we kill 'em both right now," Kiowa said again.

Falcone directed his eyes to him. "I pay you to scout, not to think. If they are to be killed, and I mean if, I'll be the one who decides. Is that clear? Or do I need to make it more clear?"

Kiowa knew Falcone's speed with a gun wasn't the equal of Patterson's, but he was still danged good. Kiowa was an accurate shot, and his rifle was in his hands, while Falcone's pistol was still holstered. Yet, Falcone had set down his glass and bottle, so his hands were now free. Dusty saw Kiowa weighing all of this in mind. Could he swing the rifle toward Falcone and squeeze off a shot before Falcone could draw and fire?

Kiowa stood his ground, but didn't move. "All right. You're the boss."

"Take them both outside."

"Should we tie them up?" Loggins asked.

"No. There's no place for them to go without horses, and nothing they can do without guns. But keep an eye on them."

At the back of the cabin the meadow dropped into a gentle grassy decline, extending a hundred more yards before being met by a stand of aspen.

Loggins directed Josh and Dusty to where the decline began, and said, "Sit."

"I thought we might walk around a bit," Dusty said. "Stretch our legs a little."

Loggins shook his head. "I don't want you boys getting too good a look at the lay of the land. If the boss says you

ride with us, then I'll show you all I know about this place. But not until then."

Dusty nodded, as if to say he considered that sensible thinking, and dropped to the grass to sit cross-legged. Josh followed Dusty's lead. The knee he had banged up falling from the roof during the gunfight protested a bit and he winced, but made it down to the ground. Loggins dropped to sit on his heels, balancing his rifle across his knees.

"You and Kiowa don't get along too good," Loggins said.

Dusty pulled a strand of grass from the earth and bit into its sweet tasting stem. "Nope. The man drew the battle lines when I was too small a child to fight back. If it wasn't for Patterson, the man would have carved me up for the vultures just for the fun of killing. Don't ever turn your back on a man who finds fun in killing."

"It might also be good advice," Josh said to Dusty, "not to egg on a man who finds fun in killing."

"Kiowa has never been able to think straight when he was mad," Dusty explained, "and he's always been too stupid to keep himself from getting mad."

"The man's a good scout, though," Loggins said.

Dusty shook his head. "He's not going to be the scout anymore. The job's mine, once Vic decides to hire Josh and me."

Loggins looked at him with surprise. "You seem awful sure of that."

Dusty nodded calmly. "That's why Kiowa wants me dead so bad. He knows there ain't room for the two of us. And he knows I'm the better man."

Loggins chuckled. "I hope Vic has the same faith in your abilities that you do."

"So do I," Josh said.

After a couple of hours, Loggins left them. He was replaced by the man with the Winchester, who had been patrolling the canyon rim with Kiowa earlier. The man was called Stew. However, unlike Loggins, he sat at a distance, smoking a hand-rolled cigarette and looking off at the trees.

Josh lounged back in the grass, enjoying the warmth of the late afternoon sun. He tipped the brim of his hat

forward to shade his eyes. "I sure hope you know what you're doing."

"I do," Dusty said quietly, so his words wouldn't travel to their guard. "Falcone is a man with very little heart. He can put a bullet in you without even thinking twice about it. In his own way, he's more dangerous than Kiowa. Kiowa is just plain stupid. He's a cold-blooded killer because he's an animal. But Falcone, he's not stupid. He's cold-blooded because he chooses to be. It's the more efficient way for a man in his walk-of-life. The only way for us to remain alive is if he thinks we're useful to him."

"So, do you think they saw you when they were spying on the ranch from off in the ridges?"

"I'm not going to gamble against it. That's why I'm playing it that you and I were hired hands, working at the McCabe spread. But I recognized some of the men who were shot, and knew it might be Sam and the boys, so we rode after them, looking for a better job."

"So, things changed awfully quick, didn't they? It's gone from trying to get the jump on them and bringing them in, to just trying to stay alive. And to do so without joining their gang. So much for taking a couple days to scout their hideout."

Dusty nodded. "Life can be like that."

Josh smirked and snorted a chuckle at having his words turned back on him.

Dusty said, "Sometimes all the plans you might spend a lot of time laying out just fall away, and you have to think on your feet."

"All right. I have another question for you. Why are you building such a reputation for me as being good with a gun? Sooner or later, one of 'em might want to challenge me, considering how good you told him I was."

Dusty shook his head. "The only time two fast guns will ever challenge one another is in them dime novels published back east. These men don't want to die any more than you or me. And in a gunfight, the lesser man usually dies. Now that they think you're hell on wheels with a gun, they'll be more likely to leave you alone."

"But what if they want me to do some target practice, to show how good I am?"

Dusty shrugged. "Then, show 'em. I've seen how good you are with a gun. You aren't bad, really."

"Not as good as you or Pa."

"Maybe not, but you're a dang sight better than a lot I've seen. Better than either Kiowa or Falcone. I know that for a fact. And the way Loggins carries his gun, I'd wager you're better than he is, too."

"What about our shadow, over there?" Josh asked, meaning the man with Winchester.

"He's not that good. Otherwise, he'd have a higher place in the pecking order. I saw that right off. You notice he didn't go into the cabin with us? Kiowa told him to go take care of the horses, and he just did what he was told."

Josh reached with one hand to lift the brim of his hat enough so one eye could focus on Dusty. "You sure do see a lot in a short time."

"You have to, if you want to stay alive in a group of men like this."

As the sun trailed toward the western rim of the canyon, the blonde girl stepped from the cabin carrying two tin plates. On each was a slab of deer steak, and a brown mess neither Josh nor Dusty could recognize by sight or smell.

She was now wearing a pair of Levi's, and a man's range shirt with the tails hanging loosely, and the front unbuttoned carelessly low. And she still wore no shoes. Her hair was now dry, falling about her shoulders in a small sea of breakers the color of sunlight.

"I've never seen a girl in men's trousers," Josh said, as she set a plate before him in the grass. The wearing of trousers and a shirt intended for a man couldn't have been more shocking than had she lighted a cigar.

She shrugged. "They're easier for riding. And besides, Loggins seems to like it."

"I don't care much about what he thinks." Josh sat up, and tipped his hat back and away from his face. "I care about what I think. And I think you're way too beautiful to be dressing like a man."

"A lot of men call me beautiful. I have yet to work a saloon where men didn't call me that. But it was all for a reason."

Josh nodded. "But we're not in a saloon now, and I'm not saying it for that reason. I'm saying it because I mean it."

She looked at him curiously, her brows dropping into a small frown. She started to say something, then stopped. After a few heartbeats, she turned away and set the second plate in the grass beside Dusty.

"What is that stuff?" Dusty asked, referring to the brown mush.

"Some sort of concoction Flossy comes up with, using roots she digs around here, and mixing it with refried beans."

Another gunman drifted down from the cabin, to drop in the grass beside their guard. He wore a floppy, beaten sombrero, from under which greasy hair fell to his shoulders. He bore a knife scar that began at one cheekbone, extending upward to his brow, and his eye was a sightless milky white.

"Who's that?" Josh asked.

Tempy glanced over, then snapped her gaze away with...what? Disgust? Fear? Josh wasn't sure. But the gunman was looking over at her, his mouth spreading into a grin.

"That's White Eye," Tempy said.

"I think he likes you," Josh said, probing for a response.

"I would never let that man touch me. I would kill myself, first."

"What does Loggins say about it? You're his girl."

"He just laughs. He tells me White eye means no harm. But I've known men like that. Harm is all they mean. Like Kiowa."

Josh shook his head. "I would never let a man look at my girl that way. I'd tell him to keep his eyes away, or I'd fill him with lead."

She looked at him at the sudden suggestion of gunplay. "Are you as good as Dusty says?"

Josh shrugged, playing it like an actor on opening night. "I never gave it much thought. But if White Eye doesn't stop looking at you like that, and if Loggins doesn't do

anything about it, then White Eye is going to find out the hard way how good I am."

Dusty put in, "It'd be White Eye's funeral."

The girl's brow knit. "I could see you maybe wanting to fight Loggins over me. Not that I'm that rich a prize, but there aren't many available women in most parts of the west. But why would you want to fight White Eye?"

"I don't fight for possession of a woman. You're not an object. I would fight to defend your honor."

Her gaze drifted to the grass beyond where she sat, and she drew her knees up and wrapped her arms about them. "I've never heard a man talk like that about me. After all, I know what I am. Most men would feel I had long since lost any honor worth defending."

"I'm no one to judge. You do what you have to, to survive in this world."

She looked at him again. "You don't talk like most men."

"That's because most men you meet are in a saloon, ready to get liquored-up and spend money to buy you. I'm not one of those men."

"You've never been with a saloon girl?"

"Well, I can't really say that." He was thinking of one in particular at Alicia Summer's establishment, who didn't mind him stopping in once in a while. But she had never charged him. "But I've never paid for one."

There was silence then, and she let her gaze drift beyond the aspens to the rocky rim of the canyon. Josh did the same, but didn't want the silence to be too long. He had gotten her train of thought moving in a certain direction, and wanted to build on that.

"How did you meet Loggins?" he asked, knowing fully well the answer. Where else would a saloon girl meet an outlaw?

She sighed. "In the saloon, back in town. He and Vic and some of the men started showing up regularly."

"Were they all your customers?"

"Some of them."

"But not White Eye."

"No. He scared me from the start. And Kiowa was rough. He likes to hurt a girl. I told Flossy about it. She spoke to Vic, and Kiowa is no longer allowed near us."

"He hurt you? He'll pay for that."

Dusty shook his head. "No. Kiowa is mine."

Tempy continued. "Flossy eventually became Vic's woman, and I became Loggins'. We spend most of our time out here at the hideout, now. We don't get paid anymore, but our meals are provided. They brought me along on one of their recent raids, to cook. And Loggins is only one man, at least. That's something, to know there will be only one man there, every night."

So, it was indeed her shoe prints they had seen at the remains of their camp in the ridges surrounding the McCabe's valley.

"So," Josh said, "what were you doing at the saloon a couple days ago? Looked like you were working."

"Flossy still runs some girls that work there. She was in town, and I went with her. I was just lounging in the saloon, having a drink."

"Not the kerosene that barkeep serves."

She chuckled. "No. He keeps the good stuff for his special customers. And because I'm with Loggins, I get to drink for free. I was just having a little fun with you when you and Dusty showed up."

"Tell me something," he said. "You told me your name was Felicia, and you have also said Sarah-Ann. How did they get 'Tempy' out of either one of them?"

She laughed. "My name was never Sarah-Ann. I said that because I was told to ride in and find out all I could from you. I don't call myself Felicia, either. That's a name Flossy thought I should use. My parents named me Temperance, but everyone calls me Tempy. I hate it, but somehow, 'Temperance' isn't quite becoming of a girl who works the saloons."

"How much of what you told me was a lie?"

"Not all of it. My father was in the Army. My parents died, and I was forced into this line of work to stay alive. Sad story, right?" Again, a bitter chuckle. "I had a sister named Faith, who was older than me. She married before Ma and Pa died, and moved back east."

"Weren't there any other children?"

"A boy and two other girls, all who died at birth."

"Wasn't there any family you could have gone to when your parents died?"

She shook her head. "My sister is all I have, and I am not going to be a burden to her. She and her husband are farmers, living in New Hampshire, and they're raising a brood of children. They don't need another mouth to feed."

"So, you took to the saloons."

She nodded. "I was fifteen. With no money. Ma and Pa had worked hard all their lives, but like most folks I ever saw, they had very little to show for it."

She got to her feet. "I've got to be going. Flossy and I have work to do. Clothes to wash, and we got a small garden we tend."

"Thanks for sitting with me. It isn't often I get to chat with a pretty girl."

She tried to suppress a smile, but her eyes betrayed her.

Before she could speak, Josh said, "Doesn't Loggins ever tell you you're beautiful?"

"He doesn't need to. He knows I'm his."

"When I tell a girl she's pretty, it's not because I have to, it's because I want to. It's because she is."

She didn't know what to say about that. She let her gaze drop to her toes while she searched for the words, then said simply, "I've got to go."

"I'll be seeing you. Temperance."

She looked at him again, this time the smile fully escaping. Then she turned and started up the grassy hill toward the cabin.

THIRTY-SEVEN

Dusty had just finished his venison and was procrastinating on the brown slop, when Kiowa Haynes came ambling his way down from the cabin. "Boss wants to see you."

Dusty glanced at Josh. "I don't think I could have brought myself to eat this brown stuff, anyway."

He set his plate down in the grass.

Josh still had a couple bites of deer steak left, but set his plate down too.

"Not you," Kiowa said to Josh. "Him only."

Falcone sat at the table. Flossy was nowhere to be seen. A whiskey bottle stood on the table before him, half filled. With a nod of his head, he indicated an empty chair across from him. Dusty spun the chair backward, then straddled it.

"You can go," Falcone said to Kiowa.

"You sure, boss?"

Falcone simply stared at him, with eyes that reminded Dusty of a hawk.

Kiowa said, "I'll wait outside, boss."

When the door had shut, Falcone slid a glass toward Dusty. "Would you like a drink?"

Dusty had never really liked the taste of raw whiskey, but his gut feeling was to play along, so he reached for the bottle.

Falcone said, "So, you two are here looking for a job?"

Dusty nodded, and took a sip.

"Tell me about this partner of yours."

And so, Dusty spun a tale of fiction about how he and the gunfighter, Josh Brackston, had signed on as hired guns at the McCabe Ranch. They had stayed for a while, punching cattle, but after the attack on the ranch, they moved on. The pay wasn't good enough for that kind of risk, and besides, they had grown tired of cows. When Dusty realized it might have been Patterson and Falcone's men who had attacked the ranch, they decided to try to find them.

"All right." Falcone knocked back the remainder of his glass, then reached for the bottle for a refill. "What do you

think you have to offer me that any of the men I already have couldn't?"

"The McCabe Ranch," Dusty said simply, and took another sip of whiskey while he let the words sink in.

"I lost a lot of men when I tried that the first time. Barely got away with my own hide intact. The place is too well guarded. Like a small fort."

"You tried it the wrong way."

"And what would be the right way?"

"Hiring me as your scout."

"I already have one. Kiowa Haynes."

"And look what that scout got you. How many men were killed?"

"All right. I'll play along. What would that ranch have that would be worth risking a second strike, which might not go any better than the first? Horses? Supplies?"

Dusty decided to stretch his fabrication further—as far as it might take to sell himself to Falcone. "How about twenty thousand dollars?"

That got Falcone's attention. That was more than most men in the west saw in a lifetime. "I'm listening."

"They have a strongbox filled with cash. Dividing it up among us, it would still be a lot more per man than McCabe was willing to pay Josh and me for risking our necks as hired guns. And that ranch wouldn't be very hard to take if you went about it the right way."

"I never would have thought a rancher would have as much as twenty thousand dollars. Where could he have gotten that kind of money?"

"A couple cattle drives were more successful than they had planned. And he had a price on his head when he was younger. He didn't get that being a choir boy. I didn't ask specific questions, but it was kind of obvious. He also has business interests in California. You know how men like that are, when everything they touch turns to gold. There's no bank in that little town, so he keeps it in a strongbox right in the house."

"So, you think that ranch can be taken? If we went about it the right way? What did we do wrong?"

Dusty took a swig of whiskey. "You and your men rode into that valley bold as brass, checking out the area and

deciding which spread to take. And in doing this, you gave McCabe time to find out you were there, and prepare for the attack. Keep in mind, that's Johnny McCabe we're talking about. He was a former Texas Ranger and a gunfighter, not just a stupid cowboy. I worked for him for a few weeks. The stories they tell about him are mostly true."

Falcone filled Dusty's glass again. "Please continue."

"You split into two groups, which wasn't really a bad idea. Against anyone else, it should have done the trick. But his men attacked the flank of one group, and caught the other in a crossfire. Like I say, he's good. But he lost some men, too. And he took a bullet himself. He has a son about my age who's trying to run things while the old man is laid up. But he's not a gunfighter. He's a cattleman.

"This time, when you attack, it should be done entirely by surprise. No camping out in the mountains for a few days to let them know you're there. And we won't ride in with torches, and with guns firing. We'll sneak in. By day. When most of the men are away from the ranch. Take the strong box, grab some horses and supplies, and be on our way."

"I don't believe sneaking onto the McCabe Ranch will be as easy as you make it sound."

"Josh is from this area. He knows the hills and ridges around that valley like the back of his hand. He can lead us in so no one will know we're coming. We take the strong box and grab some horses, then I'll lead us out, covering our trail so's it can't be followed."

"I have Kiowa for that."

"Having Kiowa for that didn't do you any good the first time. And Josh and I followed you and your men right here to this canyon. If we could do it, so could a lawman."

"It'll take time to hire more men."

"You don't need any more men. We got enough right here. Seven, including me and Josh. Any more would be too many for a job like this."

Falcone allowed himself a brief smile. "I see you learned much from Patterson."

"He was a good teacher."

Falcone looked down to his drink thoughtfully for a moment, then rose to his feet and paced toward the hearth, one hand at the back of his neck.

"You've given me a lot to think about, Dusty. But I'm still undecided."

"It's a good plan, Vic."

He nodded, and turned back to Dusty. "Of that I have no doubts. It's you I still have my doubts of."

"Why?"

"Because of Sam Patterson. He virtually raised you, and he raised you to be a man of integrity." Falcone chuckled, and raised his brows. "You see, Sam wanted you to be everything he was not, but might have been had things been different. Sam had a heart, a serious handicap in this business. He cared about people. That proved to be his greatest weakness, because he was forever leaving witnesses alive who could testify against him if he was ever caught. He also showed that weakness in the way he raised you.

"He taught you to use a gun, and I have seen you use it. Even at thirteen, you were better than anyone currently in this camp. And he taught you the art of guerrilla warfare, and indeed there was no better teacher. He taught you to survive in this wilderness, and again – no better teacher. But he also taught you that his very lifestyle was wrong, and when it came time to make a decision about which path you were going to follow, you rode away. And now, I am to believe that you have a had a change of heart, and are willing to join us?"

Dusty shrugged, and put on his best cynical smile. "I guess Patterson didn't teach me that good after all."

Falcone smiled. "If only I could believe that. I guess I want to believe that, because even as a child you exhibited a natural intelligence. As a former teacher, I find myself looking for that sort of thing in a person, and I find so little of it in the company I keep. Such intelligence would indeed be very useful to me. But I don't quite dare trust you. At least, not yet."

Dusty let out a long sigh. "Life's been hard, Vic. After I rode away, I started looking for jobs. I found some. Cow punching, mostly. I was a shotgun rider for a stage company. But it was mostly lean times. And when I was working, the pay was low. A man can't build a life that way. Sam taught me ideals. And I still have them. But life taught me reality."

"I don't know, Dusty. I want to believe you." Sam drew a breath. "You and Josh are guests here, at least for the moment, until I make my decision. There won't be any need for an armed guard."

"Can we have our guns back?"

"If and when I decide to hire you."

"And if you don't decide to hire us?"

"Then, you'll both be shot, because you know the location of this canyon."

Dusty nodded.

Falcone said, "I thank you for your time. Now, I must be left alone to think."

Dusty knew he was being dismissed, and knew it would be unwise to overstay his welcome. He wanted to stay on Vic's good side for as long as possible.

Dusty found Josh still sitting in the grass at the top of the slope. "How'd it go?" Josh asked.

Dusty shrugged. "I gave it my best shot. I hope it works. Because, if it doesn't, not only will we be shot, but I may have given him a way to attack the ranch successfully this time."

The following morning, Josh rounded up his and Dusty's horses and led them to a makeshift stable Falcone's men had fashioned out of hand-cut pine logs, with a roof thatched with pine boughs. He removed the saddles and inspected the shoes for wear, then grabbed a brush hanging by a nail and set about brushing down each horse.

"That's the McCabe brand" came a woman's voice from behind him. Josh glanced over one shoulder to see Temperance walking up behind him, and he followed her gaze to the encircled M branded onto the hip of the horse. She was still in men's pants and a range shirt, and she held a folded up blanket in one arm.

He nodded in response to her remark. "That it is."

"A man could get hanged for horse stealing," she said.

"And he could for stealing twenty thousand dollars." Dusty had told Josh of his plan.

Her brows rose. "Twenty thousand dollars?"

He nodded.

"How? Where?"

"Dusty has been talking it over with Falcone. I shouldn't say more until they work out all the fine points."

"So that's why there's no armed guard, now."

Josh nodded.

"How come they haven't given back you're guns?"

"Like I said, the fine points aren't worked out yet." Josh returned to brushing his horse.

She stepped up behind him. "Where's Dusty?"

"He decided to take a stroll, now that we're free to roam the canyon. He's a restless type." Josh turned his gaze back to her. "Where's Loggins?"

"Vic sent him into town for supplies."

A silence developed as they stood each looking into the other's eyes. Then, she turned quickly away. "Loggins wouldn't like me being here."

"But he's in town."

"It doesn't matter. I don't want to make him mad. He's not very pleasant when he's mad."

"Why? You're a grown woman. You can talk to whoever you please."

"He's..." She hesitated, as though this was difficult to say. "He's hurt me, before. I don't want to give him cause again."

"If he ever lays a hand on you again, I'll kill him."

She looked at him suddenly. "I don't want you fighting him."

"Why not?"

"It's just that..." she shrugged and turned away. "It's just that I don't meet very many men who are nice to me, and I don't want to see one of the few get hurt."

Josh dropped the brush to the ground, and took her by the shoulders and turned her to face him. "I've been in my share of fights. And you know the only way I get hurt?"

She shook her head.

"My knuckles, when the men I'm fighting smash their faces against them."

She smiled, despite her concern. "Are you really afraid of nothing?"

He grew suddenly serious. "Everyone's afraid of something, Temperance."

Her smile grew broader. "I like it when you call me that. When Loggins says it, it's because he's making fun of me."

"I'd never do that."

"I know."

They drew closer, and Josh found his lips touching hers. Lightly. Then she pulled away.

"I was heading down to the pond for a bath," she said, suddenly nervous, almost afraid. "I'd better get going, before I give Loggins a reason to shoot you."

"Like I said, don't worry about him."

"He has a gun, and you don't. I've seen him shoot a man in cold blood for less."

She turned and hurried away, and Josh retrieved the brush and went back to brushing his horse, a sudden wave of uncertainty touching him. Not at the thought of possibly having to fight Loggins, but because he was no longer as sure of himself as he had been.

He had started this situation with Temperance partly because he thought he might be able to use her to his and Dusty's advantage. It wouldn't hurt to be working more than one game. Dusty was working Vic, and Josh was attempting to gain the girl's trust. But when she spoke of Loggins hurting her, his anger had been sincere. His intention to kill Loggins was real. And the kiss had been very real.

He hadn't intended this to happen. She was nothing more than a saloon girl and a liar, and an outlaw's woman. But he was now discovering beneath the labels was a person. She was sensitive, vulnerable, even beautiful in her own way.

And as he tried to concentrate on the brushing down of his horse, he found his mind drifting to what she had said when she left. She was heading down to the pond at the center of the canyon, taking a bath...

Temperance lounged in the cold mountain water, submerged to her shoulders. Her eyes were shut, and she was enjoying the heat of the sun on her face.

"Beautiful day for a swim," came a voice from the shore of the small creek. A little coarse and gravelly, and with a slight twang that was out of place here in the northwest. She looked to see Josh standing in the patch of grass where

she had dropped her clothes, and the blanket she would use to dry off with.

"Where are you from?" she said. "You have the sound of Texas in your talk."

"My pa spent some time there. I guess I picked it up from him." Josh hoped he hadn't just said too much.

But she was smiling. "You want to come in and join me?"

He hesitated at the appeal of her invitation, then said, "I would love to. But I'd better not."

"Loggins and Kiowa are in town. Stew and White-Eye are at the pass outside the canyon, and Vic and Flossy are in the cabin. We have the water to ourselves, and no one will ever know."

"I thought you were afraid Loggins might shoot me."

"Maybe I'm just suddenly feeling brave. And the more I know you, the more I'm starting to think maybe you are as tough as you and Dusty say you are. Come on in."

He shook his head. "Thanks, but it wouldn't be right."

She frowned a bit with lack of understanding, her head lilting to one side slightly. She reminded Josh comically and yet endearingly of a confused puppy, perking its ears and cocking its head to one side. "Why not?"

"It's not the way things are done. Wouldn't be proper. It's not the way you treat a lady."

Josh turned and started away from the creek, up a small incline and into a grove of pines. Why had he gone down to the water, anyway? He knew he would have been asking for trouble. But he had gone down regardless.

He leaned his back against the trunk of a pine. Dang! Why did life have to be so complicated?

"Josh." Temperance spoke from beside him. She must have followed him up from the creek, padding softly along in bare feet.

She had wrapped the blanket about her, pulling it tightly a bit below each shoulder. He noticed the suppleness of her neck, as water beaded and rolled down. Her hair fell in a dripping tangle against her back.

He found himself being pulled toward her as if by some unseen force. Their lips touched, lightly at first, then more powerfully.

Then he pulled his mouth from her. "Temperance. This is not right."

"Why not?"

"Because...because..." he was having trouble focusing his mind enough to find the words.

"Josh, I'm just a saloon girl. It's all right."

"No, you're not." He took her by the shoulders. "You're a woman. One who has had to do some unpleasant things just to survive, yes. But you're only a saloon girl if that's how you think of yourself. And you don't have to think of yourself like that any longer."

"Take me, Josh. Right here. Right now."

"I can't. I'd be treating you no better than all the other men have."

"There's one big difference. With those other men, I never had any choice. I had to, so I wouldn't starve. And with Loggins, I don't have a choice either. With you, I do. And I choose you."

"You can leave all of this behind you," he said. "Come with me, and I'll take you away from all of it, and you can start over again."

She pulled away, a surge of panic rushing through her. "What are you saying? Leave? I can't go with you."

"Why not?"

"Because..." she found herself reaching frantically for words that wouldn't come because of the suddenness of it all, ideas that wouldn't fully form.

"Because, I can't!" she turned and ran.

That night, she stood before a mirror mounted on the wall of one of the two bedrooms in the cabin. By the light of a candle standing on a small table in one corner, she was trying to tie her hair into a fashion she had seen worn by the wife of the mine owner in town, but couldn't quite figure it out.

She was wearing a slip only, and when Loggins parted the blanket that served as a door and stepped in and planted a kiss on her neck, she did not find herself smiling. She found herself thinking of Josh.

"What're you doin'?" he asked.

"Trying to fix my hair."

"Why?" he seemed truly perplexed.

"So I can look pretty."

"Pretty?" A chuckle began, and grew into a laugh. "You? Pretty?"

She let her arms drop to her sides, her hair falling loosely to her shoulders.

"Nothin' your hair can do will make you look pretty. Not with that nose, and your eyes too close together. You're a saloon girl, Tempy. You don't need to look pretty. All you need to do is satisfy your man."

He saw her jeans lying on the bed. "I don't know what's gettin' into you, girl, wearin' that dress-thing. You know I like you better in jeans. Show's the roundness of your butt better," his hands reached for and grabbed her bottom. "Get this foolish thing off."

She did as instructed, letting it drop to the roughhewn floorboards, and he pulled her to the bed and under the covers.

When he was done, he lay snoring, the smell of his whiskey-soaked breath filling the room. She curled up under the blankets at the far side of the bed, and wept silently until sleep finally took her.

The following afternoon, Vic Falcone sent Flossy to fetch Dusty, then sent her to the garden so Falcone could be alone in the cabin with his guest.

This time, Falcone didn't offer him a drink.

"I've made my decision," Falcone said.

Falcone strolled thoughtfully toward the hearth, then turned to face Dusty. "As much as I would like to trust you, Dusty, I can't afford the chance of being wrong."

As if on cue, which Dusty realized it probably was, Loggins and Kiowa stepped from the back room, each with a pistol trained at him.

"In the morning," Falcone said, "you and Josh will be shot. I am truly sorry."

Kiowa smiled. "I ain't."

Dusty sighed, long and wearily and with much exasperation, as Loggins bound his wrists behind his back with a strip of rawhide. Loggins then did the same with Josh, and left them both sitting at the crest of the grassy slope behind the cabin.

Loggins stepped away, to where Stew was sitting at a bench alongside Kiowa at the cabin wall. Kiowa held a pint bottle of clearish liquid Dusty guessed to be corn squeezings?

Kiowa raised the bottle to Dusty in a mock salute. He called out, "Tomorrow morning, muchacho, I gut you like a pig. I've been waiting to do this ever since Patterson first took you in. I will gut you like a pig, and watch you slowly die."

"I take it your plan didn't work," Josh muttered to Dusty, with an edge of sarcasm.

Dusty shook his head grimly. "How about you? I noticed you were trying to work that girl. Did you get anywhere with her?"

Dusty didn't realize quite how loaded a question that was.

Josh had seen Temperance a handful of times that day. She had been again wearing jeans and a range shirt, and he had caught her looking at him a couple of times with open sadness in her eyes. One time their eyes had met for a moment, then she looked away. Josh called to her, but she turned and ran into the woods. That had been around noon, and now the sun was drifting low in the western sky.

"No," he said. "My plan was a complete failure. In more ways than one. I guess I made the mistake of getting too close to her. I'm still new at this."

"I can't fault you for that. I grew up in this life, and I didn't do any better."

A question occurred to Josh. "Why is Falcone holding off until tomorrow on letting Kiowa kill us? Why not do it right now?"

"Falcone is just enough of a military man to want things done by a sort of schedule. He used to teach at a military school back east, or so I'm told. A condemned man is always given a least a night to ponder his fate and make

peace with his maker before he's put in front of a firing squad."

"Hey!" Kiowa called over to them. "No talking, or I will go to work on you tonight."

"And violate Falcone's order?" Dusty called back. "You don't have the backbone for that."

Kiowa drew his knife, a Bowie that gleamed in the late afternoon sunlight. "Shut your mouth, little muchacho, or I will show you how much guts I have."

Dusty said to Josh, "We may have a way out of this, yet."

He then raised his voice to Kiowa. "You know something, Kiowa? You've been wanting to kill me ever since I was eight years old. And the sad part is, when you finally get your chance, it still won't change what you are."

"And what is that, muchacho?"

"You're a coward. A stupid one, at that. You always have been, and killing me won't change that."

Loggins said, "I'd shut up if I was you, boy. If you want to live the night."

Josh could tell where this was going. Despite the fact that he was tied up and due to be killed slowly in the morning, he had to admit he was enjoying the thrill of this. Like poker, but with deadly stakes.

"I wouldn't stand by Kiowa," Josh said to Loggins. "Not considering the way I've seen him look at your woman. And from what I hear, when he's done with a woman, he doesn't leave much left."

Loggins shot a glance to Kiowa, but Kiowa rose to his feet, ignoring Loggins, and took a few steps toward Josh and Dusty. His knife was in one hand and his whiskey bottle in the other. "Another word out of either of you, and I'll cut your tongues out."

Dusty rolled over to his knees, then rose to his feet. "Spoken like a coward, Kiowa. Only a coward would have to wait until a man's hands are tied to kill him."

Kiowa started for him. Dusty attempted to side step, but Kiowa slammed him in the chest with the whiskey bottle, whiskey slopping onto Dusty's buckskin shirt, and Dusty was knocked backward. Kiowa continued forward, standing over Dusty with his knife ready. He tossed aside the bottle.

"Now, little muchacho," Kiowa hissed. "You don't feel so brave, do you? There ain't no Sam Patterson to protect you. Maybe I skin you alive, and not wait for morning?"

Dusty raised a leg and drove the sole of his boot into Kiowa's groin. Kiowa gave a sharp, raspy inhale, and his eyes went wide as he dropped to his knees. He was well within range of Josh, who raised a foot and drove it into Kiowa's shoulder.

Kiowa tumbled down the hill, his legs now folded under him.

Stew and Loggins were making no attempt to suppress their laughter; it simply rolled from them.

Dusty rose to his feet again. "It's a good thing my hands are tied," he called down to Kiowa. "You'd be in a lot worse shape than you are now. You ain't dealing with an eight-year old boy now."

A gun went off, and all heads turned toward the cabin, and the source. There stood Falcone. A revolver was in his hand, aimed toward the sky. Smoke drifted from the barrel.

"What's going on here?" he bellowed.

"Just teaching that madman you call a scout some manners," Dusty said.

Loggins had ceased his laughter at the boss's gunshot, but he was still smiling. "He took Kiowa out of the fight with his hands tied."

"Hey," Josh said, indignant. "I helped."

Falcone looked at Dusty curiously, and holstered his pistol. He said nothing, but nodded approvingly.

From the bottom of the slope, Kiowa screamed, "I'll kill you!"

Kiowa was on his knees, still bent forward from the pain reaching upward into his kidneys, and down into his legs. He drew his pistol and cocked the hammer. "I'll shoot you down where you stand."

Falcone whipped his own pistol once again into his hand cocking it as he drew, and placed a shot that kicked up dirt inches from Kiowa. Kiowa pulled back, lost his balance, and fell onto his side.

"Not until morning!" Falcone shouted. "That is my order. Disobey it, and I will shoot you myself."

Dusty stepped forward. "Vic, I want to have a word with you."

"I am not changing my mind," Falcone said firmly.

"I have a proposal for you."

"A proposal? You are hardly in the position..."

"I want to talk to you in private."

Falcone was silent a moment, considering. Then, he said, wearily, "Step into the cabin."

Dusty, his wrists still bound behind him, stepped into the cabin, followed by Falcone.

The lighting inside the cabin was dim this late in the afternoon. Falcone struck a match and brought to life the lamp standing on the table, then turned the flame up. Its pale glow filled the small room.

Falcone walked around to the other side of the table, pulled out a chair and dropped into it. He reached for an empty whiskey bottle beside the lamp, gave it a glance, saw it was empty and set it back down.

"Vic, what's happened to you?" Dusty asked.

Falcone carried himself with a military stiffness, like he had years earlier. But now his hair was unkempt, which it had never been. There was a dark circle under each eye, and he was drinking more than he ever had. From what Dusty could determine, Falcone spent most of his time inside this cabin with Flossy and a bottle of whiskey.

Falcone looked at him a moment, as if he needed a moment for the question to settle in. Then he carelessly shrugged his shoulders. Sort of a combination of I don't know, and I don't really care.

Dusty continued. "You drink way too much, Vic. You spend all your days in this cabin, drinking and whoring. How much longer do you think you can keep a handle on those men, especially Kiowa, like this?"

"I've been learning something, Dusty. Something I suppose I knew all along, which is sometimes the hardest thing to learn. This sort of life is a dead end. I fear my demise is probably coming soon, regardless. After all, how long can a man live this life?"

Dang, but he was hard to follow, sometimes, throwing around ten dollar words. Kind of like Aunt Ginny.

Falcone continued, "Maybe the attack on the McCabe Ranch that went so poorly was part of it. I guess I felt like the wind came out of my sails when that happened. I rode in with as large a complement of men as Patterson had ever assembled, and we were more than cut in half. Thirteen went in. Only five rode away."

"Do you really think this is the end of the road?"

He lowered his gaze and nodded. "I suppose I do. Soon one of the men, probably Kiowa, is going to place a bullet in my back. Then Loggins will probably take over. Kiowa might try, but does not have the gray matter to lead men."

"So, what do you do? Just stay in this cabin, whoring and drinking and going through the motions of leading these men, waiting for one of them to kill you?"

He nodded. "I suppose.'

"It doesn't have to be that way, Vic. Listen to my proposal. It might be just what you need."

Falcone sighed, long and wearily. "All right. I'm listening."

"You need a right-hand man. Someone you can count on. Someone other than Loggins or Stew, or especially Kiowa."

"You?"

"I'm young, Vic, and have enough energy and stamina for both of us. But I need your savvy, your experience. Together, we can form a new gang."

He shook his head and chuckled. "I'd like to believe you, Dusty. Really, I would. But there's that problem with integrity, again. I just don't believe you're cut out for a life like this."

"How can I prove it to you?"

"I don't know."

Dusty turned, and began pacing impatiently to one side. He would have to make what he was about to say sound like a spontaneous idea, not something he had pieced together before he had even started baiting Kiowa.

He stopped short, then turned suddenly to Falcone. "I know. A trial by combat. Me and Kiowa. At sunrise. If I kill him, then that can be my way of proving myself to you."

Falcone shook his head. "You could never just kill a man like that. You don't have it in you to fight a man to the

359

death. In self-defense, maybe, but never just to prove a point."

"And if I do? Then will I have proven myself to you?"

Falcone was silent, letting all of this toss itself about in his whiskey-addled mind. A smile of amusement crept across his face. "Kiowa is the most deadly hand-to-hand fighter I have ever encountered, you know."

Dusty shook his head. "Second most deadly. Sam taught me all he knew, and I've learned a bit more on my own, and I'm willing to use all of it. If I kill Kiowa, then two of your problems are solved. You'll have a man you can rely on, and you won't have to worry about Kiowa. And you won't even miss Kiowa as a scout."

Falcone nodded as he let the ideas work their way through his mind. One hand went to his chin.

"All right, Dusty. I'll give you the chance. In the morning, a trial by combat it is."

It was Loggins' turn to stand guard. He crouched on his heels, his rifle balanced across one knee. Josh and Dusty sat in the grass. They were no longer tied – apparently Dusty had again won at least some trust from Falcone. The sun set behind the ridges, and the canyon slowly descended into blackness. Behind them, a window from the cabin flickered with the pale light from a lamp. Overhead, stars speckled the night sky. There was no moon this night. The wind from the mountains was cool, and the grass beneath Dusty and Josh was becoming wet with dew.

Loggins rose to his feet and said, "Oh, hell. I ain't gonna sit in the wet grass. It ain't like you two can go anywhere, anyway."

He walked over to the cabin, dropping onto the bench that rested against the back wall. Had it been daylight, he would have been within sight of Josh and Dusty, but in this darkness, all they could see of him was the faint red glow of his cigarette every time he took a draw.

Dusty whispered, "Josh?"

"Yeah?"

"Can you run fast?"

"Pa used to say I ran like a jack rabbit. Why?"

"When the fight begins, I want you to get out of here. They'll all be paying attention to me. I want you to slip past them and run like hell."

"No. I ain't leaving you."

"Yes, you are. That's why I set up this fight. You got to get back to the ranch, to warn Pa. If Kiowa kills me, then Vic and the men will be attacking with a new plan, trying to sneak in by daylight, when the ranch is mostly unmanned. Once you're out of the canyon, keep moving. Once they realize you're gone, they'll probably come after you. Find a horse somewhere, and get back to the ranch."

"Dusty, it should be me that's fighting him, not you. You're great with a gun, but I'm the better one when it comes to scrappin'. I handled you, remember?"

"Have you ever fought with a knife before?"

Josh shrugged with his brows. "Well, no."

"I have. And I've seen it done many times. That's the weapon he'll use. I'm the best one for this. Do like I ask. Once the fight begins, you run like hell."

"All right. But I'll be coming back for you."

"No. Don't bother with me. Just get back to the ranch. Warn Pa."

Loggins called over to them, "Shut up, you two!"

Dusty figured he and Josh wouldn't find another chance to speak before the fight. He hoped Josh would do as asked, or the entire plan would be in vain.

Dusty knew Falcone was right. He could never kill just to make a point. The only reason he could kill was in self defense, or the defense of others. Like back at the ranch when Falcone's men attacked, or at the way station in Nevada.

The thought of that way station brought Haley Anderson to mind. He imagined her, now in Oregon. Working a small farm alongside her father, and thinking of the young gunhawk who had saved her life. Waiting, wondering if he got the letter she left for him, and if he would be coming for her.

He didn't believe he would live to see another sundown, and he found himself feeling a pang of regret that he might never taste Haley's kisses again. Never look into her eyes again. The home he had allowed himself to imagine building alongside her would remain simply an unbuilt

dream. And she would never know what had happened to him. Just that he had never come looking for her. She would marry someone else, raise children with him, and as she grew older Dusty would become but a dim memory.

Dusty didn't know if Josh fully accepted him as a brother, but he realized it no longer mattered. All that now seemed important was Josh safely escaping this canyon and returning to the family, to warn them. And that Josh would live. For that, Dusty would kill.

He needed to make the fight last as long as possible, so Josh could get a solid head start. And he would need to kill Kiowa, who was the best tracker among them. That would leave Falcone, Loggins, White-Eye and Stew to pursue Josh. Dusty no longer thought Falcone would have the stamina for such a thing, and would not spend much time, if any, on the pursuit. Loggins and Stew might attempt to follow Josh, but they were not expert trackers, and Josh was, so he would be able to cover his trail well.

That they would shoot Dusty was to be expected, once they realized Josh was gone. But Dusty didn't care. What was important was Josh could rejoin his family. Josh was lucky. He had what Dusty had always longed for, and Dusty was determined not to see the family broken up.

Dusty drifted off to sleep with thoughts of the McCabe home, and the warmth that seemed to generate from the bond between them all. And what it might feel like to wake up every morning to a breakfast in that kitchen, and to have that house to return to every night.

THIRTY-NINE

Dusty was awakened with a boot to the ribs. The eastern sky was lightening, and the last of the stars overhead were fading.

"Sit up." It was Loggins.

Dusty did as he was commanded, stretching his arms to either side to try and work out a knot that had developed between his shoulders from spending the night on an uneven patch of earth.

"The boss wants to see you."

Dusty rose to his feet. Dang, he hoped this knot went away before the fight.

Josh was awake and looking at him. Dusty looked back, and in their silence, managed to say a lot. Dusty gave a slight nod of his head, which Josh returned, and then Dusty started for the cabin.

Loggins fell into place beside him. Loggins said, "I've got to tell you. Just between you and me, I hate Kiowa. He's dangerous. He's bad for the whole lot of us. He's a loose cannon, and will get us all killed if someone don't get rid of him. I'm rootin' for you."

"Thanks."

"Do you really think you can take him? I mean, he's the best with a knife I've ever seen. And he's cruel. Likes to hear a man scream."

They reached the cabin door, and Loggins said, "Go on in. The boss told me to wait out here."

Dusty found Falcone sitting at his table, with a fresh bottle of whiskey standing before him. He had already poured himself a glass. Flossy was at the hearth, fixing a pot of coffee, and Temperance stood at a cupboard preparing a batter for what Dusty guessed would be hot cakes. Where she had found the eggs, he didn't know. Maybe they had been taken from the nest of a wild bird. Now was not the time to put much thought into it.

"Would you like a drink?" Falcone asked. "A lot of men I've known would have a drink before battle, to take the edge off. Steady the hand."

Dusty shook his head. "Sam Patterson told me to never take a drink when going into a situation that would require all your wits."

Falcone nodded thoughtfully. "That might be wise advice."

He motioned to a chair across the table from himself. "Sit. Please."

Dusty slid the chair out and dropped into it.

Falcone looked to Flossy. "Go get it."

Apparently she knew what he was talking about, because she left the coffee and pushed past the blanket into the bedroom she shared with Falcone, and returned carrying a knife with a shining double-edged blade. She handed it to Falcone, who cradled it by the handle with one hand and held it up so the blade caught the light of the fire.

"This was given to me by my father, the late Colonel Victor T. Falcone, the First. Given to me as a reward when I chose to follow in his footsteps."

"I've heard over the years you were a teacher at a military school," Dusty said. "Some say West Point."

Falcone looked at Dusty, chuckled and shook his head. "I was a teacher, yes, but never at West Point. Never at a military school of any kind. I did attend West Point, though, with intentions of following the military tradition of my family. But I was expelled before my first year was completed. Drinking, brawling. Maybe I was never cut out for the military life. Or, maybe I was simply too young.

"Regardless, I found myself a disgrace in the eyes of the family. I moved south, attended school and eventually became a teacher in Missouri. When the war broke out, I joined the Confederate war effort, riding with Patterson and his raiders. I found a lifestyle that was much more rewarding than teaching, and more exciting. And so consuming that, when the war was over, I could not give it up and simply return to teaching little children the three R's."

Falcone handed the knife to Dusty. "I want you to use this today."

Dusty held the knife, and saw letters etched into the steel of the blade. VTF. Victor T. Falcone. "I can't use this, Vic. It was a gift from your father. It means so much to you."

"That's why I want you to use it. I want you to kill Kiowa. I want you to win this fight, because I did some thinking last night. I decided I don't want to reach the end of my trail, yet, after all. Maybe I still have a little life remaining within me. But as you said, I need a good right-hand man. As I was to Patterson. I need you, Dusty. But only if you can prove you have what it takes, by killing Kiowa."

Dusty held the knife by the hilt, and slashed at the air. "It is nicely balanced. A beautiful weapon."

"The Falcones have always been fighting men. We know our weapons. And we know our men. Now, go, and do what you have to do."

Dusty stepped from the cabin and found Kiowa standing twenty yards from the doorway, Bowie knife in hand. Kiowa had discarded his riding boots, and stood in calf-length rawhide moccasins.

He smiled, or at least gave the closest thing to a smile he could muster—his lips pulling back to reveal a row of black and broken teeth. "Are you ready to die, little muchacho?"

Loggins and Stew stood to one side, and with them was Josh. Falcone stepped from the cabin, with Flossy at his side. Dusty didn't see Temperance with them. White-Eye was also missing. Dusty supposed he was standing guard out at the canyon rim. He hoped Josh would surmise this, too.

Dusty cast a glance to Josh. Their eyes met for the space of a heartbeat. Dusty hoped Josh would follow along with his plan and not do something heroic.

"I've been waitin' for this a long time," Kiowa said.

Falcone stepped between them, and said, "Come forward, both of you."

They each advanced until a distance of only ten feet separated them, with Falcone still between them.

"This fight will be held with knives, only," Falcone said, much like a referee announcing the rules of conduct before a prize fight. Though, Dusty knew full well the prize in this fight would be life itself.

"There will be no other weapons allowed," Falcone continued. "If this rule should be violated, the violator will be

shot immediately. And this fight shall be to the death. Is this understood?"

Both Dusty and Kiowa nodded, though Kiowa didn't take his gaze from Dusty.

"Very well," Falcone stepped back. "Let the fight begin!"

Kiowa lunged at Dusty, swiping at him with his knife. Dusty leaped back, avoiding the tip of the blade by a full inch, then slashed out at Kiowa hard, nicking his wrist and drawing first blood.

Kiowa looked at him with surprise. "A lucky cut, little muchacho."

Dusty shook his head. "I'm no longer a little muchacho, a little boy. I've grown up, Kiowa. You're going to find me a lot harder to kill than you would have ten years ago."

Kiowa's smile faded, and a grim seriousness took its place as he saw Dusty for what he now had grown to be, not the frightened child he once had been.

Kiowa raised his knife, holding it out before him, and began to circle to Dusty's right. Dusty assumed the same stance, his knife ready, and circled to his own left, countering Kiowa. He did not want to stand still and be caught flat-footed by a sudden attack.

Kiowa feigned a lunge with his knife, and Dusty jumped back. Then the circling resumed. Dusty suddenly lunged with his blade, and Kiowa sidestepped, slashed downward in an arc, and cut through Dusty's buckskin sleeve.

Dusty kept his gaze focused on Kiowa's eyes, watching for any intent that might betray itself before Kiowa could actually move.

Kiowa suddenly struck, charging forward with his knife raised high as if to strike downward into Dusty's heart, but then at the last moment, dropped his strike and lunged at Dusty's stomach. Dusty had raised his forearm to catch Kiowa's wrist, but now the knife was thrusting in from a lower angle.

Dusty managed to drop his left forearm quickly enough to strike Kiowa's wrist sideways and knock away the strike, but he was unable to keep his footing against Kiowa's

weight and the speed of his attack, finding himself being pushed backward. He hit the ground on his back, and Kiowa landed on him, straddling his chest. Dusty's knife landed a couple feet away in the grass. Kiowa's knife was raised for the strike.

Dusty brought his feet up, wrapped his ankles around Kiowa's neck, and pulled him backward and away.

Both scrambled to their feet. Dusty grabbed his knife, and they stood facing each other. Dusty now took a moment to touch his left hand to the cut in the forearm of his right sleeve, and found his fingers were wet with blood.

As Dusty and Kiowa began circling each other again, Josh took a step backward. Falcone, Loggins, Flossy—none of them seemed to notice, as their attention was fixed so intensely on the battle.

Josh took a second step, this one larger than the first. All eyes were still on Dusty and Kiowa, as Kiowa lunged at Dusty again with his blade. Dusty stepped aside, and with the same motion, sliced at Kiowa, cutting a swatch across Kiowa's forearm.

Josh turned and started walking. He had to fight down the urge to run, because any sudden motion might draw attention to him. The corner of the cabin was only ten yards away. He kept his strides strong and steady, at any moment expecting a shout from one of the outlaws as they realized he was attempting to escape. But the noise rising from them continued to be the cheering on of Dusty or Kiowa.

Josh stepped around the corner of the cabin, and from the sight of the others. No one called to him. He hadn't been seen.

He drew a lungful of air, then burst into a run down the grassy slope, and into the grove of trees. He felt the wind at his face as his strong legs pounded the earth, and stretched into a strong, loping stride. His hat lifted from his head and bounced lightly along the earth behind him, but he did not take the time to go back and retrieve it.

His goal was what appeared to be a thicker grove of trees beyond the water Temperance had been swimming in. He would hide his trail, then search for a way out of this canyon other than the pass he and Dusty had been brought in through. He had noticed White-Eye wasn't among the

audience for the fight, and figured he had been assigned guard duty. And that pass into the canyon, the only entrance a rider could use, was where the guards seemed to be always posted.

Josh was leaving the canyon, and he would return to the ranch to warn Pa and the others. But he would be back. Dusty was risking his life to give Josh a chance, and would probably lose his life in the process. Josh didn't forget his debts. He would be back to resume the quest he and Dusty had set out on originally—to bring Vic Falcone and the other raiders to justice, or kill them in the process.

He emerged from the trees at the edge of the small pond, and found Temperance facing him. She wore a faded range shirt, the sleeves rolled to her elbows. The front of the shirt was buttoned a little more conservatively than usual, and she wore Levi's that conformed to the roundness of her hips in a way Josh could not help noticing, despite the urgency of the situation. In one hand was a Bowie knife which she held before her, the tip of the blade pointing toward him.

He looked silently at her. He didn't want to hurt her, but didn't want to lose time, either.

"I thought you were Loggins," she said, and lowered the knife.

She had been crying, he realized. Her eyes were reddened, and a little puffy.

"Are you all right?" he found himself asking.

"I'm not going to let him touch me again. Not ever."

"I've got to go," he said. "While they're all focusing on the fight. I'm getting out of here, but I'll be back."

She nodded.

"Will you tell them you saw me?"

She shook her head. "No. On one condition."

"What's that?"

"Take me with you."

Kiowa moved in on Dusty with a series of sudden swipes and thrusts, forcing Dusty backward. One thrust he parried with his knife, as though he were fencing, but the others he found himself continuously leaping away from.

His back collided with the wall of the cabin. This had been Kiowa's plan, Dusty realized, to pin him against the wall and rob him of his mobility. Kiowa was taller, stronger, and Dusty's only hope had been to out-maneuver him.

Dusty began a swipe at Kiowa's face, but Kiowa caught Dusty's right wrist with his left hand before the blade could find its target.

Kiowa raised his own knife for a strike, but Dusty reached with his own left, and grabbed Kiowa's knife-hand by the wrist.

A contest of strength began.

Kiowa dug his feet into the sod and drove Dusty back, slamming him into the wall. Once. Twice.

He then drove the knuckles of Dusty's knife-hand into one of the pine logs that made up the wall, and jarred the blade free of Dusty's grip.

Dusty brought one knee quickly up toward Kiowa's groin. Not exactly clean fighting, Dusty thought, but when you're fighting for your life, you toss most rules aside.

Kiowa instinctively twisted his hips at the motion of Dusty's leg, so the knee missed and caught instead the inside of one thigh, not doing the damage Dusty intended, but the momentary distraction enabled Dusty to pull his right hand free of Kiowa's grasp. Dusty then balled his fingers into a fist, and drove a right cross into Kiowa's cheekbone.

Kiowa's head rolled back with the force of the punch, and as it came forward, Dusty let loose again with his fist.

With Kiowa momentarily dazed from the two punches, Dusty grabbed the wrist of Kiowa's knife hand with both of his own, and brought Kiowa's arm down across one knee. The knife fell from Kiowa's grasp.

Kiowa shook away the cobwebs brought on by Dusty's fists, and leaped at Dusty, wrapping his arms about Dusty's ribcage and lifting him from his feet. Kiowa couldn't match Dusty's youthful speed with his fists, and was not about to waste energy even trying. He would instead use his superior strength to squeeze the life from him.

He slammed Dusty back and into the wall again, and Dusty's skull bounced against a pine log, which started his head swimming.

Dusty felt the air being forced from his lungs by the pressure of Kiowa's vise-like grip. Kiowa shook him from side to side to keep his opponent from regaining his bearings.

Dusty yanked Kiowa's shoulder-length hair but it had no effect. He raised one fist and gave a couple short jabs to the side of Kiowa's head, but the limited distance of the punches took away from their effectiveness.

Dusty then swung both hands wide to either side of Kiowa's head, and then with all of the strength he could muster, he slapped Kiowa's ears with his open palms.

That did the trick. Kiowa released his grip on Dusty, and brought both hands to his ears, howling with pain.

Dusty spread his feet wide, and sent a left jab into Kiowa's face, then another, then a wide hook punch, rolling his torso into it, rocking Kiowa's head back and opening a gash above one eye.

Kiowa staggered backward, then leaped—not toward Dusty, but to one side.

Dusty realized a moment too late what Kiowa's goal was, as Kiowa's fingers curled about the handle of Dusty's knife where it lay in the grass.

Kiowa sprang to his feet and charged at Dusty, raising the knife for a strike.

The blade began a downward arc that would bring it to Dusty's chest, but Dusty raised one forearm to make contact with Kiowa's wrist and block the strike.

Kiowa gripped the knife with both hands, and began forcing the knife downward with all of his strength, grimacing with the effort.

A stream of blood was flowing from the cut above Kiowa's eye, traveling down along his nose and dripping away. Rivulets of sweat made their way down Dusty's face, and he felt it breaking out along his back beneath his buckskin shirt.

Dusty knew this could not go on much longer. Despite the fact that Kiowa was twenty years older, he was simply the stronger of the two. Then, an idea occurred to him.

Dusty suddenly stepped back, and as suddenly pulled the knife downward. The arc of the knife brought it down and into Kiowa's own abdomen, and Kiowa's strength drove the knife in deeply, burying the blade to the hilt.

He looked at Dusty, his eyes wide with surprise. He opened his mouth to say something, but all he could manage was a gasping groan.

Dusty curled his fingers about the hilt of the knife, and pulled it free, the blade dripping with crimson. Sam had told him years earlier if you ever find yourself in a situation where you have to use a knife on a man, never leave it in him. Pull it free so he can bleed more freely. And many a mortally wounded man can be full of life right up until the last second, and Kiowa could possibly, though not likely, pull the blade free himself and use it on Dusty.

Kiowa sank to his knees, a blood stain growing about the hole the knife had made in his shirt. Dusty figured he was not only bleeding out through the knife wound, but internally as well. Kiowa's eyes rolled back, and he fell face down into the grass.

Loggins hurried forward rolled Kiowa over, and lowered his head to press an ear against Kiowa's chest. He then looked to Falcone. "He's dead."

Falcone looked to Dusty and nodded with approval, a smile breaking onto his face. "Well done."

"Hold it," the one called Stew said. "Where's the other one?"

Falcone glanced quickly about, realizing for the first time Josh had disappeared. His brows dropped. "Yes. Where is he?"

Stew had been cradling a scatter-gun throughout the fight. He now brought the twin barrels to face Dusty. "Don't you move a whisker until we figger out what's goin' on, here."

Dusty raised the knife and let it fly in one quick motion. The steel blade sank into Stew's throat, and he fell backward a couple of steps, dropping the gun to clutch the knife handle protruding beneath his chin.

Dusty raised one foot and drove the toe of his boot into the jaw of Loggins, who was still kneeling by the body of Kiowa.

Dusty then turned and sprinted for the cabin door as Falcone drew his pistol.

Falcone squeezed off a shot, but his aim was high and the bullet buried itself into the wood of the door as Dusty pushed the door open and charged inside.

He didn't slow his pace as he crossed the floor toward a window, which was no more than a three-by-three foot hole cut into the wall, with a small shutter that was at the moment open. Dusty raced toward it, raised his arms out before him, and dove through the opening, one shoulder grazing painfully against the corner of the window. His body cleared the cabin, and he rolled head-first onto the grass outside to break his fall. His momentum carried him back to his feet, and he resumed running.

A thick grove of short pines stood thirty feet from the cabin, and he knew if he could reach them without being shot from behind, he might have a reasonable chance of escaping this canyon.

He wasn't as quick afoot as Josh—a little taller and more heavily muscled—but he stretched his legs to their limits.

He charged into the thick boughs of the pines, and a gun fired from behind. He felt the breeze of the bullet as it passed inches from his left ear.

He dropped to the earth as more shots erupted from the cabin, the bullets cutting through the pines, snapping off branches and tearing off strips of bark. The shots were from a pistol, Dusty could tell by the sound of each report, and he figured it was Falcone who had followed him into the cabin was now firing from the window.

There was a slight pause, but Dusty remained on the ground, out of sight of the window. Falcone might very well have a second pistol. And that proved to be the case, as more shots exploded, Dusty counting six, tearing into the trees.

Then, when the shooting ceased again, he sprang to his feet and started running again, now blocked from the view of the cabin by the pines, but knowing it wouldn't be long before Falcone had reloaded and would resume firing, or he and Loggins took up pursuit.

Dusty ran along a wooded decline that led to a stream, which in turn led to the water hole that served as the water supply for Falcone and his men, and where the women did their bathing. The stream was too large for Dusty to clear with one leap, but he found a spot a few yards downstream where a rock rose above the water part-way across. With a

running start, Dusty leaped, stretching one leg toward the rock.

His foot landed on it to push away from it toward the far bank. The leather sole of his boot slipped on the rock, however, and he lost some of his momentum. The earth at the very edge of the stream was soft, and it was there that he landed, burying one heel and creating a footprint that would show Falcone and Loggins he had passed here.

The print could be covered, Dusty knew, by scooping some mud from the stream bottom to fill in the print with, and the current would quickly smooth the gouge this would create in the stream bed, but there was no time. At any moment Falcone or Loggins would appear with a gun aimed at him. He would simply have to be more careful.

This side of the stream formed a wooded incline, rising toward the canyon wall, which from the other side of the canyon had appeared to be sheer rock. Yet, scaling that wall seemed to be his only course of action. To hide from men like Falcone and Loggins indefinitely within the confines of this canyon would be impossible. And they would be watching the pass into the canyon too closely for him to have a chance of using to escape.

However, could he scale the wall before they located him, and came within shooting range? A chance he would have to take. His only chance, he figured.

And at least they were chasing him, and not Josh.

He resumed running, stepping as carefully as he could along the pine needle laden forest floor so that he wouldn't leave any noticeable boot prints. He stepped around any fallen branches, as even a broken twig could indicate to men like Falcone and Loggins that he had passed this way.

He emerged from the trees to find maybe three hundred feet of open ground, covered with light grass and choppy with outcroppings of bedrock, separating him from the canyon wall. Dang. Even more of a chance for one of his pursuers to get off a good shot at him before he could completely scale the wall.

He was huffing for breath. He had spent most of his years in a saddle and not afoot, and it now showed. His legs felt wobbly, and sweat was streaming down his face. A couple

chugs from a cold canteen, he thought. What he wouldn't give for that right now.

But he had no time to waste. He charged across the uneven ground, expecting at any moment for a gun to fire from behind and plant a bullet in his back. But he ran without looking back. To look back would cause him to break stride, and maybe lose a valuable second. A second that might make the difference between life and death.

The wall was maybe twenty feet of bedrock, not as sheer as it had appeared, being corrugated with rough edges and small shelves. Lots of hand and footholds, he thought. But rising at almost a perfect right angle from the canyon floor.

He noticed a crack at one point that was jagged like a lighting bolt, and it was here that he began his climb.

One leather sole slipped on the rock, but he held on with both hands and kicked around to regain his footing.

He scraped a finger, which would probably bleed, but only if he could get to the top of the wall before anyone shot him from down below. Dead men don't bleed.

The crack in the rock ended eight feet from the canyon rim, and Dusty didn't have much room from which to jump. Immediately overhead was a small pine, leaning over the edge of the wall, and this would be Dusty's goal. He knew if he missed the tree, there would be nothing between himself and a thirty foot fall to the canyon floor. And even if he managed to obtain a firm grip on the tree, its roots might not be strong enough to hold him for more than a moment or two.

He drew a breath. He needed all of the strength he could muster. Even had he been well rested, he wouldn't have wanted to bet on making this jump, but now, with his legs wobbly and his energy nearly spent, he had a feeling this jump might be the last thing he would ever do.

A bullet zinged at the rock near one hand, kicking off a chip of stone, and a moment later, the crack of gunfire from down below reached him.

He allowed himself a glance back and down over one shoulder. Falcone and Loggins had both emerged at the edge of the trees. Loggins had obtained a Winchester. He had been the one shooting, because Dusty was still out of pistol range.

Loggins was already jacking the rifle, chambering a round for another shot. Dusty turned his eyes back to the pine overhead, and sprang upward. He wrapped the fingers of his left hand about the slender trunk of the small pine. It bent under his weight, but the roots held. Dusty found himself dangling above the canyon.

With his right hand he grasped at the top of the wall, finding the earth soft. He managed to find a handhold, as a second bullet caught the shoulder of his shirt, tearing away some buckskin but missing his flesh. He let go of the pine, and grasped frantically at the canyon rim with his left, then began pulling himself upward until his shoulders were above the edge of the canyon.

Then the earth gave way, and he found himself slipping backward and down. He scrambled with his feet against the rock facing of the wall to slow his descent. His fingers clawed out at the earth frantically, but he could find no firm hand-hold.

Suddenly, a hand reached out from above, and gripped his right. It was a huge hand entirely enveloping his. He looked upward to see the bearded face of Hunter.

With his free hand Dusty clamped onto the top of Hunter's big paw, and using only one hand Hunter pulled him upward and free of the canyon, as a third shot was fired from below.

And there was Zack Johnson, a few yards from Hunter, kneeling at the edge of the canyon wall, Pa's Sharps buffalo rifle pressed against his shoulder. He was drawing a bead on the men below.

Zack squeezed the trigger. The rifle bucked against his shoulder with a loud boom, and Loggins, still at the edge of the trees, was caught squarely in the chest. Despite the distance, the force of the shot lifted Loggins into the air and dropped him backwards to the earth.

"Even the old man himself couldn't have done better than that," Johnson said, a small smirk decorating his face, and he slid the action open, pulled out the empty cartridge, and dropped in another one.

The sling he had been wearing around his left arm was now gone. He said, "Good thing it wasn't my right shoulder

that took that bullet. It could never have taken the kick this rifle has."

Beyond Johnson was Josh. And beside him was the girl, Temperance. Dusty was about to ask what she was doing here, but then he decided he didn't need to. The answer was obvious.

Zack jacked open the action and pulled out the empty cartridge, then inserted a fresh one and closed the action. He brought the rifle to his shoulder, and began sighting in on Falcone. Vic, whose survival instinct was one of the greatest Dusty had ever seen, turned and ran back into the trees as Zack squeezed the trigger. The bullet tore away a chunk of bark from the trunk of a pine.

"Dang," Zack said.

"Should we hunt him down?" Josh asked.

Dusty shook his head. "We'll never catch him. He's one of the best I've ever seen at finding a way to stay alive. By the time we can get back down and into that canyon, he'll be long gone. But I have a feeling we'll see him again, one of these days."

Dusty turned to Hunter. "I have to admit, I'm sure glad to see you. But, a little surprised too."

Hunter said, "Aunt Ginny told us where you had gone. We saddled up and followed. The way we see it, we're all family, and we couldn't let you ride after them alone. We've been a day behind you all the way, and camped out up here since yesterday, trying to figure a way to get the two of you out of that canyon."

Zack rose to his feet. "Come on, let's ride. Fred's waiting back there with the horses."

"Hunter," Dusty said, extending his hand. "Thank you."

Hunter's huge hand wrapped around Dusty's. "Don't mention it."

"If there's every anything..."

"Like I said, don't mention it."

"I don't suppose you're going to let me start paying for my beer now?"

With a big smile, Hunter said, "Not a chance."

EPILOGUE

Dusty stepped into the kitchen. His destination, the coffee pot.

He wore a blue shirt he had bought at Franklin's, tucked into a new pair of Levi's. He and Josh and the others had gone back down into the canyon to retrieve the horses, and Josh and Dusty's guns. Dusty's Peacemaker was once again strapped down to his right leg.

He had also pulled the knife from the corpse of Stew. The knife that had the initials V.T.F. engraved in the side of the blade. A memento, he supposed. It was in his room upstairs.

Aunt Ginny had cleaned the knife wound on Dusty's forearm, following Pa's old method of washing the wound with whiskey. It was a pain worse than anything Dusty had experienced fighting Kiowa. The wound was now wrapped in strips torn from a bed sheet to form a makeshift bandage, and was healing nicely.

Josh was leaning against the counter, a cup in one hand. His gun was also buckled on.

The sky outside was light with early morning gray. It wouldn't be long before Aunt Ginny and Bree would be fixing breakfast. And then, Dusty and Josh would have a full day of work ahead of them. Fifteen hours, which was normal for a working day on the McCabe ranch. And it wouldn't be long before Pa would be joining them again, Dusty figured.

Temperance was also helping with the household chores. She was staying with the family, at least for a while, finding a sort of comfort in settling into the duties of maintaining a household, working alongside Aunt Ginny and Bree. Josh had raised no complaint at all about this, or the inconvenience of having to give up his room and share one with Dusty, sleeping in bunk beds he and Dusty had been called upon to fashion out of two-by-fours.

Dusty believed Josh was falling in love with Temperance. Even though Josh wouldn't talk about what was going on in his heart, Dusty could see in the way Josh looked at Temperance that the concern he had shown her back at the canyon was much more genuine than Josh would admit.

And there was something in the way she looked back at Josh that told Dusty what her heart held, also.

Josh was a good man, Dusty had come to realize. A little head strong, and a little hampered by feeling he lived so much in Pa's shadow. But a man to ride the river with, as Sam Patterson would have said.

Josh said, "Aunt Ginny told me you're thinking about riding on."

Dusty nodded, as he filled a cup with coffee. "I'll be staying for a while, to help out until Pa is recovered enough to go back to work. But then, I've got to be going. I've got some unfinished business in Oregon."

Josh knitted his brow. "Oregon? What's there?"

"A girl. Named Haley. Last I knew, she and her father were heading there. I might take a little ride and make sure they arrived all right."

"And then, what's after that?"

Dusty shrugged. "I don't really know."

Josh dropped his gaze. "Dusty, I don't quite know how to say this. But..."

Dusty shrugged. "I've always thought the best way to say something is just to say it."

"Well, it's just that Pa and Aunt Ginny and Bree have grown awfully fond of you, and don't want you to leave."

"Is that it?"

Josh nodded. "And..."

He looked Dusty in the eye. "It's hard for me to say this, but..."

He paused. Dusty gave him the time he needed.

"Oh, hell. I don't want you to leave. I've gained a brother I never knew I had. I've just started getting to know him, and I don't want to lose him now. Once you've finished in Oregon, whether you find this Haley or not, I hope you come back. And Jack hasn't met you, yet."

"I don't know if I belong here, Josh. A place in a family isn't given to you. You have to earn it. I know that, now. Families are built over time, with love that develops over years. That's one thing I learned from you all. I rode in here wanting to be a part of all this, thinking the blood and the name made me one of you. But I've realized I can never quite

be a part of the family, not the way you are. You were born and raised a McCabe."

"I guess you haven't quite learned yet what a family is, have you?"

Now it was time for Dusty to knit his brow out of puzzlement.

"A family isn't built by time, Dusty. It's built by love, alone. Good, honest, unconditional love. You're my brother. Unconditionally. And nothing is ever going to change that. You fought alongside me, helping us defend our home. You rode with me to go after the men who attacked it and almost killed Pa, and you risked your life so I could escape. That sounds like unconditional love to me.

"Let us give some of that back to you. At least, once you're finished in Oregon, come back and give yourself a little more time to find out what a family is really all about. You belong here, not anywhere else."

Dusty nodded, and took a plug of coffee. "Thanks, Josh. I'll think about that."

A voice spoke from the doorway to the parlor. A man's voice. "You got about six more weeks to think about it."

Pa was standing there, standing strong. Four weeks had already passed since he had been shot, and though he wasn't quite strong enough yet to sit in the saddle, you wouldn't find a sign of weakness in his step. The gauntness and the grayness his face had taken on during those first few days, when he had been so near death, were now gone like they had never been there. His hair was pulled back into a tail, he was freshly shaven, and he wore a range shirt and jeans. Buckled about his hips were his ever-present guns.

He said, "I figure I have about six more weeks before I can spend a full day in the saddle without falling over. Then, if you want, you can head off to Oregon. And I'll probably send Josh with you, because that's a lot of country for a man to be covering alone."

"I've ridden over longer distances than that alone."

"Yeah, but you're not alone anymore. You're part of a family, Dusty. This family. And I hope you come back here to us when you're done in Oregon."

"You'll have to come back," Josh said, looking at his brother. "I'll be with you, and I'll drag you back."

That got a smile from Dusty.

Josh drained his remaining coffee with one gulp and said, "Let's get moving. We've got a big day ahead of us."

Josh was out the door, and Dusty a few steps behind, taking his last mouthful of coffee and setting his cup on the counter, when Johnny said, "Dusty?"

Dusty stopped and looked back. "Yeah, Pa?"

"There's something I've got to say." Johnny approached his son and laid a hand on his shoulder. "I want you to know, if I had known about you, I would have come back for you."

"I know that, Pa."

"But I never actually said it. Some things have to be said. You're my son. You're as much mine as Josh and Bree and Jack. And I love you just as much. I do hope you come back here when you're done in Oregon, son. This place will always be your home."

"Thanks, Pa. You'll never know how much being a part of all this means to me."

Johnny nodded, one corner of his mouth twitching into a half-smile. "Yeah, I think I do, because I know how much it means to me. Now, you'd better get going before Josh starts bellowing for you and wakes half the countryside."

Dusty grinned, and turned and headed out into the ranch yard.

Johnny turned toward the coffee kettle, intending to fill himself a cup and then head out onto the front porch to watch morning take the land, when he saw Ginny standing in the parlor doorway, her face glowing with a smile, tears streaming down her cheeks.

"What are you looking at?" Johnny asked, as he reached into a cupboard for a coffee mug, knowing fully well what she was looking at. She had apparently been standing in the doorway, eavesdropping on his conversation with Dusty. He braced himself for one of her barbs, such as an I-told-you-so, regarding Johnny's acceptance of Dusty as his son. But she surprised him.

"Nothing, John," she said. "It's already turning out to be a beautiful day, that's all."

* * *

Fred had left fresh mounts for Josh and Dusty. They were tethered to the corral fence. Josh took the rein in one hand and was about to step into the saddle, but then he glanced toward the house, and saw Temperance at the front porch.

He and Dusty had been rounding up strays. They had brought five hundred head into the valley, to graze on the lush, green grass growing at the valley floor. Then, a couple nights ago, a thunderstorm had sent them scattering. They had been working from dawn to dusk for the past couple of days at this. However, they were close enough to the house to allow them to return for lunch.

Aunt Ginny's sandwiches and a cup of hot coffee sure beat chewing on jerky and drinking warm water from your canteen. And, Temperance was at the house. Josh found himself taking any opportunity to see her, even if was simply to sit with her and the family at the table. He found she was occupying his thoughts much of the time.

Dusty had swung into the saddle. He and Josh were about to return to rounding up strays. But Josh wasn't getting into the saddle. Dusty saw him looking toward the porch.

Dusty couldn't help but grin. He said, "I'll ride on ahead."

Josh gave the rein a couple turns around the top rail of the corral and then walked toward the front porch. He was covered with dust. Aunt Ginny had generously allowed him and Dusty to eat at the table without requiring them to wash up and put on fresh clothes. He was wearing leather chaps strapped on over his jeans, and his pistol was at his side.

He tried to look casual and yet wanted to get to the porch before she went back inside.

But she saw him and threw a smile his way.

He stopped below the porch. "I haven't had much time to talk with you lately. Aunt Ginny keeps you busy, and there's always folks around. Hard to get a moment alone."

She nodded. Her hair was tied back in a bun, and she was wearing a blouse and a long, dark skirt. An apron was tied about her middle. She was now eating regular, well-balanced meals, and her color was good. She had been a little

washed out looking when he had first met her. Now there was no sign of that. She looked like she belonged working on a ranch.

"I love it here," she said. "I never thought I could have a life like this."

"I'm glad," he said.

"Your family is so wonderful. I'll never be able to thank you enough for bringing me here."

He raised his brows and gave her a questioning look. "The way Aunt Ginny works you..."

"The work is hard. But it's good work. Honest work. At the end of the day, you feel like you've accomplished something."

This drew a smile from him. It was what he liked about ranch work, too. At the end of the day, his butt might hurt from all of the hours in the saddle, his back might ache, but he had the feeling that he was building something.

"You know, there's a creek out yonder. A couple miles that-a-way," he nodded with his head in the general direction of northwest. "It's in a little patch of woods. It'd be the perfect place to put a little house. Raise a family. With the right girl. Maybe I could show it to you sometime."

"Josh," she said, a little sadly, catching what he was hinting at. "I'm flattered. You need a good girl to build a life with. But I'm just not worthy."

"I think you are. I don't think any of us should be judged by what we have to do to survive. We're all human, Temperance. And we're all damaged to some extent. But any man would be honored to have you at his side."

She took a moment, letting his words sink in. No man had ever talked to her like this before.

Then she said, "I'm just not ready. Not to build a life with anyone. But," she met his gaze with eyes as blue as the sky above, "when I am, if you still think you want me, I'd be honored."

He nodded. "I can wait. When something's worth it, I can wait a long time."

She smiled. A big, beaming smile. A smile that warmed his heart like none other. She didn't know what to say. Maybe there was nothing that could be said. She simply smiled at him, and he smiled back.

"I gotta be going," he said. "Gotta join Dusty. Round up them strays."

"I'll be here when you get back."

He nodded and turned toward where his horse waited for him by the corral.

"You know," she called to him, and he turned back to her, "I think I'll always be here when you get back."

He strode toward his horse. Nothing makes a man feel more alive than a woman he is in love with saying something like that. He had been hurting from all of the work he and Dusty had been doing. But at the moment, all of the hurts were gone. He grabbed the saddle horn and leaped onto the animal's back.

He looked toward the porch and found Temperance was still there, watching him. He reared the horse up and onto its hind legs. She laughed, and waved back.

Josh turned the horse and rode off to catch up with his brother.

Temperance stood on the porch, watching him shrink with the distance. For the first time since she was a child, she felt like she was home.

* * *

Johnny stood on the porch, a half-full mug of coffee in his hand. Ginny stepped out onto the porch behind him, carrying a teacup and saucer, and noticed Johnny held his mug in his left hand so his right could be free should he need to reach for a gun. Living in a perpetual state of war. She figured he always would.

The sun had set and the valley before them was falling into shadows. The breeze was turning cool, but brought with it a hint of balsam.

"My favorite time of day," he said. "When Zack, Josiah and I wintered here with the Shoshone, I would stand in front of the lodge we used and just watch night descend onto the valley. It always brought a sort of feeling to me like what my Ma used to describe feeling in church. A sort of hushed reverence."

Ginny said, "To the Shoshone, the land itself is their church. The forests, the mountains. The sky is their cathedral."

He nodded. "Not just to them. I guess it is to me, too."

"Oh, John. I kid you a lot about your Indian beliefs. But I really think you're more Shoshone than you realize. At least in your heart."

He tossed a grin back at her. "Why, Ginny. I think that might be the nicest thing you've ever said to me."

"Don't get used to it," she said with a smirk, and lowered herself to her rocker, and took a sip of the steaming hot Earl Grey. Then she grew serious. "John, how are you feeling?"

"You ask me that three times a day."

"Well, you get yourself shot and almost killed, and you have to expect people to ask you how you feel."

"I'm feeling fine. Stronger every day."

He still felt a twinge of pain when he exerted himself. Such as the day before, when he saddled one of the geldings himself, hefting the saddle and tossing it onto the horse's back, and pulling the girth tight. He could feel the exertion at the point the bullets had entered, and he could feel it deeper inside. He then stepped into the saddle and rode for a few minutes, keeping the horse to a light walk, with Fred watching should something go wrong. His bullet wounds had long since healed on the surface, but he could feel the jarring of the horse's steps internally. After a few minutes, he began to break out in a cold sweat, so he stepped down and sat in Ginny's rocker on the porch until he felt better.

Of course, he hadn't told Ginny any of this. As far as she knew, he had gone for a long walk.

He was sure, in time, he would regain all of his stamina, and the wounds would heal entirely. A concern he had, though, was that neither bullet had left an exit wound, meaning the lead was still inside. He had known men who carried lead from old wounds, and the effect it could have was unpredictable. Never affected any two men the same.

But this evening, as he stood with a cup of coffee in one hand enjoying the mountain air, he felt fine. Yesterday's discomfort and fatigue had been only warning signs, he figured, to take it more slowly.

"So," she said, "the plan, as I understand it, is Dusty and Josh are going to ride out to Oregon after the fall roundup."

Johnny nodded. "If Josh can pull himself away from Temperance for that long."

Ginny chuckled. "They're falling in love, you know."

"You can almost feel it in the air when the two of them are in the room together." He turned to face her. "What do you think about all of that? I mean, what do we really know about Temperance?"

"She's a good girl, John. A girl forced to make some bad decisions. But she's a fighter. A survivor. She was able to survive the life she had been trapped in. And I've been thinking—she and Josh sort of remind me of a couple I knew years ago."

He raised his brows questioningly. "Who?"

"Do I really have to tell you? He is your son. Dusty isn't the only one who reminds me of you."

Johnny turned back to look at the darkening valley. "Jack'll be home in a few weeks. It'll be good to see him."

"I've written him a letter telling him about Dusty."

"Good."

Johnny stood in silence for a few moments. He took a sip of coffee. The breeze picked up a bit, then died down.

"John," Ginny said. "You said something when you first woke up from being shot. You said that Lura loved me. Why did you say that?"

How could he tell her? How could he tell anyone without them thinking he was out of his mind? And maybe he had been. Out of his mind with the loss of blood, and the fever that had been setting in. Maybe it had only been a dream, as his head swum in delirium. But somehow, on a deeper level, he felt it had not been.

He hadn't realized until after he had his experience in that dream state with Lura and the old Shoshone shaman, and he lay in bed recuperating, with lots of time to think about it, it had not been grief that he was carrying all of those years since Lura's death. It was guilt. Guilt, because he had believed that bullet was meant for him. And now, the guilt was gone. He felt somehow lighter, as though a burden had been removed.

"I could never explain it," he said. "But trust me."

She nodded thoughtfully. There was probably no one on Earth she trusted more. "So, have you had any more thoughts about riding to California to visit Lura's grave?"

"I think I probably will. But I won't be gone long. I'll definitely be coming back. My life is here. And for the first time in a long time, I feel young and alive, and I intend to live my life."

She didn't know what had happened. Maybe she never would. But she knew it was more than simply coming back from near death. Whatever had happened, she was grateful. She hadn't seen him this full of life since before Lura died.

Welcome back, John, she said to herself, and brought her cup of tea to her lips. What a day this had turned out to be, indeed.

Ginny closed her eyes and took in a deep lungful of the evening mountain air, relishing the scents of balsam, and the scent of grass and earth. And the subtle yet unmistakable scent of peach blossoms.

In the next few pages is a sneak peek at:

ONE MAN'S SHADOW

The sequel to THE LONG TRAIL

On sale now at Amazon.com

Jack McCabe returns home to Montana from medical school, but the family finds he is not exactly who they thought he was. A story of one man attempting to find himself while living in the shadow of a father who is a living legend. And an old enemy of Johnny McCabe returns, looking for blood. A story of family, love and revenge, and of the redemption of the human spirit.

1

He pulled open a wooden drawer, and scooped out a load of folded socks and handkerchiefs and dropped them into a trunk lying open on the floor. He then grabbed a stack of union suits, also neatly folded like Aunt Ginny had taught him to keep them, and they joined the socks and handkerchiefs. In the trunk beside them was a hat box.

The final item in the drawer was a leather gunbelt. The belt was rolled up, the cartridge loops filled, and in the holster was a .44 caliber Colt Peacemaker. The holster had actually been designed for an older model Colt cap and ball

revolver. But on a trip to New York he had seen the Peacemaker in a gunsmith shop, and after sampling it, found the balance too incredible to resist and coughed up the cash.

The money had been left over from what Aunt Ginny had provided him to purchase text books with. He doubted she would approve of him buying a gun with it, but the gun had almost called to him. He was, after all, the son of Johnny McCabe.

His name was Jackson, after his father's grandfather, and even though Aunt Ginny called him by his full first name, everyone else called him Jack.

He had been raised on the family ranch in Montana, and could ride a horse as well as most men walked. He was not the wizard with a gun his father was, but he could clear leather quickly enough, and shoot straight and hit his target most of the time.

His fellow college boys here at Harvard knew the name Johnny McCabe. It was being spoken on a level with Wild Bill Hickok and Wyatt Earp. There were even a couple of dime novels written about him. This brought Jack a sort of fame about campus. He found himself invited to fraternity parties that he would otherwise not have been.

When he had bought the Peacemaker, he traded in the older model the holster had been originally designed for. He had originally brought the older gun with him from Montana.

Aunt Ginny had said, "Jackson, I understand why a man needs a gun out here in the West. Your father has long convinced me of the practicality of a man walking about with a gun belted to his hip. But you are going to one of the finest Ivy League schools. You will hardly need that there."

She stood barely to his shoulder in height. Mid-fifties, with spectacles perched on her nose and speech that reflected her classical education.

"I suppose not," he said. "And yet, I would somehow feel incomplete without it at least nearby."

That statement disappointed her, he knew. She was generously paying for his education with a small fortune she inherited from her father, a shipping magnate in San Francisco. She saw his departure for college as leaving behind a world of leather and guns and branding irons, and embracing a future of books, classrooms and eventually, a

career in medicine. And yet he was the son of Johnny McCabe, and that would always be with him no matter where he went.

His shoulders were wide and strong from working alongside his father in the years before college, and from belonging to the college boxing team and rowing team. His shoulders had once filled out a range shirt, and now as he stood in his room at Harvard, they filled out a gray blazer.

He stood with his trunk open before him and took a long look around him at his room. The room that would soon not be his anymore.

Summer break was upon him, and he was heading home for a visit, as he often did in the summer. He had told no one, but this time he would not be coming back.

"Hey, Jacko," a voice came from the doorway behind him.

Jack recognized it immediately. Darby Yates, his roommate for the past two years. A tangle of red wavy hair on top of his head, and with freckles decorating his nose and cheeks. Darby was always quick with a laugh, and even more so once he had downed a few mugs of beer. He held a paper bag in one hand.

"Darby," Jack said, without turning around.

"That gun is so radically impressive," Darby said. "You know, I've never actually seen you strap it on. Like a cowboy, you know?"

"And you never will." Jack set it gingerly into the trunk, not dropping it like the other items. He kept the gun loaded, even here at school.

Pa had said once an unloaded gun is of little use to you. You keep it loaded and treat it as though it is loaded. Never carelessly.

"Hey, Jacko, why so dour?"

Jack shrugged. "Got a lot on my mind."

Darby stepped in and placed a hand on Jack's shoulder.

Darby said, "My friend, I wish I was going with you. I'll be playing croquet and watching polo with the family back on their estate in New York, but you'll be out west, riding the range alongside your father. The legendary gunfighter."

Jack stood a little taller than Darby, with chestnut

brown hair. He wore a white shirt under his gray jacket, but contrary to campus rules, he had yanked off his tie and it was folded and tucked into a jacket pocket.

"I so envy you," Darby said. "You'll have to tell us all about it in the fall. We'll have to hoist some mugs of beer and you can tell us all about your adventures in the west. Maybe you'll get to ride on a posse. Maybe get into a gunfight with outlaws."

Jack said, "Killing a man is never a thing to be taken lightly, Darby."

"Hey, Jacko." Darby gave a light punch to Jack's shoulder. "I'm just funning with you, my man. You need to lighten your mood. I mean, the semester's over. We're free for the summer. And I, for one, need the break. I think you do, too."

Jack nodded, and forced a half-smile. "That I do."

Jack closed the trunk and latched it shut. "Well, I'd best be going. My train leaves in an hour."

"I got you a little going-away present." Darby handed the package to Jack.

Jack reached into the paper bag and pulled out a pint of Kentucky bourbon. He couldn't help but smile.

Darby said, "I'm a scotch man myself, but I know you have a taste for it."

"I'm sure I'll find some use for it." Jack opened the trunk and tucked the bottle into one corner.

He then extended a hand to Darby.

Darby grasped the hand, but his smile faded. Darby said, "Why is it I have the feeling that this is not just 'so long for the summer?' That it's somehow really good-bye?"

Jack shrugged. "You never know what the future holds."

"Now, that's cryptic."

Jack pulled a gray tweed flat cap on over his head. "Sorry. Don't mean it to be. Take care, old friend."

"Yeah, Jack. You too."

Jack gripped the trunk by one handle and slung it over his back. Darby was amazed at the strength Jack had, handling the trunk easily. Darby had boxed and rowed alongside Jack, but he couldn't match Jack for sheer bull strength. All those muscles built cowboying on that ranch in

Montana, he supposed.

Darby watched as Jack turned a corner, and then disappeared down a stairwell.

Jack had been a great drinking buddy, and more than once a passport for Darby into a fraternity party. More importantly, Jack had been a friend. They had lain awake many a night, simply talking of dreams. Of future hopes. Of women.

And yet, there had always been something somehow mysterious about Jack McCabe. There were times when Jack would just stand silently in the window, looking off toward the western sky.

Jack was gone, down the stairs and out to hail a carriage to take him to the train station. Then, he would be off for the wilds of Montana for a summer of sitting on a horse and cowboying, or, as he called it, punching cows. Then, in the fall, Darby would be seeing his old friend again. They were both signed up for one more year in this dormitory room.

Yet, for some reason, Darby had the feeling he was never going to see his friend again. There had been something somehow final in that handshake. Something intangible, but it spoke to Darby's gut. Somehow, he knew something had just ended.

Darby went to the window and looked down at the street below, and watched his old friend toss his trunk into the back of a carriage and then climb in. The carriage moved off, the shoes of the horse clattering along the cobble stones of the street.

2

Jack stepped off the train in Cheyenne.

This town had originally been a railhead - a place where drovers brought herds up from Texas to meet buyers who had come west from Chicago. Brothels and saloons had sprung up to help relieve the drovers of their money. Some railheads closed up, but Cheyenne had hung on and a small town had grown and become somewhat respectable. However, when a herd arrived, that respectability went out

the window as the town reverted to its railhead roots. The saloons and brothels swung into full action, and the drovers ran wild and mothers kept their daughters inside behind locked doors.

Some towns like this were little more than a single street of single-floor wooden buildings slapped together, but Cheyenne actually had numerous streets, and many of the buildings were beginning to take on a feeling of permanency. Peaked roofs were numerous. A bank was housed in a brick building. The town actually had a fully functional train station.

Jack was now four days out of Harvard. There had been train stations where he could stop and stretch his legs, but much of the trip had meant sitting and watching the world go by out the window.

However, as he stood on the platform of this train station, his trunk over his shoulder and his tweed cap pulled down over his hair, he knew this would be the last one. This was as far north as the railroad went. The rest of the journey from here to the tiny town of McCabe Gap would be by stagecoach.

He stepped off the platform and crossed the tracks and made his way across the dirt street. The sign over one doorway read, TRAIN WHISTLE SALOON. He went no further.

He stepped into a dimly lit barroom. At the far wall was a mahogany bar, and behind it was a painting of a nude woman reclining in a bed of flowers. It was still early in the afternoon and the barroom was nearly empty. A bartender was milling about, waiting for business.

Jack crossed the floor and stopped at the bar and dropped the trunk onto the floor beside him.

The bartender was maybe forty, a thin man with thinning hair but a thick mustache, and an apron was tied about his middle.

He said, "What'll you have?"

"You have bourbon?"

The bartender shook his head. "Scotch."

"That'll do."

The bartender set a glass in front of him and poured a shot. Jack leaned one elbow on the bar, and downed the whiskey in one gulp.

He had experienced his first drink in a little saloon three miles from the ranch where he had grown up. The saloon was owned by an old friend of his father, name of Hunter. Biggest man Jack had ever seen, with an even bigger smile, and a huge, bushy beard. But Jack had learned to drink at Harvard, alongside Darby.

"Want a refill?" The bartender said.

"I wouldn't refuse."

This time, Jack took the whiskey a little more easily, letting the taste fill his mouth. As he did so, he decided he was going to take a break from his journey home. He had been traveling for four days, and had probably seven more in a bouncy stagecoach ahead of him. He decided he would stay in Cheyenne for a day. Maybe even rent a horse from the livery and ride about the countryside.

He could not allow himself more than a day in Cheyenne, though. The family would be expecting him. Most every summer, once school let out, he headed home. A few weeks in the little valley in the foothills of the Montana mountains. He had to admit, though, this year he was not feeling enthusiastic about returning home. In fact, had he not already promised Aunt Ginny in a letter that he would be spending his summer at the ranch, he probably wouldn't be returning at all.

As it was, he had delayed coming home by a full month. There were some projects a couple professors needed help with. He would be home for only about six weeks this summer. Part of the reason for the delay was to help the professors. And part of it was he just didn't really want to go home.

Jack knocked back the rest of the whiskey and set the glass on the table. The bartender glanced at him and Jack nodded. The bartender strolled over and filled the glass a third time.

Two men approached the bar. One bellied up, and the other stood sideways, leaning one elbow on the bar. They each ordered a glass of whiskey. The man leaning on his elbow was unshaven, with a shirt and vest that were covered with dust. But what caught Jack's attention was he wore his gun like he knew how to use it.

Before Jack had gone east to further his education, he

had learned at the school of Johnny McCabe. The school house had been under the open sky, often involving riding through the wooded ridges surrounding the little valley where his family made their home. Sometimes he and his father camped for days in those ridges.

His father's lessons had been about survival. And one of the most important tools of survival was the skill of observation, primarily noting details that were out of place, such as the way this man at the bar wore his gun. Another skill was to adequately deduce what this meant.

In this case, the man was no cowhand looking for work. He was a gunhawk.

"Howdy, boy," the man said. "You look a little out of place, here. All dressed up in your fancy duds."

"I don't want any trouble," Jack said.

The man grinned. The man had a long face, with a long, blade-like nose. His grin showed no humor.

The man said, "Didn't say I wanted trouble, boy. What makes you think I want trouble?"

He thinks I am afraid, Jack thought. *He sees the jacket and the cap, and thinks I am a dude from the east. He doesn't know who I am.*

As if the bartender were reading Jack's thoughts, he cut in and said, "Mister, don't you know who that is?"

Jack hadn't introduced himself, but he had stopped in this town every time he returned home for a visit. Word got around as to who he was.

"I don't care who he is," the man said.

"That there is the son of Johnny McCabe."

The man blinked with surprise at the bartender, then gave Jack a longer look.

The bartender said, "I wouldn't want to do nothing that might give Johnny McCabe cause to come gunnin' for me."

The man said, "If I was you, I'd mind my own business. I ain't afraid of Johnny McCabe, and I sure ain't afraid of some dude like this, who's still wet behind the ears."

The man who had come in with him said, "I don't know, Cade. I mean, Johnny McCabe. Think about it."

"I don't have to think about nothing. It's time people got to know the name Lewis Cade. It's time people started

thinking about not wanting to do anything that might cause *me* to come gunnin' for them."

Jack wasn't in a good mood, and he had his father's temper. Not the best mixture.

He should not egg this man on, he knew. But the man thought he was afraid, which grated on him a little, and Jack simply found he had no patience for this man's posturing.

"I know who you are, Cade," Jack said, turning away from him, and back toward the bar. "I've heard your name. Now, get away from me."

"What'd you say to me?"

The second man said, "Cade, don't start nothing."

"Why? You afraid of him? I don't see him wearing no gun."

Jack said, "I don't need a gun to deal with the likes of you, Cade. Back off."

Jack knew, however, Cade was not going to back off. Jack didn't really want him to.

"Listen, boy," Cade said. "You might think I'm afraid you because of who your daddy is, but I ain't."

"I don't blame you," Jack said. "If I were you, I would be afraid of me because of who *I* am."

Cade hesitated a moment, not sure what to say.

Jack set down his glass, then turned suddenly and shot a fist out, his knuckles bouncing off of Cade's cheekbone. Cade's head rocked back and he fell backwards and into his friend.

Jack stepped away from the bar calmly, shouldering out of his jacket and flipping his cap to the floor. Cade regained his footing, and sputtered a bit while he tried to shake off the punch.

Colleges were not simply places of learning, which this would-be gunfighter was going to learn the hard way, Jack thought. They had rowing teams. Cross-country running teams. Boxing teams. Wrestling teams. All of which Jack had partaken in. And before he had gone to school, he had been trained in the school of Johnny McCabe, which also involved boxing, and wrestling tricks he had learned from the Shoshone.

Cade, his balance fully regained, his vision now clear, pulled his gun.

Jack stepped into him, grabbing Cade by the wrist of his gun hand with a grip more firm than Cade was expecting, and shot a short hook punch into the side of Cade's head. He then took Cade's wrist with both hands and drove his knee up and into it as though he were breaking a stick over his knee, and the gun fell away.

Cade swung a fist at him, putting his weight into it. A mistake, Jack knew. Using skills his father had learned from the Shoshone, how to move efficiently and use an opponent's weight and momentum against himself, Jack grabbed the arm of the incoming punch, turned, and pulled Cade over his shoulder and slammed him down hard on the barroom floor.

The Shoshone had taught Pa how to fall. Pa had taught Jake and his brother Josh. Cade, however, didn't have this knowledge and took the brunt of the fall with his back. He remained where he had fallen on the beer-stained floorboards, gasping for breath.

Jack then turned to the man who had walked in with Cade. The man held up both hands in a stopping motion.

"Hold on," he said. "I ain't involved in this."

"Yeah, you are," Jack said, and shot a right cross into the man's face.

The man was driven backward and into the bar. Jack stepped in, following the right cross with short, uppercutting punches to the man's midsection, then rocked a hook punch into the man's head, and the man's knees buckled and he slid to the floor.

Jack picked up Cade's pistol from the floor. He turned it upright, flipped open the loading gate and rotated the cylinder, letting the cartridges fall to the bar.

"A man like Cade can't be trusted with one of these," Jack said. "He might hurt himself."

The bartender, smiling broadly, filled Jack's whiskey glass to the rim. "I seen your old man in a fist fight, once. Cleaned out the saloon. You're a chip off the old block, all right."

"Maybe," Jack said.

There had been a time when Jack would have beamed with pride to be compared to his father. Not that his father wasn't a good man. It was just that Jack realized he had had enough of living in this man's shadow.

He took the glass and downed a mouthful of whiskey. Then he returned the cap to his head and slung the jacket over one shoulder and hefted his trunk over the other, and turned and walked out into the street.

3

The marshal of Cheyenne was a man named Kincaid. Tall, with black hair and a matching mustache. A badge the shape of a shield with the name *Cheyenne* imprinted on it was pinned to his shirt, and a gun was tied down low at his right side.

Jack stood behind the marshal. His jacket was once again in place. Though most men wore a tie and jacket when they traveled, Jack had removed his tie the day he left Harvard, and had not put one on since. He wore a tie every day of the year while at school, and enough was enough. He stood with his shirt collar open.

He knew disorderly conduct like fighting in public was against the city ordinances of Cheyenne, and he wanted no trouble that might delay his trip home, so he had gone to get the marshal himself.

"You done nothing wrong," Kincaid said to Jack, as he locked the cell door. Inside the cell were Cade and his partner, sitting on the bunk. "They had it coming. I wish I was there to see it, though."

The faces of Cade and his friend were cut up and bruised. Amazing what a fist can do to a man's face, Jack McCabe thought.

The marshal said, "I've seen your old man in action a couple of times. Not so much fast on the draw, as he is smooth. Fluid. And his aim is like nothing I've ever seen. Takes a lot of nerve to hold your hand steady when you're being shot at, but your old man - you would have thought he was just target practicing. And I've seen him with his fists. You're apparently a chip off the old block, all right."

"Marshal," Jack said, "all I really want is to be left alone."

Kincaid tossed the cell keys on his desk. "That's all the great ones really want. Hickok. Doc Holliday. Zack Johnson. Your father. They don't go looking for trouble. That's for small-time scum like Cade. Challenging the great ones, looking to build up his name. Cade's lucky you weren't carrying a gun, but I doubt he's smart enough to know that.

"But be careful, son. I can't hold him here forever, and my jurisdiction ends at the last building in town. Cade's not

one to forgive and forget. You should watch your back. Friendly warning, that's all."

"Thanks. I'll keep that in mind."

Jack hefted his trunk onto his shoulder and stepped out onto the boardwalk. What he wanted was to simply get a hotel room and maybe grab a little sleep.

No, he realized. What he really wanted was to change into his levis and a range shirt, and find a good horse.

There was nothing as relaxing, as cleansing to his mind, as sitting on the back of a running horse and feeling the wind strike him in the face. It was like the wind washed away his troubles.

And yet, the thought of one more whiskey was kind of appealing to him at the moment. He had downed a couple of them already, one really full, but that was a good two hours ago. With his cap in place, he strode toward the saloon down by the train station.

"Back for more?" the bartender said.

"One more."

"On the house," the bartender filled the glass, and Jack set his trunk on the floor.

"Excuse me," a man said from behind him.

Oh no, Jack thought. Not again. But as he turned, he saw the man was no gunfighter.

The man was fifty-ish, and about Jack's height. A thick mustache accentuated the thinness of his face. And where his left hand might have been once was an empty sleeve.

"Can I have a word with you?" the man asked.

He was not wearing a gun, Jack noticed quickly. He was wearing no vest, which meant he was not a horseman. If you rode a horse a lot, you wore a vest to carry your wallet, and your tobacco and rolling paper if you smoked. Maybe a pocket watch. Carrying such things in your trouser pockets could be a might uncomfortable as you rode.

The man's face was deeply tanned and lined, as though he spent much time outdoors. This, along with the fact that he was not a horseman, told Jack the man was probably a farmer.

"What can I do for you?" Jack asked, impatiently.

"You're the son of Johnny McCabe, am I correct?"

"So they say."

"Well, if you are, then I have a job proposal for you."

"Not interested in work. Now, if you'll please excuse me..," Jack turned back to the bar.

"If you'll just give me five minutes of your time."

Jack didn't really have the patience for this, but he decided to listen to the man out of simple courtesy. And it was not as though he had anywhere he actually had to be.

They took a table. The man said, "Let me introduce myself. My name is Abel Brewster."

"Jack McCabe."

Brewster grinned as they shook hands. "I know who you are, sir."

"Mister Brewster, I don't mean to be rude. Really, I don't. But..,"

"Yes, I'll get to the point. When you were coming into town on the noon train, you might have noticed three covered wagons just outside of town."

Jack had absently noticed them, but thought little of it. "Yes, I suppose I did."

"One belongs to me and my family, and there are two other families traveling with us. We are bound north."

"Looking to strike it rich in the gold fields?"

Brewster chuckled. "Oh, no, Mister McCabe. We're farmers. We have no delusions of riches. We seek only an honest living, from the earth God provided for us."

"Well, there's not much farming country north of here. Lots of open grassland. What they sometimes call the high plains. Good cattle country, but a little dry for farming."

"There is good farming country further west, though, in the foothills. Or so I've heard."

• Jack nodded. The land in the valley where he was raised was fertile, and in the ridges surrounding the valley. "In places, yes. It's a long haul, though, and it's pretty remote country."

"Let me cut right to the point. The trains don't go that far north yet. The only way to go is by wagon. But we don't know anything about the territory. We're looking to hire a guide."

Jack shook his head. "I'm not looking for work. I'm heading out on the stage day after tomorrow."

"Is there any way you could be persuaded? Your reputation speaks for you. We don't have much money, but I'm sure we could put together a fee that would make it worth your while."

"You mean, my father's reputation speaks for itself." Jack felt his ire rising. "People look at me and they see him. They hear the name and they make assumptions they shouldn't make. You see, Mister Brewster, I am not my father. Never have been. And my services are not for hire."

"I didn't mean any offense, son. It's just that I have three families with me, and I'm real reluctant to head out with them over country I know nothing about."

"You should have thought about that before you headed west to begin with." Jack got to his feet. "Now if you'll excuse me, I really am not feeling very sociable."

Jack strode from the saloon, trunk held on one shoulder.

He walked down the street and to a small hotel he had stayed at before. He thought he would check in, then maybe head to the livery to rent a horse.

The man at the desk said, "Oh, yes sir, we have a room for you, Mister McCabe. Absolutely."

Jack thought the man seemed almost giddy at having the son of Johnny McCabe under his roof. It might be a selling point he could use for future customers.

Jack dropped his trunk on the floor of his room and then stretched out on the bed. Not very comfortable. It couldn't compare to his bed in the room at Harvard he had shared with Darby Yates, or his bed at the ranch. But it sure beat being jostled about on a train.

The train was a marvel of modern science, reaching speeds previously unheard of in any other method of travel. And yet, all the jostling and bouncing about did not appeal to Jack. He found trains cramped and uncomfortable. His preferred method of travel was by horseback, moving at whatever speed best suited him and the horse. And to have the open range about him and the sky overhead.

His father, in his younger years, had traveled throughout Texas by horseback. He had spent a couple years with the Texas Rangers, then returned home to Pennsylvania in the saddle. Later on, he and his brothers had ridden clear

to California on horseback. Even now, when Pa went on a business trip, he did so by saddling up and riding out. Trains and stagecoaches were not for him. He often rode overland, and took established trails only when they were convenient. He seldom stayed in a hotel, preferring to camp under the open sky.

Jack got to his feet and looked out his window at the street below, and decided he had enough daylight hours left to take a ride.

He dug into his trunk and found a pair of levis and his riding boots. Not that he had much need for them at Harvard, but it felt good having them on hand. They were reminders of what he was coming to think of as his previous life on the ranch as a young cowhand and frontiersman, learning at his father's side.

He tossed aside his jacket, and then exchanged his trousers for the stiffer fabric of his levis, and pulled on the tattered, tight-fitting boots. A cowhand always wants his boots tight so his foot won't slip in the boot while the boot is in the stirrup.

Many frontiersman and cowboys wore their trouser legs tucked into their boots, but some were starting to pull the cuff down over the boot, which seemed to work better with levis. Jack did so, and then stood in his boots, appreciating the fit of the levis. Now he felt more like his old self.

Rolled up in the trunk was his gunbelt. He reached for it. Hello, old friend. He unrolled it, and then buckled it on. He pulled the pistol and checked the loads, and then slapped it back into its holster.

He then pulled out the hatbox, and lifted the cover. In it was a brown sombrero. It had rounded crown, and a flat brim that had lost some of its stiffness. He pulled the sombrero down over his temples.

This felt right, he thought. He had gotten used to wearing a flat cap, but it had never really felt natural.

He decided he wouldn't need the hatbox anymore, because he had no plans to put the sombrero in storage again. He tossed the hatbox onto the small trash can beside the bed. The box was too big for the can and bounced off and landed on the floor.

He then grabbed the tweed flat cap he had set on an end table, and decided he would need this no more, either. He had worn it when he and Darby went into Boston looking to find some fun. It had been perched on his head as he and Darby hit taverns on Boston's waterfront and downed whiskey and sometimes got into fights with the locals. But it represented a life Jack was leaving behind. He tossed it into the trash can.

With his sombrero pulled down over his temples, he left his room and headed for the livery.

Word was spreading quickly. The son of Johnny McCabe was in town.

The hostler who ran the livery, an older man with a squeaky voice and thin, white hair, almost fell over himself finding just the right horse for the son of Johnny McCabe.

"Is it true?" the man asked. "About that gunbattle at your daddy's ranch a year ago? Word's spreading like wildfire. Fifty men rode on the ranch. Sam Patterson's men. And your daddy and his men just shot the stuffin' out of all of 'em."

Aunt Ginny had told Jack about it in her most recent letter.

"That's what they say," Jack said. "I wasn't there."

"His legend just grows and grows. Yessir."

"Seems to."

The man saddled a sorrel gelding for him, and when Jack asked the cost for an afternoon, the man said, "Oh, it's on the house, sir."

Jack shook his head with bewilderment, and stepped into the saddle.

The horse was long-legged and liked to run. At the edge of town, Jack let it have its head, and the horse broke into a mile-eating gallop, its mane fluttering in the wind. Jack leaned forward to provide less wind resistance, and the brim of his hat shook in the wind. Jack found he was smiling.

Two miles later, he reined up to let the horse blow, and he stepped out of saddle and loosened the cinch.

"That felt good, didn't it?" Jack said to the horse, as though the horse could understand him.

On either side of the trail were low, grassy hills

stretching away toward the horizon, with an occasional stunted tree attempting to hang on. In the far distance was a low line of gravelly looking ridges.

Jack tightened the cinch and swung back into the saddle, and they were off at a spirited trot. Jack turned the horse from the trail and over one hill.

He eventually turned the horse so they would make a wide circle about town. He thought how much he would like to simply turn the horse north and make the rest of the journey on horseback, like his father. But he dismissed the thought as whimsical.

Aunt Ginny had sent him money for the train and the stagecoach, and the family would be waiting for him in McCabe Gap. The little town in a pass outside of the valley they called home. And yet, as he brought the horse to a stop atop a low grassy rise and looked off toward the sun that was now trailing low over the western horizon, the wind from the northwest catching him in the face, he found himself longing to forget the stage and simply ride on.

He dismissed this in the face of reality and turned his horse, and soon the buildings of Cheyenne were standing in front of him in the distance, maybe a half mile away.

Between him and the town were the three covered wagons he had seen earlier, belonging to Brewster and his party. The sun, now setting, was casting a soft, rosy light against the canvas of the wagons.

Campfires were being brought to life, and people were puttering about the wagons. Oxen were grazing lazily.

Jack suddenly felt a pang of guilt over the way he had talked to Brewster earlier in the day. He had been raised by Pa and Aunt Ginny to be courteous, and to assist people when he could. He had dismissed Brewster rudely.

He gave his horse's ribs a little nudge with the heels of his boots and started toward the wagons.

A man was kneeling before a fire and adding chunks of wood to it. He looked up at the sound of the approaching rider. He had a wide, floppy black hat, and a full, dark beard gave his face a fierce look. He glared at Jack, and when Jack nodded to him, the man simply returned his attention to his fire.

I guess I had that coming, Jack thought.

At the second fire, a woman had set up a pot with some sort of stew cooking, and a coffee kettle was heating. She had a round, matronly shape and her hair was hidden by a bonnet. She glanced toward Jack, and when he touched the tip of his that to her, she gave a polite smile and nodded.

A girl was there, walking up toward the woman. Maybe Jack's age, maybe a little younger. She stepped through the tall grass with a sort of lithe grace. She glanced toward Jack, her hair also hidden by a bonnet, but in the fading light of the day, he caught the light gray color of her eyes, and a face that was gently freckled.

He found himself smiling, and again touched his hat.

She glanced shyly away and continued toward the woman at the fire.

At a campfire before the third wagon was Brewster. He looked up. "Well, Mister McCabe. I assumed I would have seen the last of you."

Jack nodded. "I would have thought so, too. I was just taking a little ride through the hills. I saw the wagons."

"Yes. If you'll excuse me, I'm building a cook fire."

Brewster returned to what he was doing, dropping to one knee, and adding chunks of wood to a fire, much as the first man.

"What'll you use for wood, once you're on the trail?" Jack said. "There aren't a whole lot of trees between here and the foothills of Montana."

"I'm sure we'll manage."

"Used to be that settlers used buffalo droppings, but now that the buffalo are gone, there's little to be used."

A woman was stepping from behind the wagon. She said, "Buffalo droppings! Sounds quite dreadful."

"Mildred," Brewster said, "this is Mister McCabe. The man I attempted to hire as our guide."

Jack gave a touch to the brim of his hat, "Ma'am."

She gave a nod, curtly.

Following the woman was a boy of about twelve, and a girl closer to the age of the one at the other fire. She wore no bonnet, and long dark hair fell freely, catching the wind.

Jack touched his hat to her, also.

She gave him a smile that struck him as either teasing, or daring. She said, "So, you're Jack McCabe. The

son of the famous gunfighter."

The woman said, "Hush, Jessica." Then, to Jack, "Forgive our daughter, Mister McCabe. She's too brazen, sometimes."

Jack shrugged. "It takes a lot to offend me, Mrs. Brewster."

Her husband said, "That wasn't the impression I gained when we talked earlier."

"Look, Mister Brewster, I owe you an apology. I really do. It was uncalled of for me to talk to you the way I did. I just, well, I had a lot on my mind. That's all."

Brewster looked up at him from the fire. "No harm done, I guess. But at the risk of being rude myself, we have to get on with our evening chores. We want to get an early start in the morning."

"I wish you all the best," Jack said. "You know, there aren't many who travel so far overland by wagon, these days. Used to be there were long wagon trains that made their way overland from Missouri all the way to Oregon or California, but those days are gone."

"Thanks. But we'll fare the best we can."

Jack nodded.

"Mister McCabe," Brewster's wife said, "if there are no trees, and as you said, the buffalo are gone, then what is used to start fires?"

He shrugged. "Most of the travel these days is either by train or stagecoach. The Army travels through in convoys, but they often bring firewood with them. Freight wagons make the trip too, and they often bring wood with them. I suppose," he was thinking quickly, wanting to offer these people some last minute advice, "some twist grass together, into little twists maybe the size of a small piece of firewood. But grass burns quickly and not very hot."

"Thank you, Mister McCabe," Brewster said dismissively.

"If you have an extra sheet of canvas, you can sling it under the wagon and use it to carry extra firewood. It's called a possum belly."

"We'll make do," Brewster said.

The girl, Jessica, threw a smile at Jack. "It was nice meeting you, Mister McCabe."

"Likewise, Miss." He touched the brim of his hat, and turned his horse.

He returned the horse to the livery, and then after a steak dinner at Delmonico's, a restaurant a few doors down from the hotel, he returned to his room.

Still in his levis and boots, he stretched out on the bed, and attempted to sleep. However, he found sleep evasive, as it often had been since he received a letter from Aunt Ginny earlier in the year.

The letter was in his trunk. When he had first read it, he had thought of crumpling it and throwing it out, but then found himself folding it and putting it in his desk. When he was packing his trunk to leave, he again thought of throwing the letter into a waste paper basket by his desk, but instead it wound up in the trunk.

He now sat up and struck a match, and brought to life a lamp standing on a small table at the side of the bed. He then dug into his trunk and found the letter.

This was it. The letter that changed his life.

He thought of maybe unfolding it. Reading it again. He had read it maybe thirty times in the past few months. But instead, he tossed the letter back to the open trunk. He blew out the lamp and started for the door.

When he was troubled, he liked to move. To walk. Better still, to ride. But to ride through the barren countryside around town at night might be foolhardy. A horse could step into a gopher hole and break a leg. So he thought he would settle for walking.

He stepped out onto the boardwalk and began to stride along. The town was dark except for some lighted windows. At the Harvard campus, and the city of Boston where Jack and Darby sometimes went for drinks, the streets were lighted with gas lamps. But not here in a small cowtown like Cheyenne.

After a time, Jack found his wanderings had taken him toward the train station, and he saw the doorway to the Train Whistle was lighted, and he thought maybe he would cut his walk short. The whiskey here was a far cry from Kentucky whiskey, but it would suffice.

He leaned one elbow on the bar, taking the glass with his left hand keeping the right free. Something his father had

taught him years earlier. Keep your gun hand free. At Harvard, such a thing wasn't necessary, but here in this frontier town, as he stood in his levis and riding boots, with his sombrero perched atop his head and his gun once again at his side, he found his father's old lessons returning to him.

The swinging doors were suddenly pushed open, and Jack tossed a glance back. To his surprise, stepping through the doorway were Brewster and the dark bearded man from the wagons.

"Mister McCabe," Brewster said. "Thank goodness."

Jack was about to make a comment about the two of them being out rather late, considering they were hoping to make an early start the following morning. But he thought better of it when he saw the urgency written on Brewster's face.

"What's wrong?" Jack asked.

"It's my daughter. Jessica. She's gone."